PICTURESQUE

"The smell does something to you, doesn't it?"

Willow's soft voice brought Jake back to the present and he opened his eyes while answering yes. She had already turned back to whatever she was busying herself with since he'd closed the door. He looked amused as the normally self-assured woman fidgeted with lamps and switches, then stumbled as she walked to a wall on the far side of the room where many canvases were stored. He remained where he was, taking his fill of her.

Jake could see the heat in Willow's eyes as she stared at him, her lips parted.

"What?" Her voice was breathless.

He pushed himself off the door and was at Willow's side before she took another breath. He removed the painting from her hands and turned to her, his eyes boring into hers.

"This," he said softly as he cupped her chin, lifting her lips to his. "This, is what."

Jake's lips captured hers in a gentle kiss that deepened hungrily when he felt her body sway into his. When she lifted her arms around his neck, he caught her close, enfolding her in his strong arms, as he tasted her kisses.

BOOK YOUR PLACE ON OUR WEBSITE AND MAKE THE ARABESQUE ROMANCE CONNECTION!

We've created a customized website just for our very special Arabesque readers, where you can get the inside scoop on everything that's going on with Arabesque romance novels.

When you come online, you'll have the exciting opportunity to:

- View covers of upcoming books
- Read sample chapters
- Learn about our future publishing schedule (listed by publication month *and author*)
- Find out when your favorite authors will be visiting a city near you
- Search for and order backlist books from our online catalog
- Check out author bios and background information
- Send e-mail to your favorite authors
- Meet the Kensington staff online
- Join us in weekly chats with authors, readers and other guests
- Get writing guidelines
- AND MUCH MORE!

Visit our website at
http://www.arabesquebooks.com

WHITE LIES

Doris Johnson

Pinnacle Books
Kensington Publishing Corp.
http://www.pinnaclebooks.com

To Marvis—for something you once said. Thanks.
Also to Laura for her art counsel; and to a reserved gentleman
landscaper.

PINNACLE BOOKS are published by

Kensington Publishing Corp.
850 Third Avenue
New York, NY 10022

Pinnacle, the P logo and Arabesque, the Arabesque logo Reg.
U.S. Pat. & TM Off.

First Printing: October, 1998
10 9 8 7 6 5 4 3 2 1

Printed in the United States of America

Prologue

Irvington, New York July, 1972

There it was again. The pervasiveness of a whistle intruding upon the sleeping house. Beatrice Vaughn sat upright in the vast bed, listening. Again. The unmistakable sound of a whistling teakettle. A tea craving? At three in the morning? she questioned herself as she eyed the luminous hands of the bedside clock. Who? She was in bed alone, sensing, rather than feeling the absence of her husband. She slid her hand into the slight indentation in the pillow. His musky male scent and the heady smell of their sex from hours before filled her nostrils, which almost on cue prompted her to touch the tender bruise on her inner thigh. In the same gesture, with sudden trepidation, she moved her hand across the soft, stark-white sheets. As she suspected, the cloth was cold to her touch. How long has he been gone this time? Beatrice wondered. Every boisterous freeloader had gone hours ago. The only sleep overs were her sister Vera and the stupefying drunk and asinine man she had brought with her this time. She stilled her hand and listened. A throaty female chuckle drifted through the gray shadows of the silent house and settled unnervingly in Beatrice's ears. Once more she heard the whistle of the kettle as if it had been placed back on the flame then removed, the sound comingling with baritone

murmurs. Beatrice was on the landing outside the bedroom door, listening. She started descending the stairs
slowly. No, he wouldn't. Not in his own home with his wife
and daughter within earshot of his vile fornicating.

Beatrice unconsciously ran her fingers over her bruised
thigh. The remembrance of how it became so, renewed the
pain, forcing her to close her eyes against the memory. Her
husband's version of making love; to twist and squeeze and
brutalize the softest parts of her, until finally, unable to withstand the pain, she would cry out. As if her cry were the
trigger for his release, he would match her painful scream,
then plunge into her with all the savagery of a wild beast.

Beatrice opened her eyes shaking off what was the non-
magical reality of her love life since her wedding night
nearly six years ago. But now, who was he with? Did my dear,
dear, ex-best friend have the gall to sneak back tonight?
After she was confronted with her treachery? No. She
wouldn't have the nerve to set foot in this house again. But
who? Beatrice's heart froze. My baby sister! Her bare feet
touched the cold, sleekly polished oak flooring of the hallway, her steps soundless as she reached the entrance of the
huge kitchen. Her eyes bulged in their sockets. Shoes or
not, they wouldn't have heard me anyway. What a mindless
thought, Beatrice. She nearly laughed at her silliness. They
are oblivious. Not on my table! What another stupid
thought she chastised herself. What matters where? Mesmerized she watched her husband, New York's darling, the
great and celebrated cartoonist Michael Vaughn: the talented creator of the streetwise Spodeo, take her sister on
his kitchen table! Vera Morgan's half-clad torso writhed like
a caterpillar in the throes of shedding its cocoon. The animal sounds emitting from their throats banged against Beatrice's ears like a boxer's fists of fury, until finally, she threw
up her hands to ward off the lascivious sounds. She
screamed and screamed until the stinging slap on her face
snapped her back into reality. Her towering husband was

leering at her as if he were confronting an idiot. He wasn't drunk but stone-cold sober when he said, "Can the theatrics, Beatrice. You've known for months what's been going on with me and my dalliances and especially with your hot little sister. Like everything else you do, you chose to file it away to deal with at another time. Well you can put this on the back burner, too, my cold, cloistered innocent. Your little sister and I are going to be combustible for a mighty long time."

Hysteria evaporated, replaced by cold fury. Beatrice became as still as a trapped cobra poised to attack. Her eyes became reptilian; cold, black and watchful. Her voice was a hiss.

"Like hell you will, you vile piece of nothing. Not in my home, not ever again." Her deadly eyes pierced her sister. "You, you slut. Dorcas knew about you your whole life. She tried telling me but I couldn't, wouldn't listen. You piece of trash. Get the hell out of my sight and my home and never, never set a foot on that door sill. Now." Her voice was murderous. Stone-faced, she watched as Vera hastily scrambled past her. She followed and watched as her sister dressed and packed, her "date" standing stupidly by as if wondering what the hell was going on. When the car's taillights disappeared down the long driveway and past the iron-grill gates, Beatrice went inside the house, locked the door and turned out the lights as she walked steadily up the stairs.

She stared at Michael. He was sitting in bed smoking a cigarette. How she hated him at that moment. How she loved him. Loved him? Did she still? After six years of abuse? What was so compelling that she stayed? She knew when the soft cry reached her ears. Beatrice lingered, silently eyeing her husband, then walked softly across the hall to her daughter's room.

"Okay baby, okay, Willow. Everything is okay, I'm here,

baby," Beatrice crooned. "Shh, go back to sleep, sweet-heart."

"Mommy are we going to have tea now? I thought I heard the kettle whistling," Willow said sleepily against her mother's soft breast.

"No, darling," Beatrice whispered. "It's too early for tea. You were dreaming. Don't worry, I won't forget to wake you in time so that you can pour Daddy's tea. Go to sleep now, my little darling."

"Is my baby asleep?" Michael Vaughn asked drowsily against the pillow. "That little one is going to be as famous as her old man one day. Only four years old and already on her way up the yellow brick road. Yes sirree, she's daddy's little girl, all right."

Beatrice was standing in the doorway. A small knowing smile tugged at her full sensuous mouth, her dark beige face flushed. "I've told you before, Michael. You are not going to exploit that child. She will have a normal life and will not live it in a goldfish bowl."

"Hah. You'll thwart her creativity until she's all dried up, like you. You want to bury it. Artist, pah! You? You never had any talent, but your daughter was born with it. It's exuding from those ten little fingers. She'll become the artist you've wanted to be and which you will never come within a hairsbreadth of achieving. Shut up, Beatrice, for once and for all. You never make any sense. I'm taking over my daughter's career as an artist. She's a damn prodigy. The critics believe that lifelike wilted rose was painted by an adult for Christ's sake. All you can think of is selfishly stifling that God-given genius talent. Well, think again. Over my dead body, you will." Michael Vaughn threw off the covers and leaped from the bed, stalking past his wife. At the door he turned to her and said, "You dis-gust me. I need a drink." Bounding down the stairs, he shouted, "End of conversation."

Beatrice walked to the bed, unlocked the drawer of the

ightstand and removed the loaded revolver. Michael had
nsisted that she keep the weapon as protection against
ntruders and kidnappers. He wanted his daughter safe,
e had said.

Intruders! Beatrice smiled. You're the intrusion Mi-
hael. You've invaded my heart, used it and flung it aside.
Now you want to intrude on your daughter's right to a
happy and sane childhood. You want me to watch silently
while you intrude upon my slut of a sister. How long before
you toss her aside? How many others besides my friend
and neighbor have you intruded upon then discarded so
cavalierly? Her eyes closed on the scene earlier in the day
when she had come upon her best friend locked in Mi-
hael's arms. She rose from the edge of the bed, her long
stride propelling her from the bedroom. She found Mi-
hael in the downstairs guest bathroom, sitting on the toi-
et smoking a cigarette, a glass of brandy in one hand.

"What the . . ." he said, his eyes opening wide.

"You're right," Beatrice said softly as she raised the gun.
"End of conversation."

Dawn was breaking. The faint light in the distance that
penetrated the thick foliage of the giant oaks made Beatrice stir from her perch on the window seat. Stretching
ong-folded limbs, her feet touched the floor unsteadily as
she walked to her writing desk and looked down at the
violet-tinted envelopes. There were two. She ran a finger
over the name she had written in her long, flowing hand,
"Dorcas Williams." The other she picked up, holding it
to her cheek. She laid it down gently, running her fingers
back and forth over her daughter's name: "Willow."

She turned toward the window, listening for the expected sound of the tire-spun gravel as the housekeeper
neared the end of the driveway. No. All was quiet. But soon

she'll come. She'll be here soon. She's never late. Alwa
punctual.

It's time, Beatrice thought. With characteristic litheness
she walked from the bedroom, closing the door softly be
hind her. Her daughter's bedroom door was ajar. Pushing
it open slowly, Beatrice did not enter the room but stared
at the sleeping child. She feared touching her daughte
"I love you Willow, my little darling," she whispered. She
pulled the door closed tightly and walked silently down
the stairs. The hall floor was cold beneath her bare feet
as eyes straight ahead, she glided past the closed bathroom
door. In the kitchen, she picked up the phone.

Dorcas Williams, raising herself up on one elbow, turned
on the light before answering the phone. Mumbling about
creatures who never went to sleep before daybreak, she
said "Hello?"

"It's me, Dorcas. Beatrice. Can you hear me?"

"Beatrice? For God's sake, what's wrong?" The misery
in her younger sister's voice froze the heart of Dorcas Williams.

"Come for Willow, Dorcas. Keep her and protect her.
In Canada, no one will know her. I love you."

A soft click. The connection ended.

"Bea—tr—ice! Bea—tr—ice?"

One

Irvington, New York, June, present day.

Willow Vaughn cleaned her paintbrushes carefully before putting them away, pleased with the results of the day's brushstrokes. Her palette cleaned and oiled, brushes stored in a can she walked to the window wall of the small one-bedroom cottage where she stared unabashedly at the man working outside. She had known for some time that he had arrived and had quietly begun his work, that is, as quietly as gardening would allow. She had felt, rather than seen him. Curious, she thought, how she had become so aware of Jake Rivers in recent months. At that moment, as if feeling, rather than seeing her, he looked up from the shrub he was cutting and their eyes locked. As usual, when she stared into the depths of those odd-colored eyes like dark moist earth with the barest tint of burgundy, she felt as if she were drowning in a vat of fine wine. "Bedroom eyes" she thought, unwilling to break the stare. Even as he nodded his finely shaped head, adjusting the band that rested on his high forehead, the sweat glistening on his warm sienna-brown skin, her body did not disappoint her, in that the reaction was always the same; the rush of an erratic warmth. How long since this feeling in her began? Surely not in February when they first met; when she had acted like a shrew in panic when she noticed her beautiful gardens were all but dying under the care of Lloyd Rivers Land-scaping. Most definitely not in March, when her voice had gone shrill, when she called him about her malfunctioning greenhouse. She had not been commissioned to paint wilted camellias. The beautiful pink and white winter blos-soms had nearly died when the thermostat had dropped below the required 28 degrees. After he had recoupled the electric vent control, the proper temperature was resumed, reviving the tired blooms. Afterward, Willow had the feeling that the tall, muscular man of few words, regarded her as the proverbial high-strung artist to be avoided at all costs. Aware of his avoidance, Willow made a point of speaking, forcing him into conversation, be it about her flowers or her greenhouse. Soon these topics became sated, but still, she persisted in conversation each time she saw him. Willow could not pinpoint the exact moment that her body began reacting in that strange manner toward Jake Rivers.

Acknowledging his slight nod of greeting, she waved, no-ticing the tiny movement of his thick mustache over his full mouth before he bent his head to the unruly shrub. Willow watched as his big hands moved the hedge-cutter skillfully across the rounded shape of the bush, quickly eliminating the unwanted sprouts. The late day sun was still hot enough to warm his muscular bare arms, bringing to the fore the underlying reddish hue of his skin. When he squatted on his haunches, his thigh muscles caused a thick ripple that started from his groin and moved with alacrity down his calf, disappearing beyond where she could see to the ankle that was covered by heavy work boots. His movements were sure and filled with confidence. Willow found herself won-dering if his personal life was so ordered. Stirring herself, she moved from the window. Minutes later, after returning things to their proper places she turned out the light and locked the cottage door. She'd promised her aunt help with dinner tonight. Instead of taking the stone path that led to the back of the main house and the kitchen door, her steps carried her off the path and over to Jake Rivers who watched her approach, his face a mask of curiosity.

"Ms. Vaughn."

Willow liked the deep resonance of a voice that she heard far too little of. She smiled and she knew that her almond-shaped deep brown eyes were crinkling at the corners as she teased, "I thought we had established that me Willow, you Jake." She was rewarded with a smile in his eyes though none was on his lips. 'One would think you never smile Jake Rivers' she said to herself. She had watched unseen from her cottage window as he tended to the wildflowers in her garden. His big hands had moved gently around the tender petals and she had seen a smile cross his face. She had been amazed at the deep dimples in each cheek. *One day you will smile for me,* she thought.

Jake Rivers acquiesced. "Willow," he said.

Willow brushed at her face pushing a long black strand of curly hair from her flawless light beige cheek. She looked around and with a sweeping gesture of her hand, she said, "The place looks great, Jake. Thank you. You've done wonders in such a short time." Her smile was earnest. "I don't know what our guests would think about "Wildflowers Cove" not bearing a single flower to justify its name."

Jake looked down, but not too far, at Willow Vaughn. He had long ago guessed her to be about five inches less than his six-foot-one-inch frame. His shoulders rippled under his green plaid cotton shirt. "That's why you contracted with Lloyd Rivers Landscaping." He too surveyed the grounds with a pleasing eye. The damage that his brother Nat had done was no longer evident. He turned his direct gaze back to Willow. "My father could not afford to lose the Cove contract. Thanks for not pulling out."

Willow was about to be lost again in those eyes when she heard her name. Turning, she saw her aunt approaching them. A plump mid-fiftyish woman of average height with a beautiful round face and stark white hair, Dorcas Williams rushed toward her niece, looking flustered.

"Willow, I need you now . . . Tommy just called to say he has a makeup class tonight and can't make the dinner hour . . . You'll have to do the dessert . . . It's strawberry tarts with whipped cream," she said all in one breath. In the next, she smiled. "How are you today, Jake? My, how you have gotten this place looking normal again." She frowned. "You tell that rascally brother of yours that I'm still waiting to give him a piece of my mind; him shucking and jiving, your ailing father not able to move, thinking that Nat had the business under control. Humph, I thought my niece would never stop rampaging around here, thinking that she wouldn't be surrounded by her beautiful flowers this year."

"Ms. Dorcas," Jake nodded at the woman when she paused. "I did give your message to my brother, but Nat being Nat, well . . ." He shrugged. "He'll mosey on by one day with his apologies. You can count on it." His look encompassed Willow.

"Well, I'll be waiting," replied Dorcas. "Come on, Willow," she said, taking her niece's hand, "Let's get a move on. Jake would you like to come back for dinner at six? Love to have you." Her eyes twinkled. "Our guests this week include four women to one man. He could use a little help, I think. Besides, Willow makes a mean sweet tart." Winking at Jake and not waiting for his reply, she started back to the house pulling Willow with her. "Just show up. No formality with old friends. You know that."

When Willow turned to wave good-bye, she was surprised to see Jake Rivers giving her an appraising look. He didn't blink or play coy, but he was communicating to her, as bodaciously as he wanted to, that he liked what he saw— very much.

Willow smiled, knowing that she was sending an invitation. As she disappeared into the house behind her aunt, she wondered aloud, "Lord, where is this going to take me?"

Willow finished filling the small pie tins with freshly made dough then put the large tray in the eye-level oven. After checking Dorcas' stuffed chickens in the lower oven she turned to her aunt with curiosity in her eyes and her voice. "Old friends, hmm? Where is that coming from? You sounded like the Vaughns and the Rivers go w-a-a-y back." Willow lowered her voice conspiratorially. "Do we have a history here? Come on, Aunt Dee, you can tell me."

Dorcas Williams was glad her back was turned to her because she knew that the fear in her eyes would betray her. Recovering with a cough and a pretense of an injured air, she said, "I'll remind you my dear that Lloyd Rivers Landscaping was contracted by your father before you were born. Some of these trees and shrubs are older than you."

"Aunt Dee, you didn't know them. You were living in Canada!" Willow smirked. "Now tell me how your moving back here makes you such 'old' friends."

"Willow," Dorcas said with great patience, "We moved back to New York when you entered your first year of college twelve years ago. How old are you? One scant week past thirty! You were gone for six of those years educating yourself. Who do you think was cutting the grass? And besides, who made a rule that a twelve-year relationship is not 'old?' "

Willow laughed. "Okay, okay, I concede. But must you be so blunt about my milestone natal day? I've forgotten it already."

Relieved, Dorcas' voice turned to a light banter, "I don't know why. You need to be thinking about it every day. Haven't you ever heard of that thing called the biological clock? When am I gonna get some babies underfoot?"

Willow bantered back, "Haven't you ever heard that it

takes two to tango? I'm hardly your prime candidate for artificial insemination. I want to see and touch the father of my child."

Dorcas, who made a great show of putting on her large mitts and before bending to open the oven door, winked. "What makes you think you haven't met him already?" then ducked her head. When she removed the pans and closed the door she continued, "One of these little chicks is his if he accepts the invitation."

Willow gaped at her aunt.

"Close your mouth child before you put your foot in it. I've seen you around him. You can't deny you're attracted. And him? Don't know what's wrong with the man. I thought young men these days had it going on. But shy, he ain't." She tilted her head to one side. "Cautious. That's gotta be it. Cautious. Anyhow, I thought I'd give him a little push . . . you know . . . as if to tell him he has my blessing."

"Blessing!" Willow all but sputtered. "For what?"

"Courtin'," Dorcas said with aplomb. "Call it what you will, but in the twenty-fifth century it'll still be known as courtin'."

Willow had filled the browned shells with strawberries, baked the tarts and now was removing the large tray from the oven. After placing it on a cooling rack she eyed her aunt with much speculation.

"Do you suppose the big three-O has pushed me to the brink of irrational actions? I swear, before a few weeks ago, I never noticed the man . . . in that way. Now, I find any excuse to delay his leaving. What's this all about Aunt Dee?"

Dorcas chuckled. "I thought we had our reproduction of the species classes when you were thirteen years old."

Willow smiled at the dim memories. "Seriously, I'm thirty, employed, healthy. I have a home and a sassy aunt who loves me. I'm content, Aunt Dee."

"So a 'sassy aunt' is going to keep you warm at night?

Make you babies? Bring out the woman in you?" Dorcas pulled the salad bowl from the refrigerator and tossed the chilled mixed greens. "What you're feeling child is the ticktock of that clock. It's time." She threw her niece an I-can't-believe-you-said-that look. "Thirty? Sure, a beautiful woman, ripe for the plucking. Employed? Only one of the most sought-after successful young artists around. How many other artists do you know that at age nineteen caught the critics' eye and six years later was solely supporting herself with her art?"

"Not solely," Willow said softly, a shadow clouding her eyes.

Dorcas heard the anguish in Willow's voice and her eyes softened. "If not for the trust fund, Willow, you would still be a success by all monetary standards in this country." She added, "Your home? It's been in our family for more than a hundred years, but it was your father's success and money that restored, renovated and enlarged it." Dorcas paused, then continued in a gentle voice, "You're not content Willow. You're ready to move on to that next phase, that new adventure that I promise you will be the most rockiest and sweetest experience that you've ever tasted." She grinned. "Even better than the invention of chocolate ice cream!"

Willow laughed with her aunt. "How a simple question about the Rivers family being old friends led to a birds-and-bees lesson is blowing my mind, Aunt Dee." She filled the cruet set and took two additional dressings from the refrigerator and started toward the dining room door. "But we'll have to continue this debate another time I think. Our writers have emerged from their retreats. I wonder if it has anything to do with hunger pains?" She was still chuckling on her way into the dining room.

Dorcas loaded a trolley with steaming bowls of green and yellow vegetables and pitchers of lemonade and iced tea. She followed her niece through the swinging door that led to the dining room. Unlike her niece, she was not smiling, but chewed her lower lip in a nervous gesture. Suddenly she was unsure of her innocent but deliberate attempt at throwing Willow and Jake Rivers together. Though they didn't know it, their pasts were definitely and irrevocably linked. When the discovery about their history was known would they hate each other? Or direct their hate toward her? Fear gripped her chest as she entered the brightly lit room. How could she bear to lose the love of her precious Willow?

Dorcas massaged the facial moisturizer cream into her dark brown skin in slow motion. Her full-figured body was ensconced on the padded seat at her dressing table, but her mind was light years away. It was nearly eleven o'clock when she had retired to her room, bathed in a hot tub and donned a fresh cotton nightgown. After their guests were fed, she and Willow had joined them for dessert and soon afterward all had said their good nights. Dorcas sat thinking of the fateful day that left her niece a confused four-year-old; she hadn't seen Willow since she was two. Whenever they spoke over the phone, Dorcas had always called Willow her little "buttercup." Dorcas had marvelled at the young child's bright, alert disposition. She was a gay, contented little lady, who was intrigued by the world around her. She loved her doting parents. Dorcas' lids shuttered the pain in her dark brown eyes as she remembered the sound of her sister's voice all those years ago. She remembered the sound of her own voice as she screamed Beatrice's name over and over until her husband had to shake her back into sensibility. Even before that 'next-of-kin' phone call from the New York Police Department Dorcas was on a plane to her old childhood home. The same home that had been left to Beatrice by their parents and the home that Beatrice had chosen to live in as a young bride. It was a grand old house that had been in the Morgan family since before the

days of reconstruction, built by a Morgan, a freeman. Over
the years, renovations and additions had given the sprawling structure a unique character all its own, not to be clas-
sified as old Victorian or classic Colonial. When Dorcas had
arrived at the house late that night, the taxi could not get
past the gate at the beginning of the driveway for all the
police cars and official vehicles. She had jumped from the
car and ran, reaching the front door as a black body bag
was being carried from the house. Just beyond were two
more men carrying an identical bag. She had yelled for
them to stop and would have fallen on the bags if she wasn't
caught and held by a woman. Dorcas would never forget
the stricken look on the woman's face. Through a dim fog
she recognized the woman as being Beatrice's best friend,
Octavia Rivers. Little did she know then that later on the
thought of that woman touching her would make her
cringe. But at that moment she could only cry for her niece.
Before she could be stopped, she ran into the house calling
for Willow, running past the bloodied bathroom. All she
could remember before passing out was that there was so
much blood. When she was revived, Octavia was by her side,
tears streaking her face as she told her that Willow and the
housekeeper were at her house and that she would take her
to them. During the twenty minute drive, Dorcas could only
ask why, but Octavia appeared to be nervous and dumb-
founded and could offer nothing that made any sense.
When they had arrived at Octavia's home, her husband,
Lloyd Rivers, was there with their two sons; twelve-year-old
Nathaniel and ten-year-old Jake. When she spied her niece,
she was sitting somberly between the two young boys. It was
young Jake who let the quiet little girl use his shoulder for
a pillow. Dorcas could see that there was no recognition in
her niece's eyes when she saw her standing in the doorway.
But when Dorcas said, "Aren't you my little buttercup?"
the sound of her voice brought a cry of glee from the little

girl. She sprang from the couch and ran into the arms of Dorcas, crying, "Auntie Dee?"

Dorcas never brought Willow back to the house. For nearly two months, they stayed with long-time friends of Dorcas' parents until Dorcas had been awarded guardianship of her niece and the investigation into the deaths had been completed. The determination was as expected: murder and suicide. It was then that Dorcas took her niece home to Canada where she and her husband Thomas raised her as the daughter they could never have. For months, Dorcas could not explain Willow's fear and near panic whenever she heard the whistling of a teakettle. The sound appeared to bring troubled memories to the child but Dorcas never knew why. She threw out her whistler and thereafter coped with using a regular kettle. One thing she remembered that was curious and unexplainable, was the housekeeper's story that the housekeeper had told her; that when she found Willow that morning, the distressed little girl was sitting forlornly in the living room. She looked sadly at the housekeeper and said, "It's time to make tea for my daddy but I can't find him and my mommy. Why did they leave me?"

A soft knock on the door startled Dorcas from her troubled memories as Willow breezed inside. Parking her slender, lithe form on the bed. Lazily crossing her ankles, she appeared to be settling in for a long stay. Airily, she said, "Old friends?"

Dorcas groaned. "Willow, you're the world's greatest nudge. Just like a dog that won't let loose of a raggedy old bone." With an exaggerated sigh, Dorcas wiped the excess cream off her hands then joined her niece on the over-sized bed. "Okay pest, move over. Looks like the only way I'll get to sleep tonight is to tell you a story."

"Not any story, Auntie, the real gossip behind how you're

so buddy-buddy with the Rivers brothers." Willow shuddered. "What about the old man? The few times I've seen him, he threw daggers my way with those cutting eyes. Gave me the creeps. Good thing you're the business keeper here. I would have let Rivers Landscaping go long before now."

"Lloyd?" Dorcas was thoughtful. No need to mention her meeting with the man when she first moved back into the house. Willow had gotten an apartment in the city close to Hunter College and was never home much. The man was a cold fish when he had inquired about his company continuing the landscape contract at the "Inn." She had politely informed him that it was no longer the Oaks Bed-and-Breakfast Inn, but Wildflowers Cove—Writer's Retreat. "Lloyd?" she repeated, then shrugged. "He's harmless. As long as I don't venture from talking about business, he's civil. The minute I ask after his health or mention the boys, he's Mr. Iceberg personified. So, it's strictly business." She smiled. "Nat? Well he's something else all together. You've dealt with him a few times and as you know, Nathaniel Rivers is a charmer from the word go and handsome to boot. With those eyes and that smile he could charm a cobra right out of its own basket, and without a flute or a piccolo or whatever snake charmers blow."

Willow laughed. "Were you bitten?"

"Humph," Dorcas sniffed. "The first time he laid one of those dreamy looks on me, I said 'Oh no you don't—I'm not hardly looking for a sweet young thang to raise' and he grinned like a little boy who got caught with his hand in the cookie jar."

"You two couldn't help but become friends after that, right?"

"I couldn't get rid of the man. I became his confidante, aunt, big sister, you name it. I had to tell him to put a curb on his visits. Talk in the village had us everything but married."

"Since when did you let neighborhood gossip stop you from doing what you please?"

"Since my niece was becoming so famous I didn't want to become a cause célèbre. The taint of a scandal would never do." The minute the words left her mouth, Dorcas wished for instant recall. How could she be so gauche? The pain of her sister murdering her husband then killing herself was as fresh in her mind as if it had happened yesterday. The celebrity of Michael Vaughn had kept the story in the tabloids for months afterward. Thank God their daughter had been whisked to Canada.

Willow caught her aunt's hand. "That's okay, Aunt Dee," she said. "You didn't hurt me. But I know how much you loved your only sister and how much you miss her." She squeezed. "I only wish that my parents had had another child. The loneliness probably wouldn't have been so great. It's just you and me, Aunt Dee. What's going to happen to our family name?"

Dorcas closed her eyes briefly before answering. What had started from anger and a tiny little lie to Willow all those years ago, now had her niece believing that she had no other living relatives. Vera's dead to me and so must she be for Willow, Dorcas reasoned. Her voice was strained but bright. "Happen? Why you're going to have plenty of babies. All with the middle name of Morgan."

"Boy or girl?" Willow teased.

"Boy and girl," Dorcas affirmed, "Three of each."

"I want a family, not a basketball team." An amused glint appeared in Willow's eyes when she said, "I think your plan to get me started on this team has backfired. We didn't have an extra guest for dinner tonight," she reminded her aunt.

"Don't fret, child. It's a standing invitation. You'll get your chance with him. Bet on it."

"Do you bottle that stuff?" Willow queried.

"What?"

"That air of confidence that leaps from you like tentacles."

After a comfortable moment, Willow said, "With all the things that you had become to Nat, you never mentioned mother. Why? Does he have one? Is Mr. Rivers a widower?"

Once again, Dorcas held her mouth straight when she lied, "I've never met the woman but I heard she died some years ago." With unusual abruptness, she changed the subject. Talk of the Rivers family was beginning to pall. "So what do you think of the new crop of guests this week?"

Surprised at her aunt's sudden desire to change the topic from matchmaking, she thought about the sleeping guests who were bedded down on the top floor. In the huge house, she and Dorcas had their own spacious rooms with private baths on the main floor. All five of the second-floor guest rooms were renovated into private retreats with sitting areas and attached baths. Willow liked the setup because guests really had no reason to leave the inviting rooms unless they joined others at meals or spent some time away from their work in the downstairs library at teatime, or for a needed respite.

When she and her aunt had moved from Canada to occupy the big house, her head was only into college and its heartaches and joys. Her aunt was left to make the decision whether they would continue a bed and breakfast as did the former lessees, or live in the rambling structure by themselves. Within six months, Dorcas had decided to continue to share the beautiful surroundings but only on a part-time basis. She would work several months as a nurse and four months of the year she would run a retreat for writers. The quiet surroundings of Hudson County were just perfect. Summers, Willow would help out because, like her aunt, she loved to cook. After her master's studies at New York University she returned home where they had settled into a comfortable routine. Wildflowers Cove always welcomed its first writers on the first Saturday in June.

Some stayed for two weeks but most opted for only a week of solitude. The final guests left on the last Saturday in October.

In response to her aunt's question, Willow smiled. "George Henry is back."

With the mention of one of their repeat guests, both women doubled over in a fit of laughter.

Two

Jake Rivers was exhausted. Although it was nearly nine o'clock, he had yet to eat dinner, a fact of which his grumbling stomach was making him well aware. Rolling off the bed, he rubbed his sleep-swollen eyes and headed for the bathroom where splashes of cold water stung his face and droplets soothed his warm, bare chest. Early June at night was masquerading as a mid-July day. He stared at the five o'clock shadow-covering his strong jawline. "Christ! You look like hell," he chastised the haggard reflection in the mirror. Grabbing a towel off the bar, he swiped his face dry while walking to the kitchen and thinking of the extreme possibility that there may be something akin to sustenance in the fridge. Hoping against hope he opened the door but was not disappointed in his first assumption. He could only look in disgust at three bottles of Budweiser, a small dried-up pan pizza laden with the works, a lone egg that probably needed trashing and a partially eaten he-man size chicken dinner that he immediately tossed. The freezer yielded little else but was doing its duty imitating the arctic region. Giving up, Jake reached into the cupboard, found a can of black-bean soup and seconds later had it heating up in the microwave.

Working three jobs was hell! Jake was sitting in the living room of his two-bedroom condo, soup and beer long gone. He idly channel-surfed, before finally turning the set off

to stare at nothing. Earlier when he had left Wildflowers
Cove he had dropped off his father's truck, picked up his
own car and driven the eight miles to his complex. After
a quick shower he had sat down at his computer to take
care of his own landscaping business. When finished, he
lay down on the bed to rest his eyes, only to awaken hours
later, unrested. Wearily, Jake rubbed his forehead. *How long
can I keep up this pace?* First prize to the solver of the riddle,
he jested. Months before, when he had heeded his father's
call for help, he had had no idea of the enormity of trying
to efficiently cover three businesses—his own, the one as
an independent landscape contractor, plus his father's gardening contracts. His performance as contractor on his
primary job was beginning to show some strain. Luckily
his employer, Mac, was understanding of the situation. Jake
remembered the frantic call he had received last September from his brother Nathaniel. Their father had been
hospitalized after suffering a stroke. When Jake's beeper
had vibrated against his hip, he and Mac had been surveying a site in Soho where Mac had won the bid to plan
and design the landscape for a midsize corporation. A siz-
able garden was part of the plan.

Later when Jake finally reached the hospital in
Westchester, he had been shaken at the sight of his father
lying unconscious. At the memory, Jake, shaking himself
out of the past, flipped the TV on and began channel-
surfing again. As it would happen, nothing but a slew of
food commercials with mouthwatering dishes danced before his eyes. You're the fool he berated himself. You
could have been eating strawberry tarts with whipped
cream along with the other goodies that preceded them
and you would have had the chance to look legitimately
at a beautiful woman instead of stealing glances through
a window while she worked. You've had your chance and
you blew it, buddy. No one else to blame. Jake thought
about that. Maybe not. Ms. Dorcas did say "just show up."

Does that mean anytime? He wondered how Willow Vaughn would react to the informality of his arrival at her dinner table. When she had turned and caught his bold stare, she had surprised him with her equally bold smile and wave. He knew from his being around for thirty-six years that he had just received an invitation. To what, he wasn't exactly certain, but that smile was definitely not an invite to back off.

Jake pressed the Off button of the remote and left the darkened living room, walking the few feet down the hall to the second bedroom that he used as an office. There were several pages on the fax machine. Perusing them, he decided that all replies could wait until morning. He studied the reply from Mac, which was in response to his fax earlier that evening. He'd sent a complete update of the contractual work he'd done on the Soho job, ending the report with his intention to visit the site again in the morning.

Jake turned the light out and left the room, heading for the bathroom and a hot shower. Tomorrow was going to be a long day. Today he had noticed that a set of drainage pipes may have been laid in the wrong section. A review of Mac's master plans would let him know definitely whether the pipes would have to be ripped out.

In the morning, precisely at five-thirty, he would be parking his car at the Soho site. At day's end, tired, he would pick up his father's truck and make the necessary visits to his father's customers. The so-called supervising of his father's workers by his brother, Nat, had all but ruined the thirty-five-year-old business. His rounds completed, early evening would find him at his own apartment making and returning calls to his own customers. Tonight, when he had hit the door, it was all he could do to keep his eyes open until he did some data entry, before dropping on his bed like a rock. He was certain he'd been asleep before his head hit the pillow. But one of the last thoughts he had was that he would never make it back to the Cove to stare into a pair of beautiful doe-brown eyes.

Water pelting his torso as if the fingers of a thousand masseurs were vying for his body, Jake mused that tomorrow, come what may, he would be dining with "old friends" at Wildflowers Cove.

The next morning Jake watched as workers at the site pulled onto the lot one by one. At nearly six A.M. he was finishing his second cup of coffee. Tossing the empty cup, he pushed himself off the fender of his car and walked toward the trailer office to study the blueprints when he heard his name.

"Jake, wait up."

Turning, Jake saw Mac get out of a beat-up faded blue Chevy. Grinning, he waved. Their respective cars were a running joke between them. Both were old but while Mac's was a jalopy, Jake's was a restored classic in mint condition. A silver, 1979 Chevrolet Camaro Z/28 with 99,000 original miles, Jake beared the good-natured ribbing from the men when he pulled out a tarp cover on blustery days. He relished the stares and questions he got from collectors.

"Didn't trust me to correct the problem all by my lonesome?" he chided his friend.

"Hush your fresh mouth. You know I don't do mornings too well. You won't be able to reach me later in case you needed to. Speak to the site man yet?"

Jake eyed his employer with an amused look. Tala McCready, always known as Mac during their days at Cornell University together looked worse than Jake did in the morning. Her Native and Irish-American-inherited, straight, deep auburn hair was wind-tossed and her eyes were still sleep-puffed. "Not yet," he answered as they walked together. "When are you going to tell the prof to stop burning that midnight oil? Hasn't he ever heard of beauty rest?" Professor Brian McCready, Tala's husband, taught literature at New York University, and in Jake's opinion kept the most ungodly of schedules.

Tala McCready threw her employee and long-time friend, an evil look. "Mind your business. You get what you can get when you can get it," she said gruffly. Jake always told her that her voice could get her a job anywhere. She had the deep hypnotic sound of Marlene Dietrich and the melodious tone of Phylicia Rashad. Her long black lashes touched her olive-tone cheek when she cut her eyes up at the tall man walking beside her. "When are you going to be on the receiving end of your own advice?" Almost immediately, Tala wished she could recall her words. "Jake, wash my mouth out, I didn't mean that shrewish remark." She had forgotten his grueling schedule since his father became ill. She knew that he had next to nothing of a social life lately.

"Yeah, you did. But I'm aiming to remedy that, real soon." Jake stepped aside to allow Tala to enter the trailer first. When she stopped and stared at him open-mouthed, he gently nudged her inside. "A fly is going to find the most delicious of homes if you don't snap it shut," he said.

"Jake Rivers. Where did you find the time? And who is she?"

A rare smile brightened the burgundy hue of his eyes. "All things in time and place," he answered. "Right now, we have a customer to keep happy."

At exactly six P.M., Jake rang the front doorbell at Wildflowers Cove. *Can't cut and run now*, he told himself when he heard footsteps. As he parked his car, he had suddenly felt a little foolish showing up a day late in response to a dinner invitation. When the door opened and he found himself staring into a pair of startled brown eyes, his moments of doubt dissipated in the early evening breeze. Suddenly speechless, he could only stare.

Surprise in her eyes was replaced by a smile that spread to her lips as Willow stepped back to allow Jake to enter. "I'm afraid I polished off your tart for breakfast. Tonight, there's banana pudding but Tommy, Dorcas' student helper, made that."

Jake stood aside as she closed the door. Had she really been disappointed last night? The question unasked, he apologized. "I'm sorry. Is there a special night for tarts?"

The instant his words registered, their eyes locked and both reacted simultaneously. Willow laughed, a deep sound that came from her belly and her eyes closed as she threw back her head. Jake showed a row of fine, even teeth under the brush of mustache as a grin split his face. The dimples in his cheeks could get no deeper. His deep baritone laugh mingled with hers filling the foyer with melodies uncharacteristic to the quiet retreat.

When Willow opened her eyes, her smile broadened. *You smiled for me Jake Rivers and we've really only just met. Where do we go from here?*

"What's all this ruckus out here, Willow. . . ." Dorcas stopped in her tracks at the sight of Jake and Willow, both wearing grins from ear to ear. Flabbergasted, she looked from one to the other. Her niece looked like she was in seventh heaven and Jake, why the man was good-looking. Not as handsome as that rake of a brother of his but he should show those dimples more often. *Could that smile of his be the reason my niece is all bent out of shape?* Who'll ever understand the mysteries of the man-woman thing? Aloud she said, "Jake, you're too late for tarts, but we have Tommy's banana pudding. Now come on, my pork chops will congeal at this rate." Dorcas turned to raise a brow at the fresh peal of laughter bursting from her niece, shrugged and disappeared down the hall shaking her head in bewilderment.

Jake held out his arm and Willow slid her hand into the crook of his elbow. "Shall we go? Ms. Dorcas might be calling for help." The timbre of his voice was still tinged with laughter.

Willow's laughter ended abruptly when she touched the bare flesh of Jake's arm. He was dressed casually in slacks and short sleeves. Although she had seen him for days, bare-armed and bare-legged, there had never been any reason for such close proximity. The shudder that she felt was like electricity that passed through her to him. When it reached him, she knew it; she felt his quiver. When their eyes met, the message they shared shocked them both into soberness. They were a quiet couple when they joined Dorcas and the other guests in the dining room.

Willow savored the aroma and taste of the rich Columbian roast coffee as she sat contented as the proverbial cow. The taste of the last spoonful of banana pudding was still on her lips and her tongue darted out to taste the flavor. She couldn't eat another morsel if her life depended on it. At that moment, Dorcas' helper appeared to clear the table. "Tommy," she groaned, "that was absolutely sinful. There oughta be a law." Willow rolled her eyes at him in mock disgust.

Tommy White grinned, eating up the compliment. Coming from Willow who was pretty mean with the desserts herself was saying a whole lot. "Thanks," he said, as he stacked the rolling cart with empty dishes. His smile broadened as the other guests chimed in with their praise.

"Tommy, you put a hurtin' on those bananas, my man." George Henry, a retreat guest, gave the young man a broad wink while raising his hand in salute, then asked slyly, "Sure that's the last of it?" as he eyed the empty serving bowl. "Ms. Dorcas keeping a little on the side for a midnight snack?" Seeking approval for his jest, his large, round bespectacled eyes glimmered as he sought those of his hostess.

Dorcas felt Willow's stare but didn't look at her niece. If

she did, she'd embarrass them both. Instead, she remarked to her third season guest, "George, what Ms. Dorcas does at midnight is nobody's affair but her own. You should know that by now." To soften her words she said in a stage whisper, "Took more than three squares to make these hips though, but don't tell anybody." She grinned at the mollified Mr. Henry. Can't lose a paying guest through sheer rudeness. She pushed away from the table and stood up. "Folks, since I get up with the roosters I'm bidding y'all a good night." Turning to Jake, she smiled a genuine smile. "Jake, glad you made it. Don't be a stranger now. The invite is a standing one." Refusing to meet her niece's eyes, she left the room, plump hips moving in a genteel rhythm.

A chorus of good nights erupted, as the other retreat guests stood and followed suit; all but George Henry, who eyed Jake Rivers.

Showing no surprise that the man remained seated after everyone else had retired to their rooms, Jake sat quietly, waiting for the man's next move. He had pegged Henry's personality after the man's utterances throughout dinner. Jake had learned that this was the man's third year at the Cove. A writer, with one self-published, nonfiction book to his credit, George Henry made it plain to anyone who would listen that his first fiction endeavor had caught the eye of an industry giant. Any day now he expected to hear good news. That bit was said with a gleam in his eyes as he pointedly stared at Willow. Jake hadn't missed the look nor the meaning behind it and at the time wondered why it had bothered him so much. *Why do I keep asking myself questions that already have answers?* Willow Vaughn has captured his complete attention and also apparently the eye of that joker, Henry. When the tip of her tongue had darted out to lick her lips, she was unaware of the sensual gesture but the heat that movement generated in his body was incendiary. He wondered if she hadn't felt the warmth radiating from him, they were sitting so close. Catching the look on George

Henry's face, he had wanted to put blinders on the man's eyes. "Excuse me?" Henry had spoken to him.

"How long did you say you were gardening, my man?" George Henry's tone was more than a little condescending. He resented the nearness of Willow to the "help." His mouth was set in a curl as he waited with derision-filled eyes for an answer.

For whatever reason, Jake was suspicious of guys who spewed out "my man's" in every sentence. He almost had it down to a science when he heard the two words. Casually, he answered, "Oh, only all my life. It's in my blood." He shrugged. "Can't remember a time when I wasn't holding a shovel or digging in dirt."

Willow looked from one man to the other, fully aware of the byplay. At Jake's words she smothered the urge to laugh at the ribbing he was giving the smug-faced George. She knew from the ever knowledgeable Dorcas that Jake Rivers held a master's in landscape architecture and had his own business as a contractor. Deciding to end their not so private tête-à-tête before it turned into a verbal war, Willow stood up. "George, it's been a long day for me too, I think I'll call it a night. See you tomorrow." As both men stood, she turned back to George saying, "Hope you have a fruitful day." To Jake she said, "See you to the door?"

After he and George exchanged civil good nights, Willow preceded Jake into the long hallway that led to the foyer and the front door. She had already opened the door and was standing on the front steps casually leaning against the white wooden railing. The porch had been renovated years ago when the former lessees opened up the bed-and-breakfast. Running the width of the house, it enabled guests to sit in white or green wicker chairs and take in the beauty of the profusion of wildflowers that lined either side of the long gravel approach to the house. The meticulously kept green lawn was dotted with white tables and adirondack chairs for the guests' relaxation.

Willow did not turn when she heard Jake close the door behind him. He stood by her side sharing the beautiful view in the fading light. Just past 8:30, nothing stirred but the petals of the flowers swaying in a breeze so soft that the leaves of the giant oaks were still. She did not want the night to end though she knew he had to rise before the break of day. Sitting on one of the floral-pattern, cushioned, chairs, she beckoned for him to join her.

After a fraction of a second of hesitation, Jake sat beside her in an identical chair. As he did so, the thought ran through his mind that he must have a pretty boring life because tonight was the best evening he had had in months. Dinner with Willow and Dorcas and their guests was a very different but interesting affair. He could easily see himself imposing on their generous hospitality quite often. "You and your aunt work magic with a set of pots. Please thank her again for the invitation," Jake said.

Willow nodded in response, "I will. She loves to hear compliments about her cooking. My uncle Thomas always told her that she could 'burn' as they used to say. She taught me."

"So can I take that to mean that you can 'burn' too?"

"You can," Willow replied without shyness. "But my schedule doesn't always permit, so I mainly do desserts. That's really my specialty." She caught his stare that traveled the length of her. "What?" she asked, curious.

"You don't sample much of it, do you?"

Liking his forthrightness, Willow knew exactly what he meant. For her height, she could carry another pound or two. She was almost skinny. "I do, but it's not very apparent. Ectomorphic genes I guess."

Jake heard no regret in her voice and he liked that. She was happy with herself. He found it hard not to watch her. She carried her height well, with no slouching; shoulders back, head held high, her curly hair flowing down her back. Her long slender arms moved gracefully at her side swinging rhythmically with her shapely legs. Although she frequently dressed in loose flowing garments, he knew that her waist was tiny and her breasts were full. He'd thought once that they stood on their own, unmolested by any trappings. That thought now made him squirm in his chair. Looking away from her out into the garden that was now dark, he said, "Is this your regular routine, dining with your guests every night?" Anything to get his mind off her body.

Willow was becoming hot under his frank appraisal of her. Without words, he had told her that she looked good to him. Ignoring his uncomfortable movement, she said, "No, not every night. We give our guests privacy. We'll have dinner with them on occasion and sometimes we join them for dessert. Most times, dinner for us is informal in the kitchen. At times, Tommy will stay." She gestured toward the grounds. "We advertise as Wildflowers Cove—Writer's Retreat. The peacefulness results in a lot of repeat business. Each guest room is a retreat within itself complete with sitting area and private bath. One doesn't have to leave the room except for meals. Those who are serious about the solitude they're paying for are hardly ever seen off the second floor except at breakfast and dinner." Willow looked at Jake. "You won't mind joining us at the kitchen table?"

Jake weighed her words. "I take it you and your aunt won't mind an extra guest on occasion?"

"You already have Aunt Dee's standing invite. In my book that's not guest status. *I* won't mind," Willow answered. Suddenly, she smiled. "You're really not expected to come bearing gifts, though the wine was appreciated."

Jake acknowledged her thanks with a nod. The chilled sonoma had been served with dinner. "It was no problem but I'll remember that." Changing the subject, he asked, "You don't find the guests a distraction from your work?"

Willow was emphatic with her reply. "Not at all. My day

is scheduled around my work and the light that I may need. Sometimes my deadlines are stringent. I can't afford to be lazy."

Anything but, Jake mused, visualizing the movement of her lithe form. Still vivid in his mind was the emergency call he had made in response to a very irate customer with a malfunctioning greenhouse. "The camellias survived to your satisfaction?" He knew that they had; he had caught a glimpse of the finished painting through the window of the cottage. It was extraordinary.

His words brought a flush to her cheeks as she remembered her tirade. Her publisher would not have understood her missing the deadline for her yearly calendar. But that fact did not give her the right to act like a fishwife to a perfect stranger.

"Beautifully," she replied in a soft voice. "I can't thank you enough for responding so quickly." Leaning, so that she faced him directly, she said, "Would you like to see the results of your efforts?"

"Yes," Jake said simply. Who would refuse a private showing by an acclaimed artist? *Flowers by Morgana* calendars were awaited yearly by avid collectors. As he followed her down the steps, around the side of the house and past the greenhouse, he thought about her professional signature. Why not her first name? And who was "Morgana?"

Reaching the cottage, Willow bent to a small wooden wheelbarrow planter, and removed a key, unlocked the door, then stuffed the key back amongst the flowers. Inside the lighted room she noticed Jake's look. "I know," she said, "but it's convenient. I invariably leave it in the house. Besides, the cleaning service can come and go without disturbing anyone. The routine has worked for quite a while without incident."

"Until." Jake thought it a lousy routine given the isolation of the property. He didn't mind expressing his opinion.

Clearly surprised at his response, Willow said, "Disapproval, Jake? Surely you don't walk a caution line when you're about your daily routine?''

"All the time," he replied matter-of-fact. "What you're doing is foolish, to say the least." He continued, ignoring the flicker of annoyance he saw in her eyes. "You have all sorts coming up here, strangers, including your three-timer, George Henry. I've seen you invite him from this off-limits perimeter. What keeps the man coming back?" He almost dared her to mention the man's writing. "In October, when you close the Cove, you and Ms. Dorcas are two women alone. Who will prevent him from return-ing as a nonpaying guest? Besides, I never found that locking the barn door before the cow ran away, to be a bad thing, for anybody."

Astounded at his long speech, Willow looked at him in amazement, momentarily losing her voice. She sputtered, lapsing into fluid French,

"De l'audace, encore de l'audace, et toujours de l'audace!" Then in English, "Of all the nerve. . . ."

Amused by her flare-up, Jake's mouth twitched. "I think I like the French version better. I took Spanish myself. What's delodas?''

"Audacity," Willow blurted to her surprise in wanting to answer the man.

As if weighing the word, Jake replied "I guess I am that when the occasion arises." After a pause he said, *"Audentes fortuna juvat."* Humor filled his eyes. "Willow, I think now may not be a good time to view your painting. Agreed?" He turned to leave when her voice stopped him.

"I thought you didn't know French." Her tone was ag-grieved.

"My Spanish professor was a Frenchman. He was forever spouting phrases in his native tongue." The humor in his eyes touched his lips. "Good night, Willow. Another time?" He left her standing speechless in the doorway.

Willow stood mesmerized, stirring only when she could

no longer hear his car wheels on the gravel driveway. She turned out the light and locked the door, walking back toward the house.

" 'Fortune favors the bold,' indeed," she said aloud. Her lips parted in a smile, as she couldn't help thinking that there were going to be some ups and downs to unraveling the many sides to Jake Rivers.

Three

By the time Jake arrived at the big house on Windsley Street off Tarrytown Road, night had fallen. The black sky appeared to be awash with rhinestones. He had taken the road to his childhood home on impulse knowing that a phone call was not the best way to inform his father of his intentions. The twenty-minute drive from Wildflowers Cove gave Jake the necessary time to formulate the words extricating himself from his father's business. For several weeks he had known that the customers of Lloyd Rivers Landscaping were satisfied with the results of months of hard work. He and his father's laborers had performed a yeoman's task in keeping the company afloat. It was time that the care and management of the business revert to his older brother Nathaniel, who would once again assume the responsibility of running the company for their ailing father.

As Jake sat in his car parked curbside in front of the pale yellow house, thoughts of his brother brought a drawn look to his face. For months Nat had avoided him. Some mornings, preferring to use his father's pickup instead of the Camaro, Jake would arrive to find that Nat was either asleep or more often than not, hadn't bothered to come home for the night. Upon his return in the early evenings, his brother had made sure he was gone before Jake stopped by. Caught you tonight, Jake mused as he looked at his father's black Oldsmobile in the driveway. The only driver of the car these days was Nat, all but assuming ownership of the vehicle for his pleasures. It is certain that it wasn't used for work Jake seethed inwardly at the panache of his jobless sibling.

Shucking off the slightly guilty feeling that would threaten his decision, Jake climbed from the car and walked toward the house, painfully aware of how his own business was crying for attention.

As he approached, the telltale blue glow coming from the living room window informed Jake that he would probably find his father dozing while the TV watched him. He was wrong.

Lloyd Rivers gave his youngest son an undisguised look of displeasure when Jake entered the room. His ever-cold light brown eyes raked the casually dressed young man. His voice, when he spoke, held traces of a once rich baritone that was now a slow, gravelly rasp. "Ain't it going beyond the call of duty socializing with my customers?"

Jake steeled himself against his father's surly greeting but remained calm, sorry that he had called his father earlier in the evening about his plans. 'Just in case you needed me' he said to himself. Even then he was not surprised at the cold response. Never for the life of him would he understand the dislike the elder Rivers had for the people at Wildflowers Cove. He crossed the room, taking a seat on the sofa next to Nat who nodded at him with a surprised smirk on his handsome face.

Jake acknowledged the greeting by nodding in return. "Nat," he said, then turned to his father who sat in a big easy chair next to the sofa. "Dad, we have to talk." Without looking at his brother, he said, "This concerns you, too, Nat," and continued while staring at his father. "Your business is back in the black, so I'm letting you know that starting now, Nat is back as manager and caretaker. Everyone who should know has been informed: your suppliers, laborers, some customers. Those that I've missed, Nat can tell."

His eyes were clear as he said, "My business is feeling my absence and I've got to get it back on track before my own customers take a walk." To his brother he said, "Mrs. Benson will be expecting to hear from you first thing in the morning." His father's longtime secretary and the glue factor in the business was in Jake's memory from the time he started traveling around with his father when he was a youngster. It was she who had alerted him to just how bad the business was failing after Lloyd's collapse. He returned his brother's amused look. "Got a problem with any of this?"

Nathaniel Rivers, with a full beard and a slim mustache, gave his brother a huge smile, showing perfectly shaped white teeth. That look and his deep voice had charmed many an unsuspecting person no matter their gender. Ignoring Jake's question, he said instead, "So, Mr. Fixit himself is all through. A crusader in khakis with his trusty shovel and rake has saved the day for Rivers Landscaping." He spread his arms. "Now his big brother can play again. How can I thank you?"

"That's enough, Nat," Lloyd interrupted before his youngest son could reply with sarcasm of his own. "If it weren't for your brother you wouldn't have the price of a Mary Jane in your pocket, so shut up and listen for your own good."

A sullen look settled on Nat's face but he did not speak again. Although his father's nearly six-foot frame was a mere hint of his former muscular stature, he still commanded respect from his children no matter their age. His sharp tongue and piercing eyes could whittle down to a doughnut the most daunting of creatures. Nat waited.

"Did this sudden discovery of your faltering business have anything to do with that skinny butt woman at the Cove? Or are you turning your back on your kinfolk?" Lloyd's eyes shimmered with the gleeful satisfaction he derived from the maddening look his remarks brought to

Jake's face. His resentment for the two women up on the Hill, as he sometimes referred to the big house, was evident in every nuance of his body.

As his brother, Jake respected the older man because he was his parent but he did not take a backseat to the rapier-like tongue of Lloyd Rivers. Why the man held such hatred for Wildflowers Cove and its occupants had always been a mystery to him. "Sir," he said, "I see no need to belittle the woman who is among your largest accounts and whose business you still need to make up for that which was lost due to Nat's negligence and disinterest in your affairs, I might add, even though it's been his bread and butter for the last year."

Nat threw his brother a hateful look. "Developing a new style, brother? Stepping on the downtrodden?" He looked at his father as if seeking approval for his remark, but the older man cut his eyes and turned to look at Jake who was quick to retort.

"Who? You? Don't give me that. How many times in the past six years have I—*we*, picked you up and saved your butt from rotting in the street with the rest of the bums you hang with? Every time we found space for you in a drying out facility, you walked out of there not owing a thin dime. Don't give me downtrodden. If anybody should lay claim to that condition it is your ex-wife and your daughter Kendra."

"Leave Annette out of this," Nat said, "and my daughter is doing just fine."

"Yeah, thanks to her other grandparents."

"That's enough." His eyes raked both his sons.

"No, Dad, it's not enough," Jake shot back. "I don't know why you're so hell-bent on overlooking his problem. You've always looked the other way until it's too late. This time I'm not kicking out, not when he's about to go off the deep end again. I won't be available."

"What are you talking about? Make sense," Lloyd ordered Jake.

"Are you the one buying Budweiser now? I don't think so. There's been a six-pack carton in your fridge every week. Sometimes full, sometimes half-empty. Don't tell me the cleaning service is sending Mercedes with her own liquid lunch along with her dust cloths." Jake shot a look at Nat. "Recovering alcoholics don't imbibe. Not even a taste."

"What do you know? I'm the best judge of what my body can take and I'm handling it."

"Are you?" Jake said with disgust. He turned to his father. "I meant what I said Dad. It's up to you now. Either decide to give Nat the responsibility to run your business properly, hire yourself a manager or sell the company. Otherwise you're going to see thirty-five years of your life's work go down the tubes. I can't do it anymore." He stood up to leave. "I'll call Nat in a couple of days to see if he has any questions but I left Mrs. Benson with everything he needs to know."

Lloyd stared at Jake with unreadable eyes. He had no intention of dignifying his son's ultimatum with an answer.

Finally breaking the long stare, Jake turned on his heel and left, closing the front door softly and locking it. His leather heels on the flagstone the only sound made on the quiet street as he walked to his car, opened the door and slid inside. The soft purr of the pampered engine broke the silence of the night. Easing away from the curb, Jake flexed his shoulders enjoying the sudden feel of weightlessness. He felt as if he had shed a mountain.

During the short drive to his condo in a neighboring village, Jake played back his mind's filmstrip of the encounter with his father and brother. The sarcasm and sulks from Nat were no surprise but the biting remarks and cutting looks from his father still surprised him. What on earth had turned his father into such a bitter old man? At sixty-six he wasn't considered ancient by today's standards. Before his stroke, he was surly but afterward his disposition was down-right nasty and rude. How he kept customers was a real miracle. No, not really, Jake amended his thoughts. The man was good, one of the best at what he did. His residential customers spanned a generation and new owners of the corporate accounts remained faithful.

Thinking back, Jake surmised that his father's new atti-tude was probably a direct result of the death of Jake's mother more than seventeen years ago, the same year he turned nineteen. He was a college freshman and he re-membered his father forbidding his sons to drop out of school. That year had been the hardest he had ever faced. He had never felt so alone so far away in upstate New York. He hadn't known a soul at Cornell University. His brother had been a junior at City University and was at home every night. Jake's lips twisted. Nat's major had been marketing. He always boasted how his acumen in that area would net him the big ones. Big ideas and laziness were not a meld, Jake thought. Nat had connived his way from one bad deal to the next, always believing that the new scheme was the one that would immortalize his name in stone. Eventually the highs turned to lows and bouts with depression had led to a love for the bottle. The ensuing years did not bring riches but did bring about the loss of his wife and now twelve-year-old daughter.

Jake's forehead wrinkled in disgust when his niece Ken-dra crossed his mind. A preteen and already he could see the strain of her broken home affecting her once sweet personality. More than once his former sister-in-law had called him, exasperated with the behavior of the rebellious teen. Like he knew about kids, he had told her. She had only laughed and said that she felt sorry for his wife whom-ever she may be because Jake's love for kids would keep the patter of little feet around for years.

Jake pulled into his parking space and minutes later was unlocking his front door. Annette's words were loud in his

ear. "Whomever she may be." At that moment a larger-
than-life image appeared on the door, not unlike the ethereal vision of old Jacob Marley in the classic Dickens' story.
Where it had nearly scared Ebenezer Scrooge half to
death, Jake felt warm all over. There was nothing about
the vision of Willow Vaughn that frightened him. If anything, he fervently wished for the real thing: her soft generous lips against his; the sinfully delicious feeling of her
tongue flicking his. An audible sigh hurried him inside.
The neighbors will have me arrested for lewd behavior he
mused as he locked the door. Once inside, unlike the disappearance of Scrooge's vision, the smiling face of Willow
Vaughn continued to dance before his eyes.

Nathaniel was alone in the darkened living room, the
only light coming from the TV. More than an hour had
passed since Jake had left and without a word the old man,
refusing Nat's help, had shuffled with painful slowness to
his first-floor bedroom.

The brown beer bottle in Nat's hand held a little liquid,
which he downed in one swallow. He then set the empty
bottle on the table, next to the one he'd already finished.
Although his round, dark brown eyes were beginning to
squint from the bright glare of the tube, his thoughts were
not on the images flashing before him but on his brother.
So, after all these years, my brother has finally gotten his
nose open. His lips parted in a grin, showing his handsome
smile. "Of all people," he said aloud. "That standoffish
broad does like a man with dirt under his nails." The smile
disappeared, leaving a churlish scowl. He thought about
his own moves on the rich, snooty artist, which were re-
buffed in no uncertain terms. Now, here comes his no-per-
sonality brother with his quiet ways and moves right on
into the big house, planting his feet under the table. He

grunted, wondering if his brother's shoes had already been planted elsewhere in the house.

Nat pressed the Off button on the TV remote, stood up and carried the empty bottles to the kitchen where he placed them in the recycling can. On his way upstairs to his bedroom, his handsome face became rigid as he sent his brother a telepathic warning. *Brother, if you think you're going to make that woman a part of this family, think again. . . .*

Four

Willow was finding it extremely hard to keep the tiny smile from her lips as she sat on the porch in the dark. She'd be hard put to explain her tumbling thoughts that brought the mysterious smile. Though the evening had turned cool, she hugged herself, occasionally rubbing her goose-pimpled arms. Common sense should have chased her inside but she was sitting in the chair Jake had occupied. His tantalizing, faint woodsy scent intermingled with her fragrant shrub roses and sweet william, causing her to yearn for the flesh-and-blood man. Tonight, briefly, she and Jake had shared a special moment. *Speak for yourself,* she admonished. *That man gave you no indication that the time he spent with you was something special.* Don't lie to yourself. As sure as there is a man in the moon tonight, there is no denying the magnetism between Jake Rivers and Willow Vaughn. Willow only wondered how long and to what extent that magnetic field would become a living thing. The thought scared her. Was it only yesterday that she'd told her aunt how content she was with her life? But that was before Jake had taken her hand in his. Since then, it was as if she'd always known of the thought buried deep within her subconscious, that, as in a fairy tale of old; his very touch would make her his. A sudden feeling of dark foreboding, sent a shudder through her body. In that instant, she sensed that she was not alone.

"So it's a man with dirt under his nails that brings a smile, is it?"

"What . . ." Willow turned to see George Henry at the far end of the darkened porch, leaning against the railing. He walked toward her as Willow stood up. "George, what do you mean spying on me and what business is it of yours who and what makes me smile? I think you've trespassed one time too many." Willow stepped back when the man invaded her space a little too close for comfort.

"Trespassed? After three years of coming up here, returning at your invitation, implying that we could be something more than host and guest, you call me a trespasser?"

Willow could hardly believe her ears. The man was crazy. Invited him back? Of course she and Dorcas extended warm invitations to guests to return. To think that this man mistook their kindness and good business sense for something more was ludicrous. "George Henry, for a man who dabbles in the written word, I think you'd better study the word *obtuse* and then begin a program of self-discovery. I think then you might have better success at becoming a wordsmith." Willow paused and before she could say another word she had been pulled into the man's arms.

"Insensitive, huh? How's this for sensitivity, Miss High and Mighty?" George brought his mouth down hard on Willow's lips in a bruising kiss, keeping her arms pinioned at her side. Sliding his lips to her ear, he whispered, "Bet you been aching to feel something like this, haven't you, woman?" He yelped in pain, falling back, grabbing at his groin where Willow's knee caught him in a swift movement and immediately rocked on his heels at the resounding punch to his jaw.

Willow's tall frame drawn to its full height, taut and ready to spring, appeared menacing as she glared at the surprised man. Her voice was calm though it came in spurts. "I want you off this property at sunrise. Don't stop to say your good-byes, just leave the keys in your room.

Oh, and George, listen to this: You are not welcome back here, ever. You do understand that, don't you?"

"You . . ."

"I wouldn't say that, George," Willow said, sweetly. She watched as he shuffled slowly into the house trying to walk without clutching himself before her amused eyes. When she heard his upstairs door shut, Willow turned out the lights and locked her door, hurrying into her bathroom. She couldn't wait to wash the smell and the touch of that man from her body.

As she soaped her body, Jake's words pounded in her ears, breaking up in the waterfall, "What keeps the man coming back?"

Hours after Jake had said good night and the house was in the quiet state of sleep, Willow was still awake. Unable to fall asleep after the distasteful incident with George, she had been sitting propped up among her bed pillows for the last half hour, thinking about the events of the evening and her surprise dinner guest. Now, she noted as she peered at the bedside clock in the moonlit room, it was nearly midnight. Her eyes roamed the huge master suite. Willow loved the room where she lived. Like her guests, she had no reason to leave her quarters except to take meals and to walk across her garden to work. Her queen-size, four-poster bed filled one wall while across the room her sitting area was spacious enough for a settee, armchair and tables. One door led to a roomy master bath while another led to a private terrace facing her gardens with a brick path leading to her greenhouse. Her surveillance caught sight of the large sketch pad lying on the coffee table. Pushing away the white cotton chenille bedspread, she got out of bed and walked across the room to the sitting area where she turned on the brass table lamp. The soft light afforded enough illumination for Willow's glance to rake over the head that was taking shape on the pad. Smiling, she sat down in the armchair and picked up the pad and soft lead pencil. As her early art teachers had told her, the human form was not her forte, especially hands and fingers, but her faces were true to life and haunting. This was true, Willow mused as she stared at Jake's profile; this was true. Deftly, her hand moved across the pad, filling in the hair, fleshing out the cheeks, refining the mustache and at last, finishing the eyes. Those eyes that she'd nearly drowned in every time they had met hers. Suddenly she wanted to put his image on canvas, in oils. She would bring out the fine hue of his sienna skin and capture the fleeting glow of his wine-kissed eyes. However would she get just the right depth in those dimples? Her sketch finished at last, Willow propped the pad against the vase on the table and sat back, studying the face that appeared to be watching her. A shudder passed through her body as she rubbed her sleeveless arms and breathed a silent prayer. Willow thanked God for her talent to bring flowers to life on paper. She loved what she did and that dedication and love for her art showed in every detail of a painting. But as she stared at her drawing, she knew that her instructors were right: She had a gift for giving expression to the human face, especially the eyes. Jake's eyes bored into hers affecting the appearance of following her. As she stared back she could almost hear his deep voice, his baritone laugh. She caught herself up short when she thought she could smell his spicy aftershave. *Hold on girl, are you losing it?* she chided herself. Shades of Dorian Gray *this is not,* she thought, as she remembered the long ago story of a painting that lived and breathed all the evildoings of its real-life image. "Evil you are not, Jake Rivers," Willow said aloud. The sound of her voice startled her and she stood up, quickly walking to the foot of her bed where she snatched up her robe and pulled it on. "Talking to a picture at midnight will definitely put you in the running to model the latest in straitjackets, Willow Vaughn," she said aloud.

Instantly, her words sobered her. Her fears of mental insta-
bility in her family came rushing to mind. Unnerved, she
left the bedroom and padded softly in her bare feet to the
kitchen. She needed to steady the fierce beating of her
heart and her shaking hands, and warm her insides. Intending to prepare some hot cocoa, she walked down the dark
hallway. As she neared the kitchen door, a sharp whistle
pierced the still house. At the same instant, Willow froze
and another sharp sound joined that of the whistle. She
realized it was her own shrill screams when she saw her aunt
in front of her, shaking her by the shoulders.

"Willow, Willow, stop. Stop. It's me, Aunt Dee," Dorcas
shouted, as she held her niece firmly. She had heard
sounds coming from the kitchen and thinking Willow was
preparing a late-night snack had sought to join her when,
just as she had left her bedroom, she'd heard the whistle
and immediately after, the screams of her niece. Bewildered to find Willow in the hall, she wondered who had
put the kettle on? On the heels of her thought, the kitchen
door opened and a startled George Henry stood staring
at the two women. Willow had quieted and she and Dorcas
gaped in amazement at the surprised man.

"Mr. Henry," Dorcas said.

"George?" Willow said at the same time.

"Ladies?" George said, obvious relief flooding his voice,
but he took a little step backward as he remembered his
last encounter with Willow. "I had a little stomach upset
and I thought some tea might help. My God, Willow, what
did you see? Whatever it was you can bet it's miles away by
now," he ended, laughing, though warily keeping his distance.

"Mr. Henry, this is no laughing matter." Dorcas' voice
was filled with reproach. "You scared us half to death. You
are a paying guest for quarters that are exceedingly comfortable. Your meals are sumptuous and afternoon tea and
evening snacks are quite hefty. These are our private quar-

ters and you are not welcome to roam them at will. During each of your visits in the past three years, you have been asked to keep your distance from private places on the property." Dorcas breathed heavily as she continued rapid-fire. "In light of that fact, you are no longer welcome at Wild-flowers Cove as a retreat guest. At daybreak you can start packing and by noon I want you off this property. You will be reimbursed pro rata for the two-and-a-half days left of your stay. Are we clear on this, Mr. Henry?" Her voice and manner defied disagreement.

George Henry's normally affable facade dissipated under Dorcas' attack. Gone was the slick grin. His eyes darkened and his voice was less oily. "Crystal clear," he said. "But you're late." He laughed at the perplexed look on Dorcas' face who was standing in front of her niece like her great protectorate. He knew when to cut his losses. On returning to Wildflowers Cove for a third time, he had meant to get the snooty artist to change her mind about him. He had watched her and knew that she didn't have a man, just like the gossip columns reported. When he'd made a move on her last year, she hadn't objected all that hard, he remembered. But this year, every time he had tried to talk to her in the gardens or catch her in her studio someone had interrupted. Most times it had been that damn gardener who had had the nerve to show up tonight to wine and dine just like he was somebody. And she was hanging on his every word. *Go figure some broads,* he thought in disgust. *I'll leave, but this is not the last they'll hear from me.*

"Late?" Dorcas asked, wondering if the man had gone batty.

Willow said, "You're generous, Aunt Dee, I gave him until daybreak. But you'll have to excuse the man. He probably needed some chamomile for his stomach. And possibly some ice," she ended.

Before the perplexed older woman could answer, George said, "I don't need a second dismissal, Ms. Dorcas, though your offer to allow me to stay until noon is the most generous of the two. Rest assured I'm outta here." A malicious grin appeared. "Bet on it that I'll spread the word about the hospitable hosts at Wildflowers Cove."

"What do you mean by that, George?" Willow spoke with anger.

Cutting in, Dorcas said, "Are you threatening to besmirch the name of this retreat, George?" Her voice was deadly sweet. "If that is your plan, then you are putting your backside in a most precarious position. Get my meaning? Speak up if you want me to break it down a bit more."

George moved around the women cautiously as he made his way down the hall and up the stairs to his room without uttering another word. His thoughts were on the older woman's words. His eyes darkened at her veiled threat. Would she dare do what he'd planned? File a complaint? He didn't need that kind of notoriety with an impending book deal. "Best leave these two crazy broads in their own highfalutin world," he muttered as he tossed his luggage on the bed.

"What on earth were you two talking about? Chamomile? Second dismissal? What went on here?" Dorcas skeptically eyed her niece.

Laughing, Willow took her aunt's arm and led her into the kitchen. "I'll explain over a cup of hot cocoa." She looked at the untouched cup with a tea bag inside. "Looks as if Mr. Henry's stomach will remain unsettled." She burst out laughing again. "I'll explain, Aunt Dee, I promise."

Dorcas was propped on the settee while her niece was cozy in the roomy armchair in Willow's bedroom. Both women were quiet after Willow had related her encounter with George. Dorcas had listened without interruption except for an occasional sucking of her teeth and a roll of her eyes at certain points. "Now if that don't beat all," she said. "You mean to say that he was coming up here all this time because he thought he had a chance with you?" Dorcas looked at her niece. "Are you sure you didn't lead the man on unintentionally? Not even a little bit? You know how he was enamored of name-dropping and rubbing elbows with celebs. Why I'll bet he's spread the word in his own little bailiwick that he's got a thing going on with the famous artist at Wildflowers Cove."

"Oh, Aunt Dee, be serious. Men like George Henry don't need much encouragement to feed their egos. Let's be happy that he's gone." While Willow was telling her story, they heard the front door close and soon afterward the start of a car engine. George Henry had left long before the sun came up.

"Let's hope that he'll have the common sense to stay away," Dorcas said. After a pause she asked, "It's still with you, isn't it?"

Willow knew what her aunt meant. She shrugged. "I guess it is. But you know something, Aunt Dee? Tonight, I experienced déjà vu. As if the sound of a whistle had drawn me to this same hallway. No, not tonight. Long ago. I think it was that feeling that scared me more than the sound. So strange. How could that be?" The look on her aunt's face stopped her. "What's the matter?"

Dorcas was remembering the past. All these years she had thanked the Lord for erasing an evil memory from Willow's mind. Even when they had decided to move into the house, she'd had trepidations that bad dreams would haunt Willow. But nothing like that had ever happened. Not until now. What had happened in this house twenty-six years ago to a four-year-old was locked up in her mind. When the housekeeper had found the little girl sitting forlornly in the living room with a tea bag and a cup and saucer, asking for her parents, who knew what the child had heard and seen before then? All efforts to get Willow to talk about the last time she'd said good night to her

Mommy and Daddy, failed. Willow would only say that her parents were gone. But she never remembered preparing for tea. She'd obviously used a chair to reach the tea canister. She would have had to walk down this same hallway on her way to the kitchen, past the bathroom where her parents lay dead. Had she tried the locked door? Had she seen the little seepage of blood under the door? These questions arose and died on the lips of the detectives when Dorcas had intervened.

"Dorcas?" Willow sounded worried. "Are you all right?"

The concern in her niece's voice brought Dorcas back to the present. "I'm okay, Willow, it's just that I was worried about you. Remember you were born into this house and didn't leave it until you were four years old. Anything could have happened to make you frightened of whistling tea-kettles and other similar sounds." Quietly, she asked, "Have you remembered something?"

"No," answered Willow. "Except that never before was the fear so strong. Not since I was a little girl in Canada and you and Uncle Thomas had to remember not to let the kettle whistle." She smiled. "Until you finally said the heck with it and threw the darn thing out."

"I remember."

Willow was thoughtful. "Whatever happened to my parents the night they died had something to do with loud noises. Loud enough to reach my ears upstairs in my bedroom. Is that what you're thinking?"

Dorcas nodded but remained quiet.

"When I was thirteen, for the first time, you told me about my famous father and how he and my mother died violently, mother shooting father and then herself. You wanted to tell me before I'd learn an embellished version from others. But that's all you told me. Over the years you never said more than what was necessary to satisfy my curiosity. Why?" Willow answered her own question. "You think that night all those years ago, I saw or even heard something. You're afraid that I'm repressing a bad memory. That night has something to do with my fear of sudden whistles, doesn't it?"

"Yes," Dorcas answered, her chest constricting while her heart pumped wildly. After all this time, Dorcas didn't want to know if her dear child was a witness to her father's murder. "Yes, that's what the detectives at the time thought, but you were a frightened little girl, wanting her parents and that's all you cried for. Not once did you give any indication whatsoever that you saw or heard anything unusual that night. When the police began to force you to say things and to browbeat you, that's when I put a stop to their questioning. The child psychologist, who was present, agreed."

"But later on, in Canada, when you noticed my reaction to the kettle, didn't you wonder about such a foolish fear? Didn't you try to question me about it even though I was so young?"

"Of course your uncle Thomas and I wondered about it," said Dorcas. "The loss of your parents was traumatic enough we thought and we didn't want to go against the psychologist's warnings that you were being pushed to remember something that you may have buried. Besides, in seven or eight months you'd become such a happy little girl that I would've killed if anyone had approached you with what happened that night." She paused. "The only disturbance was the whistle and when we learned that that sound upset you, we took care of the problem."

"I was happy, Aunt Dee." Willow sighed. "I can't remember my parents or this house or anything except that you and Uncle Thomas and Grandy were my only family and I loved you. When Uncle Thomas died and then his mother, my dear Grandy, I remember thinking that you were all the family I had left." She slid out of her chair and onto the couch next to Dorcas and kissed her aunt on the cheek. "I love you and I'm glad we are family but it's after one o'clock in the morning and how we got on this subject I can hardly remember. Don't you still have four guests left to feed in a couple of hours?"

Dorcas hugged her niece and stood up. "Love you, too, buttercup. And what do you mean I have breakfast to fix? You sleeping in late?" She eyed the sketch of Jake Rivers. "Or do you intend to lay up in here daydreaming?"

Willow laughed. "I think I've done that already as you can plainly see. Not bad, huh?"

"Definitely not bad after only a few hours over dinner. I wonder what kind of inspiration would come from a 'morning to night' date?"

"Date? I think it's time we said good night, Aunt Dee." Willow had to smile at the sound of Dorcas' soft chuckle as she left the room and padded softly down the hall to her own room.

As Willow turned out the light and slipped under the covers, she didn't wonder if, but when, she'd have her first date with Jake.

Dorcas was sitting at her desk, attacked by insomnia. Her sister Beatrice's presence enveloped her. Worry lines creased her face. After years of excuses, it was time to honor her sister's wish. Her fingers trembling not a little, she opened the bottom drawer and pulled out a locked steel box. The sound of the tiny lock clicking open signaled a point of no return. This time, something kept her from slamming the lid and shutting the box up in the drawer again.

One by one, she lifted several documents and envelopes until she reached a faded violet-tinted envelope. She stared at her name. Just underneath was an identical envelope bearing her niece's name. Opening the envelope addressed to her, her eyes grew misty as she fingered the worn pages. She could recite the words verbatim if her life depended on it. Her eyes flickered. Thomas would find her fingering the pages, sobbing quietly, then he'd take them from her and enclose them in the envelope and lock it up again. His words were always the same, spoken in the same firm but gentle voice. "The time for healing is long past, Dory. Let her go."

As long as she lived, she would never forget the sound of her voice screaming her sister's name. How could she let her go? Her sister's soul would know no peace. She took a life and damned her own soul. Had she been mad? What possessed her to doom herself and that of her beautiful child? Dorcas' eyes narrowed to slits. Her sister's last words spoke of the evil she'd lived with for the last six years of her life. Beatrice would have surely gone mad had she forced herself to live with the darkness that was Michael Vaughn.

She began to read the words, still as fresh in her mind as though she'd read them yesterday.

July 1972
Dorcas, my dear sister:
   Love you. I know that you and Thomas will love and raise Willow as your own. Dorcas, I have not been completely truthful to you all these years. You suspected that I was unhappy but to keep you from probing too deeply, I only told you of small arguments and little disagreements between me and Michael. I kept the physical and mental abuse a secret. Does one really speak of these things? Please forgive me. You have always been a kind and loving sister to me though we're miles apart. I should have been forewarned the first time Michael slapped me before our marriage. But I was so in love with him I ignored my inner voice. Even as he grows cold downstairs. I think I still love him. Am I mad?

Dorcas dropped the pages. She couldn't continue. She knew every word. To finish would mean another sleepless night, her heart filled with hatred for her long-dead brother-in-law. To finish would mean that she would have to honor Beatrice's promise to give her letter to Willow. Her last words to her lovely daughter. What were they? Dorcas wondered. Would a voice from the grave hurt her little buttercup? Would she dare disobey her sister's dying wish? She put the pages back inside the envelope and locked it up inside the steel box. The envelope with her niece's name on it was put inside the top drawer. Giving the letter to Willow would mean exposing the truth. Willow would learn that after all these years, she'd been lied to.

Dorcas couldn't lose the love of the niece who was like a daughter to her. She couldn't give Willow her letter. Not yet, thought Dorcas. Not yet.

Five

Saturdays at Wildflowers Cove were always hectic. Departing guests were given an early breakfast in order to be checked out and off the premises by 11:00 A.M. The housekeeping service arrived to clean, change linens and shampoo carpets before the new guests arrived at four in the afternoon. It is the one day that retreat activities superseded Willow's painting schedule. Her hours were spent checking minute details such as the fresh flowers in each guest room and in the main floor sitting areas and keeping an eye on the meal preparations. Long ago Dorcas had decided that she wasn't in the running for a "Superwoman-of-Innkeepers" award and when the pleasure of running the retreat turned into a drudgery, she was through. So, to give herself and her niece time to enjoy their home, a catering service prepared weekend meals. Only occasionally did she get the urge to make a special Sunday dish. Culinary students like Tommy White were hired for a few hours each day to assist the caterer. While Willow was downstairs, Dorcas was upstairs, following behind the cleaning service making certain that every dust speck was gone and every toilet shined. Once satisfied that the interior passed inspection, Dorcas gave the grounds the once-over, instructing the Rivers' laborer to trim this or trim that. There was hardly anything to do in that area because of the expert manicuring done by Jake in the past weeks. The grounds and the flowers were absolutely breathtaking. As the arriving guests drove along the gravel path they were welcomed by the raucous display of wildflowers, which was carefully orchestrated by Jake. Swaying gently on either side were two-foot tall English lavenders, their perfumed fragrance lingering in the air. Brilliant yellow bell-shaped lilium; purple delphinium; the daylily in whites, yellows and rare pinks, spilled over themselves, one more eager than the other to preen in the breeze. The drooping orange-red tiger lily vied for attention with other colorful sister lilies. Months ago, Dorcas and Jake had planned the color scheme with Dorcas insisting on an abundance of her favorite, the tiger lily.

By six-thirty, the service trucks and staff had departed. Food deliveries had been made and meals cooked. Two student servers had arrived and Willow had seen the last guest upstairs.

After showering and changing, Willow decided to take a much needed respite in her garden. Ambling by the living room window, she noticed Nat Rivers talking to one of his father's laborers. Hardly surprised at his appearance, Willow rather expected it.

The day after Jake had joined them for dinner, Dorcas had received a very formal letter informing her that Nat would resume the position of manager for Lloyd Rivers Landscaping. Willow and Dorcas were surprised at the notice, for Jake had given them no indication that he would not be returning—at least not on business, Dorcas had teased.

As though Nat sensed her stare, he looked up, saw her, then waved, his butternut face breaking into a smile before he turned back to his worker. *There's a handsome man,* Willow thought, *and he doesn't give a damn who knows that he knows it.* She went to the front door and out to the garden. The worker waved, gathered his lawn brooms and rakes, said something to Nat then walked to his car. Nat waved again, then waited for Willow to reach him.

"Willow," Nat said, a devil-may-care look on his face. "Looks like the Cove won't be needing too much of my attention this summer. Appears my brother has things well in hand up here." His roving eye undressed her. "Everything is in tip-top shape. I mean *everything.*"

Nothing's changed, Willow observed dryly, as she extended her hand to the vain man. "Nat," she said, "I know you're glad to be back at work." She extricated her hand from his lingering clasp and waved it around as if to encompass the property. She didn't miss his emphasis nor his look, almost tempted to look down to see if her dress and panties were still in place. "You're right. Jake has done a fine job. The grass and shrubs are green and healthy and the flowers are blooming furiously. My aunt and I are very pleased."

I'll bet you are. Nat's dark thoughts did not match his bright and rakish smile. Aloud, he said, "Apparently, my baby brother sprung this turnover on our customers and they've been ringing the phone off the hook wondering what's up. They're driving Mrs. Benson crazy, so I'm making personal rounds." Nat's insolent look draped her body as he talked and his smile widened at Willow's growing discomfort. "I'm surprised that he didn't want to make this stop himself." Hurrying on before the fine sister exploded, he started toward the house. "Since Mis' Dorcas signs the checks, then I reckon it's her I should be speaking to." He held up a hand as Willow took a step. "No, you stay, I'll find my way. I'm no stranger, here." Smoothly, he continued, "I'm sure we'll be seeing much more of each other, now."

At the sound of a car on the crushed gravel, they both turned to watch the approach of the vintage Camaro. Nat whistled. "Well I'll be damned. Baby bro' is not lacking in the social graces after all." His eyes locked with Willow's as his smile faded. "Not lacking at all." He didn't wait for his brother to stop, but walked away without another word.

Though Willow could hear the soft laugh, there was no mirth.

When Nat disappeared around the side of the house, Willow turned her attention to Jake who was walking toward her. Some "baby" she thought of Nat's description of his younger brother, wondering if there was animosity between the two men. The older Rivers brother certainly retreated hastily from the surprise visitor. Since his departure a few nights ago, she had not seen nor talked to Jake and now as he spoke, she realized how much she had missed the sound of his voice, the faint smell of fresh washed skin with a hint of woodsy aftershave. As she extended her hand, she couldn't wait for the electric current that she expected. She was not disappointed in the reaction of any of her senses.

"Jake."

"Willow," Jake answered. He was reluctant to let her hand go, though they both noticed the faint quiver. The softness of her artisan's hands surprised him. His eyes followed the path his brother had taken. Nodding to Willow, he asked, "Did my brother approve?" His look swept the grounds.

"Very much," was her reply and wondered why the brothers did not use each other's given names. Unwilling to believe it was a "man" thing, Willow continued, "Nat's making personal appearances. 'Business,' he said."

Jake had his own thoughts about that. When he'd spotted his brother and Willow, he didn't miss their close proximity and the small step back Willow had taken, widening the distance. He looked closely at her. "Is everything all right?" In all the times he had seen her, he'd never noticed a tight jaw. *Why now? Nat's doing? Or mine?* Her smile exonerated him. It must have been Nat. If he'd said anything . . . "Are you all right?" he repeated, watching her closely.

"I'm fine. Why wouldn't I be? What's wrong, Jake?" She saw his quick look toward the house. "Nat? Oh, he hasn't changed. Always a little full of himself. People like him don't worry me."

"I just thought that he was, well—maybe acting a little out of line." His facial muscles relaxed as he saw her easy dismissal of his brother.

Ignoring his strange remarks about Nat, Willow said, "I'm happy to see you, Jake. When Dorcas showed me your letter I felt a little down."

"Why?" He was curious at her frank statement but secretly pleased.

"I thought that you would hardly return only to see a painting. With a business to run, coming here for such frivolity would be out of the question."

"I hardly think viewing a *Morgana* painting would be called frivolous, and neither do I think your following would." He threw her a skeptical look. "I didn't take you for the type to fish for compliments, Willow."

"Fish for . . . what nerve," sputtered Willow. She stopped when she saw his lips part in a tiny smile, not big enough to show his dimples but a smile nevertheless.

"No delodas?" he asked softly.

Remembering his poor French pronunciation for audacity her anger vanished. The man had a sense of humor. Laughing, she answered, *"Non."*

"No?" Jake said, understanding her French. "I like the sound of it rolling off your tongue."

Willow liked the sound of his voice and wondered how long she was going to hear it. If Nat was here on business then had Jake come for more of Dorcas' delicious vittles or what? The only way to find out was to ask. "Would you like to join us for dinner?"

"Dinner?" Jake frowned as he looked at his watch. It was well past six-thirty. He shook his head, "Sorry, for my interruption. I knew you served dinner at six, so I thought I'd stop by and take a look around and then be on my way without disturbing your meal. I had no idea Nat was stopping by." Disappointment crept into his voice. "Thanks for the invite, but I have another engagement."

"It's Saturday, Jake. New guests are tired from travel and are not ready for dinner so early. We eat at seven, today." Engagement? Does that translate into date she wondered, feeling a little twinge of jealousy. Had she really expected him to say that he'd come to see her? Her high spirits waned, a sigh escaping when she realized that it could be weeks or months before she heard his voice again.

"Then in that case, can you take the time now to visit my studio?" she asked softly. "The camellia calendar won't be published for more than a year and I really would like the savior of the blooms to see it before then."

Jake heard the change in her voice and it did something to his insides. Sadness? He didn't like the sound and knew that her mood had something to do with him and what he'd said. But what and why was she bothered? When he'd made the decision to defect he'd known that seeing Willow again by chance was a remote possibility. If anything, he would have to instigate any initial future contact. Hoping beyond hope to catch a glimpse of her was uppermost in his thoughts when he was driving here. Luck was with him when she appeared in his line of vision as he entered the gate. He didn't place that much stock in fate, believing that one made his own chances, but he'd be a fool not to walk through the door of opportunity.

"I can take the time, Willow." With quiet emphasis and an unwavering look, Jake held out his hand and Willow took it.

Jake's steps as sure as hers, Willow led him around the side of the house to the path leading to the small cottage, a path he had traveled many times. She made no comment as they walked, but wondered what was to come at the end of their short journey? When they stopped at the door, she was relieved. Walking so close by his side, her hand captured in his, she was feeling heady. *Get a grip, Willow,* she scolded herself. Bending down, she retrieved the key from its hiding place and stood to meet the reproachful look in Jake's eyes.

"Old habits die hard," she said, a smile in her voice. He was still holding her hand and his grip tightened as he pulled her close. "Jake, we're not going to argue about this, are we?" Her voice was as thick as her head was light, his maleness sending her into overdrive. Why should his nearness stir a childhood memory of her nesting her head in the soft, warm, scented bosom of her Grandy? One glance told her why and she had the decency to blush. She wanted to nuzzle her nose in the warm, soft hollow of his throat, to inhale all his essence.

Jake was losing himself in her beautiful dark eyes and was finding it extremely hard to chastise her for the dangerous habit. All he wanted to do was hold her close and bury his face in her hair. The whiffs of floral were tantalizing. Instead, releasing her he held out his hand and she gave him the key. He unlocked the door and before following her inside, he returned the key to its place then closed the door.

Neither Jake nor Willow saw the tall figure watching them from the house, his back to the closed kitchen door. Nat had just finished saying his good-byes to Dorcas and stopped when he saw his brother and Willow walking hand-in-hand toward the studio. With narrowed eyes, his look could not have gotten any blacker than his thoughts. *So I was right,* he seethed inwardly. *Baby brother* has *got a thing for Mistress High and Mighty and she certainly climbs down off that high horse around him, panting to beat the band.* "Well, if that ain't nothin'," he muttered. After glowering at the closed cottage door for another instant, Nat turned away and walked to his father's black Olds. The engine jumped to an instant purr. The gravel spun as he made his way to the gate, where he stopped to check for passing traffic before entering the road. He glanced at himself in the rearview mirror, catching the malicious gleam in his eyes. "Brother, have I got a story for you," he said aloud. The sound of grim laughter filled the car as it vanished in the distance.

Jake stood with his back to the closed door, hands in his pockets, watching Willow as she turned on the lights. The pungent smell of oil paint had assailed his nostrils when he'd stepped inside. Surveying the very private world of Morgana, the artist, Jake knew few were ever invited to her inner sanctum where she created visual beauty for all to enjoy. The current painting, on a tall easel, was draped with a rainbow-splattered cloth. A smattering of easels, some tall, some table-size, some with canvases primed and ready; as if waiting their turn to become magically washed in a raucous display of color from a masterful hand. He closed his eyes to an invading memory, when as a kid he'd tried to paint, smearing the colors on paper to create fabulous images, giving up only when his creations failed to resemble beautiful things. "The smell does something to you, doesn't it?"

Her soft voice brought him back to the present and he opened his eyes while answering yes but she had already turned back to whatever she was busying herself with since he'd closed the door. He looked amused as the normally self-assured woman fidgeted with lamps and switches, then stumbled as she walked to a wall on the far side of the room where many canvases were stored. Her mumbling was audible as she flipped through the paintings, stopping, when she pulled one aside. He remained where he was, taking his fill of her. Where before, he would catch glimpses of her body while she worked, only envisioning the movement of her lithe form, now he had an unobstructed view. She wore a long flowing, nearly sheer cotton sleeveless dress that reached her ankles. Tiny violet flowers were painted on a pale blue background. Underneath she wore a white cotton T-shirt with short capped sleeves. The dress swayed as she moved, swirling around her ankles when she tripped and dipping forward when she bent over to flip through the canvases. Her curvy hips were quite evident beneath the light fabric. Jake's thought at that moment was to run his roughened hands over the smooth skin that he knew lay beneath the layers of cloth. The thought made him wince and close his eyes briefly. When he opened them she was staring at him, her lips slightly parted, her eyes questioning. He could see the heat in them.

"What?" Willow's voice was breathless.

Jake pushed himself off the door and was at Willow's side before she took another breath. He removed the painting from her hands, placed it on a nearby easel and turned to her, his eyes boring into hers. "This," he said softly as he cupped her chin, lifting her lips to his. "This, is what." Jake's lips captured hers in a gentle kiss that deepened hungrily when he felt her body sway into his. When she lifted her arms around his neck, he caught her close, enfolding her in his strong arms as he tasted her kisses. The sweet warmth of her mouth and her darting tongue set his lips on fire, sending white hot heat to his loins. The feel of her hands on the inner softness of his neck and her full breasts crushed against his chest was nearly too much to bear. He wanted to feel the nakedness of her. They were molded together and he knew that neither of them could ignore his telltale passion. "Willow, Willow," he whispered against her moist lips, his plundering tongue seeking and finding more sweetness in the exploration of her mouth.

He showered kisses on the tip of her nose, her eyelids, her neck, while he eagerly sought and found one burgeoning breast. Jake agonized that he could only imagine the taste of the rigid bud between his lips.

Willow's body responded to Jake's every touch, straining into him, turning and twisting to make it easier for his hand to knead her aching nipples. The throb of him pulsating against her thighs made her wild to unclothe herself. She felt tortured, unable to feel his bare skin. "Jake," she murmured into the hollow of his neck, remembering that only moments before she'd wished to taste that soft flesh. She couldn't bear her hurt any longer. Her body quivered as she held him close, eyes closed as she rested her head on his chest.

As had happened before when they had touched, days ago, Willow's shiver had gone through Jake. He felt it now and the effect was the same. He stood still, letting the warmth run its course through his body. As if a move or a word would break whatever spell they had fallen under, both remained still, swaying only to what was left of the sudden passion that had engulfed them—as if they had been caught up in the tailspin of a shooting star. Jake's hand was buried in the long soft curls of Willow's hair, even as he inhaled deeply of its lilac fragrance. He was the first to stir when he heard Willow's low sigh. Releasing her with reluctance, he stepped back though he captured her gaze.

Willow stared back. She felt weak and her tongue was trapped in her throat. When she took a step, she swayed. Jake's hand shot out to steady her.

"Are you all right?" He caught her arm.

Nodding, Willow looked up at him with a smile parting her lips. "Talk about being swept away. . . ."

There was only one comfortable chair in the big room: a deep, three-cushioned sofa that was covered in a rose-splattered chintz. Willow walked over to it and sat down, her arms folded across her chest as she looked at the man whose taste was still on her lips and whose touch still seared her skin.

Jake followed and sat, leaving the middle cushion empty as he held her look. It was his turn to ask, "What?"

"Unless I've been sleepwalking these past few months, this was our first kiss, wasn't it?" She tilted her head to one side. "Anyone looking in would award both of us with the Liar of the Year prize if either of us denied it, wouldn't you agree?"

Jake smiled. "Wholeheartedly."

Willow's hand smoothed over the space between them, one finger following the design of a rose. "Look at us."

Jake knew what she meant. The magnetism was strong. Any closer proximity would be dangerous.

"Jake," her voice was a soft question, "What's this all about?" She spread her hand in an empty gesture. "I mean, I've heard of attraction, but, this . . ." Willow's voice trailed off as a thought struck her. What if she had just experienced only raw animal passion. Pure lust. Is that what months of seeing but not touching him had done? No. She wouldn't believe that. He had been as oblivious to the world as she'd been.

Almost as if he could hear her thoughts, feel her self-doubt, Jake said, "Willow, I felt what you felt. Believe me, I can't explain it either, but I do know that whatever it was, it is not meaningless." He cleared the huskiness from his voice before he continued. "I knew that when we came in here, that given the chance I would kiss you. I've wanted that. Wanted to know what you would taste like, feel like, in my arms." Jake rubbed his jaw and mouth as if savoring the lingering kisses. "I didn't, couldn't know that we would—that our—my feelings . . ."

"Ran so deep?" Willow said softly.

"Deep," Jake repeated, as if in awe. Neither spoke, nor did they try to touch, but sat, each buried in thought.

Jake couldn't believe that moments ago, the famous botanical artist, Morgana, had been locked in his heated embrace. Though he'd always known of her and when he'd finally met her months ago, he had to dispel those gossip stories of her being "cold and dispassionate," in love, with only her flowers. He'd seen for himself how warm and friendly she was. And now—what could he say about what had just happened between them? What was she thinking, feeling, now?

Jake knew that now was not the moment to examine those

feelings. Not with her so near, gazing at him with those doe eyes, full of fire. Did she realize the passion she bared? His breathing heightened and he shuttered his lids to hide the heat of his own desire. With both of their emotions bared, he didn't believe he was that strong, to ignore the taunting current of desire that threatened to carry them away beyond reason.

Finally, Jake stood up, looking down at Willow who returned his stare. She stood, and in silent agreement they walked toward the door. Willow put her hand on the knob then looked into Jake's eyes as his hand held the door shut.

Though she was a breath away, he did not touch her. "We'll talk about this. Tomorrow?" At her nod, he opened the door. "I'll call."

Willow pulled the door closed, bent and retrieved the key, then locked the door. She returned the key to the plant holder. As they walked along the path leading to the front of the house and to Jake's car, Willow shook her head, her curls bouncing as her shoulders shook with laughter. Answering Jake's silent question, she said, "The camellia. You never saw it."

The dimples in Jake's cheeks deepened as his baritone laugh mingled with her deep tones, the sound causing birds to twitter and butterflies to take flight.

Jake kissed Willow with his eyes as he left her standing at the edge of the driveway.

Willow watched Jake until his car disappeared from view, then turned toward the house. She stopped when she saw her aunt watching her from the curtained living room window. Continuing into the house, Willow wondered why on earth her aunt wore such a somber expression. For months she'd been planting the seeds of a matchmaker and when her efforts began to take root, she was having second thoughts. What could possibly be wrong? An uncharacteristic frown marred Willow's forehead as she entered the house through the kitchen door.

Dorcas hadn't seen her niece since they'd both taken a breather from the day's earlier hectic activities. She wondered if Willow was making herself scarce until Nat Rivers left, knowing how she couldn't stomach the vain man. By the time the caterers had served the guests dinner and there was no sign of Willow, Dorcas went in search of her. Spying Jake's car and no sign of either him or Willow in the gardens, Dorcas decided that they could only be in one place; Willow's studio. She returned to the house and waited. Soon she saw them. Though the young couple walked not touching, they were not the same two people who had really only met a few nights before. Dorcas guessed that they had finally discovered each other. Her heart thumped wildly as she watched the look on Jake's face as he left Willow. A man with some serious feelings.

Nights ago, when Dorcas had decided to give her niece the letter from Beatrice Vaughn, something had held her back. After all these years why should she honor her dead sister's request? What would be the harm in tearing it to shreds, pretending that it never existed? Suppose Beatrice's words to her daughter soured Willow on relationships? On marriage? But Dorcas' heart wouldn't allow her to dishonor her sister's wish. Why, even her husband Thomas, from his grave, would haunt her disloyalty to Beatrice. He would tell her to stop meddling and tempting the fates where his beloved Willow was concerned. At the thought of her husband, Dorcas' eyes grew misty. He had loved Willow like the daughter he could never have. If it hadn't been for her playing the role of ogre once in awhile, Grandy and Thomas would have spoiled the child rotten. No one would have wanted her. It so happened that Willow, after a few months with them, had developed the sweetest and most sunny disposition for one so young. At four, she had come to them a somber, self-possessed little lady; almost too grown-up, until coddling from three lovestruck adults nurtured the little girl in her. Dorcas would give the letter to Willow and pray to God that Beatrice's message from the grave would not ruin her daughter's chance at happiness.

Now, as she eyed her niece, Dorcas put a smile on her face and in her voice. "Jake didn't want dinner?" Exaggerated furrows appeared on her forehead. "Because there were no tarts for dessert?"

"Tarts?" The student assistant sounded puzzled. "Were tarts on the menu?" She was stacking the dishwasher while her helper washed the pots.

"No, Amy," Dorcas answered as she sat down at the table, Willow joining her. They both burst into laughter at the shared memory.

As Willow filled her plate, she glanced at her aunt who was already biting into a piece of the succulent roast lamb. Dorcas smiled and winked. Willow smiled back, still wondering why Dorcas had stared at her and Jake so strangely. Before the night was over she had to know.

Later, after leaving the Cove and making an unscheduled stop before driving home, Nat Rivers sat at the kitchen table glaring at his father. Since he'd entered the house, sat down to the meal prepared by Mercedes the part-time housekeeper, his father had harangued him, dragging after him from kitchen to den to kitchen. "Just leave it alone, can't you, Dad? Leave it alone." His voice rose in exasperation though he was careful to modulate it. He was in no mood to incur further wrath with tones of blatant disrespect.

The sudden crack of wood on wood pierced the air as Lloyd brought his cane down hard on the natural pine table. His painstakingly slow, raspy voice was swollen with the anger he felt toward his oldest son. "You no-good puppy dog! Leave what alone? You? You'll know alone when I kick your sorry ass out of this house for the last time!" He rapped the cane against the bottle of beer on the table, tilting it over, but it was quickly caught by Nat before the golden liquid spilled out. Exhausted from his effort and leaning heavily on the cane, Lloyd lowered his pain-racked frame onto the spindle-backed chair. "Miz Benson called. Yeah, she told me. Apologizin' all the way. Makin' excuses for you. Smelled your stink-butt yesterday but didn't squeal on you. Thought you just needed some more time. Humph! Time is what you ain't got a whole lot of, son. You take what I'm sayin' as the gospel, for your own good." Lloyd breathed in short, heavy spurts but stubbornly continued berating his sullen thirty-eight-year-old child. "She got nervous when a customer called, firin' us," he thundered as loud as his weakened voice would allow. "Said she didn't want no drunks comin' around her grandkids." His dark look impaled Nat. "Fired! That Gladstone clan has been with us for damn near as long as I been in business. Their money kept you in school." In disgust he said, "After all that hard work your brother did, holdin' us afloat . . . nearly killin' hisself doing it. He was right about you all the time and he was right to pull out when he did."

"Right," Nat spat. "Righteous Jake why don't you call him? He could never do wrong as far as you're concerned. Always the brightest and the smartest. Well if it's all the same to you, I'm sick of hearing about my little brother's goodness." A malicious grin appeared on his face as he stood up, bottle in hand. "Well I'll tell you one thing, I'm certainly making it my business to be around for the show when he brings a certain piece of baggage through that door." A loud laugh erupted from his throat as he left the room with his father's eyes boring into his back.

Lloyd sat spent after his long diatribe against his son. His breathing had slowed but his chest still heaved rapidly. Listening to the sound of Nat's heavy footsteps on the stairs, he couldn't help wondering what his son had found to be so funny. What kind of baggage was he talking about?

Six

At exactly eleven-thirty the next morning, Jake was sitting in the intimate dining room of a small hostelry off the beaten track that hardy tourists to Sleepy Hollow inevitably discovered. Although Willow was no stranger to the neighborhood, the Moose Inn was a place known for giving privacy to those who desired it. He knew she wouldn't suffer scrutiny from the obnoxious.

Earlier, before eight o'clock, Jake had called Willow. When he would have gone for her, she'd demurred to meeting him for brunch. He knew why. Her own mind had to be free of all doubt before she told her aunt she'd fallen in love. *Love? Are you so sure?* "Yes, dammit, I am," Jake answered himself, his words audible to none but himself.

Inevitably, Jake's thoughts drifted to the scene that had taken place in her studio. He'd been shaken to his core and with the passing of several hours, straight on to morning, his body wouldn't let him forget. He'd lain in the dark trying to figure out how, in a light minute, his life had changed; their lives had changed.

Yesterday, a man and a woman had walked into that cottage, each aware of the pervasive, almost animalistic sensuality of the other. To deny it would be to call oneself a fool. The couple that had emerged had been a man and a woman falling in love. Though undeclared, he'd not been mistaken. Jake was as certain of that as he was that the sun would rise in the east in the morning.

While driving to their meeting place, Jake had experienced an instant of doubt. What would their lives be like and what drastic changes must they make? She was a famous artist as beautiful as she was talented. She was young and rich with whole worlds to explore; untapped talents to discover. He loved his work and his own career was beginning to take hold. Must there be choices?

From the secluded table by a window, Jake saw her drive up and park. As Willow walked toward the door, pausing to look with appreciation at the mounds of impatiens in glorious reds and pinks, she stopped and looked up almost as if she sensed his stare. When their eyes met, the mutual silent greeting brought a smile to her lips. Soon she was inside, coming to him. They did not touch as Jake held her chair. He sat down across from her, capturing her gaze. A smile touched his lips.

Willow grew warm all over as she read Jake's message, wondering if his night had been as restless as hers. That thought so satisfied her down to her soul that a soft sigh escaped.

"So, it's like that, huh?" Jake said softly. "Me too," he added, when he saw her embarrassed flush.

"Jake, I'm in love with you." Startled at her own words, Willow flushed, though she hadn't lied.

"I know, darlin'," Jake answered, matching her somber tone. "And don't be embarrassed. You've stolen my words . . . and my heart . . . I've fallen in love with you."

Willow shivered at the endearment. The dropped *g* made the word roll off his tongue much like the drawl of a cowboy. She delighted in the sound . . . and his confession.

Moments passed without words or touch as a soft-voiced waitress, briskly took their order, then disappeared.

"Where do we start from yesterday?"

Jake considered her words. For all the world, he didn't

know, but did it matter? He knew that they just were. He voiced his thoughts and smiled at her reply.

"Doesn't matter at all."

"Willow, you do know that this one afternoon is not going to do it for us, don't you?" Jake said, husky-voiced. "There's so much for us to discover."

"We've a lifetime, love," Willow answered with a shy smile.

The unpretentiousness of her reply was like a caress on her lips, filling Jake with deep emotion. Thankful that their orders were brought at that moment, he busied himself with his food until the lump disappeared from his throat. He realized she was just as overcome with emotion when she made such a show of examining the stuffing in her jumbo shrimps. They ate in silence.

"First things first," Jake said, finally. Preoccupation with eating had conveniently prevented them from sharing their thoughts. "How do you feel about kids?"

Willow sputtered on a sip of water she was about to swallow. "Before or after the wedding vows?"

Jake shrugged. "I prefer after, but if it happens before, will it change anything?"

Willow's look was searching as she studied the brightness in his eyes. She expected that the look of love she saw in them would be the first thing she saw every morning and the last thing she'd gaze upon at night. He was waiting for her answer. "No, nothing at all," she replied.

For the first time, they touched. Jake reached out his hand and she took it. As expected, the now familiar current did not disappoint either. Hands clasped, eyes locked, they both waited until the blanket warmth ran its course. Willow wondered about the possibility of such deep feelings being sustained for a lifetime. She didn't know anyone who'd been together for what was deemed a lifetime.

Jake was the first to speak. "How can we be so matter-of-fact? I hope this doesn't prophesy a certain dullness."

Jake looked so morose at his sudden thought that Willow laughed. Lifting her glass of mimosa, she said, "Bite your tongue. Here's to a cornucopia of pleasant surprises between us."

Touching her glass with his, Jake drank the perfectly mixed champagne and orange juice. "To a lifetime of delicious discoveries, darlin'."

The tone of his voice and the endearment on his lips, made her insides sing with the delight of newborn songbirds. She was no longer content, sitting in this public place, unable to wrap herself in his strong arms and nuzzle the softness of his neck, inhaling his male essence.

As though capturing some of her thoughts, Jake in answer, nodded. "I know, me too." They knew that returning to the Cove was out of the question, at least not for a few hours. Jake would leave the decision to Willow.

Willow sat back in her chair and stared out the window, watching the butterflies light from flower to flower. The serenity of the garden scene with its perfumed blooms was in perfect harmony with the love in her heart for Jake Rivers. *We are going to be lovers,* Willow thought as she turned her gaze on Jake. Perhaps she'd known it months ago, or maybe even weeks ago. It's not important now. She only knew that it was to be. A tiny doubt marred her confidence. What if these feelings are as false as fool's gold?

Jake knew the very moment Willow's mood changed. "What are you thinking?" he asked.

Willow shuddered. "A moment of fear just washed over me, Jake. Suddenly, I'm afraid. Suppose what we feel is pure naked lust? Before this moment, we've never been together, never explored each other's thoughts, dreams, or desires; never discussed the expectations of a life partner. We're talking about doing and becoming all these things based on one kiss." She stared at him. "It's almost not normal," she whispered.

Jake understood her fears and uncertainty. He, too, had

probed his heart and soul since their embrace only the day before. Had it really been less than twenty-four hours since he'd silently committed himself to her? He knew that he had never had such deep feelings toward any woman in his past. The thought of living a day without this woman in his life caused such angst in his soul that he quickly rid his mind of the sickening images. He reached for her hand again, holding it tight. "Shh, don't even think about what's normal. We can't even explain to ourselves what's happening between us. What we do know is that it's not fleeting. We have our whole lives together to try and make some sense out of it."

Willow squeezed his hand. "I'm ready," she said.

Jake took her other hand and as he held them both, he looked at her with such intensity that the burgundy hue of his eyes turned the color of mulled wine. "Are you ready, Willow? You know that I want you, now. Are you ready to let me love you?"

Willow returned his heated gaze. "Yes, Jake Rivers, I want you to love me, now," she answered.

Jake summoned the waitress and soon they were in their cars, Willow following behind Jake. In less than a half hour, by mutual agreement, they were parked at Jake's. They walked hand in hand to his front door where, before they entered, Jake bent down and whispered in her ear, "Don't be afraid of me, darlin'. I'll never hurt you."

Jake wanted Willow in his arms without the passing of another second and it took all of his resolve to restrain himself from ravishing her. Sensing her sudden shyness once the door had been closed and locked, he led her straight to the wide sofa in the living room where they both sat at opposite ends. He was quiet as he watched her silent appraisal of the big room dressed in bold hues of earth tones, navy and beige. She turned to meet his stare. He waited.

"Strong, like you," Willow said. She reached over and took his hand.

Holding on tightly, Willow pulled herself toward Jake,

kicked off her shoes, and stretched supine on her back, her head resting in his lap as she looked up at him. She lifted her hand to his cheek. Brushing her fingers over his mustache, she said, "There oughtta be a law against anyone having such a sexy mouth." Her fingers trailed down his neck passed his broad shoulders to his nipples where she traced the tiny hardening nodules through his thin cotton shirt. The gasp he emitted emboldened her to continue with her ministrations. Slowly, she loosened the buttons until his chest was bared before her. Lazily, she dragged her hand from one nipple to the other, massaging, squeezing, tickling each bud until she felt Jake's thigh muscles tighten beneath her head.

Jake closed his eyes against the gentle assault on his body. The indescribable sensation made him feel that a loveless void deep within, of which he had been unaware, was filling with each sensuous touch of her hand. He was unprepared for the sudden warm moist touch of her mouth on one nipple. When her tongue darted in a rapid, swirling motion, the agony was too much to bear.

His hand had been buried in her long curly hair. He brought her head to his, finding her mouth, crushing her moist lips against his. "Willow," he murmured, as he sought her breast. Restricted by her clothing, only seconds passed before her breasts were bared to his touch. Their naked warmth shot a current through them both that sent Jake's head reeling. He kneaded the soft circles until they hardened to ripe peaks at his touch. He traced the faint outline of the tawny beige flesh that had been unkissed by the sun, making a delectable-looking contrast to the peach-colored skin of her neck and arms.

"You're lovely," he whispered, as he sought and captured one swollen nipple between his teeth, tasting, then sucking each one in turn.

Willow had turned her hips until the soft fabric of her long skirt had bunched around her thighs. When she felt

Jake's hand on her skin, moving slowly beneath the fabric, she squirmed into him, willing him to hurry and ease the ache of her feminine core. "Jake," she murmured against his searching tongue, "Oh, Jake, you're teasing me, please . . ."

"Mmm," Jake said, releasing one nipple and staring into her eyes. He had slipped his hand inside her panties and his fingers were feathery light on the soft hairs of her mound. "Don't you know about those guys, 'Slow and Steady?' " he whispered.

"Jake Rivers," Willow gasped, "I don't believe you. . . ."

"I don't believe me either," Jake said as he suddenly stood up with her still in his arms and swiftly walked across the room to the door leading to his bedroom. Pushing it open with his foot, he had Willow on the queen-size bed in seconds, then commenced to finishing undressing himself. Almost immediately, he stood naked and barefoot before her. Willow, whose eyes were on his, began to undress. Jake steadied her hands with his. "Let me." His voice was barely audible. He finished removing her blouse, bra and skirt. He lay her down, then slowly slid her panties off, his hands skimming over the silken smoothness of her thighs. Jake eased himself atop her, raining kisses on her temples, eyelids, the soft pulsating hollow of her throat. He couldn't contain his grunt of contentment when he felt her hand begin to pleasure his body, and at last, firmly grasp his throbbing manhood, seeking to guide him into her moist center. Jake, unwilling to stop her, knew that he must. "Willow, my love," he said, brushing her lips, "one second more." That was all he needed to reach for, and provide, protection. Soon, they were meshed together again and amidst her cries of anguish, he entered her.

"Jake!" His name exploded from her lips as she raised her hips to cement their joining. Their legs entwined, she clasped his tightly, as if they were the leverage she needed to keep her in this world. Their rhythm was symbiotic; they were one entity.

Jake knew the very moment she had reached her zenith because he felt the jolt at the same time. For a moment that hovered in eternity, they ceased to breathe as each clung to the other, allowing their bodies to hurtle wherever their passion took them. With his last masterful strokes, determined and explosive, murmurs of delight escaped Willow's lips until she screamed his name. Like a passing storm, the turbulence subsided, leaving an inner warmth like liquid fire. Their burning ache had been satisfied.

Spent, and awed by his high state of emotions, Jake slid from her warm body and lay quietly by her side, one arm up over his head, the other flung loosely across her stomach. He stared up at the ceiling, then closed his eyes. He would never have believed he could feel so into a woman and have a woman so into him. He was suddenly scared of the strong feelings that touched the very core of him. The same thoughts that had nagged at him earlier, plagued him now. How could he go on with his life as though nothing had happened? And she with hers? They lived in such different worlds. He had his career and a young business; she was a celebrity, accustomed to the trappings of fame. Before allowing oneself to fall blindly into love, shouldn't one weigh all the pros and cons and do an in-depth analysis before making such a soulful commitment? He opened his eyes at her small shiver.

"Jake?"

Shifting until he had covered them both with the sheet, his response was a lazy, "Hmm?"

"There are no doubts about us." She spoke in wondrous tones, almost as if giving voice to her thoughts would end the magic. "Yesterday, after we . . . well, when we realized that there was such strong chemistry between us . . . well, I never dreamed that this day, this hour, would become so momentous, marking us so indelibly."

Jake held her close until she was snuggled into him, her head resting on his chest. He kissed the top of her head, inhaling her woman smell and a delicate flowery scent.

He expelled a breath that was dredged up from his soul as he knew the truth of her words. "I can't blame you for questioning this . . . this mysterious feeling that has captured us. I don't mind telling you that I'm more than a little scared by it." He reassured her when he felt her slight movement. "It's an awesome thing to go to bed as one person as I did last night, knowing that the new dawn would forever change my ordered world. I wonder that for months we barely spoke, never touched. Strangers." He paused. "But not really, were we, love? We knew." He kissed the smile on her lips. "And now, I'm laying here wondering how I can continue to act normally when you leave me in a little while. I know where you're going, where you will always be, but that doesn't stop me from feeling lonely already. My insides are doing a dance that you wouldn't believe, Ms. Vaughn."

"No more than mine, Mr. Rivers," Willow answered softly, then fell silent. How could she have let this happen? Easy, she told herself. Did she really have any control over her heart? Her longtime fears dissipated while she lay in his arms. How could there ever be anything wrong with her when she felt so strong and loving? Never before had her fears caused her to think about her past. Before she left here today, she had to see his reaction to her story. How much had he heard about her and how much did he believe? And would it matter now? Willow eased herself from his arms and slid from the bed. She had to watch his face when she talked. Wrapping herself in a lightweight spread, she sat in the big chair across from the bed. "We have to talk, Jake," she said.

Jake eyed her with surprise, propping himself up against the headboard, and waited, though wondering why she was trying so hard to mask the sadness in her eyes.

Seven

"What do you know about my parents, Jake?"

Her odd voice caused Jake to sit up a little straighter against the pillows. Matching her steady stare with an unwavering look, he said, "I know that your mother shot your father, then killed herself, Willow." Except for a flicker of her long lashes, her expression did not change. He waited.

"I've always wondered whether she was mad, Jake. Insane." Willow's voice had dropped to a whisper. "There's not a shred of evidence attesting to that." Clouds of doubt crossed her face. "I'm a thirty-year-old intelligent, successful careerwoman; teacher; and part-time hosteler, yet I've harbored this ignorant, unfounded fear about my mother for years, so much so, that I've governed my life by it." At his puzzled look, she said, "My love life . . . until now."

Instinct told him that she would reject his touch. Distance was what she needed. "What has Dorcas told you?" he asked quietly.

"The fear is all in my mind, Jake. There is no insanity in my family as far as my aunt knows. I've never let her know my thoughts. My questions were always posed in the guise of wanting to know about my family history, not because I thought that there was tainted blood."

Jake weighed her words. Thoughtfully, he said, "You avoided close relationships because you may have fallen in love, married, had a child, only to discover that there

is a strain of madness running through your bloodline."
She nodded. "Yet you have no proof of this." She shook
her head. "Tell me what happened to you, Willow. When
did you start feeling afraid?"

Willow looked closely at him. "Don't you want to know
why I'm telling you this?" A slight tremor in her voice belied
the calm look on her face as she waited for his answer.

"I already know why," Jake answered, spearing her with
an intense look. "You've fallen in love, want to marry and
have a child. You want the same things that I want: to live
our future together and share our love with our children.
Now tell me what happened to you, Willow."

"Audestes fortuna juvat," said Willow.

"Not bold," Jake answered simply, "just truthful." After
a pause, he prodded, "Do you remember your mother, Willow?"

"Only in shadows," she answered. Closing her eyes as if
willing the image of her mother to appear behind her lids,
Willow shook her head, repeating, "Only shadows." Frustration filled her voice as she opened her eyes to Jake's, his
own filled with understanding. "I remember smells and music," she said suddenly, as if she just realized she had such
a memory. "I do, Jake." She was in awe of herself. "Everything appears to be soft, quiet too. Rather, serene." She
hesitated. "Visuals escape me. There's simply nothing
there."

"What are the smells like?" Jake deliberately kept his
voice low and even so as not to jar her into losing the
fragile memory.

"Familiar. Pleasant. Like something I smell all the
time . . ." She straightened in the chair. "Paint," she said
quietly, "it's oil paint."

"That's not so unusual, given the nature of your father's
work. He probably held you on his knee many times while
he drew."

Willow shook her head as she strained to see herself as a young child. "That's not it, Jake, I just know it."

"You'll remember, Willow," Jake answered. "Can you hear the music?"

Her shoulders lifted. "Soft, low and soft. That's all." She left the chair and walked back to the bed where she joined Jake beneath the sheet, snuggling against his broad chest. Her gesture was the most natural of movements and she gave it not a second thought. Combing his dark chest hairs with her fingers, she said, "What do you make of this, Jake? Never before have I had such thoughts. Not even those times when I belligerently accused my aunt and uncle of keeping things from me about my parents."

Jake kissed the top of her head, smoothing back the hair from her face. She smelled like her art, warm earth and scented flowers. He gave her a gentle squeeze. "What precipitated your aunt and uncle finally telling you about your parents. Had something happened? You'd heard something?"

"Yes," Willow answered, as she pondered the long-ago memory. "My early years in Toronto, I never drew. Years later, I discovered why. I apparently associated something distasteful with making pictures. Upon reflection, I believe my aunt and uncle were relieved. They'd believed that I had squashed my talent and therefore all association with my father and how he'd died. But that all changed one day when I was thirteen. Art was a part of the curriculum, so I had no choice but to participate. The instructor was marvelous. When I started drawing, it was as if I'd always done so. He spent special time with me, encouraging, teaching, and always amazed at my productions, especially my flowers." Willow moved impatiently against Jake's chest, uttering a deep sigh. He hugged her and she kissed his shoulder.

"It was my interpretation of a rose that piqued his interest. My signature Willow was what did it. He remembered the nearly ten-year-old story of the budding genius,

Willow Vaughn. The daughter of the murdered cartoonist, Michael Vaughn. With my answers to his questions, he realized that I knew nothing of which he spoke. He arranged a meeting with my aunt. It was then that my aunt voiced her fears about dredging up the old memory, fearing that I'd be emotionally scarred. My teacher, Mr. Fieldings, expressed that more harm than good would come from keeping me so ignorant about such an important part of my life. Later, Aunt Dorcas decided that he was right. That night, she told me about my mother and father."

Jake and Willow were silent, each with their own thoughts about her admission.

"Is that the reason for your professional signature Morgana?"

"Yes. Just like Mr. Fieldings, eventually, others would begin to associate a flower painted by Willow with the remarkable painting made by the four-year-old daughter of Michael Vaughn. My aunt suggested the signature, Morgana. After her maiden name, Morgan. It was my mother's too. It's been my signature, since. My young classmates scoffed that I was affecting the role of a great artist and teased me unmercifully. But Mr. Fielding and I thought it our own secret." Willow smiled. "He was ever protective of me after that. Whenever anyone inquired about my art, he took on the role of agent. It was he who screened and with my aunt's approval, agreed on the agent I presently use. I was seventeen at the time. Later, while still a college student, I was earning quite a nice sum from my commissioned artwork." She paused. "I've really had a comfortable and fantastic life, Jake. One that others could envy. I'm indebted to Our Father for my talent."

Jake heard the underlying sorrow. "But, deep inside you've harbored this fear that loving another and bearing children would result in disaster." She nodded against his chest. "Now something has occurred to bring that fear to the surface. What was it, Willow? Don't be afraid. I'll do my damndest to help you fight past the fright."

"It may not be so easy, Jake."

"We can give it our best shot, darlin'."

"Teakettles," Willow said. "I always connect the sound of a whistling teakettle to something, unexplainable terrifying." She shuddered. "Recently, I was scared almost senseless." Briefly, she described her encounter with George Henry in the hallway, omitting the disgusting meeting on the porch. Unconsciously, she wiped her mouth.

The gesture was not unnoticed by Jake. He swore under his breath. Dismissing the obnoxious man in the middle of the night hardly seemed punishment for his want of a cup of tea. His jaw tightened. "Tell me what you left out, love. What else happened?"

Unsurprised by his insight, Willow related the scene that took place when she'd returned to the porch. "You were right. I should have been more alert." When he didn't reply, Willow looked up into his eyes. "I know you're not the type to say, 'I told you so,' but go ahead, you're entitled."

Jake smiled, "Consider it said."

Willow suddenly laughed, her shoulders shaking.

Infected, Jake grinned, "What?" he asked.

"Something my Grandy always told my aunt when she was annoyed with visitors. 'Dorcas, guess it's true what they say about company and fish—after three days they start a stinking.' " Willow's smile broadened. "Guess in George Henry's case it took three whole seasons." Jake's deep laugh matched Willow's own, the sturdy bed surviving the fits of laughter.

Sobered, Willow sighed. "But, after all, there's still the mystery. Do you think, together, we can solve it?" she asked, burying her nose in the soft hollow of Jake's neck.

"I have no doubts about that, darlin'," Jake whispered in her ear. "But I do doubt solving this present crisis on my

own." Her leg pressing up against his thigh and her un-
mindful rubbing of her hand against his belly, had stirred
his arousal. Gasping, as her hand closed around his swollen
sex, he growled, "I take it you plan to help me out here?"
In answer, Willow's hand tightened around him, searing
the tender flesh. An erotic sound escaped her lips as she
suddenly fell flat on her back trying to pull his bulk with
her, seeking to guide him into her. "I want to feel you inside
of me, sweetheart. All of you . . ." she whispered.

Jake touched her damp mound with his fingers, caressing her until she squirmed her pleasure, her body ready
to accept more. Adroitly, he maneuvered himself over her
and slipped inside. "Willow," he breathed as she welcomed his heated passion, "You are my life." Willow's
words were inarticulate as she met Jake's powerful thrusts
with the harmonious movements of true lovers. Like the
sweet strains of a symphony, they experienced the cresen-
dos, the swells and finally, with exquisite shudders, fell to
an almost silent rest.

Then, Willow murmured, "As you are mine, my love."

When the phone rang, Dorcas knew that she would hear
her niece's voice on the line. Lunch was hours gone and
the caterer was preparing dinner for a six o'clock serving.
For the past hour Dorcas lay on the chaise, eyes closed,
thinking about Willow and Jake. It was an hour spent in
anguish. At the thought of them together, a sudden fear
gripped her chest and she shivered as though a hand had
reached inside of her and was massaging her heart. An
unknown fear for what the future held for her niece per-
meated her body and she wanted to know why.

"Aunt Dee, is everything quiet?"

Dorcas expelled a breath. "Running smooth. Got my
feet up, lazing away Sunday. How about you," Dorcas
teased half-heartedly. "Brunch was so good that you can't

resist dinner?" Her chest thumped at the happiness she heard in the soft voice.

"You might say that," Willow replied, wondering what was wrong. Her aunt did not sound like old her usual ebullient self. "Aunt Dee, are you sure you're okay?"

"Of course, I'm fine. Enough about me. Just tell that handsome man that kidnapping is a punishable crime." She paused. "You're still with him?" She rubbed her hand across her chest as if to give it warmth.

"Yes," Willow answered, then smiled, listening to the sounds of Jake in the shower. She had showered, dressed and was keeping a vigil for the delivery of their gourmet Japanese cuisine. "Aunt Dee," she said softly, "Jake and I . . . well, Jake, he . . . Oh, shoot, Aunt Dee, we love each other. Believe it, if you can, then that will make three of us," she ended with a soft laugh. "What do you think? You never really had to play at matchmaking. It was going to happen anyway," she ended, simply, then added, "Destiny."

Dorcas swallowed. "Love, Willow? After one day together? Didn't I teach you that true love is forever?"

"This is right, Aunt Dee, I know it is." Willow heard the bathroom door open and from her view of the street from the living room window, she saw the restaurant van. "We'll talk later, Aunt Dee."

"Wake me, if you have to. Oh, I almost forgot—Oscar called. He wants you to call him back. Something to do with the wildflowers calendar."

"Oscar? I wonder what could be wrong?"

"Don't know," Dorcas answered. "You know how bent out of shape your publisher gets at the least little thing. That's why you have Oscar. Anyway, if not tonight, he expects your call in the morning."

The door buzzer sounded. "I have to go, Dorcas, but I'll wake you. Bye." As she walked to the door, she couldn't help wondering what had gone wrong? Next year's wildflowers paintings were completed and had been out of mind for more than a year. They were all beautiful. Willow's frown deepened. Something was terribly wrong to prompt her longtime friend and agent, Oscar Germany, to call about business on a Sunday afternoon.

Eight

Dorcas sat spellbound on the chaise. Tiny beads of moisture appearing on her upper lip, belied her outer calm. Something terrible is going to happen to my Willow. Without warning, that cold apprehension caught hold of her upper torso, squeezing her chest with fingers of icy steel. She gasped aloud as though her cry would set her free. At that moment, a cloud passed over, shutting out the sun and blanketing her room in a cloud of gray. Over her frightened panting, like an uninvited guest, she almost heard an ominous quiet settle itself in the big room.

Dorcas closed her eyes, willing herself to breathe easily as she massaged her chest. There's nothing wrong . . . nothing wrong . . . nothing wrong. . . . Silently she chanted until her breaths were normal and the blood flowed warm in her chest. She stood up. Never one for fanciful thinking, Dorcas couldn't shake the sense of foreboding that clung to her like a shroud. With the sudden need to hear a human voice, she left the disturbed sanctity of her bedroom.

Thirty minutes later, at six-thirty, the warmth of peppermint tea putting a fire in her belly, Dorcas was sitting on the front porch, lulled to peacefulness in the low, sloping adirondack rocker. Her eyes were bright, free of the clouds and a smile touched her lips. Her sigh was content as she gazed at the still bright, cerulean summer sky. "Foolish woman," she muttered. "What could happen on this beautiful day that God has brought?" She chuckled at herself and sipped her tea. She had chalked up her queasy feelings to the inevitable pangs of an impending empty nest.

The sound of a car engine, and then spun gravel, caught Dorcas' attention. She watched as the unfamiliar vehicle approached. Someone lost, she surmised. Unless one of the guests is expecting a visitor? Dorcas stood, waiting to greet the stranger, but frowned at the discernible shapes of two women. She remained on the steps, waiting, and watched as the driver opened the door and got out, looking intently at Dorcas as she neared.

At the foot of the steps, the woman stopped. Her deep brown eyes in an equally brown face were intelligent-looking but full of reproach as she stared at Dorcas.

Taken aback by the skinny stranger's unveiled dislike for her, Dorcas stared back. The mixed-gray cornrows pulled back into a bun were too stern a look for her long, gaunt, cosmetic-free face. She stood unmoving until Dorcas asked, "Are you looking for someone?"

"My name is Alma Manning."

Her voice was as devoid of personality as she was, thought Dorcas. She didn't extend her hand, but asked, "Have we met?"

"You are Dorcas Williams." The flat statement was spoken without a smile.

"I am," Dorcas replied.

Alma Manning nodded. "You still favor your old pictures." She sniffed as though there was something bad in the air. "I accompanied your sister here. She's too sick to travel by herself. We flew in from Illinois. Can she come inside?"

Dorcas froze. All the turmoil she experienced earlier came tumbling back with a force that caused her to sway. She would have fallen if Alma Manning had not reached out to steady her descent off the steps. Dorcas sat down, covering her face with her hands until the dizziness subsided.

"Are you all right?" Alma Manning's tone implied that she could care less about Dorcas' state of health.

Dorcas raised her eyes to the woman, who involuntarily took a step backward. The hatred blazed as a bush afire. "No, I'm not all right." The cold voice sent Alma Manning back another step.

Dorcas turned her heated look to the still figure in the car. Vera Morgan. Her baby sister whom she'd disowned all those years ago. Her sister who'd been part of Beatrice's last tormented hours was here!

"Can she come inside?"

Dorcas had forgotten the tense woman standing a foot away. Without a glance in her direction, she nodded. She felt, rather than saw the woman moving quickly to the car, immediately reaching inside to grasp the arm of Vera Morgan.

As though in pantomime, she watched the two people moving in slow motion toward her. Dorcas gasped, and her eyes widened. Vera? This skeletal female is not my sister! "What kind of sick scam are you two running?" Dorcas demanded, an ocean of relief engulfing her; anger quickly taking over. "Who are you?"

The rail-thin woman, raised her eyes. "I'm Vera Morgan, Dorcas. Twenty-six years is a long time, but you look the same, Dory." The long statement left her breathless and she leaned heavily on Alma Manning.

Dorcas closed her eyes. It was baby Vera who had nicknamed her Dory. The name stuck. She used to love the way her husband Thomas used it almost as an endearment. When she opened her eyes, Vera had sat down on the steps, too weak to stand. Dorcas swallowed, her normally heavy voice only a whisper when she beckoned to Alma. "Bring her inside," and turned to open the door.

Alma Manning looked at her watch. It was just past seven-thirty. Earlier, she had been led to the kitchen where the cook had been instructed to serve her dinner. After her meal, she'd wandered back outside to the porch where she now sat. A plate was fixed and brought to Vera who was in Dorcas' bedroom. The two women had been in the closed room for an hour. Alma sat with her expressionless face, waiting and rocking in the adirondack chair.

Dorcas waited until her sister finished picking at her food before she spoke. Quietly, she watched Vera slowly consume the mashed potatoes and the spinach, hardly touching the baked ham and finishing a glass of milk. When Vera, exhausted, pushed away the plate, Dorcas removed the soiled dishes. When she returned, Vera had moved to the big easy chair by the window, apparently seeking the last of the sunny warmth. Dorcas sat across from her on the plush love seat. She did not mask her stare of incredulity. This emaciated woman was indeed the once-gorgeous, voluptuous, Vera Morgan, stacked like the proverbial brickhouse. Her baby sister with the huge dark eyes under the longest, silky lashes, with a dimpled chin, and a smile to break men's hearts. Jet-black curly hair that tickled her butt. Gone.

Dorcas' throat swelled with emotion. Half of her hated this woman for what she once was. The other half pitied her for who she now was. Her nursing experience told Dorcas the story.

"How long have you had AIDS?"

"More than a year."

Dorcas drew in a breath. "What's your count? Any infections?" She exhaled slowly when she heard the soft-spoken answer. Vera's T cells were practically zero and she'd recently recovered from a serious infection. Vera took advantage of Dorcas' speechlessness.

"You know that I'm dying, Dorcas. I can't give you a 'when' but we both can see I won't be putting fifty-one candles on a cake come November." Vera tried to put strength in her voice. "I was almost twenty-six when you threw me out of your house in Toronto; three months after you buried Beatrice. I only wanted your forgiveness. I wanted to see my niece. I needed my family, Dorcas. With Beatrice dead, we're all we had. Why did you do that to me? Did you really always hate me so much?" Her once-bright eyes were cloudy with sickness and pain as she watched her oldest sister. Her only sibling.

Dorcas listened impassioned to Vera as she remembered the last time she'd seen her. The name of her dead sister coming from her lips, hardened her heart again toward this shell of a woman. "I've never liked you, Vera. Not since you were fourteen and thinking you were a woman." Dorcas' eyes flashed. "But you were, weren't you?" She saw the flicker of hurt in Vera's eyes but she didn't care. "You were doing everything a grown woman was doing anyway and probably more than I even thought about doing at twenty."

"You're hard, Dorcas."

"Hard? Hell, yeah. Where you're concerned, I always had to be. How and where you'd learned to become such a hateful and manipulative young person, escaped me. Me . . . who baby-sat you . . . loved your cute cuddly ways. You changed overnight. One day I looked and the baby sister I'd known had disappeared. Suddenly living under the same roof was this . . . thing . . . that was pure slut. At fourteen! You wouldn't listen to me. Mother would never have believed me if I'd told her. She worshipped you. Father would have died had he suspected what you'd become. Sneaking around, sleeping with his best friend, a man old enough to be your father!"

"That's all in the past, Dorcas," Vera said wearily.

"Past," Dorcas exploded. "Your 'past' and your slutty life helped kill your sister!" Dorcas struggled to still her heaving chest. Her fingers tingled with the fury that she sought to squelch, along with the long-ago urge to pummel Vera Morgan, given the opportunity. She was not really surprised that her hatred for her sister had survived all these years.

Beatrice Morgan Vaughn had been the sweetest person Dorcas had known; ever willing to comfort, please, become the peacemaker to all who knew her. In today's world, she'd probably be considered a "loser," a "soft touch." Her husband had known and used her personality to torture her into sudden madness. Dorcas would always believe that Beatrice's finding Vera and Michael in intercourse on her kitchen table, was the catalyst to her eventual breaking. Yes, all these years she'd hated Vera for that. And yes, she did chase her out of her home.

Only three months after her parents' death, Willow was finally able to smile, adjusting herself to her new family and learning strange new words. When Vera showed up, thank God, Willow was out with her Grandy and never saw her aunt. If Dorcas had anything to do with it, Vera Morgan would become but a fairy-tale memory in a child's mind, and she had succeeded. Until now. A worried frown appeared. Suppose Willow saw Vera. As if a boulder just landed in the pit of her stomach, Dorcas slumped in her chair. No! That can't happen. *Then Willow will know I've lied to her all these years. She believes I'm all she has.*

Vera sat watching the panoply of emotions wash over her sister's face, at last, the guard falling away. Her shoulders drooped, if that were at all possible, her body was so shrunken. The hatred was still there! Sadness erupted through her, filling her with hopelessness. *What should I have expected,* she thought. For at least two years after she was kicked from her sister's house, like someone's trash, she'd tried in vain to make contact with Dorcas. She'd finally given up. But now, she had to make things right. There was someone else's life to be considered in this weird equation of her life. She had to make Dorcas understand. Her eyes never wavered from her sister's when she finally spoke.

"I have a daughter, Dorcas. Your niece, Dolores. She's the daughter of Michael Vaughn . . . and Willow's half-sister."

Silence.

For the rest of her life Dorcas would remember the time her heart stopped beating—yet she lived. Almost like an out-of-body experience, she hovered over the room, watching herself, sitting, dumbstruck.

"What are you saying, Vera?" Her voice was ethereal, belonging to someone else.

"Her name is Dolores Jones." Vera's eyes flickered and the muscles around her mouth moved in an attempt to smile. "Jones is the name of the man I was living with at the time she was born, in Rockford, Illinois. My daughter is your niece . . . and a Morgan." Her look defied her sister to challenge the truth.

Willow's cousin? And . . . half-sister! Dorcas shuttered her eyes against what she knew was not a dream. Vera was dying. To whose good would such fabrication benefit? This was no lie.

"That night in July . . . in the kitchen . . . I was impregnated by Michael. Our baby was born on the seventeenth of April, the next year. Two months later, in June, Willow turned five. My baby had a big sister; one she would never know."

Dorcas' look turned black, a storm brewing behind her dark eyes. "You want them to meet? Now?" Her voice was low and dangerous. "It's not going to happen, Vera."

"Why, Dory? Because Willow will know the truth you've hidden from her all these years? That you're not her only relative . . . that she has close family? She's going to hate you for your deception . . . whenever she finds out." Vera shifted her bony weight in the easy chair, rubbing at the soreness in her thighs. "All these years, they could have been friends. But you wouldn't listen to me when I visited you in Toronto. You closed your mind, allowing your hate for me to poison your good sense. You wouldn't let me stay long enough to tell you that I was carrying Michael's child."

"How long were you and Michael . . . lovers?" Dorcas

tasted bile as she said the word. At her sister's curious look, she said, "I need to know for my own sake, that I was right in keeping trash like you out of Willow's life. How long? How many times in your sister's house?"

"Why torture yourself . . . ?"

"How long?" Dorcas barked. "Humor me that since I've been righteous for so long."

Harsh reality told Vera that Dorcas was, and would always be, unforgiving. The last bit of hope she'd had of reconciling with her bitter sister, vanished. Relenting, she told Dorcas what she wanted to hear, wondering if her sister would feel that somehow, in the telling, there would come vindication for the dead Beatrice. "Not long. Not as long as all the others. And not as long as the gardener's wife, Olivia, Bea's best friend." Vera shut her ears to the sound in Dorcas' throat, like the gurgles of a drowning person, gasping for air. "Since their news making New Year's Eve, bash. That was when he really noticed me. That night we used the floor in his daughter's room. Who would come there? Beatrice was acting the effervescent hostess. Willow slept through it all. After that, we always met in Manhattan, which wasn't a problem for him, since he conducted a lot of his business there. I answered to only me." Vera paused. "He stood me up a few times and I would get mad as hell. But that didn't stop me. He had a thing for me and I loved it."

"She was your sister!"

Vera shrugged. "You know, Dorcas, I think that Bea was miserable in that marriage but wouldn't let on. I think she was relieved that he had other women. Nothing she'd ever said, just a feeling I had." She continued, her words coming a bit slower. "Beatrice sent me one of those coveted-by-everyone invitations to that posh party in July. Come for breakfast and leave when the champagne stopped flowing. A party for no other reason than just because. That was Michael Vaughn." Though Dorcas had quieted, her eyes never left Vera's face. "The party was only a few hours old when I realized that Michael was smelling himself again. There must have been eighty or more people there at any given time but I knew the women he'd been with. They all were so obnoxiously obvious. Michael was loving it and I was hating it. But the gardener's wife was hating it more than me. Apparently, she found a way to let him know because I saw when they disappeared into one of the enclosed cabanas."

All true. All true. Beatrice's letter was coming to life. Dorcas could see the next scene, confirmed by Vera's halting speech.

"Bea came down to the pool. She had a smile on her face for her public, but I could see she wanted Michael. She saw a woman enter one of the cabanas. Almost as if she knew, she headed for the other one. I watched, wondering what my sister would do. I already knew Michael would do nothing but laugh. Not a sound came from that building but in minutes, Olivia came flying out of there like all the residents of Hades were after her. Her face was frozen with fear. A long time later, Michael came out, then Bea."

"What did Beatrice do?" Dorcas was feeling the pain.

"Nothing." Vera's short laugh was a harsh croak. "She was the lady of the manor, remember? She went around like good hostesses do, asking in her pleasant voice if anyone needed anything." Vera made a grim sound. "She was ice, Dorcas. She'd just found her best friend in the arms of her husband, in only the Lord knows what state of lust; and she was asking if people's bellies were full."

"She was in shock, Vera. Of course you wouldn't have understood why."

The sadness she felt, reached Vera's eyes. "Not then, Dory. Not then," she replied, softly.

"What happened, next?"

"Michael avoided me after that. I thought that his getting caught, in his own backyard, so to speak, cooled his avarice for sex for a while. I was willing to wait until he came down to the city." She looked squarely at Dorcas. "He wasn't. Later, when everyone was asleep, he caught me by surprise when I was in the kitchen. The water hadn't started to boil in the kettle, and I was just sitting there. He just appeared. He came on to me, and as always, I didn't back off. I wanted him as much as he wanted me. Besides, I wanted to let him know that whatever Olivia was giving him, I could give better. I was jealous. I knew then that she'd been the reason for him standing me up those few times. He wanted me right there and I let him. The kettle started to whistle. I teased him, saying he'd have to wait until after tea. He turned off the burner and grabbed me again. Laughing, I pushed him away and turned the burner back on. The whistle was so loud, I thought sure we'd woke up the house. Michael only laughed, this time, taking the kettle off the burner. Before long, we forgot about tea, and everything else."

"Until Beatrice found you lusting on her table." *Willow had heard the whistle,* Dorcas was sure that her niece had long ago associated whistles with the disappearance of her parents from her life.

"Until then. But, she was too late. Michael had left his seed in me." Vera's low voice rose. "And she's every bit as precious to me as your Willow is to you, Dorcas Williams. I'm glad I didn't abort her. She's everything that I was not, and I love her."

Dorcas was shaken at the venom in her sister's voice. Though her heart was hardened to Vera, what of her child, the niece she'd never known existed?

"Where is she?"

"She lives in Jersey City, New Jersey. She's a journalist and she found a job at a small newspaper, there. She's bright and I know she'll be moving on to bigger things." Vera almost knew the next question. "No, Dory. I never told her about you or Willow . . . or who her real father was. The man who let me give her his name, moved on soon after she was born. She thinks her father was a victim of a mugging. She's ignorant about her once-affluent father and famous big sister."

Dorcas was silent.

"That's the way you want to keep it," Vera said, flatly.

"Yes." Dorcas stood up. It was late, after eight, and Willow was probably on her way home. Vera had to leave. "Nothing good for either of them would come from their meeting at this stage of their lives, Vera. Nothing."

Vera stood and reached in her handbag, pulling out an envelope. She handed it to her sister. "I had a gut feeling that you would still be the unforgiving woman you've always been toward me, Dory. So I'm leaving you with details about my daughter. Just in case you may find it in your heart to forgive me . . . and to give your niece a family, and roots." Vera walked to the door of the bedroom and opened it. Dorcas followed. "Good-bye, Dory," Vera said.

"Vera," Dorcas said, but was stopped.

"There's nothing more we have to say, after all, is there Dory?"

She was right. "No, there really isn't, Vera." Dorcas followed her sister out of the room, then lead the way to the porch, where Alma Manning was waiting.

Dorcas would remember later, but for the simple fact that taking care of bodily functions, delaying the departure of two women, Willow Vaughn would never have lain eyes on Vera Morgan Jones. Jones, the name she'd simply "borrowed" for herself and her daughter.

The precious minutes needed to get the two women to their car and off the grounds, had been used up. They were at the steps, when Willow's big black Mercedes entered the drive. The sound of her tires spinning gravel, would haunt Dorcas for a long time.

Nine

Willow pulled the big car easily into her reserved parking space alongside of the house, eyeing the strange car with curiosity. The visitors standing with her aunt, piqued her interest even more. The dusky light hadn't afforded a good look at the two women, but somehow she sensed that their departure would not leave her aunt bereft of friends.

"Good evening," Willow said, as she approached the threesome. Without stopping their measured steps toward their car, the tallest of the two women, simply nodded her head. The other looked as if she wanted to stop, but was caught in the grip of the grim-faced woman who propelled her along.

Vera Morgan Jones' fleeting glance caught the eyes of her niece. "Hello," was all she said. Allowing herself to be buckled in, she never looked back as her silent companion drove steadily away from the big house, and a pretty, perplexed, young woman.

Hours after the house settled for the night, Willow was still awake. The miniature crystal grandfather clock's delicate black hands moved in suspended seconds toward 11:00 P.M. Brushing her hair with long methodical strokes as she'd been doing for the last ten minutes, Willow laid the brush on the dressing table and stood. Catching a glimpse of her face in the mirror, she was not surprised at the tightening she saw around her jaw; the tenseness, an indication of rarely used muscles doing heavy-duty work. Her usually bright eyes were fraught with worry. She walked the few steps to her sitting area and lay on the sofa, staring at the ceiling. Pulling a throw over herself, she searched her brain for a clue to what was happening.

Never, except for the years at school—the times she'd studied abroad, and as long as they were under the same roof—had her aunt ended a day without saying good night. When as a child, she'd have her tantrums, and even as a sulking, know-it-all teenager, stalking to her room, her aunt would follow. Only when the disagreement was discussed were good nights said. Dorcas would say that the 'morrow the good Lord brings should begin with sunshine and smiles, not grumpy frowns and scowls. It was much harder the next morning to set ugly things right, once they became part of one's dreamworld during the night.

Earlier, when the strange women had gone, Dorcas turned to Willow who could only stare at her aunt. It was the haunted eyes that caught Willow's breath. With an unsteady voice, she'd asked if Dorcas was sick. Who were those women and what had they said? Her aunt's face had grown ashen and she'd hurried to her room. All she'd said in her hasty departure was, "No one. She's no one, Willow."

Shifting herself, Willow reached over and picked up a pencil sketch from the table. Staring at her were the brooding eyes of her aunt. Willow had captured the look of terror so clearly, that the picture frightened her. What could have put that naked fear there? She laid the sketch back down on the table and sat up. Though it was late, her conscience wouldn't allow sleep to come before she spoke with her aunt. Something was torturing her aunt and Willow knew that Dorcas would not be sleeping peacefully tonight. Not with demons chasing her into tomorrow.

I have to speak to her tonight, Willow reasoned, *otherwise*

I'll have to wait until late tomorrow night. And that would be too long for her aunt to suffer in the silent world she'd chosen.

When Dorcas had closed the door of her room, Willow went bewildered, to her own room. She'd decided that after making her call to her agent, she'd see to her aunt. Whatever Oscar Germany had on his mind, he obviously felt it important enough to disrupt both their weekends. When they spoke, he asked her to come to his office in Manhattan. It was important that they meet. Apparently, her publisher was disturbed by one of the paintings. Why? she wondered. Those paintings had been completed more than a year before the calendar was published. Without Oscar giving any additional information, she'd readily agreed to a ten A.M. meeting. After their thirteen-year, agent-client-turned-friend relationship, they had no compunctions about their mutual honesty and commitment to each other.

Willow would have to be up and out early if she meant to be prompt for her appointment. Before turning in, there was something she had to ask Dorcas. There had been two women leaving. Why then had Dorcas spoken in the singular? As she opened the door and walked down the hall to her aunt's room, the words milled about in her mind. *"No one. She's no one, Willow."*

Dorcas lay wide awake in her bed. It had been hours since her lifelong nightmare had finally surfaced and she still hadn't recovered from the shock. Her body was cold down to her soul and her hands trembled. To keep them still, she had them clasped over her chest. The red wine she'd drank—how many glasses, she'd lost count—hadn't done anything more for her chills than make her woozy. As the hours passed, she was far from sleepy and her mind was crystal clear. *Do you think you can sleep your troubles away,*

Dorcas Williams? You're a hypocrite. What was it you always told your little buttercup? No good nights on ugly thoughts?

Dorcas rubbed her hands over her cotton nightgown, seeking to gain warmth from the repeated friction. What was she going to say to her niece? When Vera had looked into her eyes, had there been some flicker of memory from Willow? The beginning of long repressed images flashing at precipitous moments? At that moment, Dorcas had frozen and did not move until somehow, she felt herself navigating on unsteady legs toward her room. *What had Willow asked me? Was I sick?* Dorcas nearly laughed with that thought. Sick? *Oh, God, forgive me. What I've just done is sick. My sister is dying and I have no forgiveness in my heart for her evil deeds. But, Willow, bless her goodness, will hate me if she finds out what I've done. The lies all these years and then to turn her dying aunt away—no, she can't know.* Dorcas shuddered at the low knock on her door followed by the soft voice.

"Aunt Dee. Can I come in?"

Dorcas did not answer.

Willow frowned. She knocked again. "Aunt Dee? I won't stay long. Are you okay?" Willow waited, uneasy at the stillness surrounding her in the dim hallway. Not a sound inside her aunt's room. Somehow, Willow felt that her aunt was listening. The uneasiness heightened as she turned away, wondering what was scaring her aunt to death?

Ten

Jake frowned as he glanced at his watch and then the big wall clock. It was still eight-thirty. Mac was late. The fax she'd sent last night emphasized the eight A.M. sharp! meeting, so he was surprised at the empty offices. Rarely making the drive from her West Village apartment to Twenty-sixth street, it wasn't the traffic that kept her. It wasn't like her not to call if something came up. He was worried. The faint ring of the elevator bell sounded, signaling its stop on the second floor. Jake stood when Tala McCready opened the door and without a word, rushed by him, racing for the ladies' room. He could only stare, flabbergasted.

Jake was staring out the window when he heard Tala enter the room. He turned. "Good morning." He kept all questions out of his voice.

"Good? So you say." Tala sat heavily in the big chair behind her desk, wiping her forehead and the back of her neck with a damp cloth. Brushing wisps of deep auburn hair from her ashen face, she looked up at her friend. "I'm pregnant."

Jake left the window and took a seat across from her. "I guessed." He still kept his voice level, not knowing how she felt about her state—this time.

"Don't be so cautious with me. Not after all these years." Tala spoke softly as she looked with moist eyes at him. "We go way back, remember?"

"I remember." Jake's voice was equally low.

"I had to abort that first time. A senior, planning for grad school, Brian starting his first teaching assignment; I couldn't hang him out like that. He and I agreed it was the right thing to do in our situation at that time. But later," Tala saw the flicker and her expressive brown eyes clouded as a small sigh escaped. "I never told you. I miscarried two years ago."

"I'm sorry, Mac." Jake was sorry. He knew that Tala had put herself on a guilt trip during these last childless years of her marriage. She'd conceived once, so why not again? She just knew something had gone wrong with the abortion. Jake realized now that the miscarriage must have affected his friend deeply.

"How does . . ."

"We want this one," she interrupted, teeth clenched. "Nothing is going to take this one away from us. We won't let it, Jake." Tala swiped at her damp cheek.

Jake stared thoughtfully at his friend who returned his stare. "This meeting. It's all about me, isn't it?"

Tala nodded. "I need you, Jake. Like never before." She added softly, "I can't lose this baby."

"The project?" Tala had been excited when she'd first told him the firm had won the bid on a national sorority's conference center complex. Nothing more was said, until now. He felt he knew what she was going to ask. He waited.

"You know." Tala read her friend's face.

Jake nodded.

"Would you take over the complete project, Jake? Be the architect, contractor? Run the show?"

"It's your design, Mac."

"My design, my plan, my vision, yes. But how long before it becomes your vision? We've done this together in the past. We think alike, Jake. You won't have a problem with this." Tala continued, "For a year. One year is all I need."

"When are you due?"

"I'm two months. By the first of the year you'll be an uncle for another go 'round. A nephew this time." Tala grinned at the smile that leaped into his eyes.

Jake laughed. "You're so sure about that?"

Tala opened her desk drawer and pulled out a folder. Opening it, she pushed some papers across the desk. She looked at Jake with unwavering eye. "You know my dad was a giant in the business and left me a solvent company. Very solvent and its been kept that way thanks to you and Larry and the rest of my talented staff. The firm's lawyers drew up a new contract for you, Jake, in the event you accepted my proposal."

Tala cleared her throat and stood up, pushing back her chair. "Look it over. I hope you accept. Be right back." She went into another office and closed the door.

Jake had not moved since putting the contract back in the folder except to rest his elbows on the desk, burying his head in his hands. He shuttered his eyes against everything but the thoughts whirling around in his head. What of his plans to marry in a matter of months? Though he hadn't officially proposed to Willow, they both knew that before the year ended, they would be husband and wife. It would be a fait accompli. Of that he had no doubt. Overnight, he'd mentally planned his movement in the next six months, deciding to immediately accept two major interior landscaping contracts. His reputation for excellence was spreading throughout the metropolitan corporate world. Before Willow—his thoughts stopped at those two words—wondering now if all time would be separated by "before" and "after" he found her. He hadn't planned to spread himself so thin while completing Tala's contracting schedule. After all, he was in her employ. Jake rubbed his forehead. But this? How could he refuse her generous offer? The mileage he'd get from completing this giant undertaking would cement his name and the caliber of his work in the field. He heard Tala enter the room.

Without looking up, he knew she was standing at the window, hands jammed into the pockets of the baggy chino pants she loved to wear, complete with striped cotton shirt and navy leather loafers. He'd always teased her about the improbability of a deceptively, reed-like woman creating such mammoth landscapes. This project included a giant waterfall. He turned and watched her stiff back, recognizing her stance. She was nervous.

"Tala." Jake stared as she turned and walked toward him. Her lashes were damp. His glance touched the folder. "You'd do that for me?" He was standing, towering over her slight frame.

"You'd do it for me." It was a fact, stated simply.

"But a year's salary for my contractor to run my company . . . and almost doubling my salary?"

Tala walked behind her desk and sat down in the big swivel chair. "I told you Jake, the company is in excellent shape and I want you to act in my stead. To make decisions. I'll be around to consult with. I'll assist."

"You already have an assistant." Larry Norman had been with the firm for nearly thirty-eight years. Always on the brink of retiring, he just couldn't take that final step. Jake sympathized with the aging bachelor who'd be lost without his work. "He'll feel like he's being edged out, Mac. He's still a damned good architect." He frowned. "You're certain about this?"

"As I'll ever be, Jake." Tala shook her head while drumming her fingers over the folder. She knew Jake was surprised at her offer and sensed he wanted to accept. He was holding back and she wondered what was gnawing at him.

Since their freshman year of college, Tala had been able to look beyond Jake's quiet reserve and pinpoint his mood. She'd been there when the news came about the death of his mother. Of his few friends, it was to her, and Buddy Carter, that he'd finally opened up to, unwilling to grieve alone. They'd been a threesome. While she and Jake were still close, Buddy dropped out of touch when he followed the love of his life to Hawaii. Once in awhile he'd shout at them via postcard.

But now he was worrying over something. Wondering if it was his father, she said, "You'll accept the proposal, but . . ." She waited.

"Can't fool you, Mac. Though me and Buddy tried like hell." Jake walked back to the chair and sat down. The half-hearted smile was replaced by a sober look as Jake stretched out his long legs and crossed one foot over the over. "I started planning the rest of my life, Mac." He hesitated. "It's not only about me, anymore."

Tala McCready stared at him. It was only when he spoke again that she realized she'd been holding her breath.

"Mac, it's all right, you're not hearing things. Now calm down or else I'm not saying another word. My god-nephew can do without the shock wave." His voice was sharp and he watched her until he was certain she'd recovered.

Tala narrowed her eyes. "Repeat that, Jake Rivers." He was about to stand, but stopped by her voice, he remained seated. "Jake Rivers, you tell me while you're looking me in the eye." In a calmer voice, she added, "Tell me how in the hell you went and fell in love right under my eyes and I didn't suspect a thing." She glowered at him. "You are in love."

"I'm in love, Mac." Hearing the words on his lips startled Jake, causing a strangeness to suddenly envelop him. Was it only yesterday that he'd claimed his love, making Willow a part of him? Their coming together had been the most natural act of his life.

"Yes," she said, peering closely into his face, "it's love." Instead of crackling fire, her eyes were soft as mist as she asked, "Who is she, Jake?"

"Willow Vaughn. She's also known as Morgana." Her name on his lips brought on that pang in his chest.

Tala's voice sputtered. "The snooty flower painter?"

"I thought you weren't one for the gossip rags, Mac," he said dryly.

Instantly, Tala apologized. "Sorry, Jake. My mouth, again. But you have to admit, she's hardly ever seen out in public, socially, I mean. Never dates. . . ."

Jake shrugged. "That's soon to change. Wonder what they'll say then?"

"Oh, forget them, whoever *they* are. Just tell me all about her, Jake," Tala said, eyes gleaming. "How in the world a looker like that ever looked at your sober mug more than once, and fell for it to boot, is a mystery to me." She chuckled. "This, Brian will not believe."

Jake's berry-brown eyes hinted at a smile. "Are you going to shut up and listen?" Airily, he checked his watch. "We can do this another time . . ."

"Jake . . ."

"Okay, okay." Spreading his hands in a gesture of confusion, he shrugged. "Mac, believe me, it just happened."

"Not for you, it didn't 'just happen' Jake Rivers." Her tone warned him to come up with a better line.

Jake considered her words. "You're right. For months I worked at the Cove, but all I cared about was fixing whatever damage Nat had done." He grimaced. "Or should I say what he didn't do." His anger disappeared in the next instant. "I'd see her come and go, catch glimpses of her working, but she was just another of my father's accounts— one that he needed to keep. One day, early in the spring, I watched her walking in the woods on her property. She was oblivious." Jake paused. "She stooped to smell the flowers, Mac. It was late April and the wild blue phlox clustered around her ankles. She touched the awakening trees as she walked by them." He spoke in a low voice as he remembered. "I could swear she was talking to them." Jake caught the look on Tala's face. "Yeah, I know. Anybody else would have run in the opposite direction."

Tala laughed, nodding in agreement. "But, you're Jake Rivers."

"That I am," he said, laughing with her. "Since then, I found myself really taking notice, but really not, if you can understand what I'm not telling you."

"Yeah, you were 'scoping.' I remember when, friend."

Jake grinned. "After that, she appeared to go out of her way to make conversation. I didn't know what to make of it. But, I didn't act on it."

"Not because you were playing hard to get?"

Impatience clouded his face. She knew him better than that, so he didn't address her remark. Instead, he said, "I just let it go, not knowing how she'd feel about me coming on to her."

"Cautious Jake," Tala murmured. "What happened?"

Jake related the conversation that led to Dorcas' standing dinner invitation. "When I looked into her eyes, that did it for me." His stare was enigmatic. "Everything afterward is private, Mrs. McCready," he said.

"Whew. You do fall hard."

Jake mused in silence until Tala interrupted.

"What do your father and brother think?" Tala was aware of the family friction. She'd met both men and was none too impressed with either of them. Pretty-boy Nat hid his surliness with an outward layer of charm and Lloyd Rivers looked upon the whole world with disdain. She'd often wondered how hard it had been for the resilient Jake to resist being tainted by his sour relatives.

"I guess I'll find that out tonight," Jake answered. "I promised to look in on my father before heading home." He shrugged. "But then, does it really matter?" Bitterness edged his voice.

"What matters is you and Willow," Tala said in her deep voice.

Neither disturbed the comfortable silence that followed for several minutes.

Tala was the first to stir. They still had unfinished business. Now she understood her friend's hesitancy. His plan had been to leave her in another year, to stand on his own. The only way to fly, he'd told her, was to spread your wings, get on those toes, and go. He'd find out soon enough if he had what it took to stay airborne. But, Mac had to hit him with her left-field offer. No wonder the man's mind was buzzing like a chainsaw. Cementing a business and a new relationship was already visiting Stress City. Taking on her giant project with a new wife at home was asking for a divorce lawyer, but knowing Jake, he would put his heart and soul into making all three a success. Tala sighed. She couldn't put her friend through that. She'd have to find someone else.

"Jake, I understand if you can't accept. I know what your business means to you. Leaving it in the hands of someone else . . . and a wife to keep happy . . ." She paused. "It's not easy trying to find someone who would mind your business like you would. I know about that." She lifted a shoulder. "I wanted you, but not if it means retarding your company's growth."

Jake listened intently. Where before his thoughts stumbled along wide paths of confusion, he now exuded a quiet air of strength and self-confidence. Opening the folder, he leafed through the contract until he reached the last page. He stared at the line where his signature was required. Lifting his pen from his shirt pocket, he scrawled his name. Handing his pen to Tala, he pushed the contract toward her.

Tala bent her head as she signed, hiding her tear glistened eyes. Wordlessly, she gave Jake his pen.

"My company will grow, Mac. I have the perfect managers in mind. I must admit I was floored by your generous proposal." His voice was low and thoughtful. "I wondered if the undertaking would consume too much of me. I'd fail you, my future wife, and not the least, myself." He cleared his throat. "I was overwhelmed at your faith in me." A moment passed. "Thanks."

"You're welcome." No other words were needed.

Tala stood up. "I'm starving." She rubbed her stomach. "No. I'm ravenous!"

Jake frowned. "You mean you didn't feed the little guy this morning?"

Tala threw Jake a nasty look. "Have you ever had morning sickness?" Before he could snap on her, she picked up the phone on the first ring, a malicious grin spreading over her face. She listened. Her grin widened as she handed Jake the phone. "It's for you," she said and left the room, curiosity replacing her smile.

Willow's voice was a melody in his ear. "Hi, yourself," he said in answer to her soft greeting. Almost immediately, he stiffened. Although he'd told her the name of his firm, he'd never given her the number. "What's wrong, Willow?"

"Jake." Willow's voice, lower than normal, was almost a whisper.

Jake felt the intake of his breath. His voice was sharper as he asked her again, "What's happened? Are you all right? Talk to me." He remembered her appointment with her agent. "Are you still in town?"

Words came hard as Willow tried to speak in a normal tone. Each time she opened up her mouth she felt as if little puffs of hysterics would float from her mouth like a million billowing clouds. She had to calm down. She was scaring Jake.

"Yes," she managed in a steady voice. "Can you . . . can you get away?"

Jake swore. "Yes, I can get away," he barked. "Where are you? Are you hurt?"

"I'm not hurt." Willow's eyes teared. At least not physically. "Jake, someone's tampered with my work. They mean to discredit my name."

Her words didn't make sense but all he knew was that

she needed him. "Tell me where you are, I'll come to you." He listened. "Stay put. I won't be long."

Tala heard his last words. She knew enough to wait until he was ready to give an explanation. On rare occasions she'd seen those thunderclouds settle in his eyes.

Jake picked up his leather briefcase and jean jacket and walked briskly to the door where Tala stood. Her forehead was crinkled with worry lines. He tried to reassure her without knowing what he was talking about.

"Mac, stop worrying. I don't know what's going on, but Willow needs me. I'll call you tonight."

Tala watched him rush away. The thump of his boots resounded on the stone steps as he bypassed the elevator. Long after the sound subsided, Tala wondered what else could possibly go wrong in that man's life—and to the people that he loved.

Eleven

Willow patted her water-splashed face with a paper towel. Pushing dampened wisps of hair off her forehead, she stared at her reflection, not so much for vanity, but rather to see if her eyes still held the bewilderment that she felt and wondering when the numbness in her body would reach her brain. She hoped not before Jake got to her, suddenly needing the security of his arms around her. The whimsical thought played in her mind that if this news had come before there was Jake, what would she have done then? *Taken it like the resourceful woman you are,* she chided silently. But oh how comforting to be able to share one's pain. Pushing away a stray curl, she left the restroom, returning to her agent's office.

Oscar Germany rose from behind his desk when Willow entered the room, watching as she sat down on the low pillow-backed sofa. After a moment, he joined her, sitting at the opposite end. His thoughtful perusal told him she had not completely recovered from his bombshell. He knew she wouldn't have. Not Willow. While being so self-assured, she was also the most sensitive woman he'd ever known, holding hurts close to her heart, always bewildered by intentional cruelty. He knew this like he knew himself. After thirteen years, he knew Willow Vaughn. After thirteen years, as he'd so orchestrated his feelings—she did not know him. She was unaware that she'd hit him with her own bombshell news: *she had fallen in love.*

"Germany," Willow repeated, realizing her agent and old friend was in as much shock as she was.

Oscar smiled. Her name for him when she was seventeen, and they'd formed a partnership. He'd thought "Mr." was too formal, and her aunt wouldn't hear of Willow using his given name. They were hardly peers. He was thirty-nine. Now, he responded. "I know, Willow. Beats the hell out of me. Why now?"

"Why, at all, Oscar?"

'Oscar' was reserved for somberness and mirthless situations. Like now. "Hard as it is to believe, you've finally made an enemy."

"Oh, stop, Oscar. You make me sound like some Goody Two-shoes, tip-toeing through my life like the Grandiloquent Grande Dame," Willow sniffed. "I'm plain old me. Uncomplicated Willow. You're sounding awfully like those news rags, making me into something that I am not. *Entendez-vous?*"

"*Au contraire,* Willow," Oscar said. "Yes, I understand, and you're anything but a pompous old lady. I only meant that there's someone out there who's not a fan. Substituting your original art and almost getting away with it was not the work of a Morgana admirer."

Willow's frown disappeared at the low, calming sound of her friend's voice. Her blood flowed warm again as fear was replaced with anger. Morgana had an enemy. Or was it Willow Vaughn? She said, as much to Oscar.

"It's no secret that Willow Vaughn is Morgana," Oscar said. "The question is, which one is the victim? Willow the person or Morgana the artist?"

There was no answer to the disturbing question. After a moment, Willow said, "Poor Anna Pratt. Even in death, more than one hundred years later, she's linked to controversy. How ironic. Her floral art when published was thought not to be her own, an unfair judgment by one opinionated man. Now someone intends a similar fate for me." Her glance rested on Oscar's disturbed dark brown eyes. "Suppose it had slipped through? Gone unnoticed?" she said softly. "Next year's calendar, instead of becoming a once-in-a-lifetime piece, could have meant the ruin of Morgana." She watched as he worried the thick brush of salt-and-pepper hair on his upper lip. She'd always teased him that with a tad more gauntness to his cheeks, he could double for the tall, good-looking actor Sam Elliott. Only months after they met, Oscar married for the first time. His wife was eight months pregnant the summer Willow graduated high school, soon after she turned eighteen. Oscar had urged her to begin studying with a master, French botany artist. While she was in Paris, Oscar was widowed. Geneva Germany died giving birth. His son died hours later. Over the years, Willow always wished that he could've found someone else to love because he was such a kind and giving person. Now he showed his deep concern for her.

"You're probably right," Oscar answered, then with vehemence, "What a damn, vicious trick. The whole thing doesn't make any sense!"

Willow, unaccustomed to the ever-calm man's outburst, only nodded in agreement.

"Thank God, an astute proof editor was not sleepwalking through his job. If he hadn't been accustomed to your signature he would never have noticed the insignificant little loop was missing from the *M* in your name."

"Thank God," Willow echoed. She inclined her head. "There was something else that puzzled him? Something about a smudge?"

"You know the copy that you sent was the true botanical illustration, complete with the tiny numbers identifying the various parts. They had been whited out, but obviously not very cleverly. That and the curious signature, alerted the editor. He did a very thorough job of investigating before he called Fran with his findings." After a pause, he asked, "How long since you finished that project? One, two years ago?"

"Almost two years," Willow answered. "It's next year's calendar so the finished product should be rolling into the stores as we speak. I had to have all the paintings completed the year before." Willow frowned. "It is strange, though, Germany," she said softly. "Someone knew that I was doing a watercolor. Fran, my editor, agreed with me that a surprise watercolor amongst the usual thirteen oils would surely destine the edition for collectors item status. And for someone to substitute that particular piece?" Willow shrugged. "Why not? Anna Pratt was considered one of the greatest botanical illustrators of her time and gender. Besides, it's no secret that floral artists, including me, have admired and studied her work."

"That someone took a hell of a chance in making the substitution without getting caught. To have gotten as far as it did was certainly a coup." Oscar stood and walked to the desk. He returned with the Morgana painting and the illustration by Anna Pratt. It was a watercolor of brilliant purple foxglove and vibrant pink and yellow snapdragons. Like Pratt, Willow was known for her flamboyant use of color. Holding the two pictures close together, he sat beside Willow.

Willow looked hard at the paintings. Although foxglove and snapdragons dominated Willow's painting, the brushstrokes hardly were those of the Victorian artist. She recognized the Pratt painting because she'd used it as a model when she sketched out her thirteen paintings. It was her habit to give her editor an idea of what to expect as the calendar's theme. It was then she'd introduced the one watercolor idea, sending the Pratt picture along as an example. It appeared that same Pratt picture was substituted for Willow's original art. How it came to be mixed up with the final paintings, ready to be printed and published remained a mystery. She hadn't seen that picture since it had been sent to Fran.

"Are you going to see Fran today?" Oscar interrupted Willow's thoughts. "She's anxious to talk with you about this."

Willow was mentally exhausted. All she wanted was a hug from Jake, a warm bath and sleep. "No," she answered. "I want to talk to her but not today. I'm blown away by this." She hesitated, but because she was speaking to an old friend, she continued. "I really wanted to be at home today, Germany. Something . . . there's something that's bothering Dorcas and I'm worried about her. It's not like her to keep secrets from me." She raised her eyes hopefully. "Has she . . . called you . . . about anything?"

Oscar was clearly taken aback. "No," he answered, "We haven't spoken lately." Dorcas Williams and he had become friends over the years. He admired her staunch and loving support for her niece, whom she protected with all the fierceness of a lioness. In the early years, when Willow was still a college student, she would check out every gallery tour that he'd set up. If she didn't approve, Willow was dropped from the schedule. It didn't take her long to learn that he was a respected professional and good at his job. She left it to him to agent Willow. There was one time that Dorcas had confronted him. They were both at JFK Airport to greet Willow's return from a monthlong Holland tour. After her own greeting, Dorcas stood by, watching him greet Willow. He didn't know what happened, but after all the years of iron control, he'd clung to Willow a second longer then propriety allowed for a professional relationship. Willow never noticed. When he'd lifted his head, his eyes met the enlightened ones of Dorcas. Later, when Willow was off saying good-bye to fellow travelers, Dorcas spoke softly.

"Does she know?"

"No."

"Do you want her to know?

"At one time, I did. Now, it wouldn't be such a good idea. She doesn't think about me in that way and she would be distressed if she knew. We could no longer be friends."

"I agree," Dorcas answered. "How do you plan on handling it?"

"Say nothing. She's young, talented and beautiful. She'll fall in love soon."

That was five years ago. The relationship he had been in at the time was long finished. He was fifty-two and still unmarried. And Willow had finally fallen in love. Her low voice filtered through his reverie.

"Germany," Willow repeated. "Please call Fran for me? Tell her I'll get in touch with her, tomorrow?" The door buzzer sounded in the outer office. "That should be Jake," Willow said as she stood up. "I asked him to park in your garage. I want you to meet him, Germany." She opened the door and waited for the receptionist to buzz Jake in. When she saw him, her heart skipped a few beats as she went to him. "Jake," she whispered, as she was enfolded in his arms.

Jake held Willow close, burying his nose in her hair. Aside from the slight tremor of her body, which he tried to quiet with a crushing hold, she appeared to be calmer than she had sounded over the phone. He murmured against her cheek, "Are you feeling better, Willow?"

Willow pulled away and looked into his eyes. "Now, I am," she whispered. She took his hand and led him into the office, shutting the door.

When Willow shifted from his arms, Jake lifted his head, catching the quiet figure standing in the doorway, watching them. Too late, the man moved away, but Jake had seen his face. Once the door closed, Jake's eyes were knowing but he kept his face expressionless, as Willow made the introductions.

Oscar Germany stuck out his hand. "It's Oscar. Good to meet you."

Jake nodded. "Thanks. Call me Jake."

"Germany, we're not staying. I want to take care of that thing I told you about. I just wanted you two to meet." She began gathering her purse and jacket off the sofa and turned to Jake. "I'm starved. Can we stop to get a bite before you go back to the office? I want to explain what's happening."

Jake stared at her. "I'm not going back. You needed me," he said simply.

Willow swallowed hard as she fought back the moistness in her eyes. She loved this man who was going to become her husband. "Thank you," she whispered.

"Germany," Willow said, "I'll call you tomorrow." She took Jake's hand and walked toward the door. *"Au revoir."*

Oscar repeated the good-bye in French, then in English, with an outstretched hand to Jake, said, "We're confident that this mess will be cleared up. See you again?"

Jake took the other man's hand. Their gazes held. "I'm sure of it. And yes, we're certain to meet again."

As Jake led Willow to the elevator bank, he couldn't help wondering how long Oscar had been in love with Willow.

Twelve

Jake's arm around her waist as they walked the deserted hall, was not enough for Willow. Halting their approach to the elevator, she twisted herself fully into his arms, resting her head against his chest. Wrapping her arms around him, she leaned into him until she felt the strength of his rock-hard body flow into hers. Here was where she'd yearned to be since the moment her ears rang with the shock of Oscar's words. The sound of Jake's strong voice when she'd called, gave her the strength to carry on as a sane woman until he came to her. He was all she'd imagined he would be: her own personal tranquilizer. His soothing effect upon her was evident in her subsiding shivers. An involuntary sigh escaped.

Jake held Willow close, careful not to bruise her slender body. Although she was stronger than she looked, his hold on her was nearly crushing. The need for her to meld her body to his, seeking his comfort, was evidence of the great fear she must have experienced. He'd never seen her so shaken and he sought with all his being to protect and reassure her that she was safe with him. Safe from anyone intending her harm. That thought brought such fiery fury to his eyes that he closed them against the dark, vicious acts of anger that he knew he was capable of inflicting. He prayed to God, nothing—or no one—would bring him to that.

Willow loosened her arms and tilted her head up at Jake. The sudden calm of her body was mirrored in her once fear-filled eyes. She didn't speak but gripped his hand as they waited for the elevator doors to open. Silently, they stepped inside the empty car, Jake never relinquishing his hold.

On the slow ride down from the sixth-floor offices, Jake spoke. "Darlin'," he said thoughtfully, "Can you ward off those hunger pains for a bit? You need to talk to me and you can't do it with any kind of privacy around New York City lunchtime chatter."

Willow stood on her toes and kissed his mouth, hard. "Just keep calling me 'darlin' like that and your every wish is granted, and then some," she whispered against his lips.

Startled, Jake instinctively nudged his tongue deep inside her mouth, but just as suddenly stopped when the elevator doors opened. He growled low in his throat at the deprivation of sweets.

Willow laughed. "I got mine," she teased.

Jake spoke softly as they exited. "Uh-uh," he said. "You will get yours." His wine-hued eyes glittered brightly in anticipation.

Willow turned her head and lazily watched Jake walk to the trash can to deposit the remnants of their impromptu picnic: deli-style cold roast beef sandwiches, bananas, grapes and Evian. Her gaze clung to the smooth roll of his hips in his body-hugging denims topping western-style polished black leather boots. His stride was slow and easy and the rolling motion brought visions of those hips moving in quite another provocative manner. The short-sleeve black cotton T-shirt strained against his chest accentuating the strength in his powerful biceps and long arms. A smile touched her lips. No wonder some women strut and slow down to a crawl while passing construction sites. If all the men looked like Jake, however would the city grow? But this was not Jake's working costume. She'd seen him when he arrived at the Cove, driving his father's pickup. He favored chinos and long sleeve-shirts rolled to the elbow. Either way, he was a very sexy man.

He was coming back to her. He was smiling and she knew that those rarely seen dimples were meant only for her. Leaning back against the slatted bench, she closed her eyes and inhaled deeply, the garden scents invoking pleasant memories, and waited for him to join her. When he did, she said, eyes still closed, "I know about this place, Jake Rivers. A more quiet romantic place in the middle of the city, doesn't exist. You appear to know it very well."

Jake chuckled as he looked around. They were in a secluded area of the Central Park Zoo. He was surprised that on a bright, sunny June afternoon that there weren't many school groups or tourists visiting the area. It was just past noon, a time when the little zoo was a favorite haunt of residents occupying the tall buildings bounding Fifth Avenue and 105th Street. The section he chose was just steps away from the Conservatory Garden, one of his favorite quiet places, with sweet-smelling blooms and the scent of wisteria perfuming the air. Because the garden was a "quiet space" meant only for contemplation and soft whispers, he chose the little alcove just outside it so Willow would be free to talk. The only other occupants in the secluded place were an elderly couple who were oblivious to all around them, whispering to each other. They soon left, leaving Willow and Jake alone. While they ate, Jake had listened without interruption to Willow's strange tale.

Now as he sat down beside her, Jake brushed Willow's eyelids with his lips, then whispered in her ear. "Don't be jealous, honey, you're the last."

Willow's eyes flew open. "What . . ." Her protests stopped as his mouth covered hers.

Jake's kiss was long and slow as he slipped his arms

around her, pulling her close, desirous of more seclusion than this place allowed for how he wanted to love her. Breaking away, he said, "You're only my alpha and my omega." His eyes burned into hers. "Don't ever forget it."

Willow traced his cheek where the dimple would be if he were smiling. "Not likely to, sweetheart. I hope you won't ever regret it."

In answer, Jake kissed her cheek. Then, his eyes were serious as his voice when he said, "Willow, none of this makes any sense." Smoothing the wrinkle that appeared on her brow, he continued, "The tampering of your picture had to have taken place almost a year ago. It actually sat among the other twelve waiting in the final stages of production, undetected?"

"Until now," Willow answered tunelessly.

"How was that possible?" His tone implied contempt for less than professional operation of a supposedly well-oiled business.

"Oscar said that Louie, the copyeditor who discovered the plant, was mystified as to how the pictures were switched. He thought it was a joke at first and went looking for my picture, but couldn't find it. Not right away, anyway. He said that the amateurish obliteration of the tiny numbers used in the botanical illustration and the forging of my signature was so blatant that the bogus was surely to be discovered in the final production stage, just before printing." Willow shrugged. "You're right. No one understands who, or why."

Jake made an impatient sound. "Obviously to discredit you."

"That's just it. Me? Or Morgana?" Willow voiced her agent's question. "If Willow Vaughn, then I haven't a clue who it could be. If Morgana, the celebrated artist, is the victim, then it could be any of a myriad of jealous workers in the industry." Again a shoulder lifted. "Where does one look, Jake?"

"Always at the beginning." Jake appeared deep in thought and it was moments before he spoke. "Tell me, how does your work get from Wildflowers Cove to your publisher?"

"Different ways," Willow responded. "At the onset of a new project, I send several sketches to my editor. Later, I send color drawings. These are sent by mail. I'll do it myself or sometimes I leave it to Dorcas. Other times, a messenger service may be used. At the publisher's the originals are turned into slides and sent to the printer's for lithographs, which become the calendar. Once or twice I've done preliminary slides so that I can get a sneak preview."

Jake listened and then frowned. "Not much control once they leave your studio." Reproach tinged his voice.

Willow heard. "Who would think it necessary, Jake?" Willow answered, not without a little anger. She was hurt that he thought her to be so irresponsible. "I never received any ominous notes warning me that someone was out to get me. If I had, don't you think I would have been more cautious?"

She was angry, Jake knew, but she had a right to be. He had so much as accused her of running her affairs with careless aplomb. Warning or not, she should take more care about what went on around her. Like leaving the key to her studio in such an unguarded place. Anyone could gain access in her absence.

Jake's silence was telling. Willow sensed what he was thinking. "The key," she said. When he nodded, Willow sighed, "You're right, as usual," as she settled back against his broad shoulder. At the sound of his voice, she sat erect, immediately.

"Stop that, Willow," Jake rapped suddenly. "What you and I have is not a contest on one-upmanship. If that's what you think we're all about, you have the wrong idea about us."

Stunned at his outburst, Willow didn't answer, but pon-

dered his words. Of course, she didn't think their relationship was based on such shallowness. A more honest give-
and-take between two new lovers was not possible. They
were born to be together, come what may. A week ago, Willow had thought herself a happy and complete person.
Working daily at what she loved best, the days were not long
enough to enable her to create beautiful canvases. Not the
least, she had her family, her only living relative, Dorcas;
her writer's retreat, bringing strangers, only to have some
return as friends; her international tours, seeing the magical cities that so many others only dream about. She was an
extremely lucky woman and she was grateful to the Lord
above for what she'd been given. But never would she have
believed that without the advent of Jake into her life, true
happiness had been elusive.

Willow looked at Jake. "Never," she finally said. "Never,
will I have the wrong idea about us, Jake. Two days ago,
when we bared our souls, that was our beginning. It will
never be possible for us to go back to who we were. Or to
doubt what we are to each other. Never."

Jake listened intently to her words. She was right. There
would be no world for either of them without the other. It
was as if each had been waiting to reach this crossroad in
their lives. No marriages or near attempts, no serious lovers;
almost as if fate had lain in wait for them. For some inex-
plicable reason, some nagging thought, he felt a strong desire, no, a command, to protect Willow Vaughn from harm.
The inner voice was so strong that he shuddered, shaking
off the dank feeling. He encircled her shoulders and pulled
her head onto his chest. "Never any doubt."

After a moment, Willow murmured, "Life can't be all
roses, after all."

"We have to do our best to make it so. If not," he
shrugged, his words hanging in the perfumed air. Stirring,
he said, "We won't solve the mystery this afternoon, so I
think I'd better get you home before your aunt starts wor-

rying." He paused. "Did she know the nature of your meeting with Oscar Germany, today?"

"No. Only that he wanted to talk about the calendar. She doesn't know what's happened." The mention of her aunt brought a shadow to her face. After the shocking news that Oscar had given her, she was not mentally ready to confront her aunt about her odd behavior. Willow knew deep down that something or someone had seriously frightened her aunt. But she knew that she wouldn't allow another night to pass without speaking to Dorcas.

Jake held out his hand and pulled Willow to her feet. Her somber look did not escape him. As they walked away from their secluded space, he said, "Put the picture out of your mind for a minute before you give yourself a monster headache. We'll attack this thing once we've both tried to absorb this nonsense."

Willow shook her head. "It's not that, Jake. Aunt Dee's odd behavior last night has been bothering me. Something heavy is weighing on her mind and now I don't know if I should hit her with my dizzying news. I really think she would be very disturbed."

Jake thought. "You'll have to tell her soon, Willow. You realize that." Whatever had happened, had affected Willow, deeply. When Willow nodded, he pulled her closer into the circle of his arm that hugged her waist. Their bodies touched, bumping gently with each step. Jake realized that in the space of hours, she'd been hit in areas of most importance to her; her family and her career. She was hurting inside but he was determined that before they parted there would be no good night between them until she shared her burden with him. He wasn't opposed to her sharing his bed either, if she so desired. He knew that that was out of the question, considering what she faced at home.

Soon, after skillful maneuvering out of the city and midday traffic, Jake drove the silver Camaro north. Traffic was moving easily on the Hutchinson River Parkway. Jake shot a brief look at Willow. Though her eyes were closed and she seemed at peace, small wrinkles marred her forehead. Jake reached over and brushed her cheek softly. In a low, unhurried voice he asked, "What bothered you last night?"

Her eyes still closed, Willow smiled, reaching for his jean-clad thigh. The concern in his voice so stirred her that she wondered if she could possibly love this man more. Willed to touch him, her hand caressed his firm thigh until heat sparked the tips of her fingers. She squeezed. She felt him jerk involuntarily. "Don't do that, darlin'," she heard him say softly. Willow opened her eyes. Jake's face was taut with control as he kept his eye on the road.

"Not now, darlin'."

"I love you, Jake Rivers," Willow said. In answer, his face broke into one of those rare smiles, warming her all over. "I know," he said. A thought came to her that she knew she'd never share: when they argued—and there would be such times—she'd lose every time, once he flashed her that look. She'd just be a big old-fashioned ball of Silly Putty. Irresistibly malleable.

"Willow?"

Taking a deep breath, Willow spoke. "When I arrived home last night, Aunt Dee was obviously saying good-bye to two women." Faltering, she continued, "Jake . . . it . . . was the strangest scene to come upon. Those silent, strange women chilled me through." Willow was suddenly filled with the need to unburden herself. The words flowed into the telling of the unsettling encounter of the strangers in her driveway—and the haunted look on Dorcas' face.

Silent throughout her relating of the strange story, Jake was as mystified as Willow, frustrated that he had no explanation to offer when she finished. Obviously the two visitors had upset Dorcas, but to the extent of shutting out her beloved niece?

"She never answered your knock on her door?"

"Not a word, but I suspected she wasn't asleep." Her

dark eyes filled with pain from the memory of her aunt's cold behavior. "I really don't know how I'm going to approach her or what to say when I see her. She was just so . . . into herself . . . like I suddenly ceased to exist."

"Impossible," Jake responded. The two women meant too much to each other. It was hard for him to imagine either living distant existences. Although they would be under separate roofs when he and Willow married, they would still be emotionally connected.

"I'm not so sure, Jake. You didn't see her face. Her body appeared drained. You know Dorcas."

The truth was, the little he did know made it hard to visualize Willow's description of her. Meek and frightened? To him Dorcas represented the take charge, dependable, don't-give-me-no-guff person who was as reliable as old slippers. "Yes, I think I do." After that, he drove in silence until a short time later, he passed the Elmsford exit that would take him to his father's house. He'd thought about taking Willow by to get acquainted with her intended father-in-law, but thought better of it. Especially since he knew there was no love lost between the two of them. He would wait until Willow was in a better frame of mind and after he'd had a chance to break the news to his father and brother. Neither would be too thrilled at welcoming her into the family, but that would remain their problem as far as he was concerned. Jake frowned. The major upheaval in his own world of work would take huge adjustments. He would have to put in motion the turnover of his business to his new managers. That meant contacting his choice immediately, before the day was over. Jake turned onto Broadway. Nearing Wildflowers Cove, he couldn't help thinking that with their marriage would come a lot of unwanted baggage. The thought nagged at him that they should wait until the clouds hanging over Willow disappeared. Just as suddenly as it had appeared, that thought dissipated. She was his and they belonged together, come what may. His? Jake pulled into the Cove driveway and stopped, turning off the ignition.

Willow, perplexed at his strange behavior, turned to him. "What's wrong, Jake?"

"I never asked. Willow, will you marry me? Be my wife for eternity?"

Willow stared at Jake. "What?" she said, stupefied.

"I never asked," Jake repeated, "and right now, I don't have a diamond to give to you, but I refuse to take us for granted."

Willow's eyes misted. "Hadn't you noticed I'm not a diamonds kind of girl?"

Jake had noticed. She could drape herself in the precious jewel but the only adornment on her fingers was an ages old, thin gold band with two tiny rosebuds, vines entwined, like two hands.

Willow removed the ring from her right hand, middle finger. "It belonged to my mother." Offering it to Jake, she whispered, "Yes."

Jake took the slim band from her and slipped it on her ring finger. Bringing her hand to his lips, he kissed her fingers. "I love you, Willow."

"I know."

Jake turned on the ignition and slowly drove the length of the driveway, a small frown etching his brow. How could he leave her now? They hadn't come close to a resolution of how, or who, tampered with her art. Approaching her aunt required a clear head, and Jake knew that Willow's own mystery would definitely be a distraction. Wishing he could lighten her burden, he made a decision, parking behind her big Mercedes.

Willow was surprised to see Jake turn off the ignition and walk around to help her out. She'd expected him to leave the motor running while they kissed good-bye, knowing he'd want to get to his own business. Wondering at his determined expression, she waited.

"I feel helpless and I don't want to leave you. Not this way." His voice dropped to a husky rasp. "I want to hold you, love away all the hurt inside of you."

The frustration in his voice, though it did not surprise her, touched her deeply. Her pain was his pain. The love they'd shared two days ago was beginning to become a cherished memory. She didn't want memories, she wanted, now. Silently putting her hand in his, they walked to the cottage. Willow glanced briefly at the big house then stared straight ahead. Dorcas would be waiting for her, but Willow needed the wisdom of Jake's words and the comfort of his powerful arms, just as he needed to know that she believed and trusted in him to be there for her. It was important to their tender relationship. Afterward, she would be ready to help her aunt deal with her own shadowy demons.

Thirteen

When Willow and Jake left the cottage, dusk had fallen, and the warm June evening air was scented with the perfume of hyacinth and delphinium. Hands clasped, speaking in low voices, they walked along the brick path leading to the big house, when Jake stopped. Willow followed his stare. They looked at the white truck with the red lettering, advertising 'Lloyd Rivers Landscaping.' It was parked on the path leading to Willow's greenhouse.

Jake frowned. "Trouble?" he asked. Willow hadn't mentioned any problem.

Willow shrugged, as curious as Jake. "None that I was aware of. Dorcas must have called Nat." The sound of laughter coming from the kitchen further piqued her curiosity. When she opened the door, Willow could only stare in amazement at her aunt. The Dorcas Williams of the night before bore no resemblance to the woman whose body was shaking with laughter. Beside her, sitting at the big table, was Nat Rivers, obviously, just as convulsed with glee.

"Aunt Dee?"

"Buttercup." Dorcas stood, and grabbed her niece in a bear hug, while trying to control her laughter. Her smile included the surprised man by Willow's side. "Hello Jake."

Jake nodded. "Dorcas," he said, as he shared a look with a bewildered Willow. He then nodded to his brother. "Nat."

"Don't mind us, you two," Dorcas said, wiping at her

eyes. "Come, sit down. Your brother should do stand-up, Jake. He's hilarious. Tommy and the cooks were in stitches and could hardly serve dinner. But we got through it."

"You called the caterers?" Willow was not surprised. She'd known that Dorcas would probably call for help. But, she wondered at the presence of Nat. "What went wrong?" She looked at Nat.

"Oh Willow," Dorcas quickly answered. "A careless accident this morning. Not long after you left for the city. Somehow, two of the glass panes got broken by one of our guests. Luckily, I was able to get a glazier here today. About an hour ago it dawned on me to have the greenhouse checked. Lord knows we don't want anything happening to your beautiful blooms, honey." Dorcas looked at Willow and Jake. "I was surprised when I went outside to see your car, Jake. Had I known you were here, I could have saved Nat a trip." Before Jake could answer, she said with a wink and a smile, "But, I'm glad I didn't know." To Nat, she said, knowingly, "I think we're going to hear some page one news."

Since his brother had walked in the door with Willow, Nat couldn't stop staring at them. As long as Nat had been out there, messing with the honeys, he knew the look they got when they thought they were in love. Miss High and Mighty was lost in the clouds. He watched now as his brother looked from Dorcas to Willow. *Waiting for permission to speak?* Nat wondered. *Oh, you just wait, Brother. This is only the beginning. You'd better get used to being called, "Mr. Vaughn."*

Jake, except for the low greeting to his brother and Dorcas, had been silent. He was concerned for Willow, apparently mystified by her aunt's normal behavior. He could see the changing expressions on her face as she stared at Dorcas. Somehow, he'd thought the announcement of their engagement, would have been done with a little more panache. Standing in the middle of the kitchen at Wildflowers Cove was not the way he'd planned to tell his family that Willow had consented to be his wife. He sat down beside Willow, and took her hand in his.

"I've asked Willow to marry me, and she's accepted." Jake looked at Dorcas. "We hope we have your blessing." He wondered at the fleeting look of fear that her lashes had hidden. Maybe it was his imagination?

Dorcas was on her feet and hugging her niece. "Willow," she cried. "I knew it. How wonderful!" She kissed Willow's cheek, and then hugged and kissed Jake. "Welcome to our family, Jake."

Tears sprang into Willow's eyes, as she hugged her aunt. Disbelief, joy, apprehension, roiled around in her stomach, then shot through her like a geyser, so that her breath escaped in small gasps. Was she taking a bizarre trip through the twilight zone? Had it only been mere hours ago that she was determined to demand that her aunt open up to her? Tell her what had frightened her so badly the day before?

"Aunt Dee?" Willow said. "You're really happy for me?"

"Happy? Honey, I'm ecstatic," Dorcas said, pulling Willow into her arms again. She brushed away a tear. "I only wish your uncle Thomas and your Grandy were here, honey. Happy? Shame on you, for asking!"

Jake and Nat stood up together, each eyeing the other warily. Jake waited.

"Congratulations, Brother." Nat held out his hand, and Jake took it.

"Thanks," Jake answered. He couldn't help wondering where the humor was in the situation. His brother was silently cracking up.

"Here I am, an old man, and I finally get me a sister." Nat had walked around the table. He put an arm around Willow's shoulder, pulling her close, then bent and kissed her cheek, brushing her lips when he straightened up. "Welcome, to our family, sis," he said.

When she sensed what he was going to do, Willow couldn't move fast enough away from Nat. She cringed from his embrace with such distaste, she instantly regretted it because Jake's look was murderous. Ignoring Nat, she caught Jake's hand. "I think we'd better call it a night, Jake. It's getting late and you have that call to make." To her future brother-in-law, she said, "Don't believe the hype, Nat. You really don't have the magic touch." With a see-you-later look at Dorcas, she and Jake left the house.

Willow was in Jake's arms, her head resting against his chest as he held her tight around her waist. They were leaning against the Camaro. It had taken some minutes for the muscles in Jake's jaw to relax. Willow could feel the tightness ebb away when she caressed his cheek. She gave him a squeeze, to let him know that she understood, and that she was glad he was feeling better. In response, Jake kissed her forehead.

"I don't know that you'll need me to champion for you, Ms. Vaughn. You are a ferocious army all by yourself." Jake slid his hands down her arms. "Let's see those dukes.' "

Willow made fists with both hands.

"Hmm," Jake said, squeezing them in one of his big hands. "Just as strong as the lady's tongue." He grinned, broadly. "I was worried about leaving you alone some nights while I burned the midnight oil. Now, I see I don't have to worry about a thing."

"No, you don't, sweetheart. You don't have to worry about me taking care of myself." Her eyes sparkling, Willow stood on her toes and whispered in Jake's ear. "But, did you ever wonder what happens when the oil in the lamp dries up?"

Her meaning did not escape Jake, and he threw back his head and laughed. "Not a chance of that ever happening, darlin'. Not if I have anything to do with you. Not a fat man's chance." The laugh was smothered as he crushed his lips against the mouth of the love of his life.

Willow basked in the embrace of her lover, wishing that the night was still young. She longed for a command per-

formance of their past few hours. For her, Jake Rivers had
no peer.

It was a grim-faced Jake, who for the last twenty minutes
had been driving toward his father's house in Elmsford.
When he parked the car, he saw the company truck and
the Oldsmobile parked in front of the garage. He was surprised. When Nat had driven off shortly after he and Willow had left the kitchen, Jake had guessed that he would
not find Nat waiting in for him. "Guess I was wrong about
that, brother," he muttered. Anger filled his heart again,
as he unlocked the front door and went inside.

Lloyd Rivers glanced up at his youngest son, but did not
speak as he turned his attention back to the TV.

"Dad," Jake said, ignoring his father's sullen look.
"Where's Nat?" Jake shook his head in disgust at his father's lack of response, then took the stairs two at a time
as he headed toward Nat's bedroom. Without bothering
to knock, Jake pushed opened the door. Nat was on the
bed, ankles crossed, lounging against the headboard,
watching TV. He put down the bottle of stout when Jake
neared the bed.

"Second thoughts, Brother?" He laughed. "I'm not surprised. Happens to the best of us, whe . . ."

Jake slapped Nat's bare foot so hard, his hand stung
from the impact. In the next second, he had a fist full of
undershirt in his hand as he sat, eye to eye, with Nat. His
unhurried voice was low. "You keep your damn, smart-ass,
street ways in the street . . . where you belong . . . not, I
repeat, not, around me and mine. Understand? And . . .
if you ever touch her like that again, pray to God, that
you'll be far away when I find out." Jake released his
brother and stood up.

"What the hell's goin' on, in here?" Lloyd stood in the

doorway, breathing heavily from the effort of climbing the stairs.

Nat and Jake stared at their father.

"Dad," Jake said, suddenly concerned for the strain on his father's heart. He was stopped by the older man's voice.

"Answer me, dammit all. At each other's throat all the damn time. What are you up to now, Nat?"

Nat was on his feet, glaring at his brother, as he pulled on slacks over his underwear. He had never been comfortable standing before his father, half-dressed. "Why is it me all the time? I haven't done a thing. Why don't you ask him? Remember the baggage? Well, it's comin' in here, sooner than you think!" He laughed and sat down on the bed.

Jake looked at Nat. What the hell was he talking about? When he turned to his father, the ashened skin alarmed Jake. What was going on?

Lloyd was leaning heavily against the mirrored dresser by the door, waving off Jake's attempt to get him to sit down. "What are you talking about?" he asked.

Nat's voice turned surly as he looked from his father to his brother. "Well?" he said. "You gonna wait until the church bells ring before you tell him he's getting a new daughter-in-law?" To his father, he said, "Your baby boy is getting married. To the lady up at the Cove and I don't mean the old one."

Lloyd closed his eyes, wishing he could drown out the sound of his son's voice just as easily. A Vaughn, in his family? When he opened his eyes, he stared at Jake. "Is this true?" His voice was almost inaudible.

Jake was bewildered at his father's and brother's reaction to his engagement. What was their problem with accepting Willow as his intended bride? Firmly, he answered, "I am marrying Willow Vaughn."

"No." The word spewed from Lloyd's mouth. "You will not give that woman the Rivers' name," he spat. "You will not bring her into this family. She's the child of the devil

himself, and you'll regret the day you ever laid eyes on her!"
Lloyd, righted himself, and turned to leave the room. His
eyes burned bright with hate as he stared at his youngest
son. Without another word, he lumbered out of the room
and made his way clumsily down the stairs. The sound of
his bedroom door slamming shut penetrated the silence in
the room upstairs.

Stunned, Jake turned to his brother for an explanation of
their father's bizarre behavior, and was startled by the bared
look of malevolence on Nat's face. "You hate her too." The
statement was spoken in awe. What had Willow done to either
of them to make them hate her so much? They didn't even
know her. Jake sat down in a chair by the window. "Why?"

"You're so dumb, Jake. You've always been so dumb. All
your life you've never questioned anything. Anything." Nat
shook his head. "You were the baby and you had to be
protected. I was old enough to understand and to help
shelter you. Mother wanted it that way."

"Mother?" Jake's eyes narrowed. All his life, since her
death, he had cherished her memory, grieving in silence,
never sharing his thoughts with his father and brother. He
had loved his mother and had missed her terribly when she
died. That void was still a special place in his heart. Now,
what was his brother mentioning her for? "Mother?" he
repeated.

"You never wondered why mother left us? Then returned when father begged her to?" Nat laughed at the
stupid look on Jake's face, then answered his own questions. "No. You didn't. You were so happy that you had
your precious Mommy back. Never asked any questions.
Dumb Jake." Nat got off the bed. "I need a beer." He
walked to the door.

Jake stood up, following his brother, heated at the implied
words that his mother had kept some dark secret from him.
In the kitchen, he asked, "What's mother got to do with
anything? She's been dead for almost seventeen years!"

Disgust spread over Nat's face as he drank his beer from the bottle. "Ah, grow up, Jake. It's time to grow up." Brushing past his brother he headed for the stairs. "If I were you, brother, I'd be asking Miss High and Mighty all about her precious family. You might have those second thoughts that I mentioned about bringing her home to Daddy."

"I already know about how her parents died," Jake shouted at Nat's back. Nat answered by letting out a loud laugh. Jake could still hear the laughter through the closed bedroom door.

Frustrated, Jake left the house. "They've both gone crazy," he muttered as he walked to his car.

But he really didn't believe that. His gut was that something was very wrong in both houses—the Vaughns and the Rivers. Whatever it was, how could it possibly affect his love for Willow and hers for him? Impossible, he thought. They would live together as man and wife until their last day on this earth. He knew that with all that he had ever believed in.

After Jake had driven away, Willow had gone straight to her room. She'd showered, dressed in a nightgown and robe, then waited until the house settled down for the night. She knew that she and Dorcas would talk tonight. It was after eleven o'clock when she walked to her aunt's room and knocked on the door.

Dorcas had prepared herself mentally for Willow's visit. When she heard the knock, she was ready. Ready for more of her little white lies.

"It's open, Willow," she called. When her niece entered the room, Dorcas patted the sofa cushion next to her and gestured. "Come, sit beside me, and have some tea. It's fresh-brewed and hot."

"You expected me."

"Now, don't you think your old Aunt Dee knows she

wasn't going to escape the nudge tonight?" She winked and laughed, then poured the hot liquid in a mug and handed it to Willow. She filled her own mug, stirred in honey and took a sip. Settling herself, she said, "I wasn't myself, Willow, and I hope that I never let another night pass without saying good night . . . when we're under the same roof. If you even think that that's going to happen, be your nudgy self and don't let it happen."

"I did try, Aunt Dee," Willow said softly. "There won't be a next time, I promise you, that." She drank from her mug. After a moment, she asked, "Tell me now?"

"Those ladies brought bad news." Dorcas sighed. "Threw me for a loop. The shorter of the two used to be . . . a . . . friend of mine. We grew up together."

"Used to be? Where does she live now?" Willow was surprised. She'd always associated her aunt with Toronto and Dorcas had never spoken of any friends from her childhood years in Irvington.

"She moved away years ago. Lives in DC now."

"She's moving back to Irvington? What was the bad news she brought?"

"She's dying."

"Oh no," cried Willow. Briefly, the image of the sad-eyed woman appeared. "I'm sorry, Aunt Dee. You were close?"

Dorcas exhaled. Close? To Vera? Never! Glibly, she answered. "A very long time ago. My best friend. We had a falling out, the year we graduated high school. We haven't spoken since."

"Is that why she came to see you? To make things right before she died?" Willow thought there was more to be told. Her aunt had been nearly comatose yesterday.

"Yes. She wanted my forgiveness for the hurt that she caused me. It all seems so silly now. She told my then boyfriend lies about me, and he believed them. It was all a ploy for him to turn to her." Dorcas grimaced. "It worked, apparently, because he of so little faith, called me everything but a child of God, and walked out of my life." Dorcas winked at her niece. "Silly kid stuff. But if it hadn't happened, I would never have met and married Thomas. So, as the saying goes, 'Things work out for the best.' "

"What else, happened? You're not telling me everything she told you, Aunt Dee," Willow accused.

Dorcas breathed heavily. Where will the lies stop? she wondered. *How long can I keep this up? Why did I even start this damn charade? Do I really have so little faith in my Willow that she will disown me for what I've done to her?* Dorcas shivered. *I can't take that chance.* "She's been in prison practically all of her adult life," Dorcas lied. "She murdered the boy she ran away with. My old boyfriend. She caught him stepping out on her and she shot him in a jealous rage. She became ill while in prison. She's served her time and she's been released, to die a free woman."

"Oh, my God, Aunt Dee. How awful!"

Dorcas had to end this. No more lies! She waved a hand as if to dismiss any further discussion. "I can only add that she's been sorry all these years for what she'd done to me. She apologized. Said she can die now with one less burden on her soul."

"God bless her," Willow murmured.

Dorcas sighed. She hoped the subject would never surface again. She was nearly shaking with relief. "Now, tell me what Oscar called you into the city for on such short notice."

Willow reached over and patted her aunt's hand, relieved that Dorcas was her old self. "That was a horrible shock for you. But thank God, you've both made your peace." Sitting back, after pouring fresh tea, she tucked her feet beneath her. "Get ready for this and see if you can make sense out of it. We can't." Willow related the details of the story Oscar had told to her, leaving out nothing. When she finished, she had to laugh at the expression on her aunt's face. "You look like I probably looked to Oscar," she said. "Bizarre, isn't it? Maybe you can figure it out."

Dorcas couldn't help but laugh at the weird story. Who in his or her right mind would even attempt such a thing? There were less elaborate ways to discredit a celebrity, other than that, botched-up scheme. "Lord, where do all the weirdos come from? Do you suppose there's some kind of underground school for nuts operating in the city?" Willow's laugh joined hers. "Why, if I thought it had started here, the first person I'd accuse is that, 'wanna-be,' George Henry . . ." The words died on her lips as she stared at her niece.

"George Henry?" they chorused.

The two women looked in stupefaction at each other. Their thoughts spilled out.

"He wouldn't . . . how could he . . ." Willow sputtered.

"He was here two years ago when you were doing those paintings, but how on earth could he have gotten his hands on your work?" Dorcas asked.

They were silent, trying to think about the times George had to be escorted away from Willow's studio. He'd been found several times peering through the window and had even invited himself into the studio when she'd been working. He could very well have seen her work. But he'd shown no animosity toward her at that time, thought Willow.

"I don't know," Willow said in answer to Dorcas' question.

"Think back. I know he's wandered into your studio. Did you let him stay? Talk about your work to him?"

"No," Willow answered. "But you remember how nosy he was. He saw the color sketches I'd completed. He even remarked about the odd watercolor, asking if he was the first person to see the only watercolor by Morgana. He wouldn't shut up about it." Willow added, "That doesn't explain how in the world he ever got his hands on my work. I never worked on those pictures outside of my studio, and the door was always kept locked."

Dorcas' eyelids fluttered at a vague memory, but she couldn't quite pinpoint the reason for her sudden anxiety.

Something Willow just said. Unable to remember, she let the nagging moment pass.

"I never heard of anything so ridiculous," Dorcas said. "What did Oscar think? Did Fran have any clues? After all, the prank must have happened right there in those offices."

"Oscar is as bewildered as we are, and Fran doesn't know anything, according to Oscar. I wasn't in any state to talk to her today. I'll call her tomorrow."

Willow yawned and was about to get up, when Dorcas caught her arm.

"Not so fast, young lady. Aren't you forgetting to tell me all about your whirlwind romance? And I thought that that young man was too slow for my liking. I want to know everything!"

"I'll bet you do." Willow smiled, remembering her aunt's attempts at matchmaking. "You knew before I did that I was attracted to him, didn't you?"

"Sure did." Dorcas beamed, pleased at her astute observation. She leaned over and pecked her niece on the cheek. "I hope you'll be very happy, Willow. Jake's a good man and he'll treat you like a princess."

"I'm a woman, Aunt Dee, and that is the way I want to be treated," Willow answered in a firm voice. "Why do people always want to treat me like I'm a delicate glass object?" she added in disgust. "I'm far from being tiny and I'm not that skinny!"

"You've got a sweet disposition and people just want to please you, buttercup, so let them."

Willow grimaced. "I suppose it's the fawners I abhor. Their behavior is so obnoxious. Especially some men, who think that all they need do is turn on the charm, and I'll hop into their bed." She smiled. "Jake's never been anything but honest and natural. That's just the way he is with everybody. I think that's what attracted me to him from the beginning. Especially since he appeared not to even notice me." Willow laughed. "He's a pretty foxy guy, pulling that old act on me, and I fell for it. I'm sure glad I did."

Dorcas grinned. "I could've told you he was working his mojo."

"Oh, sure. You think I would have listened?"

"No!"

Both women laughed.

"I love that man so much, Aunt Dee, I hate to even think about him not being a part of the rest of my life."

"Have you set the date yet?"

"Not yet. We want to wait a few months. That is, Jake wants to wait. His boss just made him an offer that he doesn't want to refuse. He thought about his new duties, then decided that it wouldn't be fair to ask his new wife to bear the stress. He asked if I wouldn't mind waiting a few months. Besides, in twelve months or so, he intends to sever the ties and develop his own company. He'll be ready then."

Dorcas raised a brow. "A year? That's a hardworking young man doing his own and his father's business too. I would've thought he'd be more than ready to do his own thing in less time than that. Especially since he's turned everything back over to Nat."

"You're right, Aunt Dee. You don't miss a thing. But, Jake's meeting this morning . . . well, he's decided to stay with his boss for another year. He's taking over one of her giant projects."

"What?"

"Let me explain. You'll understand why he wants to do this."

Dorcas listened without interrupting to Willow's explanation of how Jake planned to spend his time for the next several months. She admired Jake's dedication to his friend and his friend's faith in him to carry out her plans. "Remarkable," she said, when Willow finished.

"I think so," agreed Willow.

"So, does that mean, depending on how smoothly the

project goes, you two will be willing to set a date in less than a year?'' Dorcas' voice was hopeful.

"That's right. Neither of us really wants to put off the wedding. But to give a new marriage a chance, we think our decision to wait is best."

"Oh, how practical, the young." Her eyes twinkling, Dorcas said, "You two are going to make me wait anyway, aren't you?"

Willow laughed. "Suppose I buy you a baby doll for Christmas? Would that help a little?"

Dorcas stood up. "Fresh," she said, bending over to kiss Willow's forehead. She cleared the table and picked up the tea tray. "When I get your little munchkin in my arms, you'll regret letting me have her."

Willow followed her aunt, opening the door. "Oh, and you're so sure it's going to be a girl-child?"

"Well, I'm really hoping for twins. One of each, thank you," Dorcas said.

"We won't mind, if you don't mind playing great-aunt to our babies, Aunt Dee. Jake loves kids and can't wait to have his own. Like me, he always wished his mother would have given him a baby sister."

Dorcas was in the kitchen and would have dropped the tray had she not set it on the counter just then. She listened to Willow walk down the hall and heard the soft click of her door closing.

"She almost did, Jake, she almost did," Dorcas whispered.

When Dorcas closed her own bedroom door and got into bed, she wondered what the next few months would bring. The same feeling that she'd gotten the day before, before her sister Vera suddenly appeared at her doorstep, was invading her senses now. Something terrible was about to happen, and Dorcas knew that whatever it was—she would have to bear the sole responsibility.

Fourteen

The ache in Jake's head was enough to send him to the medicine cabinet in search of a painkiller. Finding one aspirin, he swore, but downed it anyway, knowing it wasn't going to make the least bit of difference. During the drive from his father's house, Nat's laughter had rung in his ears until Jake had wished, God help him, for eternal silence. There was a sense of unknown doom that Jake had associated with that awful sound. As hard as he tried, he couldn't shake that feeling, yet he had to; he still had work to do. Late as it was, he had to get the ball rolling for his new managers, that is, if his friends would accept the job offers.

Scott Anderson and his wife, Irene, were fellow landscapers and had been friends of Jake's for several years. They had met when Jake had successfully bid on his first interior landscaping job. The husband-and-wife team had had their own business for a few years. The three had established an instant rapport, becoming friends, while remaining competitive business associates. Scottie, at thirty-seven, was a year older than Jake. Irene was thirty-five.

When he had decided to accept Tala's proposition, Jake had known who he would ask to take over his business for a year. Scott had sold his business and was in the process of relocating to South Carolina. He and his wife had decided to forego the hustle and bustle of the city, opting for a quieter environment in which to raise their three-year-old daughter. While making their long-range plans, they both had taken jobs with independent contractors.

Jake dialed the number and waited, praying that he would get a positive response to his request. If his friends refused, Jake would be at a loss because he knew of no one else to whom he could turn his business over, and have peace of mind.

"Hi, buddy," Jake said. Scott had picked up. "I know it's late, man, but I had to reach you tonight. How's it going?"

Scott Anderson was not annoyed at receiving an eleven o'clock call from Jake Rivers. Whatever it was, it was important. He'd learned over the years that his friend was a no-nonsense guy who took care of business and was not about wasting his or anyone else's valuable time. He only hoped the call wasn't bad news. He knew that Lloyd Rivers had been sick.

"We're all okay on this end," Scott replied. "How about you? Things okay?"

"Sure," Jake answered. "Nothing like that. My dad's okay." Jake almost crossed his fingers when he spoke again. "Scottie, I need your help. Irene's too. Got a few minutes to hear me out?"

"Sure thing," Scott answered. "Mind if Reenie listens in? She's right here."

"No, that's great. Hi, Reenie. Okay, here it is, guys. I want both of you to take over my business for me, running it like you ran your own, successfully, the only way you know how. I need you to commit for at least a year." Jake expelled his breath.

"What's going on?" Scott asked quietly, as he turned on the speakerphone. He and his wife stared at one another, perplexed. Their friend needed a friend.

Jake responded with a question of his own. "Have you solidified any plans to move yet? If you have, then I can't ask you to reverse them."

Scott heard the tension and sought to ease his friend's

mind. "No. We haven't made any concrete plans. We've still got feelers out on a couple of businesses looking to sell. As far as the house, we've just made a final decision on the plans. We're not going to start building until after Labor Day."

Jake began to breathe easier, giving silent thanks. "Scott, Reenie, here's the deal."

When Jake stopped speaking, Irene Anderson looked at her husband, surprise etched on her face. Scott's look mirrored hers. Before either of them could speak, Jake's voice came over the speaker.

"Think about it, but you'll have to let me know soon, so I can make other arrangements if you don't accept. I'll be in an all-day meeting with Tala tomorrow, but you can always beep me."

"Tala's offer is more than generous, Jake," said Scott. "Reenie agrees with me. Let us sleep on this, hash out a few things and we'll get back to you tomorrow, without fail."

The underlying meaning of his friend's words, alleviated the tension in Jake's body, so that he slumped back in his chair. "Call me anytime, Scott."

Jake hung up the phone. Somehow, he knew that everything would be all right. His friends were going to come through for him.

Jake stood up, and for the first time since he awoke this morning, until he ended his call with Scott a moment ago, he began to feel the chaos of the day ebbing away. Not totally, because he knew that he was not finished with his brother. Nat's words had disturbed him and Jake knew that it was a matter of time before he confronted his brother.

Jake was in the shower, rippling his back muscles, under the stream of hot water. Nat would have to wait, Jake thought. He was concerned about what was happening between the two women at Wildflowers Cove. Willow had been justifiably confused about Dorcas' elastic return to her normal behavior, almost as if the night before had never happened. Although he wanted to call her, Jake was keeping his promise. Knowing he had the important business call to make to Scott, she knew that it would be late before he was through. Willow had made him promise to clear his head of everything, and get some rest. Tomorrow was the day that he was taking over Tala's project.

Jake turned out the bathroom light, and was soon in bed, wearing nothing but pajama shorts. He turned off the bedside lamp, but instead of turning onto his side in his favorite fetal, sleeping position, he lay on his back, staring at the shadows dancing on the ceiling. Try as he would to dispel them, the day's events intruded on his slumber. Tala's act of faith in him; the revelation of Willow's unknown enemy; Oscar Germany's mask slipping, revealing his love for his young client; Dorcas' strange visitors who had sent her into a tailspin. None of it made any sense to Jake. But the most bizarre happening of all, was his father's vehement reaction to Willow becoming his daughter-in-law and Nat's veiled implication that their mother had held some deep, dark secret from Jake.

The same feeling of impending doom that had shot through him on his anguished drive home, lay-heavy on his chest now. His mother had been nothing but completely honest with him all his life. What evil had his brother hinted at?

Jake's eyes were closed, but they flew open as he realized he'd dozed off. He had been dreaming. It had been years since he'd dreamed of his mother. Tonight, she had called his name.

Hours after his father's door had slammed shut, and his brother had left the house angry and frustrated, Nat sat, propped up in bed, drinking beer and staring at the TV screen. He had dozed many times, only to wake up to the inane chatter of a talk-show host and his publicity-seeking guests. Now, he turned his attention to the big, black wooden trunk that sat beside his bed. Its usual place was under the window, covered with an old woolen throw that his mother had knitted many years ago.

Earlier, Nat had been infuriated at his brother's threat and had felt like kicking Jake's ass. Except that their father had butted in. When Nat had returned to his room, laughing at his brother, he had pulled the trunk to his bed, thrown off the cover and unlocked it. His immediate thought was to dig to the bottom, pull out what he wanted—and ruin his brother's life. But, controlling his anger, he'd stopped himself. He locked the trunk and left it untouched, resting on the floor beside his bed. He stared at it from time to time, but never unlocked it again.

A smile appeared on his lips. "All in good time, Jake. I'll show you your future, crystal clear," he said aloud. The laugh that followed came from the dark side of his heart.

Fifteen

Willow was in her studio, her back to the window, blocking out the strong, August daylight. She critically viewed her painting. Not that she wanted to find any mistakes, because she knew that she might, she viewed it for overall beauty and effect. Finally, emitting a sigh, she moved closer to the easel. The painting was ready for her signature. After careful study, she'd decided that the best spot for it was at the bottom right-hand corner. Mixing black paint to a smooth consistency, then dipping her brush, she began to paint each letter with her signature flourish, with lots of loops and curly endings. She always used a different color, depending on the tone of the picture. She chose black because it picked up the color of the huge, black glass vase.

Sometimes, she had to rework her name before she was satisfied that it blended with her painting, rather than upstaging it. Finished, she gave it a critical look. She was satisfied.

Willow was pleased with her finished work. Normally, she didn't include large paintings in her shows, because they required many long hours of hurried work. But this arrangement, she'd visualized, called for the life-size 44x48 canvas.

The picture was a large floral still life. The dominant flower were pink roses with colorful sprays of gerberas and white and pink chrysanthemums. Willow chose the hardy chrysanthemums for their long survival rate. The drooping roses, she'd had to replace from her greenhouse stock, careful to select just the right size rose in bloom, with the identical delicate shading as its wilted sisters. The lifelike flower arrangement was full, blooms spilling from the vase onto the ivory cloth-covered table, strays, strewn next to floral decorated china bowls.

A sigh escaped Willow's lips and her eyes danced with excitement as she envisioned this painting as the focal point of her upcoming show in Toronto. Over the last year, she had completed a total of sixteen paintings for the show, in varying sizes, ranging from small 9x5s to medium 36x30. Oscar had already had those shipped. It was only weeks ago that she had informed Oscar that she was including this large piece. He'd balked, telling her it would not be ready in time and that it really wasn't necessary.

Now Willow was glad she'd remained steadfast in her decision. The painting was gorgeous, but she sheepishly remembered Oscar's legitimate complaint, and immediately began planning the removal of this painting. She would wait a few days before having it packed and crated, because there were some thick areas of oil that might smudge with careless handling.

Though most of her paintings took from six months to a year to dry, she refused to spray them, for quick-drying purposes. She didn't want her canvases cracking in years to come, but wanted her beautiful floral paintings to be enjoyed for eons.

Willow washed her brushes and cleaned her palette. That chore finished, she straightened up her studio, covering paintings and closing blinds, because she would be gone for weeks. Happy that her calendar commitments had been completed for the next two years, she was free to take on other projects and to tour.

When Oscar had made plans for this Toronto tour, at first Willow had been reluctant, having gotten used to her routine at home. She hated leaving Wildflowers Cove and Dorcas. But her agent had convinced her that it was good business for her to meet the people who, for years, have continually bought her paintings. Now, Willow was happy that she'd made the right decision. She considered some of those paintings to be among her best works.

Fluffing the pillows on the sofa, Willow's cheeks colored as she thought of the many pleasant hours spent there with Jake in the past few weeks. Suddenly, anxious to be in his arms as she knew she would be tonight, Willow quickly locked the cottage door and hurried along the path to the house. A duty call to her agent was necessary before she and Jake whiled away the night in each other's arms.

"Oscar, it's finished," Willow said in one breath the second she heard his voice. "Finished!"

"I don't believe you," Oscar said in amazement. "You couldn't possibly be." *She sounds so happy,* he thought. *And why shouldn't she? She finished with one week to spare before she leaves. One whole week to be with her lover.*

"Germany, didn't you hear me?"

"I'm sorry. What was that?"

"Germany, I swear, you must be in love. How many times I've had to pull you back into reality the past month . . . I don't know . . ." Willow's eyes gleamed. "Germany. You've met someone!"

There was a moment of silence before Oscar said, "I'm found out. However did you guess?" Oscar was glad for the distance between them because he knew the pain in his heart had reached his eyes.

"You can't fool me, Germany, I've known you, too long. Who is she, if may I be so nosy?"

Oh, but I have fooled you, little one, all these years, Oscar thought. "Someone I knew years ago. She recently moved to New York, and we, shall I say, have rekindled our interest?" Oscar had gotten careless, and it had scared the hell out of him. The day he had let his guard down and had looked square into the eyes of Jake Rivers had added years to his life. Where had that come from? For years he had buried his feelings for Willow. Why had they surfaced on the day he met her lover? Admiration for the man filled his gut. Jake Rivers was the perfect gentleman, never betraying him, but Oscar had seen the look of surprise in Jake's eyes.

"No, Willow, she didn't live in Toronto." He had been listening to her guess the name of his lover. "You two never met. She was a teacher in Montreal when I lived in Toronto. We lost touch when I married and she moved out west to California. She's now a dean of students at Hunter College."

"My alma mater," Willow said. "You must introduce us soon, Germany, I'd love to meet her."

"Very soon. She'll be up one weekend to view your show. She's anxious to meet you too."

Willow was quiet for a moment. She was happy for Oscar. But there was still that nagging question in the back of her mind that had the potential to mar her happiness. Before the question formed on her lips, Oscar spoke.

"I know what you're thinking, Willow, and the answer is no."

"Nothing?"

"Nothing," Oscar repeated. "Your publisher assembled a crackerjack team to uncover the identity of the prankster."

"Wrong choice of word," Willow replied dryly.

"For lack of. Bear with them, they're working hard on this. Believe me. They've got a stake in this, too, if any of their top moneymakers come up dirty."

"Oh, I realize that. It's just that I feel so unsettled. Now that the tour is so near, I can't help wondering if . . . if, well, you know, anything might happen."

"Don't worry, Willow," Oscar reassured her. "Precautions have been taken. Get that out of your mind and just enjoy yourself. When's the last time you've traveled? Years," he answered himself.

"You're right, Germany. I am looking forward to seeing my old friends."

"Good. Oh, and before I forget, the name of that guest you and Dorcas gave me? George Henry? He's a bag of wind and harmless. Even though he played postman like everyone else from time to time at the Cove, apparently, he wasn't the one who tampered with the print."

"You're sure?" Willow was disappointed. Without George as a possible suspect, who else was there who wanted to hurt her so badly?

"Yeah. The company's being very thorough on this. They've lost interest in him as a suspect and they're still looking. The report that I've gotten about their investigation gets kudos from me. I'm confident that they'll crack this thing before long."

"Let's hope."

"Willow. Have you and Dorcas taken my advice about your mailing system?"

"Yes, Germany. We've learned from this nightmare experience. If we don't use the pickup and delivery service, we handle it ourselves."

"I know your guests are treated like family, but even family members get careless about other people's property. We can't always be so trusting."

"Yes, Germany," Willow answered teasingly. Then, "I'll call you tomorrow, I've got to run. I don't want to be late."

"Date?"

"What do you think? Bye, Germany."

Her deep laugh resounded in his ear as he hung up the phone.

Oscar closed his eyes, as he rested his chin on his steepled fingers. For the past six weeks, since the day Willow had appeared in his office, he had seen to it that he conducted their business via telephone. He had given serious thought to severing their professional relationship. The only reason he hadn't so far is the thought of causing her distress. Willow looked upon him as a dear friend. He had thought of another solution to his dilemma, and that was to tell her flat out of his feelings. Then, it would be up to her to decide whether or not to end their business ties—as well as their friendship. But, he had squashed that thought the moment it had entered his mind. Giving her career over to someone who would exploit her genius was unthinkable, because he knew that the full extent of her talent was yet to be discovered.

Not long after he had made the decision to stay with Willow, Oscar had called Maria Hall. When the attractive woman in her late forties, had been receptive to him, he had suddenly felt that he had been there before. Nearly fourteen years ago, soon after he had met Willow Vaughn, Oscar had married Geneva.

Somehow, Oscar knew that he would soon marry. He'd asked himself if that were the only way that he could continue his friendship with Willow.

He opened his eyes and leaned back in his chair, looking around the room, staring at the art of Morgana that, covered his walls. He'd know soon enough what kind of man he was. Weak? Declaring his love for her? Strong? Burying his feelings as though they'd never existed? The test of his strength and caliber was near. He would be accompanying Willow Vaughn to Toronto. In one short week, Oscar was going to find out who he really was.

At two in the afternoon, Willow and Dorcas were on the lawn, sipping lemon iced tea, while Willow waited for Jake to arrive.

"How in the world did you convince that man to steal time on a Tuesday afternoon?" Dorcas said shaking her head.

Willow winked and smiled. "The man's in love, Aunt Dee. I bet Uncle Thomas did some crazy things when he was dating you. Care to tell me some of them?" Willow teased.

"No, I do not, young lady," Dorcas protested, but she winked and smiled back.

"Seriously, you know how hard Jake's been working. He's been at the site almost from the beginning, working closely with the builders and the engineers. Thank God, none of them have any hang-ups and they can all work together. All the pipes for the lake and the waterfall have been delivered and they're scheduled to start laying and connecting them next week." She smiled. "I convinced him that his assistant can manage without him for one afternoon."

Dorcas heard the pride in her niece's voice. "You're really excited about his work, aren't you?"

"Oh, yes. I think his job is such a challenge. Each day brings something new. You never know what's going to go wrong or who'll screw up or if deliveries will be made on time. You've got to be alert twenty-four seven, even when you're home in bed."

"Humph," Dorcas snorted. "In bed? Tell this old lady anything, huh?"

Willow laughed. "Well, maybe I exaggerated just a little. But, my saving grace is the site location. I'd never see him if Tuckahoe weren't so near. We've been able to have quality time together these past weeks."

"I have eyes," Dorcas responded. She'd seen his navy Ford truck with the white lettering parked out back quite a few afternoons. It was never there for very long.

Dorcas was happy because Willow was happy. Since that period of upheaval in June, life was unhurried and uncomplicated. The scorching days of July had turned into soothing, almost balmy, days of August, and things were right in their world. Or so it appeared.

"Aunt Dee?"

"Hmm?"

"You know, I'm glad you made the decision to change the Cove's routine. I think it was time."

Before the end of June, Dorcas had completely turned the running of the kitchen over to their favorite catering service. They cooked and served all meals and cleaned up afterward. The housekeeping chores had also been contracted out.

"I don't regret it, buttercup," Dorcas agreed. "But, I do miss Tommy White and some of the other students. I heard he was out in Arizona for the summer. Hope he's still doing his thing with the desserts." A sigh escaped. "Now that I think about it, I was knocking myself out. You too." She grinned. "There's only so much love for cooking that one has before it begins to wear you down. A once-in-a-while cooking frenzy, is my speed now."

"There's always the holidays," Willow said. "That's going to be a good time for us, Aunt Dee. You, me, Jake, together . . . we'll be a family."

Dorcas frowned. Willow did not include Lloyd and Nat in her description of family. "Have you been reintroduced to Lloyd as his future daughter-in-law?"

Willow hesitated before answering. Jake had told her of his father's feelings toward her. He objected to her being potentially verbally abused by Lloyd Rivers and was reluctant in bringing Willow to the Elmsford home.

"No," Willow said. "I'm in no hurry to meet Lloyd Rivers again. When Jake and I are married, will be soon enough to put up with that man's surliness. Right now, Jake and I are happy with things as they are. It doesn't really matter to us if his father refuses to bless our relationship. We're going to be man and wife, no matter what."

Dorcas and Willow heard the car at the same time and watched Jake's approach on the gravel driveway. As always, when Dorcas saw Jake, she pushed to the back of her mind some unknown fear. A feeling that she'd learned to smother whenever she thought of the two lovers. She prayed to God, that their love for each other would be strong enough to sustain them both in the future. Now, as he walked toward them, she summoned a smile in her voice that she hoped would also reach her eyes. "Hello, Jake. It's been a while," she teased. She'd said good night to him only the night before.

Jake grinned. "Dorcas," he said. "Too long." He looked at Willow, and as usual, his inner self sang. Once, when he'd gotten that feeling as he stared at her, unseen, he had gotten the foolish thought that if he were a bird, he'd burst into song. He'd cracked up at his silly thought, until Willow had stared at him like he'd gone a little crazy. He sat down on the flat arm of the adirondack chair, and bent to kiss Willow's forehead. "Hello, darlin'," he said.

Before he could straighten up, Willow brushed his lips with hers. "Hello, yourself," she murmured.

Dorcas stood up, "Okay, okay, you two, I'm making myself scarce." To Jake, she said, "If you plan to spirit her away for more than twenty-four hours, I want a phone call. You know how I worry," she admonished.

"No need, Dorcas, I'll have her back in a few hours."

"A few hours! Is that all I get?" Willow said, pouting.

Jake winked. "That's only in this twenty-four hour period, sweetheart. We didn't say anything about tomorrow, or the next day, or the day after that."

"Oh, it's like that," Dorcas said. "You're really gonna make up for the four weeks she'll be away, huh?"

"Something like that," Jake said. His eyes twinkled.

Dorcas picked up the empty glasses and started toward the house. "Okay, Mr. Rivers," she said sternly, "I trust you to take care of my child.

Willow watched her aunt until she entered the house through the front door. Then, looking up at Jake, she said, "You heard her. When are you going to start taking care of me?"

Jake laughed. "Right now." He pulled her up and into

his arms, holding her close to his chest. Breathing in the fresh, clean smell of her hair, he whispered, "But, sweetheart, the way I want to do that requires strength. I'm going to feed you first. Then, later on, when you swoon, I'll know it's not for lack of sustenance."

"Mmm," Willow murmured, hugging him tight around the waist. "Later on? What about right now?" She could feel his struggle to maintain control, but she devilishly wiggled her hips against him.

"Darlin', don't test me," Jake said huskily, pulling her from him. Taking her hand, he led her to his car. "After I've loved you, then you can hit me with all you've got . . . if you have the strength."

"Oh, ho," Willow said. Laughing, she slipped her arm around his waist as they walked. "An endurance match, I see. I agree, Mr. Rivers. Feed me first. You're going to feel my strength."

Jake gave her a hopeful look. "I can hardly wait, Ms. Vaughn."

Willow was propped up on her elbow, watching Jake sleep. He expelled soft breaths, as his chest rose and fell evenly. Gently, so as not to awaken him, she rubbed her foot against his hairy leg, delighting in the erotic transfer of electricity from his body to hers. She bent and kissed his forehead, finding it too cool against her kiss-swollen lips. Frowning, she slid easily out of bed and walked to the air conditioner and turned it off. Earlier, at four o'clock, when they'd arrived at Jake's apartment, they had turned the unit on High to escape nature's heat, and their own fierce body fires. After a two-hour, leisurely meal at the popular Chart House in Dobbs Ferry, they left still unhurried. How they planned to spend the rest of the evening was all the more tantalizing with anticipation.

At six-thirty, the hot sun had waned, and as she looked

through the glass patio door, Willow could see the fronds of the potted ferns, rustling in the gentle evening breeze. She loved the serenity of the private backyard, remembering occasions, when after making love, they had ambled out to the chaise lounge to plan their future. She was going to miss these quiet times while she was in Canada.

"I'm going to miss you, too, darlin'," Jake whispered in her ear, guessing Willow's thoughts, as he came up behind her. He slipped his arms beneath his plaid, cotton shirt that she was wearing, and pulled her against his body. She was bare underneath, and his hands moved over her smooth belly, then fondling her breasts, he squeezed the tender nipples. "A hell of a lot," he added. Jake kissed her nape, and inhaling her scent, smelled himself on her. He lifted her hand, then softly licked her palm, and tasted himself there.

Jake had covered his nakedness with a short cotton robe. Willow reached behind with both hands, and pushed the robe apart. She lifted the long plaid shirt, then pressed her buttocks into his bare flesh. Her hands kept his body meshed tightly to hers. "Not more than me," she whispered, tilting her head to the side to look up at him.

Jake dipped his head, capturing her lips in a crushing kiss. The rumbling in his throat, burst through with a tortured groan. Quickly turning her around, he moved away from the glass doors. "You are for my eyes only," he muttered, leading her to the bed.

Robe and shirt fell to the floor as Willow and Jake walked, their arms entwined. When they reached the bed, Willow stopped, and smiled.

"What?" Jake asked, wondering at the gleam in her eyes.

"Feel me," Willow said.

Puzzled, Jake said, "I will in just a little bit, sweetheart."

"No. I mean *feel* me. Like this." Willow took his hands and placed them on her shoulders. "Now, slide them down, s-l-o-w-l-y," she said. When she felt them on her biceps, she flexed her muscles, until the tiny ripples moved under Jake's hands.

Dawning, shone in Jake's eyes as he threw back his head and laughed.

"You're not finished yet." Willow lifted her leg and rested her foot on the bed. She put Jake's hand on her thigh, holding it as she guided it slowly down to her taut calf. She flexed the muscle, so that it too, rippled under his hand. "Strength," Willow said. Then, with a teasing smile, she said, "The rest you'll be feeling in just a little bit."

Jake was still laughing at Willow's little show, when, in seconds, he deftly had her laying on her back. He stood, fists on hips, looking down at her, his eyes twinkling. "So, this is the big showdown huh? Gonna show me what a fortified lover can do?"

"Don't you want to know?"

Jake was beside her in the twinkling of an eye, whispering in her ear. "You can tease me anytime sweetheart, as long as you're in this state of undress. Any other time and you're asking for trouble," he rasped. Immediately he shuddered, when he felt Willow firmly grasp his erection. She moved her hand up and down, squeezing, while her tongue did delicious damage in his ear. Her warm breath brought stars to his eyes at the double onslaught to his nervous system. The message received by his brain urged him to relieve his throbbing sex, while his masochist self wanted to prolong the agony of the sharp tiny nips, with which she was now assaulting his nipples. Her every move surprised him until he ceased trying to guess where her soft breath or feathery touch would land. He surrendered his body to her.

Willow was on her side, kissing Jake's lips, his eyes, his mouth, while her hand traveled the length of his body. Exploring smooth planes and rough hills at will, had her nearly delirious with pleasure. She longed to feel him suckle her breasts, but she would selfishly wait for that exquisiteness because the love words and sounds that poured from his mouth were like soulful music. He was loving her with every sound. She knew that he loved the way she made him feel and she wanted to continue to give him pleasure.

Willow eased herself on top of him and lay lengthwise. Her tongue caressed the soft, hollow of his throat and Willow continued to taste him in her slow descent to his stomach, leaving a damp trail on Jake's salty skin.

When Willow's tongue flicked the softness of his inner thigh and her teeth tugged at the hair around his groin, Jake was tortured and could stand no more. He had to feel himself inside of her.

"Willow," he rasped through clenched teeth, "I have to have you now, sweetheart." Jake caught her by the shoulders and eased her up his body, exhaling, when her breasts met his chest. Shifting her upward, he then caught each breast in his mouth, tasting the sweetness of them, and inwardly smiling at her moans of pleasure. He knew she'd deprived herself for him when she strained into him, savoring his strong kisses on her tender flesh.

"Jake," Willow whispered, "Now, love." She moved easily onto her side, and Jake just as smoothly, moved on top of her. A moment later, protection in place, Jake entered her. His excruciating wait was rewarded as she tightened against him and with an involuntary spasm, arched her hips to meet him.

The unleashing of their passion sent Jake and Willow to an emotionally foreign place. The depth of her feeling for this man, awed Willow, as she followed Jake through the unexplored valleys that revealed hidden pockets of her love. She'd thought she had bared all. "Jake," she cried out. "Jake."

Jake heard the cry of his love and responded with intense, deep thrusts, giving as she did, until the point of oblivion. Almost quietly, like a broken fever, the fire abated, leaving them spent, each clinging to the other.

Jake reluctantly moved from her, positioning himself

close to her side. Both were silent, each with private thoughts. Willow stirred, and Jake opened his eyes. "What's wrong, darlin'?"

"I love you, Jake."

"That's wrong?" Jake teased.

"Never." Willow answered with a vehemence that just materialized.

Startled at the aggressive response, Jake hugged her and kissed her mouth. "I love you, too, sweetness. You're my whole world."

"Shouldn't be like this, Jake. Sort of scares me."

Jake reflected on his words. She's right, he thought. Our world is one. What if— Jake squashed the negative thought. The only separation that he would accept, painful as it would be, was the Toronto tour. Any others, he would have to think long and hard about.

"We're going to be okay, Willow. All we need to do is believe in each other and we'll be okay."

Willow sighed. "Sounds like such a simple recipe." Swinging her legs over the side of the bed, she stood up. "What'd you think?" At his inquisitive look, Willow touched some of her muscles, and sent a provocative glance down at others. "Some kind of strong, huh?"

The sound of Jake's deep laugh, made her smile as she sashayed saucily to the bathroom.

It was after nine o'clock when Jake and Willow finished tidying up the kitchen. Jake turned on the dishwasher, turned out the kitchen light and followed Willow into the living room. It was time to get her home. He joined her on the sofa.

Willow caught Jake's hand in hers. "You know, when you first told me about this mammoth task, I had doubts."

Jake was surprised. "You never told me."

"I didn't want to give negative vibes. That was the last thing you needed."

"True. But what bothered you?"

"That in the back of your mind, you would be worried about your own business. That if things went wrong, you would begin to second guess your decision."

Jake was thoughtful. "I would have had to have taken the consequences. My decision was a conscious one. There was no turning back."

"I know. I'm glad there have been no problems and that Scott's even brought in some hew accounts."

"That's Irene. She's a great idea person and even better when presenting her interior design plans to a potential customer." Jake paused. "They've done wonders with the company in such a short time. I don't know that I would be feeling so comfortable if they hadn't been able to accept this deal."

"And Tala?" Willow squeezed his hand. "Is she any better?"

Jake shook his head. "I'm afraid not. She's been battling not to lose this baby. She can't understand why her body reacts so adversely to what is supposed to be so normal for a woman."

"What does her doctor say?" Willow felt compassion, knowing how much Tala and her husband wanted a child.

Jake shrugged. "She tells Tala that no matter how many times a woman gets pregnant, each is a different experience. In Tala's case, she's one of those women that requires constant bed rest, and avoidance of stressful situations."

"Which is an impossibility in her profession," Willow replied. She kissed Jake's cheek. "I'm glad she has you."

Jake kissed her back. "Thanks. I'm glad I have you." Then, "She has backed off the project almost completely. Only in the most dire situation will I contact her. She prefers it that way."

"So, you made the decision to reroute and change the direction of the waterfall?"

"Yes. The project engineer pointed out that the structure was too close to the building's sleeping quarters. Not everyone likes to fall asleep to the sound of running water."

"What did the customer think?"

"Oh, the sorority was in agreement. Actually, they liked the new arrangement. The original woodland style, with rock and plenty of natural greenery, can now incorporate two additional styles of the formal and informal gardens."

"Sounds like it will be beautiful," Willow said.

"It will be. The house will be in use all year round. It's not only a meeting place, but it's a small conference hotel. They've designed it to accommodate fundraising events and weddings. They expect that outdoor weddings in the gardens to be a big draw. They'll have the proper flowering foliage, year-round."

"You sound pleased with making the decision."

"The customer is happy. That's the determining factor in how successful any business will be," Jake said seriously.

"Will Tala maintain it?"

"No. She's already made arrangements to sign over the contract to J. Rivers Landscape Contracts."

"Jake!" Willow exclaimed. "That's wonderful! You make me so proud. This just comes so easy for you. You love it, don't you?"

Jake smiled. "Thanks, and yes, I do." He stood up. "And now, I think we'd better get out of here."

"I think, sir, that that is an excellent idea," Willow said, as she stood. Their closeness and touching had made them both well aware of the ever-present electricity between them.

While Jake drove, a sudden thought made Willow frown. With marriage, would this feeling become old and stale, then wither away? Simply impossible, she told herself. Simply impossible!

Sixteen

The early August morning at eight-twenty was not so cool. It was Jake, who suddenly felt a chill as he walked to the JFK Airport parking lot. Although he had watched Willow's Air Canada plane take off at seven-thirty, he did not leave the terminal. Instead, he had sat at a small café table, drinking coffee and playing with a prune danish, thinking. When he checked his watch, he had been surprised at how the minutes had fled. In a short time, Willow's hour-and-a-half flight to Pearson International Airport in Toronto would land.

And just what kept you here, thinking, Jake Rivers? he had asked himself. He produced his parking ticket, paid his fee, and drove west to the Van Wyck Expressway. His assistant was expecting him at the site this morning. Jake knew exactly, of what—or whom—he had been thinking. Oscar Germany. Somehow, when Willow had told him that she and Oscar were not traveling together, he felt relieved. Why? Had he not told Willow not to worry about their relationship—that they would be just fine—all they needed to do was to just believe? A classic case of one's being able to give advice and not live by it, he chastised himself.

Jake had not laid eyes on the man since they first met in Oscar's office weeks ago. Other than Jake's own astute assumption, that man had never given Jake any reason to believe that he was pursuing Willow. Certainly, Willow was ignorant of Oscar's feelings. Of that, he knew he was right.

Mindful of the heavy morning traffic, Jake drove with
caution, braking several times to avoid the obnoxious lane-
changers. His thoughts soon turned to the conversation
he and Willow had a few nights ago. With the work on
both jobs going so smoothly, Jake had given thought to
setting the date for the wedding. When he broached the
subject, Willow had been pleased. He recalled her words.

"Are you certain, Jake?" Willow sounded hesitant.

"I'm certain."

"Then, I think that's wonderful! Let's not wait too long,
sweetheart. A quiet ceremony and a small reception at the
Cove would be just perfect since neither of us has large
families. What do you think?"

"I don't see a problem," Jake answered.

"What about our home, Jake? I haven't given the slightest thought to where we'll live. I thought we had a lot of
time to plan. Have you thought about it at all?"

"You wouldn't want to live at the Cove? You love it so
much," Jake said.

"No. I want to raise my family where we will have new
beginnings. I've already willed the property to Aunt Dee.
Upon her death it will revert back to my offspring. I want
it to always belong to a Morgan."

Remembering her words, Jake realized they'd never decided where they wanted to raise their own family. Pru-
dence told him to remain in the general neighborhood.
Especially since his corporate accounts were growing lo-
cally—and then some. Scottie had just accepted an interior
account in Montclair, New Jersey.

Once the traffic thinned, Jake reached the Yonkers area
in less than an hour and was soon driving on Main Street
in Tuckahoe. Turning on Chestnut Hill Place and onto
the site, he parked his car. While covering "Ancient," Willow's name for his old car, Jake was still at a loss as to where
he and his future bride would make their home. Tonight,
when he called Willow, he'd remind her to start thinking

hard about the matter. He wanted to become a married man while the New Year was still an infant—preferably, before it was a week old. What better way to begin the new year—and the rest of their lives—than as man and wife?

"Sweetheart, I miss you already," Willow said breathlessly into the phone. It was after eleven o'clock and she'd showered and was in bed.

"Miss you, more, darlin'," Jake replied.

"Jake Rivers, don't you dare call me that. You know very well, that there's not a thing I can do about my feelings at this long distance."

"I'm glad for that, sweetness."

"Ohh," Willow groaned. "Anything you say is not going to make it better!" After a pause, she asked, "What do you mean, you're 'glad'? Don't you trust me?" Willow sounded hurt.

Jake mentally kicked himself. *What an idiot you are, brother.* "Willow, please forget I said that. It was a stupid thing to say. Guess I was trying to say that I miss the hell out of you and four weeks has grown to four months in my mind. Forgive me?"

Willow was silent.

"Willow? Talk to me."

The thumping in her chest ceased, and her breathing returned to normal. In a light minute, her life without Jake had passed before her eyes. It wasn't a pleasant space to be in. She pitied the woman she had seen.

"Willow? Dammit, talk to me!" Jake was getting scared. Had he hurt her so badly?

The fear in Jake's voice penetrated her senses. "Jake, I'm fine," she answered. "Don't worry. I'm okay."

Jake expelled his breath. "Are you sure?" he asked, quietly. "Tell me what you were thinking. Please? I want to know." He waited.

Willow tried to be light and sassy. "Suffice it to say, my life without you doesn't make a pretty picture, Jake."

"You thought that!" Jake grimaced. "Willow, we didn't even have an argument. Don't ever think that." He paused. "Not ever," he said quietly.

"Nevermore," answered Willow. The smile was back in her voice.

Jake heard, and smiled. "Going poetic on me now? Toronto does that to you, huh?" His smile broadened at the sound of her deep laugh. Thank God, he breathed—and wondered—how in the world he was going to get through the next twenty-eight days and nights without her.

Before they said good night, they discussed Jake's idea for their wedding date and their future home.

Jake stepped into the shower. Willow had the same thoughts as he did about staying in the general area—only, she wouldn't mind going up the road a piece. Sleepy Hollow? Hmm, he thought. Not so bad. Be a great tale to tell the kids that one night, he had had a nice chat with the Headless Horseman. Jake was chuckling when he let the warm spray soothe his tired muscles. At the thought of muscles, his grin broadened.

"Didn't I tell you, Mademoiselle?" Oscar said, in a low voice. "Look at them. They came to see you."

"Incredible. I had forgotten how it could be. I just love it, Germany," Willow whispered back. Her eyes sparkled and she felt her cheeks grow warm with excitement. The reception in her honor at the prestigious midtown Blaum Arts gallery on Dundas Street, was an overwhelming success. Throngs of art lovers, eventually made their way to her, congratulating her and thanking her for continuing to provide them with so much pleasure.

When a moment came, she said to Oscar, "This is almost like Paris."

"You remember Paris?"

"Oh, Germany, don't tease. If it hadn't been for your guidance, I would never have grown so fast. There, I learned so much under the master. Years later, when I returned for my first Paris showing, it was like a homecoming. He was so proud."

"As he should have been. We are all proud, Willow."

"I know. Thanks for pushing me to do this tour, Germany. I was ready. You knew so long ago that I would be."

Oscar shrugged. "I have ears and eyes, and besides, what do you pay me for?"

Willow laughed. "Because you're the best."

"Just remember that if you get it into your head to give me the boot, I'm the last of my kind."

"You wish," Willow said. "We're stuck." Her eyes gleamed with devilment. "That is, unless you get married and Maria demands that you retire so she could have you all to herself." Then, "She really will come up next weekend?"

"She's promised," Oscar answered.

"I can't wait to talk to her in private. How you managed to escape the ladies all these years, is a mystery." Willow scanned the room. "Now don't tell me, you're missing the femme fatale looks coming your way. I can assure you they're not aimed at me."

"Humph," was Oscar's response.

"Why, Germany, you're blushing."

"I think it's time for you to mingle, Willow." His mixed gray brows were drawn together. "Do you have your pen? Go sign some calendars."

Willow made her way through the crowd, stopping to greet her visitors. The people who engaged her in conversation were from all walks of life, with varied interests, and exotic professions. A retired mountain climber who "finally came down to earth," he said, was now dabbling in paints, though he admitted he "didn't do flowers." They both laughed when Willow said, "Rocks?" She'd guessed right. He was in love with Arizona's *Painted Desert* landscape.

She accepted a glass of wine from a passing waiter, when she heard her name. She looked in amazement at the young woman pushing through the crowd, arm waving in the air.

"Willow. Willow. It's me. Willow, over here."

The amused crowd parted for the exuberant woman who at a stretch, just made five-two.

"Mellie? Oh, my God, Melva Pearson?"

The two women hugging, made an amusing picture. The shorter woman's head just barely reached the taller woman's neck.

Willow hugged her childhood friend tight. Releasing her, she cried, "Mellie, I wondered if you'd come. How are you?" she said, giving her friend another squeeze. "How is my goddaughter Valerie?"

Melva Pearson caught her friend by the hand and threaded her way through the crowd to a less noisy corner. They found an unoccupied upholstered bench just outside in the lobby.

"She's doing just great, though you wouldn't know her," replied Melva.

"I most certainly would. You sent me a picture when she turned eight, in January."

"That was more than seven months ago, Willow. She's grown inches since then. I think she's going to be a bean-pole like her godmother."

"Is that what you call me behind my back?" accused Willow.

"No, silly. That's what old smarty-pants, Ilsa called you. If you remember, I got a bloodied nose for standing up for you."

Willow smiled. "How could I forget, Mellie? You were my true friend. My first friend."

"Only the first and the best," said Melva. She nodded

her head in the direction of the crowded room. "You really attract a crowd, don't you?"

"Something, isn't it?" Willow agreed. I'm still amazed."

"You shouldn't be. Torontonians know you grew up here. We're proud to call you one of our own, though you deserted us."

"Not really," Willow answered. "I'll always remember growing up, here. I have fond memories, Mellie, and I think of it as my other home."

Melva looked at the tall, slender man approaching them. "He's still handsome, isn't he?" she said. "I was surprised when you'd mentioned in your letter that he was still un-attached."

Willow watched her friend as he neared. "I'm hoping that will be remedied in the near future," she said.

"Here you are, Willow. I have someone I want you to meet," said Oscar. He acknowledged the petite, dark brown-skin young woman sitting beside Willow, then looked in surprise. "Mellie Pearson?"

Melva held out her hand and Oscar took it. "How are you, Mr. Oscar? It's been a long time."

Oscar winced. "Ouch, Mellie. You make me feel ancient. Won't you call me 'Oscar,' now?" His lips parted in the crooked grin that only enhanced his good looks.

"Okay, Oscar." Melva laughed with Willow. They were both seventeen the first time they met Oscar Germany. Like Willow, she was too young to use his given name as he had suggested. 'Mr. Oscar' seemed just right.

Oscar had always liked little Melva Pearson. She and Willow had been inseparable. If you saw one, the other wasn't very far away. Both had been serious, intelligent students. When Willow had seriously pursued her art, Melva had taken an interest in modeling. Then, the two began to go their separate ways, though they'd always re-mained steadfast friends.

"Mellie, I have to go take care of a little business, now.

Can we meet again? The show officially opens tomorrow. Will I see you?"

"Mmm, afraid not. Thursday is my long day. I have to close the shop tomorrow. But I've checked the exhibit schedule. Maybe we can meet this weekend after the gallery closes? I can get here by six o'clock."

"That'll be even better," Willow answered, as the trio was caught up in the hubbub of the big room. "Then, you can come by the hotel and we'll talk the night away. Unless, of course, you bring Valerie."

"No, not Saturday. Her grandmother is picking her up Friday and bringing her back on Sunday afternoon."

"Your mother?"

Melva grimaced. Her expressive, large dark brown eyes, clouded. "No chance of that happening." She hugged Willow and gave Oscar a smile. "Nice to see you again, Oscar Germany. I'm sure to see you soon?" She waved and walked away.

Willow and Oscar watched the shapely young woman walk away, stopping to greet acquaintances.

"Her mother never came around?" Oscar asked. Willow had mentioned years ago that when Mellie became pregnant out of wedlock, her mother had shut her daughter out. The strong-minded young woman had refused to abort her child and had raised her daughter alone.

"No," Willow answered. "But Mellie is doing just fine." Looking around, she said, "Where's this person you want me to meet, and what's it all about?"

Oscar took her by the elbow, and guided her toward the giant floral painting. "Hold on to your socks," he said. " 'Roses and China' has been sold. Even I had to keep a straight face at the offer."

"Offer?" Willow was puzzled, because all the paintings were already priced.

"Yes." Oscar's eyes glinted with pride. "There were two potential buyers. Neither would give in to the other. The gallery owner suggested an impromptu, two-party auction. The highest bidder won. She wants to meet you."

"Incredible." Willow was flabbergasted.

"No," Oscar said, in a low voice. "You're incredible."

Willow looked at him, curiosity filling her eyes, but before she could speak, Oscar turned from her and greeted the obviously wealthy buyer of her painting.

Oscar Germany was still awake at two o'clock in the morning. Normally, he wasn't a drinker, because it was too easy to get caught up in over-imbibing at the numerous social functions that he was required to attend. But, now, the well-stocked hotel room bar was at his disposal and he was utilizing it. About to prepare his third drink, he stopped himself, got up and locked the bar. The two delmonico cocktails he'd mixed had held more brandy and less Italian vermouth. On top of the wine he'd drank hours before, he was beginning to feel the effects. This age-old mistaken panacea for whatever ails you, is definitely not the way to solve a problem, he thought. A clear head and quick mind would be needed when he breakfasted with his client in the morning.

Oscar had been very proud of himself yesterday when he had met Willow at the airport. She'd been tired but excited at the exhibit. She expressed her delight at finally seeing him again, instead of communicating via phone all these weeks. She'd talked nonstop about her work, the tour, her upcoming marriage and the new woman in his life. Oscar had responded as he normally would. Very professional. He had silently breathed a prayer of thanks. He'd passed the test. But what happened? Tonight, he'd slipped again. That one tiny emphasis placed on one tiny word, had been enough to pique her curiosity. Though he'd never looked into her eyes, he'd felt her stare.

In just a few hours, he was going to have to confront

those beautiful, dark eyes. Honest eyes. Would he be able to keep the truth out of his?

Willow sat up in bed and stared at the clock radio on the nightstand. What had disturbed her sleep at two-thirty in the morning? She got up and walked to the convenience bar. She poured a glass of bottled water and drank, then walked to the window. Night lamps twinkled across the city. The street below her seventh-floor window was quiet now, but in a few hours, it would be bustling with early morning traffic.

After the cocktail reception, she'd taken the short walk alone to the Metropolitan Hotel. Oscar had been preoccupied with the gallery owner and she'd waved and turned away. Apparently, he did not try to follow her, and somehow she'd felt relieved. Once in her room, she had called Jake. They talked for a long while. He was as excited and happy as she was at the success of the reception. Before the official opening of the exhibit, six of her paintings had "sold" tags beside them. When they'd hung up, she'd showered and got into bed, exhausted. She was expected to attend a breakfast in her honor before the gallery opened at eleven o'clock.

Willow planned to meet Oscar in the beautiful Hemispheres dining room at seven-forty-five. She wondered what she was going to say to him. Back in bed, a long-ago memory surfaced, that brought a frown to her brow.

Years before, after she'd returned from a long trip, Dorcas and Oscar had met her at the airport. She was young and excited about her adventure and was overjoyed to be with her family again. Oscar was part of her family. She'd kissed and hugged her aunt, and kissed and hugged Oscar. Had he held her just a tad too tight and a tad too long? Then, she'd thought it was her overactive imagination. He had not shown the slightest change in his professional demeanor toward her, and she'd pushed any disturbing thoughts from her mind. Oscar Germany was her agent-turned-friend, and he had never given her any reason to believe otherwise.

Until now. Willow closed her eyes. She and Oscar had to talk.

Willow was standing at the window, looking at the same view she'd stared at only a few hours before. Only now, the sun was still bright in the sky and hordes of people and vehicles filled the street below. Without turning, she whispered, "Oscar, I'm so sorry."

Oscar sat nearby in a high-backed, Queen Anne-style upholstered chair. His elbows rested on the arms; chin resting on steepled fingers. His eyes were closed. Twice before in his lifetime he had felt this alone. When his parents had moved back to France, leaving him to flounder on his own, and when his wife, Geneva and their unborn child had died. Now, he was about to lose a friend. He opened his eyes because he heard Willow turn from the window.

"I'm sorry, too, Willow."

Willow sat down in the matching chair on the other side of the round, cherry-wood table. She was still dazed at what her friend told her. She'd known. When their gazes had locked at breakfast this morning, she'd known. The only personal comment Oscar had made was, "We'll talk, later." She had only nodded. Now, it was later, and they were in her room, after ending their long day at the gallery. Very quietly, almost without emotion, he had told her of his feelings toward her all these years. She let him speak, amazed at how he'd been able to maintain an ironclad, unemotional, professional relationship with her. She was always spontaneous in her actions and wondered how anyone could live, holding back such strong desires and emotions. She would never have been able to pull off such a charade. Never in her life. Now, she could only feel compassion for her dear friend. And he had truly been her friend. There was no denying that. She looked at the pain on his face and wondered if she looked the same. What were they going to do? His next words voiced her thought.

"The exhibit is a smashing success, Willow," Oscar said. "You don't need me here with you. Your scheduled appearances are confirmed, and Judy, my personal assistant, is arriving on Sunday evening. Whatever problems that might arise, you know she is perfectly capable of ironing them out. She'll call me with anything she can't handle." He brushed his thick mustache as he caught and held her gaze. "I'll have the concierge try to find a flight for me for anytime tomorrow. When I get home, I'll have my attorneys start the paperwork to sever our contract as painlessly as possible."

"Germany," Willow whispered. "You're leaving me?"

Oscar swallowed. "I have to, Willow. I've explained to you my loss of control weeks ago. That was a breach in agent-client relationships. Meeting you yesterday, was a test. I failed. I would be the last one in this world to deliberately cause you hurt or pain." Almost woodenly, he continued. "I never wanted you to meet Maria because I knew that with your sharp powers of observation, you would see through the sham of a relationship. It wasn't fair to her that I was about to repeat my cowardly act all over again."

"You mean, Geneva?" Willow asked sadly.

"Yes. Though eventually I loved her, that wasn't the case when I married her. You were seventeen, and had me exploring my feelings that were nonexistent with women twice your age. I scared myself into becoming a married man . . . fast." He stood up and walked to the door.

"Germany . . . ?"

"Good-bye, Willow."

Willow sat for a long time, staring at the door. Tears stung her eyes. She had so few friends. She couldn't afford to lose one. Before Jake entered her life, the only other people who honestly cared about her were her aunt and Oscar. Now, there was Jake and Aunt Dee. Willow resolved right then, that she was not going to wait to have children. A minimum of four. This time next year, she quickly calculated, she was going to be a mother. When she and Jake made love on her return, Labor Day weekend, she was going to conceive his child. Convention be damned!

Seventeen

After three weeks, Dorcas missed Willow fiercely. Whenever they could, they talked, her niece giving her a detailed description of her appearances and the interesting people she'd been meeting. Her excitement was barely containable. Dorcas was glad that Willow was finally able to talk about Oscar.

Two days after the opening, she'd finally called, hoping that Willow had calmed down enough to describe the gala. The sadness in Willow's voice had not escaped Dorcas, and at her insistence, Willow had explained. Dorcas had no words that could soothe her niece. She told her that in his way, Oscar had always been there for her, giving her professional guidance and his friendship. It was to his credit that he had succeeded all these years in hiding his emotions. Severing their ties was the only way the man could now try to find some happiness.

Dorcas never revealed that days after arriving in New York, Oscar dropped by. They, too, had developed a friendship, and they talked as friends about what had happened, and how it would affect Willow.

After assuring Oscar that Willow's inner strength would see her through, she reminded him that without it, that young woman could not have carved her niche in the world at so young an age. Before he left, Oscar had thanked her for her wisdom and understanding.

Now, Dorcas left the kitchen after checking on the dinner preparations and went to sit on the porch. She was pleased with the well-kept grounds and had complimented the gardener. Dorcas had made it a point that Willow's flowers, especially those in the greenhouse were not neglected. A week from today, Labor Day, Willow would fly home. Dorcas was excited, but no more than Jake Rivers, she smiled. Only last night he'd stopped by for a hot minute, just to see if she was okay. As hard as that man worked, he always had a thought for someone else. He'd spoken briefly about the wedding plans he and Willow were making during their long phone conversations. New Year's Day was a splendid time for a wedding celebration.

She looked up the drive to see the mail truck coming toward the house.

The driver walked toward her with a letter. "Afternoon, Ms. Williams. Special delivery." He handed her his pen.

Dorcas signed. "Thank you." He was in his truck, driving away as swiftly as he'd appeared. Dorcas sat down and the minute she saw the Illinois return address, her heart fluttered like the wings of a tiny bird.

Dorcas Williams,

Your sister Vera Morgan Jones, died last week. She was cremated this past Thursday. There was no need to call you because you didn't care anyway. There was nobody but me with her when she went. She never mentioned your name since we left your steps. But the last time she spoke to me, her last words ever, two days before she died, were that her daughter Dolores was alone in the world. I know she wouldn't want me to because she knew how much you hated her, but, I'm sending you your niece's address and phone number in New Jersey anyway. Vera said what's

the use. You probably destroyed the papers she gave you.
You can do with it what you want.

Alma Manning

Dorcas dropped the letter. Dead. Her baby sister was dead. Dorcas was the last of her generation of Morgans. Picking up the letter, Dorcas stood and went into the house. She felt cold. Finding warmth on the sun-drenched chaise in her bedroom, she laid down and closed her eyes.

Dorcas must have fallen asleep from mere mental exhaustion because when she opened her eyes the sun had disappeared. She shivered and the slight movement caused the paper on her chest to flutter to the floor. She picked up the letter and read Alma Manning's words again. The harsh, cold words leaped at her. "You didn't care . . . Nobody but me . . . You hated her . . . cremated . . . what's the use."

A knock on the door startled Dorcas and she answered it. The food-service workers had served dinner to the guests, cleaned the kitchen and were leaving. Dorcas thanked them and locked up after they left. Although it was nearly eight o'clock, she turned out the kitchen light and went back to her bedroom. The thought of eating nauseated her. Instead of preparing for bed, she sat down at her desk and opened the drawer. The envelope Vera had given her lay unopened.

The last few hours, Dorcas had not been in a deep sleep, because her mind played back some scenes and words she'd seen and heard through a haze. Was it a dream that she'd heard Beatrice's voice? Seen Thomas' stern look? Heard Grandy's cluck of disgust? She knew what she must do. She prayed to God to help her to get through the rest of her life. Because she knew that once she gave Willow Beatrice's letter, her niece's love for her would turn to hate.

Dorcas dreaded what she had to do. She had to make right the wrong she'd done. A small white lie so long ago had escalated into so many more. The wound in her beloved Willow's heart would be deep.

Removing paper and pen from the drawer, she began to write, praying that the right words would come easy. She couldn't help wondering if Beatrice had had similar thoughts, so long ago.

The next morning, Dorcas greeted the cook, gave instructions for the day's meals and when the housekeeper arrived, gave similar instructions. She then left a taped note on each guest room door giving them a security number to call in case of an emergency. Dorcas put Vera's envelope and Alma's letter in her bag and left the house. It was nine-thirty.

Turning the key in the ignition of her car, Dorcas looked in surprise at the red and white truck coming down the driveway. Recognizing Nat Rivers, she wondered what he was doing here so early. She hadn't seen him for days. His excellent workers had been doing all the gardening chores. Rumor had it that Nat had taken to the bottle again and was really messing up his father's business. She knew for certain that this time Jake would not be able to bail them out of trouble. His plate was full enough. Lloyd would really have to seriously think about selling now, before he lost his life's work. She frowned. Nat was blocking her exit.

"Good morning, Nat," she said, impatiently.

"Mornin' Mis Dorcas. Beautiful day, ain't it?" His speech was thick.

Started already, Dorcas thought. "I don't have time to talk about the weather, Nat. What's wrong?"

"Nothin', Mis Dorcas, just came to see if Willow's greenhouse is doing okay. I know how she clucks over her flowers. When's she due back?"

"Your men have been doing excellent work here, Nat. Willow will be very pleased. She's due in on Labor Day.

Now if you'll excuse me, I'm late." She rolled up her window and turned on the air conditioner. When Nat turned around, she followed the truck up the driveway and onto the road. On North Broadway, she wondered which route she should take to Jersey City, New Jersey.

Willow hung up the phone. She picked up her purse, and took a sweater because the mornings were now so cool, and left her room. "Wonder where Dorcas got to so early on a Tuesday," she muttered. No call last night, and gone this morning. Hurrying to the elevator, she pressed the button, glancing at her watch. She hoped she wasn't going to be late. How would that look? Late for her own dedication ceremony. The small gardens near her old high school, where she'd spent so many hours learning to draw flowers, was being named The Morgana Gardens. That was a surprise that Oscar had kept from her. When his assistant, Judy, told her, she'd fought back the tears. There were so many memories: with him first meeting her, standing over her shoulder in the park, looking so amazed at her talent. Willow was sad that he would not be there. When she reached the lobby, Willow was happy to see Judy waiting. Oscar had promised that his assistant could stay until the end of the tour, if Willow wanted. Willow was grateful, because without Judy and Mellie, she would have felt so alone.

When Dorcas returned to Wildflowers Cove, it was after one in the morning. The woman who looked back at her in the bathroom mirror was not the same one who'd left this room hours ago. Shame for what she'd done to those young women filled her eyes so that she looked haunted.

Dorcas dumped the contents of her big handbag on the bed, pushing aside the Polaroid camera. Turning the snapshots over, she began to study each one.

Unable to reach her niece's house before she left for work in the morning, Dorcas had driven straight to the small newspaper where she worked. The Black Press was housed on the first floor of a beige, nondescript building on Kennedy Boulevard. The tiny snapshot inside Vera's envelope was a couple of years old, but Dorcas immediately recognized Dolores Jones, whose face was stamped with the features of her mother and her father. Willow's dark eyes stared back at Dorcas.

Dorcas was in the building on the pretext of placing an advertisement for a two-bedroom apartment. Her eyes scanned the wide-open room as she waited for an ad-taker. Apparently there was only one and he was busy. Dorcas didn't mind, because she'd yet to spot her niece. Suppose she was out on an assignment? A door marked Staff opened. Vera's daughter was walking toward her.

Dolores Jones, was not as tall as her half-sister. She was heavier and had a figure that would do a bikini proud, Dorcas thought. Her skin was darker than Willow's, closer to Michael Vaughn's butternut coloring. Her jet-black hair was curly and had it been hanging loose, would have reached her butt, just like her mother's. Her movements were like Vera's, but more ladylike. Quiet, like Willow. Dolores Jones would have been a beauty but for one noticeable feature: her eyes were the saddest Dorcas had ever seen, and smiles seemed rare indeed. When the young woman reached her and spoke, Dorcas was startled at the sound. The voice was a Morgan's, deep and melodious. If she closed her eyes, she would hear Vera when she was a young woman.

"May I help you?"

Dead voice, dead eyes. *I wonder if she just returned from Vera's funeral?* "I'm waiting for an ad-taker," Dorcas, answered.

"I can help you. We're short-staffed due to vacations. It's a bit slow today, so I can help out up front." She led

Dorcas to a desk. "My name is Dolores Jones." She extended her hand and Dorcas shook it.

The contact felt strange. This was her flesh and blood, thought Dorcas. "Dorcas Williams," she answered.

"What an unusual name. Pretty, though. From the Bible, right? I don't read that book much, but I wish I did. It would have helped me a great deal this past week." She looked at Dorcas. "I'm sorry for rambling, I'm sure you don't want to hear about my problems."

"That's perfectly all right. I'm not in much of a hurry. It's cool in here and scorching out there, so take your time. Now what happened this past week to upset you?"

"My mother died."

"I'm sorry."

"Thank you." Dolores gave Dorcas a rate sheet. "This explains our fees for the number of lines. Your ad can be as big or as small as you want, depending on how much you want to spend."

Dorcas took the sheet and perused it. She glanced at Dolores who sat back and waited, a faraway look in her eyes. "You must miss her very much," Dorcas chanced. She was relieved when Dolores appeared to want to talk.

"I do. She lived in Illinois and we rarely saw each other. It happened so fast, that I wasn't notified in time. We never said good-bye."

"Oh, honey, you must be devastated."

Dolores Jones looked closely at the woman before her. Had they met before? That voice sounded so familiar. She looked familiar. And she was so pleasant. *What's wrong with me?* she wondered. She never spoke to strangers about her personal life. It was she, as a journalist, who ferreted out information from other people.

"Have you decided?" Dolores asked Dorcas, who seemed confused. "Maybe I can suggest something?"

Before Dorcas could answer, Dolores was interrupted by

one of her coworkers. "Excuse me, Dory. Someone's calling long distance. Says it's urgent."

Dory! The young woman excused herself. When she returned, Dorcas said, "Dory is your nickname?" At last, a
tiny smile appeared.

"Yes. My mother used to call me that when I was very
young." She looked at Dorcas. "Do you know someone by
that name. It's not very common."

Suddenly, Dorcas became flustered. What was she doing
here? The plan she'd concocted seemed so bizarre now.
She stood up. "Dear, I'm not ready for this. On second
thought, I changed my mind. I'm sorry for taking up so
much of your time." Before the young woman could speak,
Dorcas hurried from the building.

Dolores looked after the woman with curiosity. She was
beginning to like the stranger. Walking back to her desk,
she wondered if she would ever see her again.

Dorcas was sitting in a luncheonette, directly across the
street from the building. From her window seat, she could
see people coming and going. At noontime the street was
crowded and she wondered if her plan was going to work.
When her niece exited the building and started across to
the luncheonette, Dorcas held her breath, not believing
her luck. This was meant to be, she thought, as she stood
up and waved to the startled young woman.

"Ms. Williams." Her smile showed her pleasure at seeing
the older woman again.

Dorcas breathed easily upon seeing that smile and said,
"Ms. Jones, Dolores, would you mind joining me on your
lunch break? There's something I must say to you."

"Why, no, of course not," Dolores answered, though
she was puzzled.

"Would you mind eating at the place on the corner? It
appears to be a quieter place to talk."

"Hanratty's? It's a little upscale for lunch. Generally, we
use it for special occasions," replied Dolores.

"That's the place we want to be," Dorcas said, gathering her things and heading for the door.

During the delicious seafood meal, the two women talked about generalities, until Dolores checked her watch.

"I'm due back shortly, Ms. Williams. Thanks for the delicious meal. But . . . you had something to tell me?"

In answer, Dorcas removed Vera's envelope from her bag and handed it to Dolores. "Open it." Watching her carefully remove the contents, staring in awe at her picture, recognizing her mother's handwriting, she stared at Dorcas.

"What is this?"

Softly, Dorcas said, "I'm your aunt, Dolores."

"No! That can't be! My mother was my only relative," Dolores cried.

"Look at the letter, Dolores," Dorcas said softly. Lord, she prayed silently, let me handle this right.

After reading it, Dolores Jones let the letter drop from her hands. Her eyes stayed on Ms. Williams, no, her aunt, Dorcas Williams. That face. That voice, she thought. So familiar to me. My aunt! When she spoke, her voice trembled. "It's true." She began to cry softly, then harder, as the tears streamed down her face until finally, she rested her head on her arms and sobbed.

Dorcas slid around the booth and put her arms around the young woman and held her until the sobs quieted. The pain and bewilderment she must be feeling, thought Dorcas. Her mother's death. The discovery of family when she thought she was all alone. Finally, Dolores lifted her head and in a low voice, excused herself. When she returned, her pain-filled eyes were still damp with tears.

"I've called my office. I won't be returning for the rest of the day." She hesitated. "Would you mind coming to my apartment? Do you . . . have to leave . . . ?"

Dorcas' own eyes filled. She's accepted me . . . for now. "Not at all, Dolores. I'm free for the rest of the day."

Dolores lived a few blocks from her office. Though they could have walked, Dorcas preferred the coolness of her car to the hot pavement of the streets. Her niece lived in a modest condominium complete with doorman. They had little conversation until they were inside the small one-bedroom apartment.

Dolores entered the living room carrying two glasses of ice water. Handing one to her aunt, she sat down across from her.

"Your voice reminds me of my mother's."

"That's not unusual. All the Morgans have a similar sound."

"All? There's more of you?"

"Us," replied Dorcas. "You're a Morgan, too, Dolores." Her eyes clouded for a second, before she said, "One more. You have a sister. A half-sister." *Or should I have said, 'cousin,'* Dorcas wondered.

The glass nearly fell from her hands as Dolores exclaimed, "A sister! I have a sister?" Her eyes watered again. "You don't realize how, all my life, I wished mother would have given me a brother or a sister. My goodness! Is she the oldest? Am I?"

Her tears fell, as the joy in her niece's voice, cut through her. Her emotion distressed her niece. Dorcas controlled herself.

"Your sister is five years older than you. She was thirty this past June. Her name is Willow Vaughn. Pausing, she added, "She's the artist Morgana."

"Morgana!?" Dolores fell back against the sofa. "My sister?"

Dorcas and Dolores spent the rest of the day, and all night, talking. Many questions were asked and answered. Dorcas had finally left the woman, close to midnight. They had promised to talk again in the morning.

Now, at one-thirty in the morning, Dorcas stared at the pictures she'd taken of her niece in various poses in her apartment and outside of her job. Willow could not deny the truth, she thought.

Clearing the bed of all the paraphernalia, Dorcas turned out the light and covered herself. Tomorrow was going to be another big day and she had to have a clear mind for what she had to do. The wrongs she'd done over the years were going to be put right. Before she left this earth, she was going to her maker with as clean a slate as she could make it—and pray that she would be forgiven.

Eighteen

On Labor Day morning, Jake could have slept late, but he was up at first light. Willow was flying home today and it was all he could do to keep himself from camping out at JFK Airport the night before.

During the past few weeks when he'd taken days off, he'd thought about making a quick flight to Toronto. But as luck would have it, he'd spent many of those days, poring over paperwork and conferring with Scott. Before he knew it, weeks had passed. But, the joy of it was that his love would be in his arms before the day ended.

At eight-thirty, Jake had showered, dressed, breakfasted on a lumberjack's meal—he'd been ravenous—and was now washing dishes when the phone rang.

"Hello?"

"Hello, yourself, sexy man," Willow breathed, doing her best Toni Braxton impersonation.

Jake's body heat rose. "Hmm. What was that?" he murmured. Her deep voice tickled his ear. "Wanna run that by me once more? Slowly?" Memories invaded his senses.

Willow laughed. "I will not. I'd hardly have time to cool down before I have to leave. Might miss my flight."

"That won't happen." Jake's voice was firm and no-nonsense.

"Hmm, so sure, are you?" teased Willow. "Just what would you do?"

"I'm one-hundred-percent sure, darlin'." He added, "And you don't want to know." In the next breath, he said, "Willow, this has been hell. Tell me you're not going to tour for a long, long time."

"I love you, sweetheart, and I'm staying put for a long while," answered Willow.

"Thank you, Jesus," breathed Jake. He cleared his throat. "Did you call to hear my 'sexy' voice, or are you calling to tell me you're coming in on an earlier flight? Any other reason and I don't want to hear it."

"I'll still arrive on the twelve-forty flight, sweetheart. But," her voice dropped to a whisper, "I want to make love to you, the minute I see you and . . . I can't very well do that with a crowd looking on."

Jake smiled. "I wonder how we always have the same thoughts?" Then, "Okay, what plan have you hatched?"

"I want to drop my bags home, hug Dorcas, then I want to say a proper hello to you . . . in your shower. I expect that will take the rest of the night."

"Say hello? I'm meeting your flight, honey." Jake frowned. "Is someone else picking you up?"

"Oscar will have a car waiting."

"You've spoken to him?" Jake was thoughtful. This is the first time she's mentioned his name in weeks. She'd never spoken about the reason for the dissolution of their partnership. Jake was certain he already knew.

"No," Willow answered. "Judy returned yesterday. She called to tell me that this service is part of the contract and that Oscar hopes that I will accept. I told her I would."

"I'm glad," Jake replied. "Willow, you've never told me what happened between you and Oscar, and you don't ever have to. But you do need an agent, honey. I've heard they don't come any better. Any chance of repairing the rift?"

"I can't say. I think that the choice he made was . . . best for . . . him. Jake, I've had weeks to digest what happened. He's spent years . . ." She hesitated. "Sweetheart,

I want to tell you everything, but only, I want to be with you when I do. Okay?"

Jake heard the sadness and felt her pain. He would agonize at the delay in seeing her. But, maybe, by not rejecting his offer, Willow will be making the first overture to what could lead to eventual healing for Oscar.

"Okay," Jake answered. "But from the minute your plane lands, I'll be missing you every second that we're apart, darlin'."

"Oh, you know me so well, honey. Thanks for understanding. I promise I'll be with you soon."

"Dorcas gets only one hug now. You hurry on over here and give the rest to me." As an afterthought, he said, "She'll be there when you arrive?" Willow had called him when she hadn't heard from her aunt for three days. Almost immediately she'd called him back. Dorcas had called, saying she'd gone out of town, and she would be back early Monday morning.

"Yes. She'd gone to visit friends on Fire Island who were giving a bash this weekend. She's had enough and is anxious to get back to the peacefulness of the Cove."

"I think something else is hurrying her home."

"I miss her too," replied Willow. She longed for her home, also. "Sweetheart, I've got to finish packing one more bag. Gotta ring off, now. I love you, Jake."

"Hurry to me, love."

Two hours after Jake had spoken to Willow, he was unloading his car with groceries. He had all the fixings for a holiday barbecue that would rival the best of 'em. Something Willow had said about "taking all night" had set the wheels turning in his head. He wasn't about to interrupt her hello with something as mundane as their needing to seek nutrition in a crowded restaurant. Uh-uh. That sce-

nario was definitely all wrong. He was going to be true to
his boy scout motto: "Be Prepared."

The spuds and eggs were boiling for his best potato salad,
the pork ribs were parboiling and fatback was frying to season his frozen collards. Gotta cheat somewhere, he thought.
This food is going to be *finished* when she rings that bell.
Jake went to the small enclosed backyard, uncovered the
tripod grill and filled the container with charcoal. When
the coals began to burn, he replaced the grill top. After a
careful look, satisfied, he went inside. He peeled the husks
off the corn, washed it and set the ears in a colander, in the
sink. He'd boil those when it was time to eat. Breathing
easy, he sat down at the kitchen table and began to cut up
the washed vegetables for his green salad, which included
cucumbers, onions. He then washed and dried some tomatoes. Grinning at himself, Jake wiped his eyes on his sleeve.
Unlike any observer would think, he knew that it wasn't
only the fresh onion that made his eyes water.

Willow welcomed the cool comfort of the limousine.
The return of the heat in Toronto was a surprise. The heat
in New York had been predicted. Both Pearson and JFK
airports had been noisy, crowded and hot. Excitement at
seeing the two people she loved made her wish like a child
that her plane could have landed on the lawn at Wildflowers Cove. Smiling at her foolish thoughts, she sighed and
closed her eyes. Soon.

Standing by the window, Jake checked his watch for the
umpteenth time in the last five minutes. It was after three,
and Willow should have been at his door. He'd called her,
though he didn't want to interrupt her reunion with her
aunt, but he was impatient to get some of those kisses for
himself. There had been no answer. He could only assume

that Dorcas had not arrived and Willow was on her way to him. When the phone rang a few minutes before, it was Tala asking if he was sure he and Willow wouldn't join them for dinner tonight.

"Absolutely, positively not," he'd told her. Laughing, Tala had hung up.

The phone rang and Jake answered in a rush. "Hello?" His heart pounded.

"Just wanted to see if you were in, brother. Got something for you. Stay put, now." Nat Rivers hung up.

"Nat?" Jake yelled angrily at the silence in his ear. "Damn you," he yelled, slamming down the receiver. "What are you up to, now?"

Dialing Willow's number, he waited. Nothing. If he left, he might miss her. If she came, and he was gone, she would run into Nat. Jake sat down and waited, furious at feeling so powerless. But, most of all, he felt fear. For himself—and for Willow.

Nat Rivers closed the lid of the black trunk, after lifting out a large brown envelope. He tucked it under his arm and left the bedroom, walking slowly down the stairs. He was in no rush. Little brother wasn't going anywhere. Nat chuckled, and his father heard him from his seat in the living room.

Lloyd looked at Nat in disgust. The relationship between the two men had deteriorated to a point of non-civility, since the night Jake had stormed out of the house. Lloyd had demanded that Nat tell him what he'd done to infuriate his brother. Nat had only laughed. Since then, Nat came and went as he pleased, speaking only when it was necessary. Instead of sitting at the kitchen table drinking beer, Nat did his drinking in his room. Lloyd began to notice the rum bottles piling up in the recycling can. For weeks, since Ms. Benson had brought some papers over for his signature, and had given him some reports, Lloyd knew that the end of his business was near. When he had confronted Nat, his son had walked upstairs, grinning like he'd heard a funny joke. A few times, Lloyd was tempted to call his youngest son, but stopped himself as the thought of Jake and that woman together blurred his mind. Never.

Nat looked at his father. Shifting the bag under his arm, he said "Wondering about this, huh?"

Lloyd remained silent. Nothing that foolish man ever said made any sense anymore—just making riddles out of his words.

"I started to give this to my brother weeks ago when he came storming in here to whip my ass." Nat smiled a crooked smile. "I almost gave it to him then, but it wasn't the time. I wanted him to get so deep into that honey, loving her until he thinks he can't live without her. Loving her until it hurts his soul."

"Shut your dirty, mouth."

"Uh-uh. Too late for that. But, maybe I kept my mouth shut too long, huh?" Nat sat down on the bottom step in the hallway, staring hard at his father and holding the bag on his knees. "Maybe I should have woke him up. All those years ago, maybe I should have brought him down the stairs with me when I heard you take mother into the kitchen." Nat cocked his head. "You remember. The night you brought her back . . . two years after she left us?"

Lloyd looked stricken. "You . . . heard . . . ?"

"All the noise you made? Hah! You were crying more than she was, even with her being so sick. You never heard or saw me. The next morning you told me and Jake that she was recovering from pneumonia and was very weak." Nat rolled his eyes. "I was fourteen years old and you tried to treat me like a baby!" He jumped up off the step, fury blazing in his eyes. "I heard you, Dad. I heard you crying to her. That if the baby had lived, it would have hurt too many people . . . it was better that Michael Vaughn's baby died at birth!"

Nat turned toward the door.

"Where . . . are you . . . going?" Lloyd rasped.

"Your son is waiting for me. It's time my brother knew the truth about this family. Don't you think he'd want to start his marriage with a clear mind?" Nat closed the door, ignoring his father's pleas.

Jake opened the door and Nat entered, tossing the envelope, which Jake caught before it hit the floor. He sauntered inside and sat down, swinging one leg over the other. Jake looked at the envelope.

"Open it," Nat said. He laughed.

"What's your story now, Nat? Or should I ask, how much and to whom?"

"Not mine, brother, yours. Go on. Take a look at your family history. Great bedtime story for the kiddies. That is, when they're old enough. Lurid stuff in there." He swung his foot, back and forth. His eyes glinted with glee.

Jake sat on the sofa and dumped the contents of the bag on the low table. He knew Nat had been drinking. He'd brought the smell of rum inside. Jake glanced at the letters and pictures on the table, wondering what garbage Nat was into now. He stared, as his mother's handwriting caught his eye. Moving the papers about, most of the letters had been written by Olivia Rivers. Jake stared from the table to Nat and his stomach churned. An old picture of a painting was amongst the papers and he picked it up. Even with age, the wilted rose was so lifelike. It was signed in a child's scrawl. It was signed "Willow."

"What . . ." Jake had no words for what he was holding. He could only stare at his brother.

"There was a note clipped to that," Nat said. His voice

had hardened to cold steel. "See there? The one with the paper clip? Read it!"

Jake picked it up and read.

Olivia
   This is what the critics are screaming about. My baby is a genius. Meet me tonight. Same place.

                                                   Michael

Jake stared at Nat with lifeless eyes.

"Mother?"

Nat stood up. "Our mother."

"All these years, you knew this and never told me?" Jake thought about the time he was ten years old and his mother had disappeared from his life. When she'd returned two years later, he had been the happiest kid in the world.

"You were too young. Mother made me swear to take care of you. To protect you."

Jake was bewildered. "She didn't tell you about . . ."

"No," Nat sat with scorn. "What decent mother is going to tell her fourteen-year-old about her lover? I found out by accident and she discovered it. What she wanted to protect you from was that you never find out." He walked to the door and opened it. "You're a big enough boy now. I think you have the stomach for the rest of that stuff. Good day to start growing up, Jake." He pulled the door shut and walked to his father's Oldsmobile.

It was almost seven o'clock when Jake stirred from the sofa. Almost dazedly, he looked at his watch and frowned as he realized Willow had never come. Or called. Something was wrong. Had Nat visited her first? "Oh, my God," he whispered, "he wouldn't." Slumping against the sofa, he dropped his head in his hand, shaking his head in disbelief. What other reason could there be? This vile filth

would be the only thing that would make her run from
me, he thought. To learn about her father and his mother,
in the way Nat must have told her—

Jake's glance fell on the scattered papers. The whole
sordid mess his mother had made of her life was all there;
in notes to Michael Vaughn, in letters to her husband, in
letters from her husband.

Jake pieced the events of twenty-six years ago from these
yellowing scraps of paper. He almost laughed at how an
innocent flirtation one day between two married people
eventually ruined the lives of so many people. That's how
it began, his mother wrote in a letter to his father; after
she'd run away and had written to beg his forgiveness. Jake
rubbed his forehead as he thought about his father's reply,
calling her every dirty name he could think of.

Why couldn't he have forgiven her? Jake asked himself. The
damage had already been done; Michael Vaughn was dead.
He could have let her come home. No one would've known
that the child she was carrying was not her husband's. He
gave no thought to his two sons who needed their mother,
Jake thought bitterly. His eyes filled with anger as he suddenly stuffed the papers back inside the envelope.

Jake swore at the way he manhandled the ignition when
he'd started the Camaro. Even as the engine began to purr
softly, and he pulled off, he would never have heard the
soft, insistent ring of the telephone.

Nineteen

The black Oldsmobile was not in his father's driveway. "Why am I not surprised?" Jake muttered as he strode purposefully to the front door. Once inside, he wasted no time in searching for his father.

The living room and kitchen were empty. Pushing open the door of the first-floor bedroom that his father had used since his stroke, he strode inside. It was empty. Jake frowned. He's got to be here. He raced upstairs and hurried down the hall to the bedroom that had once been his parents'. Lloyd Rivers was there.

"What . . . ?" Jake exclaimed.

Lloyd was sitting in a big easy chair by the window, boxes at his feet, the floor strewn with papers and documents. Family matters accumulated over years. The closet door was open where more boxes lay opened, their contents in a jumble. Lloyd looked up at Jake.

The look in his father's eyes made Jake cringe. If he'd never seen death before, he was looking at something very close to it. His father's skin was ashen and his cold eyes stared at Jake.

"All . . . these years . . ." Lloyd gasped. "That thievin' boy stole my things, my letters, your mother's things . . . he knew all that time. . . ." He looked at the bag Jake held. "He told you." The statement held no emotion.

Feeling drained, Jake dropped down on the bed, pity,

replacing the anger he had in his heart. The old man before him was sad and broken. His secret, the one that had made him hate for so long, was not really a secret at all. His oldest son had known of his mother's betrayal. And had laughed at him. And had hated him.

"He told me," Jake answered. "He told me that when you brought mother home, you cried, you were so happy." His voice hardened. "If you loved her so much why didn't you forgive her when she begged? Why did you make her stay away from us? You cheated yourself and your sons," Jake said bitterly.

"You don't know what you're talking about, so stop . . . just shut up!"

"No!" Jake shouted. "I want to know why you allowed that hate inside of you to hurt all of us! Tell me why."

"Because your mother didn't want to!"

"What? I don't believe you."

"You don't know nothin'." Lloyd pointed at the envelope. "You think you know everything from what's in there? That's not my whole life. Or your mother's." His voice trembled.

Jake could only stare, his head whirling with doubts, his temples beating furiously as his blood raced. He couldn't speak.

Lloyd's voice was low and strained as he spoke. "Your mother loved you boys and you better not ever forget it. What she did . . . well, she paid for it with her life. If his wife hadna shot him, I would've killed that evil man, myself." Lloyd's eyes glazed with an old memory. "The day he died, was the day, Michael Vaughn impregnated my wife with his seed."

"Jesus," rasped Jake.

"She didn't know nothin' was growin' in her body the night she brought the devil's child here. When she got the call that our friends were dead, I let her go over there by herself. Figured there was nothin' I could do for them."

He saw Jake's eyes flicker. "Yeah, we were friends. All four of us. I wasn't as close to him as your mother was to Beatrice. We went to some parties over there. Your mother liked that kind of stuff." His mouth twisted at the memory. "Later on, she came back here with that girl."

"Willow," Jake murmured. He had been ten years old. Why hadn't he remembered that day?

"What happened?"

"Your mother was like a nervous chicken. She kept that child up in this room the whole day, feeding her in here, not letting her speak to you boys. The child slept practically the whole time she was here. I think your mother was tryin' to find out what the kid had seen. If she saw her mother shoot her father."

Jake winced, his heart going out to Willow. What had a four-year-old child seen? Heard?

"The police came, asked some questions and left. Said they'd probably come back to question the kid, but they were waiting for the next of kin to arrive. Your mother followed them, saying she wanted to be there when Beatrice's sister arrived."

"From Canada?" Jake was surprised.

"No. Not Dorcas Williams," Lloyd spat. "The other one. Vera. She never showed up that night. Was the one from Canada they called and were waiting for."

"Impossible! Willow has no other relatives! Who in the hell is Vera?"

Lloyd gave his son a mirthless smile. "Told you everything wasn't in them letters." The smile disappeared. "Listen to what I say. Those Morgans were born in that house and grew up there. Three girls. The oldest one, Dorcas, moved out years ago when she got married. Beatrice was the one who got the house. The youngest was Vera who lived God knows where, or with whom, but it certainly wasn't 'round here." Lloyd sounded curious when he said, "Never saw her until she came for one of those parties. Only for the big ones, when she thought important people would be there. Shaking her butt at every man who passed."

His father's voice made Jake feel as if he were just sucker punched. Never saw the blow coming. His breath escaped with a whooshing sound. He'd lived here, grown up here, how could he not have heard rumors about the important family that lived not twenty minutes away? Siberia, it was not. He'd paid minimal attention, he supposed, as a teenager or as a young man, about something that was ancient history. A woman shoots and kills her husband then kills herself, leaving their daughter an orphan. News like that died after the first hours of sensationalism. And the dead were not only the victims. What of those left behind?

"Willow," Jake said aloud. He looked at his father, "You hated a little girl? Then hated her twice as much when she became a woman? What had she ever done to you to deserve your scorn and bitter hatred? She was the victim in all of this, Dad!"

Jake stood up, leaving the envelope on the bed. "If Nat has been over there filling her head with his filthy version of our 'family history' as he calls it, I will hurt him, Dad. I swear it." At the door, he shot a look of disgust at his father.

"You're an old man swelled with a hate so old, that you've lost all sense of who you once were. A proud and loving father. My whole life, and Nat's, you stole your father's love from us. We, or I should say I grew up in this loveless house without knowing the reason why. Wondering why, or when things changed. I was a bewildered boy, who lost, then found his mother, but still never had her because for the seven years she lived after she returned, she was dying from shame. Because you brought her back but she knew that you never forgave her. Why did you even bother? Your pride? Oh, I read the letters you wrote, asking her to return . . ." His father's voice stopped him.

"You . . . didn't see . . . them all!" Lloyd shouted. In a ragged whisper, he said, "She didn't want to . . . come back. She stayed down there in South Carolina with her cousins . . . because she was ashamed. But she refused to . . . abort her child."

Jake's face was grim, when he asked, "So how did you make her come back? Knowing what she'd done to you, what kind of life could she expect, living with you?" His voice was bitter.

"The baby. When her daughter was born dead. Six months after that baby died, her cousins called. Your mother was willing herself to die. They couldn't take care of her anymore. I went and got her."

"She never wanted to come back, knowing what she'd done to you."

"She came back because she loved her sons."

"What?"

"She . . . missed her boys."

"My God," Jake whispered, his eyes filling with pain. She endured his anger for us!

"I loved . . . your . . . mother." Lloyd's breath came in soft spurts.

"Loved? You wanted her to be grateful to you for wanting her. She probably died knowing how much hate was in your heart because she saw you change into a cold, unloving man." Jake gestured at the paper strewn room. "These are your memories. Hold on to them. I'm going to the only woman I'll ever love, and I pray to God, that she'll let us have a happy life together."

Jake did not hear his father's broken whisper. "I . . . loved you Olivia."

If Jake never prayed before, he was praying now, as he drove to Wildflowers Cove. Because he hadn't heard from Willow, he was certain that Nat had paid her a "friendly" visit. The thought of what might have transpired between them made him swear. Willow was probably traumatized.

All that had happened since his brother's cryptic phone call at three o'clock, until now, whirled through his mind. At nine-thirty, he was still dazed, speeding dangerously through the dark, curving streets out of Elmsford, as the words of his brother and father feathered his ears.

Memories of that traumatic day flitted in and out of his consciousness. He could hear excited cries coming from his mother's and father's booming voice, shouting. Unintelligible shouts. He saw strangers come and go. Some women he'd never seen before. One was there early in the day and another strange lady appeared later that night with his mother. Jake remembered now. The first lady was the housekeeper who had found the little girl. The lady who came later had been Dorcas William.

Jake could see himself now when he was ten years old. He was sitting on the couch with Nat. The little girl, Willow, sat sleepy-eyed, leaning against Jake's shoulder. As clear as if it were happening now, he heard Dorcas say from the doorway, "Aren't you my little buttercup?"

"Willow." Jake was filled up. For years, he and Willow had been connected. Neither knowing what strangeness caused the electricity to crackle between them when they touched. Years ago, their fate had been decided. He had unknowingly offered comfort to a sad little girl who would become part of his destiny.

Jake was in awe and somehow knew that he was not supposed to question what was. He slowed his speed. He was humbled.

Twenty

When the limousine entered the gate of Wildflowers Cove, at 2:45 P.M., Willow looked puzzled as the driver neared the house. The guest parking area to the far side of the house was empty except for her aunt's Buick sedan. It should have been filled with Saturday's arrivals, Willow thought. As the driver deposited her bags on the porch, Willow couldn't help but feel the sinister aura that surrounded the Cove. A shiver passed through her. Refusing the offer of help with her bags, she thanked the driver and watched him drive away.

Willow's initial impression that something was wrong was made tangible with the absence of her aunt greeting her at the front door. It should have been flung wide open and she should have been in her aunt's arms by now. Drawing a breath, Willow unlocked the door and stepped inside. The ominous shadows were inside the house, covering Willow with a shroud of fear.

"Aunt Dee?" she called. Her voice trembled.

"I'm here, Willow."

Following Dorcas' voice to the living room, Willow stared at her aunt, who was sitting in a chair by the window. She was so still. "Aunt Dee. What's wrong?" Where is she going? She just got back. Willow was confused, not understanding the two pieces of luggage by the chair, and her aunt dressed for travel in a cotton slack set. She crossed the room to her aunt, leaned over and kissed her. "Aunt Dee, I've missed you. Don't I get a hug?"

Dorcas raised her arms and caught her niece in a hug, then kissed her cheek. "I missed you, too, buttercup." Her normally deep voice sounded harsh and raspy.

"You've gone and caught a cold and sore throat at the shore." Willow sounded hopeful that that was the only thing wrong with her aunt.

"No, just a little hoarse. I've been doing a lot of talking the past few days." Dorcas smiled and gestured. "Sit down, Willow. I have a lot to say. Please, no matter what you think, let me finish. If you interrupt, I might not be able to go on." Rubbing her forehead as if to clear her thinking, she continued, "I suppose I should begin at the beginning, but I'm going to start at the end, which began last week."

Waving a hand to encompass the interior as well as the exterior of the house, she said, "I know you're wondering where the guests are. There aren't any and there won't be any, ever again. Unless of course, you decide differently in the future. That will be your sole decision. Since last Tuesday, I, and two temp agency workers, did what was necessary to cancel every confirmed reservation; from this week into the end of next season. As the calls were made, and letters of regret typed, I wrote the checks, returning all monies. There are no loose ends! Everyone was notified, so don't fall for any okeydoke hassles that someone was cheated."

Willow was stunned. The fear that had followed her into the house, sat heavily on her chest. Her aunt had told her not to interrupt, but how could she? She had no words. She only stared as Dorcas continued.

"With the exception of the gardening, all services, including the daily catering, have been stopped. One housekeeper will come five days a week to cook and clean." Dorcas frowned. "Of course, all of this is reversible if you see fit, Willow." For the first time, she looked away, unable to meet her niece's confused stare. Falteringly, she said, "I . . . know by now . . . you realize that . . . I'm going away."

"Aunt Dee, why? What went wrong?"

Dorcas turned her gaze back to Willow, then wearily, she reached inside the purse on her lap and opened it. "This is the beginning, Willow." She was holding the aged lavender envelope. Laying it on top of her purse, she then rested her clasped hands on it. "The beginning is still not where I can start." She patted the envelope. "This is a letter that your mother wrote to you before she killed herself. She left it to me to decide when to give it to you. I never did because I was a coward. I was afraid of losing your love and respect. I was afraid that what she'd written would reveal the lie that I'd told you." Dorcas looked at the young woman sitting frozen in fear, and her heart wrenched, knowing that she'd caused it. "Now, I'll tell you the end."

Willow felt her eyes mist as she stared at the letter on her aunt's lap. My mother!

"That day in June, when you came home and met those two women leaving? Remember?" Not waiting or needing a reply, Dorcas said, "Of course you do. That's when I went half-crazy and worried you to death. Well, the frail woman, the one who looked at you so strangely . . . well, I received word last week that she is dead."

"Dead?" Willow did not know the woman, but yet she felt saddened. Those thin legs could hardly support the weight of her body.

"Yes." Dorcas looked intensely into Willow's eyes. "Her name was Vera Morgan Jones. She was my youngest sister."

Willow broke the mesmerizing stare and turned her head to look outside of the window. Her attention was caught by a white butterfly flitting from flower to flower. The silence surrounding her, allowed her to imagine that she was hearing the soft fluttering of its wings. When it took flight into the woods, she turned her gaze to Dorcas.

"My aunt?" Willow whispered.

Dorcas nodded. "Yes. She was fifty years old when she died." The look she gave Willow was one of bewilderment. "The woman you saw that day, was not the beautiful Vera of twenty-six years ago. That woman was but an apparition of Vera Morgan." Resignedly, she said, "Now I'll tell you the middle."

"That weekend," Dorcas continued, "the July fourth holiday weekend, she was here, at the big party. She was an overnight guest." Dorcas stopped. "Willow, your mother left me a letter too. She explained everything that went on in this house, her relationship with her husband, and his affairs."

Willow's heart thumped wildly. Did she suspect what was coming? No, please don't let it be true, she prayed silently.

Dorcas saw the facial expression change from fear to dread, and she agonized. She must go on. "Yes. Your father and Vera were lovers. Late that night, everyone was asleep when a noise awakened your mother. She found your father and her sister having intercourse on the kitchen table." Dorcas knew she was being blunt, but there was no way to pretty up a sordid truth. "Later on that night, my sister Beatrice killed Michael Vaughn. Hours later, near dawn, she shot herself."

A tear slid down Willow's cheek.

In an unsteady voice, Dorcas told Willow the circumstances, over years, that led to her parents' deaths. From memory, she practically quoted Beatrice's letter word for word: from the years of sexual, and then verbal abuse, to the night she took their lives. Dorcas left nothing out. The time for secrets was over. No more lies.

Willow listened to her aunt's voice as if she were a total stranger come to visit, a paid teller of tales. A griot telling her family history. Willow had been transported to a dark place that was full of hurt and deceit. She was stuck there, unable to arouse herself to return. Shouldn't she return to answer the phone? It wouldn't stop ringing. But she

couldn't. She was held captive, hypnotized by the
stranger's voice. A movement caught her eye and she
looked to the window. The white butterfly was back. Willow
thought that if only she could fly away, too, she would
escape the stranger's vile words. But, the butterfly flew
away and Willow was left behind. Again, the phone rang,
but she was powerless to answer it.

Dorcas saw the glazed look in Willow's eyes and her heavy
breathing. Worried, she rose and quickly went to sit beside
her. Her forehead was damp. Dorcas took her pulse, breathing a sigh of relief. It was not dangerously rapid, but Dorcas
went to the kitchen and returned with cold water and a
damp cloth. She pressed the cloth to her niece's forehead,
then made her bend her head down for a few seconds.

Dorcas gave the glass of water to Willow. "Drink some,"
she said. Satisfied that Willow was breathing easier, Dorcas
returned to her chair. She spoke in a low voice as Willow
watched her, almost curiously.

"I arrived at this house late that night. You were gone."
Dorcas did not go into details which Willow need not hear—
at least, not now. "Olivia Rivers waited for me to come."

Willow's eyelashes flickered, but she remained silent.

Dorcas saw, but she continued. "After the police . . .
well, when they were finished with me, Olivia Rivers took
me to her house. You were there." She continued, explaining all that happened that night when she saw her sitting
on the couch with the Rivers' boys. When she mentioned
Jake's name, her niece looked at her.

"Jake," Willow said. She repeated his name as if testing
it on her lips. "Jake was there?"

Dorcas nodded.

Willow didn't speak for a long time after Dorcas finished
talking. This time, when she looked outside, there was no
sun and no butterfly. She looked around the room, then
at her aunt.

"I wonder if the sofa I sat on that day, was sitting in this same spot. Just curious," she added, looking at Dorcas. She stared for a long time at the woman who'd raised and loved her. The only relative she had in the world. Or so she told her. Now, Dorcas wanted to walk out of her life. Leave her alone, again. Somehow, Willow knew that there was more. She shifted on the couch but fastened her eyes on Dorcas.

Quietly, she said, "The beginning you're holding in your hand. The end came with the death of my aunt Vera. But, the middle isn't complete, is it Aunt Dee? There's more. Is it so terrible? What could possibly be more devastating than the horrors you've just told me?"

Dorcas had wondered how she was going to make complete, her circle of white lies. Willow provided the way.

"The day you saw Vera, the day I turned her away for the second time in her life, she begged for my help. I refused her again."

"Begged for help? She was dying!"

"Not for herself; for her daughter. She wanted her daughter to know that she was not alone." Dorcas hesitated. "She wanted you to meet her."

"I have a cousin?!" Stupefied, Willow repeated, "A cousin? Vera had a daughter and she is my cousin?"

"Willow," Dorcas said in a whisper, "she's your half-sister too." Her voice almost inaudible, she added, "Michael Vaughn impregnated Vera the night your mother found them together." Dorcas' head shot up as the scream pierced the quiet house.

"Aieeee . . . oh, no . . . no . . . no. Stop, Aunt Dee . . . no more . . . Aieeee . . ." Willow's screams had turned into uncontrollable cries. Deep, gut-wrenching cries that burned her throat before hurtling out, overshadowing the soft ring of the phone.

Ignoring the insistent ring, Dorcas went to her niece, catching her in her arms. "Willow, Willow, stop. Stop. Shhh . . . shhh. My baby," Dorcas said, rocking Willow in her arms. "Shhh, now, shhh."

Dorcas held her until the cries became sobs and then soft hiccups. Glancing at her watch, Dorcas frowned. It was after seven o'clock. She knew it could be no one but Jake calling, probably worried sick about Willow. The creases in her brow disappeared for a minute as she thought about Jake Rivers. He would stay with Willow, no matter what. Wherever Dorcas finally settled, she knew that she would not have to worry about her Willow being alone. She had set in motion the meeting of the two sisters. They would have each other now. *Willow is hurting, but she is strong and will soon forget me and begin to live with Jake and her newfound sister,* Dorcas silently assured herself.

Dorcas released Willow as she felt the tremors subside and went to the kitchen. She heard footsteps and saw Willow enter the kitchen and sit down at the table. Dorcas continued to pour apple juice in two glasses and set crackers and cheese on the table. She sat down across from her niece, pushing the food toward her.

"We both need this, Willow. Try and eat something before you make yourself sick. You haven't eaten since this morning."

Willow looked at the wall clock. The reality that it was nearly seven-thirty in the evening, surprised her. Vaguely, she remembered where she should be at this very moment. Jake. She should be with Jake, she thought numbly. Slowly, she drank the juice, nearly emptying the glass before setting it down. She pulled the dish toward her and began to nibble on the food. She tasted nothing, but forced herself to eat. Finishing the juice, Willow looked at her aunt.

"All these weeks you've known about your niece and you didn't want her? Didn't want me to know her?" Willow spoke softly, with a note of incredulity lacing her voice. "You've known I have wished for a sister all my life, Aunt Dee." She grew thoughtful. "Had my aunt Vera not died, would you have continued to lie to me about you being my only relative? For how long, Aunt Dee? How long?"

Brushing her long curls off her face, she wearily rubbed her forehead. Her eyes were angry.

"You could have died with that secret, Aunt Dee. Mine and Jake's children would have been deprived of an aunt. Just like my aunt Vera's daughter was."

"Willow—"

"Do you know her name?" Willow interrupted. "Where she lives? Have you met her?"

"Dolores Jones is her name. She works for a small newspaper in Jersey City, New Jersey."

Dorcas stood up and cleared the table, leaving the kitchen when she finished, walking back to the living room. It was time she left. She'd done all she could to help her niece get through the inevitable emotional storms that lay ahead.

Willow followed her aunt and sat down on the sofa, staring at the woman whom she'd loved as a mother.

Dorcas picked up the lavender envelope, walked solemnly to Willow and put it in her hand. "I don't know what your mother wrote to you Willow, but I was wrong to keep this from you. I hope that I did not destroy the rest of your life by my cowardice." She turned to go, preparing to pick up her luggage. The strained voice stopped her.

"I think you're right, Aunt Dee."

Dorcas turned.

"To leave me," Willow answered Dorcas' look. "You couldn't possibly want to live with me; watching my love grow into hate, whenever I think of your lies."

Dorcas' eyes filled, the impact of her niece's words cutting her as she'd known they would. She opened the front door.

"You've left her number?" Willow's voice stopped her aunt.

Dorcas nodded. "Everything is on your desk, Willow. Everything." She hesitated, then lifted her bags. "Good-bye, Willow," she said, and closed the door. "Buttercup," she whispered as she walked to the car. As Dorcas drove up the driveway, she wiped the tears from her eyes. It was getting dark now and she didn't want Willow to be alone. Not in that house. Years before, a sad little four-year-old had waited anxiously for her parents to come home. Would she remember? Dorcas felt a hard knot form in the pit of her stomach. She wondered what was keeping Jake. He had to feel something was wrong. "Hurry, Jake," she murmured. "She needs you."

The envelope was lying on the seat cushion where Willow placed it. Willow could only stare at it, not daring to open it to hear her mother's voice speak to her from the grave. Great feelings of trepidation spiraled her body, wrenching her heart. Unable to sit still, Willow stood and walked around the room, touching things, straightening knickknacks, plumping pillows. She sat down again, putting her head in her palms. Her sobs were muffled as the tears began to flow again. She rocked herself back and forth, moaning softly. Her body quivered and she wrapped her arms around her waist, hugging herself tightly, but the tears still flowed. "Mother," she whispered. "Why did you do this to us?" Her cries sounded loudly in the still house. Willow lay down, tucking her knees, as big sobs shook her shoulders. For a long time, the piteous sound resounded through the room in the big empty house.

It was dark when Willow woke up. Her heart thumped wildly, as disoriented, she looked about in the dark. Hurrying to a floor lamp, she turned it on, casting a soft light in the living room. The darkness outside the window frightened her, and she rushed to the wall switch and turned on the floodlights. Why was she so nervous? She'd never been afraid to stay in her home alone. Alone! The realization hit her; she was really alone for the first time in her life. Except for those few hours she'd spent alone in this very room, so long ago. Waiting.

Willow walked to the kitchen and turned on the light.

The wall clock read nine-thirty. She then walked into all the rooms on the first floor and turned on every light.

Willow was in her bedroom, sitting on the sofa with clasped hands in her lap. Her feet were planted firmly on the floor as if to root herself to the spot. After so many hours, a sense of calm was beginning to enter her body and she refused to give in to any fears. The fear of the unknown was in the stack of envelopes, and small, neat piles of papers and letters that her aunt had left for her. Somewhere, in that order, which represented a part of her own life, she would find a part that would be her relative. Only one of two that she had in the world. A wan smile touched her mouth. What shall I call her? Willow asked herself. Would she prefer to be my sister? Or my cousin? A mirthless sound escaped as she closed her eyes against that moment of discovery as it replayed.

"Dolores Jones," Willow said aloud. Then she whispered, "Alone now, like me."

After staring at it for long minutes, Willow was drawn to the desk, where she sat down. Almost afraid to look, she didn't have to search at all, because an envelope, neatly marked "Dolores Jones," was on the top of the pile. Her normally steady hands shook, as she picked it up and unfastened the clasp of the large envelope. She pulled out its contents, then quickly dropped them, startled; staring at her was the face of a Morgan—and a Vaughn.

Recovering from looking at the young woman who was so much like herself, Willow put aside the pictures and began to read all about the woman who was her younger sister. As she read, the tears began to fall once more.

At times in the past, when Willow needed to clear her mind for a new project, she sought solace from the hum of activity around the Cove. She would find herself in the greenhouse, where she was now.

She'd left the dossier of her sister sitting on the desk, and walked from the bedroom. The warm, moist, earth-smell inside the greenhouse had stung her nostrils when she'd opened the door. This was a familiar place. She felt safe here. Willow touched a hanging, bright pink and red fuchsia, thinking vaguely that the gardener had started to bring inside some plants. She fingered the white azalea. All my beautiful flowers are well, she thought, as she looked around.

A long ago memory stirred, and she remembered camellias—and Jake. The man who would soon become her husband. The man who'd captured her very soul and whom she'd love until she died.

How funny life is, she mused as she walked about touching, sniffing. So long ago, a young boy comforted a little girl. Who knew then that those two lives were destined to come together years later, for all eternity? Jake. He was her protector.

A grim thought invaded her senses. But will he still want to hold and caress that little girl, now grown, and his lover? His lover, he'll learn, who comes from tainted stock?

Willow Vaughn, the daughter of the respected artist Michael Vaughn; unknown as wife abuser, but notorious, in his role as a seducer of women. The niece of Vera Morgan, beautiful temptress, who coveted her sister's husband. The daughter of Beatrice Vaughn, murderess. What decent man would want the spawn of such people to father his heirs? Willow agonized over the history lesson her aunt had given her. Years of lies and secrets. Would her lover comfort her? Love her as he'd sworn? Could he look at her and who she was—and not at her sires? With all her heart, Willow wanted to believe that all the sordidness that had touched her past would not make a difference in their love. But somehow, she knew that she was wrong.

Because, she'd not yet had the courage to hear her mother's voice. What more was there left for her to discover? What unspeakable horrors waited for her in the digesting of her mother's last crazed thoughts after she'd murdered her husband and was about to murder herself?

What sense could she have made in a letter to her little girl who lay sleeping only yards away—and who would soon be orphaned? Willow dreaded setting her eyes on those words.

Her thoughts began to numb her, making her feel nothing. Why didn't her aunt have the courage to carry out her sister's wish years ago, Willow thought. When I was young and more tolerant of the character flaws in others? Not on the brink of beginning the rest of my life with the man I love. Why? Why did she do this to me?

Willow's head throbbed with pain and she felt as delicate as a flower petal.

"W-h-y . . . Dorcas . . . ?"

It was a scream of pain as the world grew dark. For the first time in her life, Willow dropped to the floor in a dead faint.

The first thing Jake noticed when he pulled onto the gravel drive of Wildflowers Cove, was the blaze of lights in every room on the first floor. Usually, even at ten o'clock at night lights were on in the upstairs guest rooms. But Jake was happy that Willow would be there. As he neared and parked, he was curious at the absence of cars. None. Neither Dorcas' or guests'. Willow's had been inside the garage since she'd left, so it was no surprise that it was probably still there. Jake walked to the door and rang the bell, wondering why Willow hadn't been at the door by now. His earlier thoughts of Nat coming here—.

Jake tried the doorknob and the door opened. His mouth went dry. Without going into the interior, he felt that something was wrong. The house was empty!

"Willow?" he shouted. "Willow, where the hell are you?" Jake scanned the living room, his sharp gaze catching the envelope laying on the sofa. Dismissing it, he walked briskly down the hall to the kitchen back into the hall, opening doors as he went. Dorcas' room was empty.

Willow's room was empty. He took in the mounds of papers on her desk and wondered at the chaos. He'd never seen her space in such disorder. The studio!

Jake's footsteps were heavy on the bare oak floors as he strode to the kitchen door. The cottage was dark. Why would she be there in the dark? His heart pounded wildly. He ran the rest of the way, found the key in its dangerously welcoming spot and unlocked the door. One glance in the now lit room told him that Willow had not been in here. He would have known. He would have felt her.

"Willow, darlin', where are you?"

Jake left the cottage, looking toward the dark woods surrounding the house, quickly dispelling the morbid thoughts that sprang in his mind. He ran toward the house. He hadn't checked the upstairs rooms. Of course! No guests. Why wouldn't she be up there? His heart told him no. Why would she be up there in the dark?

Jake stopped in mid-run, as he passed the greenhouse. He backed up and peered inside, past the hanging foliage. A small light burned as he scanned the room. His breath caught in his throat. Willow was as still as death on the tiled floor.

Jake never remembered how he'd gotten to her so fast, but he was sitting on the floor; she lay in his arms, unmoving. He almost fainted with relief when he felt the warmth of her body. She was alive!

"Willow," he whispered as he shook her gently. "Willow, wake up, wake up." His hand moved cautiously over her body, feeling for anything that would give him a clue. Was she injured? An attack of some kind? What? Squelching the panic in his chest, he nearly cried when she made a sound. That moan was one of the sweetest things that he'd ever hear in years to come.

"Willow, love. Can you hear me?" he asked in an even voice. The last thing he wanted was for her to wake up to his panic. She must have fainted. Something must have scared her badly. Nat? he thought. His eyes burned brightly.

"J-Jake?" Willow opened her eyes.

"Yes, sweetness, I'm here with you." Jake held her still, when she sought to sit up. "Hold still a minute, Willow. Does anything hurt you? You must have fainted." Once again, he felt her, probing gently up and down her body. When his hand touched the back of her head, she cried out in pain.

"Oh!" Willow lifted her hand to her head. She felt the same knot, Jake had touched. "Ow" she said, her eyes closing against the pain.

Jake was worried. A knot that size meant she'd fallen hard, without warning—and—she'd been unconscious. She needed to see a doctor. He helped her sit up slowly. He stood up, then helped her to her feet, where she tottered into his arms. With his arms around her waist, he walked her out of the greenhouse and into the house. In the living room he sat her down on the sofa. He sat beside her, moving the envelope to the table, watching her curiously as she looked at it. With fear? he wondered. Before he could speak, she wound her arms around his neck.

"Oh, Jake," she whispered. "Hold me. Please, hold me here where I belong." Willow's body suddenly started to shake with soft sobs and her tears slid down Jake's neck.

He held her close. Oh, God, how good she felt against him. How could he have let her go for so long? He was a damned idiot. He was caught up in his work when he should have stolen a day here and there to be with her. Only a fool could be so dense.

"I'm here, darlin'," Jake crooned, and rocked her back-and-forth, gently, holding the back of her head. Careful, not to hurt her, he ran his fingers around the small mound, feeling for evidence of bleeding. His fingers came away clean and he wasn't sure that that was a good sign. Dorcas would know. Where was she? Jake frowned, brushed the hair away from Willow's cheek, and held her

until the sobs stopped. She clung to him as if she would
never let go, almost as if he were her lifeline. She trembled,
and words spilled from her mouth.

"Jake," Willow cried. "She left me. Aunt Dee left me. . . .
She . . . lied. She's a liar . . . all my life, I . . . had an aunt.
I . . . I have a sister! Jake . . . Dorcas is gone!" Willow buried her head in Jake's chest, the loud cries, muffled in the
dampened cotton of his shirt. "Oh, Jake, please, don't
leave me."

Anger smoldered in Jake's eyes as he held her close,
caressing her and soothing her with soft whispers of love.
He was there, he told her over and over. "Don't be afraid,
Willow, I won't leave you," he said, kissing her brow. "I'm
with you, darlin'."

Willow's heart ached. Her body ached. She felt that
she was losing her soul. Her mind was a jumble of the
horrible words she'd heard, the lies she'd been told,
and the terrible thoughts she had about herself. Suddenly, long-buried feelings surfaced, lifting her like a
giant wave, enfolding her, wanting to take her back out
to sea with them. Feelings of being alone. She didn't
want to be alone. People were always leaving her. People
who loved her for a while and then left her. Maybe if
she held him tight, Jake wouldn't follow all those others
who'd left her behind. She'd make him stay. She would.

Willow's sobs turned into soft moans as she rained kisses
on Jake's broad chest, straining to feel his warm flesh.
While her tongue pushed its way inside between the buttons, her hands groped at his shirt, tugging until it was
out of his jeans. She pulled it up, not waiting to unbutton
it, but ducked her head beneath and kissed his bare skin.
The taste of the salty flesh and the feel of the prickly hairs
on her cheek, made her groan. Impatient to feel more of
him, she began to loosen his belt buckle with one hand,
while the other was squeezing his hardened nipples.

Jake was unprepared for the fevered onslaught of his
person. She could not be stopped. He knew that intuitively.

Whatever was driving her, she needed to run with it until she left it behind. He could only take the ride with her. Jake unbuttoned his shirt, finished opening his belt buckle and unzipped his jeans, even as Willow's hands tugged at them and held on, as if he was going away. Her grip was strong.

"Willow," he said, putting her hand on his stomach so that she could still feel him. "I'm not going away. See, I'm still here." Jake stood up, kicked off his shoes and was out of his jeans and shirt in seconds. Willow was holding on to his thighs now, and he sat back down. She pushed him down on his back and threw herself on top of him.

"Love me, love me Jake," she cried. "I won't ever leave you. Love me," she moaned.

Jake closed his eyes and his mouth was a grim slash as he wished the person who'd made her feel such pain was within his grasp. He winced as Willow's teeth closed on his nipple a little too hard. She must have sensed the pain she'd caused because she caressed it with her tongue and then kissed it gently before she moved to taste the hollow of his throat. She kissed his mouth, seeking his tongue, suckling it and drawing it deeply into hers. Suddenly, she was crying again. Tears of frustration.

"Willow, love, I'm here. What is it, love?" Jake murmured in her ear. The tears were flowing heavily.

"I can't feel you," she cried.

Willow was fully clothed, wearing the sleeveless blouse and short skirt that she'd traveled in. Her skirt was bunched up around her thighs and her blouse and bra prevented her from getting next to him.

Jake, still holding her, pushed both of them up from the sofa. Holding her around the waist, he walked her to her bedroom and kicked the door shut even as he unzipped her skirt and let it fall to the floor. He lifted her arms and pulled the blouse over her head. Her bra was on the floor by the time they reached the bed. Jake pulled off his briefs and while she lay on her back looking up at him, he slipped off her panties. Jake lay down beside her, pulling her into his arms.

"Feel me, now, sweetness," he said, husky-voiced. The words were barely spoken before he felt Willow's naked form slide over him. Without a word, she began to love him with the same fierceness. Only now, she was so silent, no cries of pain, but moving as with a purpose. Jake lay with one arm flung over his head, the other resting on her back. He closed his eyes against the sweet pain.

Oh, Jake, Willow thought, *I feel you. I do feel you.* Willow tasted Jake again, never lingering in one spot long enough to savor. From his mouth to his ears, to his neck, she moved like a ferret, darting to its next delicious morsel. Her stomach was flat against his and her mound was pressed against his thickened flesh. She was rotating her hips in a slow, circular motion. Then, spreading her legs, her knees dug into the bed as she pushed herself up on her hands. Pressing down on him, her hips sped up in rhythm and she cried out at the friction of his hardness against her softness. Feverishly, she sought him, and then sitting up, she guided him into her secret place, then sank down. Her body accepted him begrudgingly at first, but at Willow's insistent pressure, her body softened and accepted Jake fully. Jake called her name, and she basked in the sound of his voice. *He is here, with me,* she thought. *He won't leave me.*

Willow's hips moved wildly as her hands clutched at the taut flesh covering Jake's ribs. At the moment when she thought she could stand no more of the exquisite pain, the fire inside of her was quenched with one last deep thrust from Jake that tore a scream from her throat. She sat, unmoving, until the quivers ended. Then, she fell.

Willow lay on top of Jake, her breasts heaving slightly. She was exhausted. But she closed her eyes with a smile on her lips. The voices in her head were gone—and Jake did not leave her.

Twenty-one

It was past midnight, one-thirty on Tuesday morning. Jake was thankful that he'd arranged to take some long overdue days off while Scott and Irene took care of some business in South Carolina. Jake wasn't due back to the site until Wednesday and he said a silent prayer. Willow would need him like she'd never needed anyone in her adult life. He only hoped that he was all she'd need.

When she'd fallen asleep almost two hours ago, he'd been grateful. Hopefully, sleep would quiet those demons that had chased her to that dark place where she'd sought to free herself so ferociously. He was glad he was there to be of use. She hadn't made a sound when he dressed her in a short cotton gown and covered her. The night had grown cool. He dressed himself then went through the house, turning out the extra lights and securing the doors. After checking each room on the upper floor, he left a hall light burning and returned to the kitchen where he prepared a meal of sausage, eggs and coffee.

Jake looked in on Willow and found her sleeping soundly. Satisfied, he went into Dorcas' bedroom. He had to make some sense of what had happened here. When Willow awakened, he wanted to be able to help her as much as possible.

The room had a lonely feeling, as if Dorcas had been gone for more than a few days. The closet held a few blouses and dresses. Two laundered uniforms were still encased in plastic. Jake frowned at them. If she wasn't returning, wouldn't she need them for work? he wondered. The dresser drawers were empty of a woman's lingerie and other things that needed dresser space. The top drawer held a few pieces of odd jewelry. The desk drawers held writing paper and envelopes, ledgers, and other business papers. Nothing of a personal nature had been left behind. Jake was puzzled. Dorcas had taken care of the paperwork. The running of the retreat, hiring personnel. Where was her directory? As though a fog lifted, Jake turned out the light and left the room. The chaos on Willow's desk!

Willow was still sleeping. He smiled when he noticed that her breathing was no longer choppy. At last, the demons were finally leaving. His gaze took in the desk. Much as he did not want to pry, what he was about to do was to save his love's sanity; give her peace of mind. He sat down and began to put the papers in some kind of order when he stopped. At second glance, he noticed that only the top layer of papers were laying helter-skelter. Underneath envelopes and clipped papers lay in neat piles. Picking up the largest envelope, Jake turned it over. He read the name aloud. "Dolores Jones."

Jake then stared at the picture of the woman who without a doubt could definitely be related to Willow. He didn't need to be told that he was looking at a picture of Willow's sister . . . the one she'd never known she'd had. As he began to scan, he shook his head, reading the birth certificate of a child born twenty-five years ago.

"Dorcas Williams," Jake said in a hushed voice. "What have you done?"

Now, Jake watched Willow awaken. He was sitting on the sofa and her eyes opened and she was staring at him. She smiled when her eyes focused, then filled with recognition. He went to her.

"Hello," he said simply, bending over to kiss her lips. Sitting down, he asked, "How are you feeling?"

Willow held out her arms and Jake caught her to him, holding her gently, mindful of her head. He felt the lump and it was not nearly as swollen.

"Fine, now," Willow said, sleepily. She hugged him around his waist. "Feel much better, now." Then, "What time is it? I feel as though I've been gone a long time," she said.

"It's one-thirty on Tuesday morning. You needed that time away." He held her from him. "Are you sure you're not hurting anywhere? Your head?"

Willow shook her head. "I don't have a headache. I'm okay Jake." She struggled to get out of bed. Jake stood by and steadied her on her feet. When she stood without wobbling, he let her go.

"See?" she said again. "Fine." She walked slowly to her adjoining bathroom.

Jake listened. Satisfied that she was fine, he sat down on the sofa and waited.

Willow washed up and brushed her teeth. She rinsed her mouth and ran her tongue over her teeth, liking the smooth, clean feel. She stared at herself and drew a breath at the look in her eyes. There was no bright smile. They looked haunted. What would Jake see when he finally looked at her? Really looked? She shivered at the feeling of revulsion that coursed through her when she remembered. His mother and my father! Lovers! Had he known and kept silent?

She turned out the light and returned to the bedroom. Jake was sitting on the sofa, waiting. She felt the wildest urge to take flight into the dark woods surrounding the house. She hesitated to go to him.

Jake saw the uncertainty in Willow's eyes. She was frightened. He held out his hand and she came to him. Pulling her down beside him, he pressed her head against his chest. She shivered. He frowned, feeling the goose bumps on her arm. Jake stood up and got the comforter off the bed. Soon, she was laying with her head on his lap, snuggled beneath the blanket. Jake smoothed the hair from her face and started caressing her cheek.

"Willow?"

She heard the soft rumble when it started in his chest and rose to his throat to emit that soft breath that ended with her name. Willow loved him more than ever at that moment. He would not pounce at her, demanding an explanation of her incoherent, rambling and wild behavior. He was a caring man.

"I felt so alone. I needed you and you were there."

"Always."

After a moment, Willow turned her head toward her desk. She looked at it then looked up at Jake.

"I read most of it," Jake said, answering the question in her eyes.

"I'm glad," said Willow. "I wouldn't have known how to start, without you thinking I had gone quite mad." Lifting the blanket, she caught his free hand and pressed it to her stomach.

Jake freed his thumb and slowly rubbed it back and forth against her hand.

"You know that Dorcas has left me. She did not tell me where she was going," Willow began.

Jake didn't answer, letting her speak without interrupting because he knew that with the telling, would come a semblance of acceptance.

"She's made everything so . . . so . . . final." Willow still felt confused. She knew her bewilderment sounded in her voice. "Closing the retreat, resigning from the hospital, putting the household business in order; she was very thorough." A low sound of frustration escaped. "There's not a thing for me to do or worry about." Beneath the blanket, Willow was still holding Jake's hand. She caught the thumb that was moving gently back and forth. "Jake? Do you remember one night, when you were a little boy, you were so patient with a little girl? Do you remember . . . me?"

"I'd forgotten, Willow. Until tonight," Jake said solemnly.

"Tonight?" She stirred on his lap. "Why, tonight? What happened to make you remember that night so long ago?" Willow looked up at Jake, and her heart started to race when she saw his wine-hued eyes grow dark with anger. *Something's happened!*

"Jake," Willow whispered, "what's wrong?" She sat up and stared at him, suddenly afraid. Could she bear any more horror stories?

Jake caught her against him and covered her again. Then placing an arm around her shoulders, settled her in the little hollow, pressing her head against his chest. "You've a right to be scared and confused Willow, but don't worry. We'll see this thing through, together."

In answer, Willow shuddered.

"Nat paid me a visit today about three o'clock. Around about the time you should have been ringing my bell. Instead, you were, I guess, listening to Dorcas bare her soul to you." His laugh was short and harsh. "How ironic that we should learn of our family histories together. As if they'd both planned it for years. The day. The time. Like a reaction to a hypnotic response."

"What, Jake?" She wished she could fall asleep, to dream, to drown out the words that would come to hurt her soul again.

"For years, Nat knew about my mother . . . and your father." As he spoke those words, Jake suddenly realized a truth about his brother. "His knowledge filled him with hate, warping his personality," Jake said in wonder. "Circumstances and chance make us who we become, after all." Pity began to take the place of hate and anger in Jake's heart for Nat.

Absently, Jake twirled a dark curl around his finger as he spoke. He told Willow everything. Repeating, almost verbatim, the words Nat used to taunt his brother with the family's dark secrets. Jake described the scene with his father, becoming incensed all over again at Lloyd Rivers' abnormal hatred for Willow. Jake told her of the years that his mother was gone and how he had felt like a little boy lost; and how after her return, she had lingered in illness, never to return to being the mother he once knew and loved. But Jake did not tell Willow why Olivia Rivers left her family. The words wouldn't come easily and he knew that he would have to regurgitate them. He knew that Willow would insist. Jake sucked in a breath because no sooner than the thought came and went, she was asking him.

"Why, Jake? I know she was embarrassed because of her infidelity with my father, and her best friend's husband. But why did she leave her two sons behind? I know she must have loved you very much." Willow was perplexed at a mother who would desert her children. Could she not have put her shame aside for the love of her boys?

"When my mother left us, Willow, she was carrying your father's child."

Willow's temples began to throb with the absorption of Jake's words. She sat up and rubbed her forehead, trying to erase the pain. If she could, she would dig inside of her head and pull out the damning ache. Pushing herself away from Jake, she sat so that she could see his face, watch his eyes.

"What did you say?"

Jake watched her closely. "That's why she left us."

A coldness, strange to Willow's body, enveloped her, wrapping itself around her heart. Later, Willow would remember thinking that the mind was a very strong part of the human body, built to withstand almost countless mental assaults. She was strong not to cave in to the compelling desire to be swept away into a sea of oblivion. To let the world carry on without her while she sought relief in the warmth of a cocoon. Neither the blanket nor the hands of her lover could warm her. The cold she felt was inured. Would she never feel warm and alive again?

Willow could hear a voice, then realized it was her own. It didn't sound like hers, she thought.

"So which is it that you have, Jake? A twenty-five year-old brother? Or sister?"

Jake's body almost recoiled at the sharp sarcasm coming from his warm and sensitive Willow. The voice was like a razor. If he closed his eyes he'd think that he was listening to a stranger. But his eyes were locked with her haunted ones. Oh, God, don't do this to us!

"My mother's daughter died at birth," Jake said quietly.

"Died?" Willow sounded puzzled. Not here to suffer? Never to wonder why she was ever born? Her voice was but a whisper. "How merciful."

"Willow!" Jake rapped. He grabbed her by the shoulders and held her tight. "Willow, snap out of this. That happened so long ago and has nothing to do with now . . . or us. Don't let past history sour you. Do you hear me?"

Willow looked at Jake. Then, in wonderment, looked down at his hands on her shoulders. He was holding her, touching her bare skin and she felt nothing. There was no electricity coursing through her body. But it was always there, she thought, dazedly. Always. Nothing could ever make that current between them die. Amazed, she looked into those burgundy-hued eyes. For the first time, she felt nothing; and she froze. There was nothing inside of her that spoke of warm feelings and love for this man. He was alien to her.

Jake died the moment she looked into his eyes because he knew the exact instant her love for him ceased to exist. She looked at him with the eyes of a stranger. Their link to the past so repulsed her that her mind closed the door to anyone or anything remotely connected to those shadows.

Jake let her go. What could he say now that would penetrate? That would mean anything to her bruised mind? How could he live without her? She was a part of who he had become since they declared their love. He watched as she shifted away and stood up. She swayed, but righted herself immediately, waving away his outstretched hand. His throat burned with the cry that was waiting to be released.

Willow walked to the bed and got under the sheet, shivering for the lack of warmth. She closed her eyes. *In the morning,* she thought, *I'll awake and the sun will be shining so brightly that tonight will only have been a nightmare. The whole day was just a bad dream.*

Jake walked to the bed with the blanket and covered her. His hand brushed her skin. She was ice-cold. He undressed to his briefs and slid into bed. He wrapped her in his arms, letting the warmth from his body spread to hers. When he closed his eyes, he prayed that this would not be the last time that she would fall asleep in his arms.

The sun shining through the curtained windows, awakened Willow. She sat up, looking about in confusion, suddenly remembering. Jake had been here. Where was he now? It was past nine-thirty in the morning when she glanced at the clock on her desk. She swung her legs over the side of the bed and stood up. Had he left her? Gone to work? She listened, but heard nothing. She was all alone again. Putting on a robe, Willow opened the door and instantly knew Jake was in the house. She smelled coffee and heard the sounds of breakfast being prepared. She closed the door. He did not leave her.

Willow undressed on her way to the bathroom. Under the shower, she closed her eyes and let the warm waterfall work its magic. But could it get inside of her brain to erase a day's sadness? No. There was nothing that powerful, she decided. She toweled herself dry then began to blow-dry her hair.

Jake walked down the hall to awaken Willow. He had a feeling she would stay in bed, hiding from a new day and what it would bring. He would not let that happen. He would help her as much as she would let him. At her bedroom door, he listened, but all was quiet. He knocked, then opened the door. He heard the sound of the dryer and immediately closed the door. Satisfied, he returned to the kitchen. This was a start, he thought.

Jake was at the table when Willow entered the kitchen. He was drinking from his cup of coffee. When he saw her, he stood up. "Morning, Willow," he said easily as he walked to the fridge and took out a container of orange juice. "Suppose you start with this before your eggs." He poured the juice and put it in front of her.

Willow had sat down, looking solemnly at Jake. "Good morning, Jake," she said. She lifted the glass and drank thirstily. She was hungry. "Thanks."

Jake was preparing her eggs the way he knew she liked them; over-easy, a little salt and pepper. He put them on a plate, added two strips of bacon and set it down. He'd found a pan of frozen biscuits in the freezer and had baked them. He buttered one and added it to her plate. He sat down across from her, buttering a second biscuit for himself and pouring a second cup of coffee. He'd already eaten.

The smell of food awakened a ravenous appetite in Willow. She ate hungrily, thinking that it seemed like days since she'd eaten a meal. The last food she'd tasted had been cheese and crackers with Dorcas, she remembered numbly. She ate in silence, savoring every bite, aware of Jake's watchful eyes. When she finished, she pushed her plate away and drank the last of her coffee.

"Thank you." Willow looked at Jake with appreciation. How thoughtful and unselfish he was, she thought.

"More coffee?" Jake asked.

"Thanks," Willow said, nodding, and holding out her cup.

Drinking deeply, of the stimulating brew, Willow closed her eyes, then opened them to meet Jake's eyes. She set down her cup.

"Thank you, Jake." Her meaning went deep.

Jake only nodded. She should know that her thanks was not necessary. Not with him. He waited for her to speak because he knew she wanted to talk. He sensed her continued bewilderment.

A bemused smile touched Willow's lips as she looked around the kitchen. It was a big room, enlarged since her parents' day. Her hand traced the whorls in the big pine table. "This is not the same table," she said. Her eyes met Jake's. "I remember when Dorcas bought this table. The one that my sister was conceived on, must have been thrown out years ago, when the former renters took over the place." She gestured in the general direction of the pool area. "Your half-sister must have been conceived in the cabana." She tilted her head. "You remember. I told you what Dorcas told me. That my mother caught my father and your mother together?"

"Willow, don't do this to yourself," Jake said.

"I have to talk about it, Jake. Otherwise it will fester inside of me like a smelly old sore. I have to be free to talk. It won't change what's happened, but I will learn to deal with this." She stood up. "Let's leave this place." She looked around and shuddered, as if she felt the touch of the specters hovering about, and quickly turned and left the room.

Jake followed her onto the porch. He sat next to her, in the same chair he'd occupied that night, months ago, when he'd come for dinner. How long ago that was, he thought. A happy time, when he'd first known he had deep feelings for her. So long ago.

"Jake?"

"I'm here, Willow."

Willow smiled. "I know you are."

"What are you thinking, Willow?" he added softly.

"Why do you think that this . . . this . . . thing that has happened to me . . . to us, has hit me so hard?" Her voice was low and halting as she sought to verbalize her jumbled thoughts. Neither waiting for a response, nor expecting one, she said, "Every day you can read about a story like ours." She laughed. "Secret love-child story lines, run rampant on the soaps. If not, they'd dry up and disappear from lack of viewer interest. Infidelity? What's that? It's almost expected, and is something that just is. No great shakes or something to lose sleep over." She looked around the gardens, her gaze sweeping the property. "I think that I've sheltered myself in here, behind these gates, believing that my whole world existed here." She turned to Jake. "Don't misunderstand me. I'm not ignorant of what goes on out there. It's just that I never associated myself with the sordidness that happens in normal people's lives. That's something that went on out there. Whenever I leave here, I have a purpose that concerns me and what I do. I love my work, the people I come in contact with because of my work. I love the volunteering that I do with the students. I love the interaction with Tommy and the other culinary students. I love traveling to the city occasionally to meet with my editor and my agent. But you see, all those things have to do with me and what I do. It's all about me. Whenever I returned here, I was coming back to my shelter where I knew that I was safe. Dorcas was here. My work was here. That's all I ever needed or wanted." She smiled. "Until you happened to me."

Jake smiled.

She continued. "I had no worries. Nothing disturbed my peace. I was blessed that I had a happy and contented life. My world was not tainted. Not even with how I'd become an orphan. That was a time before I remembered anything of significance. I could only remember happiness with Aunt Dee, Uncle Thomas and my Grandy. I was a loved little girl, and I knew it."

"You're loved now, Willow."

Willow's lashes flickered at the pain she heard. Loved? But, for how long? she wondered. She was cold inside now. Cold to him and his love. Because of whose children they were, they could never be wholly free of the repulsive link to the past.

As if he knew her thoughts, Jake spoke. "Willow, you're wrong. I've told you that this is now. We're now, and the future. Our children will only know love because we'll show them. Nothing will harm them. You have to believe in us and that we can have a good life together. A happy life." He stood up and went to her, forcing her to look into his eyes, when he cupped her chin in his hand. At that moment, he knew that she was right. The warmth that electrified him whenever they touched, was nonexistent. He felt nothing. Her closure was like a magnetic field keeping him out. His heart was suddenly filled with sadness. He felt desolate. Earlier, when he'd sensed the death of her love for him, he'd continued to hope that he could turn things around; make her see that her thinking was wrong, almost abnormal. But this lack of feeling on his part, told the tale. Could they never get it back? That feeling that had made them part of each other? He dropped his hand and leaned one shoulder against the sturdy porch pole. He watched her.

Willow nodded her head. "See," she said. "It's gone." She'd felt the instant of his understanding—and his withdrawal. She met his eyes. "You felt it, too." The statement was said softly.

"It would seem so," Jake answered. His voice was strained.

Willow stood up. The morning was fast turning into noon and the sun was shining bright and hot. Willow removed the light sweater she'd donned before going outside, and tossed it on the chair. She inhaled the faint fragrance of the last remaining wildflowers, her gaze scanning the well-kept gardens. She frowned. The beauty of the Cove did not have the same meaning for her anymore. There was no beauty here. It was all false. Her look spanned the old structure. There was no beauty inside. It's held ugly secrets all these years. It was just a house. Not the loving, safe haven her aunt had made it out to be.

But, she thought, there is a place I was always happy here. Walking pass Jake, she stepped down off the porch.

"Where are you going, Willow?" He knew, and he despaired.

Willow looked up at him as he stood on the top step, watching her intently. "I have to go Jake." She gestured toward her studio. "I must think. Must work." Her eyes pleaded with him for understanding. And forgiveness. "Jake. I need this time. To sort myself out."

"Alone?"

"Yes."

Before she walked away, Jake asked, "What of your sister, Willow? What do you intend to do about Dolores Jones? You're doing to her what your aunt did to her sister. You're family. You need each other now." He winced at his next words. "If you won't let me back inside of you, Willow, open up your heart for your only sister."

Willow listened. Here? Bring her here? Why in God's name would she want to visit this place where she began in lust and shame?

Willow looked up at Jake. "Why do you think that that would be good for her, Jake? Bringing her here to live?" She lifted a shoulder. "What good could come from that? She already has a life. Why disrupt it now?"

"Because you're all the family she has. You and Dorcas. She has a right to make up her own mind whether she wants to welcome you into her life."

Willow only shrugged.

Jake gestured about the grounds and the house. "This

is not the only place you can live, Willow. You must know that. Begin again, somewhere else. Just the two of you. Try to find some peace and make something positive happen out of all of this." He hesitated. "Maybe one day, you'll let yourself try to love again."

Willow thought, maybe, one day. She turned to leave. "Good-bye, Jake. I'm sure I'll only need a little time, then everything will be okay. Just a little time," she murmured. She walked around the side of the house and toward her studio. Willow never turned around. If she had she would have seen him standing at the edge of the house, watching.

Jake had to smile at old words and memories when he saw her bend to get the key from its hiding place, and unlock the door. When she disappeared inside, Jake stood for several seconds, his gaze fixed on the cottage. He felt that she'd walked away from him forever. It would take just about that long before he would forget her. He turned and walked to his car.

Jake opened the door but turned and looked back at the house. The structure was beautiful, but imposing. It was haunting. As he slid behind the wheel and closed the door, he wondered if Willow would find it so. The gravel crunched beneath his wheels as he drove to the gate. He fervently wished that she would leave this place before it withered her soul.

Time passed by so quickly, Willow thought as she dried the last dish and put it in the cupboard. She opened the door of the dishwasher, leaving it open so that all the water would evaporate. She tied the garbage bag and took it outside, disposing of it in the big trash barrel. Inside the kitchen, with one final glance, satisfied that she had left nothing undone, she turned out the light and shut the door.

It was two weeks ago yesterday, that she'd returned home

from her Canadian tour to find that her life had changed. Two weeks ago today that she had walked out of Jake's life.

That Tuesday, when she'd heard him drive away, she did not feel anything. She had tried, but she was numb. She had walked to her easel, uncovered her brushes, oils and palette and prepared a canvas. Willow had stayed for hours in her studio, painting. When she tired, she slept on the couch, only to awaken and begin painting again. Dawn arrived before she left the cottage. She walked to the house where she was startled by the housekeeper. She'd forgotten. Dorcas had arranged for the housekeeper to come for five days a week to cook and clean. Willow mechanically ate the meal prepared for her before she returned to the studio. For the next two days her routine was the same. By Saturday, exhausted, she returned to her bedroom where she slept, dreamless. On Sunday, Willow fixed leftovers from the housekeeper's previous meals. On the following days, Willow had walked about the grounds, and strolled into the nearby woods. She'd taken the Mercedes for servicing, then walked in and out of the village shops. She would stay in her room for hours, sketching. She was not surprised that several of her pictures were of Jake, in various moods. She was surprised that there were several of her aunt. Dorcas, smiling and happy. Dorcas, angry. Dorcas, the last time she'd seen her: sad, as she closed the door on her life at Wildflowers Cove.

For days, while she painted, Willow couldn't shake the feeling that she had to remember something. An insistent nagging that fought to surface. She only felt it when she was painting and the pungent oils penetrated her nostrils. She'd leave the studio, thinking the memory would appear like magic, but it never did. When she picked up her brush, the feeling reappeared. Frustrated, Willow tried to banish it from her mind, but like a bad dream, it stayed, toying with her, laughing at her. Willow threw the brush across the room. She shouted, "Damn you, whatever you are. What do you want from me?'' Feeling foolish at her actions, and her anger that was directed at no one within earshot of her ridiculous outburst, she went to pick up the brush.

The moment she had it in her hand, she remembered. And heard the voice. *"Patience, little Willow. You won't learn it all in one day, baby. Patience."*

Willow froze. Her mother! That was her mother's voice. She sat down on the sofa, brush in hand, and she remembered. It had been her mother's paints that she'd smelled all those years ago, not her father's. Memories fell in a jumble before her, and she watched the pictures play, as if she were a spectator at a movie.

Her father's workplace was full of pens and colored pencils and inks and funny characters on big boards hanging on the walls. Her mother's workspace was a small room that smelled of oil paints and brought a warm feeling to Willow. It was her mother's paints that she smelled but had always associated with the great sketch artist Michael Vaughn!

Where was that room? Willow wondered. She left the cottage and ran to the house. She raced up the stairs, running into the huge room that had once been her parents' bedroom. She stood in the middle of the floor, looking about, trying to see the room from a four-year-old's eyes. The bed, the dresser, her mother's dressing table. She remembered where they'd stood! But there was no little painting corner that she could remember. Not in here. She raced down the hall to each of the rooms. Finally, she found it. It was the smallest of the guest rooms.

Willow stood in the doorway and remembered. She closed her eyes and saw her mother in the little window alcove, an easel placed to catch the light. She saw herself, with her own little easel, dressed in a smock like her mother's. She saw herself wiping paint all over it to imitate the colorful splotches on her mother's easel. Willow heard her mother's laugh at her daughter's antics. A silvery laugh that tickled Willow's ears whenever she heard it. "You sound like Santa's bells, Mommy," she heard herself say, and the tinkle of the pretty sound again.

Willow walked to the room next door. *This was my room,* Willow thought. She went inside and walked around, feeling herself here as a little girl. She couldn't remember her years spent in this room and turned to leave when she stopped. The door was cracked and she could hear something. Noise. Then her mother's voice telling her to go to sleep. It wasn't time for tea. The teakettle! I heard the whistling of the teakettle that night!

Willow closed her eyes, forcing herself to remember. What happened after she left me? What did I hear? Or see? Willow stepped back into the room trying to see it as it was back then, but she couldn't. She didn't remember how the furniture was placed or what it looked like. Now, there were voices. Loud, angry. Then quiet. She was sleeping. Or was she dreaming when she thought she heard her mother's voice again? But the image and sounds suddenly vanished.

Frustrated, Willow left the room and went downstairs into Dorcas' bedroom. This had been Michael Vaughn's studio. She stood for a long moment, eyes closed, inhaling deeply. After a while she opened her eyes. She had felt nothing of her father in this room. Only the essence of Dorcas Williams. She turned and left the room closing the door with finality.

In her room, Willow pulled her luggage from the closet. The housekeeper had unpacked the bags from her trip and put her clothes away. She searched her storage closet for warm clothing then began to pack her bags. She'd decided that she was going to a place where she'd known happiness for most of her life. Maybe she could find it again. For a few short months she had been blissfully happy with the man whom she thought would become her husband. But, since that was not to be, she was going back to the place where she'd spent her happiest days. She was going back home!

That was yesterday, and now Willow was ready. She'd contacted the housekeeping company, canceling their service, but arranging for them to close up the house. The gardening and greenhouse service would continue until further notice. The proper calls were made to the utility and the phone companies. After closing, locking and securing everything she could think of, Willow carried her luggage outside, unlocked the trunk of her Mercedes and started loading it with her bags.

Once she'd decided to leave, Willow had started to make plane reservations but thought better of it. She would need her car in Toronto. After a few weeks in a residence hotel, she expected to rent a small house in the suburbs. She loved the countryside. She slammed the trunk.

Inside the house, Willow went into the living room. She found what she wanted, then walked to the front door, and locked it.

Willow slid behind the wheel of the big car. She placed the lavender envelope inside her oversize, red leather handbag and placed it on the passenger seat. She started the engine and with one last look at Wildflowers Cove, drove onto the gravel driveway.

"Whatever you had to say to me mother," Willow said out loud, "I'm not ready to hear. Sometime in the future, maybe, but not now."

Without a backward glance, she drove onto the roadway, heading up North.

Twenty-two

When Dolores Jones left work at six-thirty, the evening had brought with it a brisk and cold wind. The whole month of October had been unseasonably cold. She pulled her scarf tighter around the collar of her red wool coat and hurried the four blocks to her apartment. On the eve of Halloween, she wanted to be indoors, not colliding with premature ghosts and goblins who meant more harm than mischief. She was grateful for the doorman because that meant no surprise visits from the would-be pranksters.

She retrieved her mail, glanced at it, then took the elevator to her third-floor apartment. Her pretty face was marred with a frown, and her heart sank.

An hour later, Dolores was on the living room sofa, dressed in baggy sweatpants and a long-sleeve turtleneck. She had finished her meal of tomato soup and tuna fish sandwich and was sipping hot tea. Her gaze scanned the mail that she'd placed on the long glass table. Bills. That was all.

No matter how many times she looked at the envelopes, the one that she wanted to see was simply not going to materialize merely because she wished it.

Every day for almost two months, she allowed herself high expectations only to be let down with a bang.

Since that day in August when she'd received a visit from a relative she'd never known existed, she lived from day to

day hoping. Hoping that either of her relatives would contact her. She reached over to the table and picked up some
papers that were worn from handling. Dolores had read
them many times, the letter and other information that
Dorcas Williams had brought to her on her second visit. It
had been the last week in August, and Dorcas had been
waiting for her when she arrived home from work. Dolores
had prepared a light meal and then spent the rest of the
evening talking and listening to the history of her family.

Dorcas Williams left late that night, after midnight.
She'd said that she wouldn't visit again, that she was going
away. She'd urged Dolores to put away her pride and contact Willow Vaughn. Both sisters would be hurting, she'd
said, but someone had to make an effort in taking that
first step toward healing.

Dolores did. Three days after Dorcas' visit, Dolores still
had not received a call or letter from her sister. She'd decided to be the one to break the ice. She called. She'd
been so nervous. What would they say to each other?
Would they like each other?

There was no need to worry because there had been no
answer. Only the message machine. After leaving two messages and writing one letter, Dolores had given up. Never
had she felt so desolate. Not even when her mother died
had she felt so alone. Her mother had been ill and Dolores
had come to accept that one day she would be alone.

But that had changed with the visit from a stranger. She
had family, an aunt and a sister! Neither of whom had made
her a part of their lives, she thought bitterly. *Why didn't
Dorcas stay away? Why come into my life, then abandon me?*

Dolores got up, cleared the table and washed the few
dishes. She turned out the light and went into the bedroom.
Although it was barely eight-thirty, Dolores prepared for
bed. Lately, she found herself retiring earlier than was really
necessary. She wasn't overworked or tired. She knew that
she only wanted to close her eyes against the awful loneli-

ness that she felt. She'd discovered that sleep was the perfect cure-all. When she awakened each morning, she hurried to work, knowing that there would be no time for personal lamentations. Her mind was kept busy with other people's problems. She put on an act of being bright and inquisitive while gathering information for her stories. Before she knew it, the day was over and she prepared to leave for home. Only then did that void in her life present itself. But she'd learned how to deal with it.

Now, as she lay in bed, she closed her eyes, but wiped away the dampness before settling into a deep sleep.

Twenty-three

Jake heard the elevator and then the footsteps in the corridor. When the office door opened, he looked up in surprise at Tala McCready. He jumped up and went to her.

"Are you crazy?" he yelled, as he helped her to a chair, relieving her of the shopping bag that she carried. "Does Brian know you're out in this mess?" he asked in dismay. "And what is this you're lugging around?" He already knew, because the pungent aroma of roast turkey filled the room.

Tala unzipped her jacket and removed her wool cap. "Whoa! Emotion. At last I got a rise out of you, fellah. Sorry I didn't think about doing this, weeks ago." She patted her protruding stomach. "Guess this little girl is feeding on my brain food."

Jake looked out the window and gestured. "You didn't drive here?" Last night, new snow had fallen on top of old, and the streets were slick with icy snow. It was still snowing lightly.

"No, father hen. I used the car service. The driver is waiting for me, and yes, Brian knows where I am and he's expecting me back in no more than an hour or else." She pointed to the shopping bag. "Now open that up, and eat. I'm not leaving here until you finish." Her eyes narrowed. "If you don't want Brian on that phone, you'd better start now," she threatened.

Jake grimaced but opened up the bag. Immediately, he

felt hungry and wondered when he had last eaten a real meal. Yesterday, Thanksgiving Day, he had stopped by the hospital briefly, then had driven here to the office. The building was deserted and he'd left soon after arriving to eat a Thanksgiving meal in a nearby restaurant. The food tasted like cardboard and he left without finishing it. Back in the office, he wondered if the real reason he'd hurried out of there was because he'd heard nothing but laughter, and the friendly chatter that families made.

"You made this?" he asked, as he looked at the spread on the plate. The food had been kept hot by benefit of a warming plate and he dipped into the steaming corn pudding and tasted. "Uh-uh," he said, taking another forkful. "You didn't make this."

"Bite your tongue, you ingrate." Tala laughed then smiled as she watched her friend dig hungrily into the food. A traditional holiday meal with yams, cranberry sauce, collards and the works, including sausage stuffing. "My usual caterer. She never fails me. If it wasn't for her keeping Brian fed, I would have been divorced long ago," she said.

"Not a chance. He's a smart man," Jake said between bites of turkey and stuffing.

Tala remained quiet, letting him eat in peace. She got up and walked to the window. Although it was just past three o'clock, the gray skies made it seem much later. She was glad she made this trip. Yesterday, when she'd phoned him to wish him a Happy Thanksgiving, she'd thought he was visiting his father. When she'd tried again later and had still received no answer, on a hunch, she'd called the office, and lambasted him for being there. There was no good reason for him to spend his holiday, poring over drafts and plans that could wait for a normal workday. On second thought, she contradicted herself, there was a good reason. He didn't want to be alone. At home.

Tala heard him get up, remove the remnants of his meal

and go to the rest room where she heard him washing up. When he returned, she sat back down.

"Well?"

"Delicious, Mac," Jake said gravely. "Thanks. How'd you know I needed that?"

"Mother's intuition."

Jake scoffed. "You're not a mother, yet."

"All right then. Woman's intuition."

Jake looked at his watch. "Hour's nearly up," he said.

"So it is, but I'll skedaddle in a few, now that I know you won't pass out from starvation." She looked intently at him. "Jake, you're taking care of yourself, aren't you? I mean physically. Mentally, well, that takes a mountain of time to get better." She cleared her throat. "Has he changed any?"

Jake stared back, trying to keep the pain hidden from his dark eyes. He knew what she meant, but chose to respond to her mention of his father. "He's still in the coma. Of course, there's no telling when or if he'll ever come out of it." He shrugged. "It's been nearly two months, with virtually little change. I never stay long when I visit. He doesn't know I'm there."

"Are you sure of that?"

Jake shrugged again. "No." He looked away. "But maybe, I don't really care one way or the other."

Tala didn't disagree with him. His father had hurt him badly and Jake was still feeling the pain. He'd told her all that had happened on that day in September. His brother's taunts. His father's admissions. And Willow. How much could one man take and not become bitter? For all his quiet ways, Jake Rivers had a big heart and much love inside to share with others. She only hoped that not too much time passed before he found happiness again. One thing she would not do was interfere and lecture. He needed her to continue being the friend she'd always been.

"Tala?"

She turned from the window and slipped on her jacket

and cap. "Okay, okay, father hen, I'm going." She walked to where he was sitting, one hip on the desk. She kissed him on the cheek and hugged him, then walked to the door. "Lights out soon for you, too, friend. Otherwise you might be bunking with us tonight. See ya," she said and closed the door softly behind her.

Jake listened to the elevator door close then went to the window. The snow was falling heavier than it was when Tala had arrived. She was right. He'd be snowed in if he didn't leave soon. He went to the desk and tidied up, putting the drafts back in the cabinet. He checked his watch. It was after four, but maybe Mrs. Benson had not left yet. He pressed the numbers for his father's office.

"Hello?"

"It's Jake, Mrs. Benson, I'm glad I caught you. Is it bad up there?"

"Hello, Jake," answered Mrs. Benson. "You caught me putting on my coat. It's coming down-pretty hard, so I thought I'd better leave now. I left a message on your voice mail."

"Oh, anything wrong?"

"No. I'm glad I came in today because I think we may have a buyer. The people who were here early in October. Well, they're interested and asked if the business was still available. I told them it was. I left all the information for you in my message."

Jake said a silent prayer. "Thanks, Mrs. Benson. I'll try to get in there on Monday. Mrs, Benson," he added, "thanks for all you've done. You know we appreciate it."

She'd hung up, clucking her tongue. He knew that she'd been embarrassed at his words. She was a fixture and considered herself family she'd said firmly. Weren't nothing at all.

Jake reached Westchester after six o'clock, but instead of heading home, he drove to Elmsford. At his father's

house, after checking windows and doors, he checked the
water in the boiler. Satisfied, he then cleared the walk and
the drive, put the snowblower in the garage and returned
to the house. He'd forgotten to check the refrigerator. He
always looked to see if there was any sign that his brother
had returned. As usual, the refrigerator was empty. There
had not been any edibles inside since the week of his father's stroke. Jake had only seen Nat once during that time
and that had been at the hospital. After that, Nat had simply disappeared. Nat's ex-wife had said that she'd seen him
once when he stopped by to say good-bye to his daughter.
He was leaving New York, he'd said. He didn't say where
he was going, or when he would return.

Jake hesitated at the front door, deciding to check upstairs for any sign of roof leaks. Two years ago, his father
had had some shingles replaced. They may be worn by now,
Jake thought, especially with the damage the winter had
wrought so far. He looked for signs of seepage in every room
and on each ceiling and wall. He stopped in his father's
bedroom longer than necessary. Standing in the doorway,
he recalled the last time he'd seen his father in this room.

After leaving the Cove on the day he'd lost his love, instead of heading home, he had gone to Elmsford. To this
day, he never knew why. He couldn't remember whether
he wanted to beat up on Nat or berate his father. He wanted
to lash out at someone for the anger and betrayal that had
swelled up inside of him, causing his blood to boil. He
thought then that he knew what an enraged bull must feel
like being goaded to attack. He'd entered his father's house
feeling that murderous rage. The downstairs was quiet. Jake
had raced up the stairs, hoping to find Lloyd in the bedroom where he'd left him, agonizing over his dead wife.
The woman he'd maligned until her death.

Jake had stood in the doorway, looking down at the inert
form of his father, still clutching the letters written to him
by his dead wife. Lloyd Rivers was still breathing. Jake saw

the slow rise and fall of his chest and saw the shallow breaths. He went downstairs and called for help, then went back to his father and waited. He never touched him. Jake sat down on the bed, staring at the man who had hated his sons for so many years—for no good reason other than his own miserable, pent-up hatred. This man was his father. He should show some sadness, care that he might die. But Jake's heart was hardened against the man who claimed to have loved his wife. How could he? How could a man treat the woman he loved with such disdain and coldness? Small pictures of memory glided across Jake's mind. Now, that he was older, he understood. But then, when he was a little boy, he had wondered at the cold voice, filled with disdain whenever Lloyd spoke to his wife. His mother's voice, always soft, never loud or angry. Jake put a feeling to that voice. Thankful! His mother was grateful to her husband for allowing her to return home to her sons. And his father had relished her constant air of humility. He had loved it! Jake's lips curled in disgust. *Love? He says he loved her? God help me if I ever treat my lady like that in the name of love,* he thought.

Jake left the room. As he locked the door and walked to his car, he thought, almost absently, that he would have to get back over here in the morning to clear away the new snow.

Two hours after he'd reached home, Jake was still at his computer, checking over the faxes he'd received from Scott and then inputting the information in his computer files. Jake was relieved that he did not have a worry in the world where his business was concerned. No, that wasn't true. He grinned. When Scott left in a few months, Jake was going to have to seriously think about hiring a manager to help run the business. Irene had secured so many new contracts that Scott had had to put a rein on her. Overload could be almost as bad as not enough. Jake smiled at that conversation, recalling Scott's words. "She'd better not fall down on the job when we move south," he'd playfully threatened.

Stretching, Jake turned off the computer and stood up. His friends were still in South Carolina. They'd taken the week off to oversee the building of their new home, which was scheduled for completion in the spring. Jake frowned. A few months later, their commitment to Jake would end and they would leave New York. Jake wished that they would stay. He was going to miss them. Besides them and Tala and Brian, he had no other close friends. He shrugged, wondering why he felt so sad about that. That's the way it had always been. He had never been gregarious. He was all about working and making a success of himself. He'd never thought he had been lonely. Until recently.

Since that first week in September he had worked hard at the site and from there had visited the hospital almost daily, checking on any change in his father's condition. By the first of October, his father had been moved to a nursing facility where his condition had not improved. There had been several trips back and forth from the facility to the hospital for various tests and treatment. That was the routine. Jake had stopped making daily visits and made it a practice to visit once a week, relying on calls to the nursing staff for updates. Otherwise, he would not have been able to function properly at work. He made sure he kept himself busy. He did not have to think about other things—or people. Or her.

Jake hurt inside whenever Willow's name came to mind, so he tried to train his inner voice to keep the refrain silent. But, sometimes, it didn't work. Like now. He had more time to think, with the weather keeping him inactive on many days.

On Thanksgiving Day, he'd wondered where she was and how she was spending the family holiday. Was she okay?

Jake was in the kitchen, watching the last of the water drip into the coffeepot, making that final gurgling sound that signaled the end of the brewing process. The aroma stung his nostrils. Pouring the strong brew into a mug, he took it into the living room. He sat, tasting the dark liquid, then picked up some papers. He'd copied down the information Mrs. Benson had left concerning the potential buyers of Lloyd Rivers Landscaping. Jake had made the decision to put the business up for sale when it became evident that his father was no longer responsible or capable of making decisions. Jake had refused to compromise on the selling price. Probably because of the memories he had when he was a boy following his father around, or maybe because of the years of sweat and hard work his father spent to make it a success. That had to stand for something, in all of this mess, Jake had thought. The buyers, obviously were going to accept Jake's asking price. On Monday he would know for sure.

Once the business was sold, Jake would see to it that Mrs. Benson could retire comfortably. She had been the mainstay of that business ever since Jake could remember. As for Nat, Jake shrugged, well, his share could go to his former wife and his daughter. That's little enough that Nat could do for them. If Nat ever returned, he could take the matter up with his brother.

Jake replenished his mug and returned to the living room where a sudden gust of wind rattled the glass doors leading to the patio. He walked to the doors, checking for security. His glance fell on the covered grill and his thoughts flashed back to the day he'd doused the hot coals, listening to the searing heat. The ribs had long been cooked and he'd waited in vain for her to appear, never thinking that she would never step foot into this place again. Later, days later, when he was tossing the spoiled food into the trash, he had gotten a strange thought. How many hungry people could have enjoyed a decent meal? Afterward, he had laughed at himself. He had lost his life and he was standing in the middle of his kitchen, wondering who could have enjoyed the remnants of a picnic meal? He had thought then that he was going a little crazy. Going? He *was* crazy, wondering where the love of his life had gone.

It was weeks later, that Jake had stopped cold in his tracks at work. He remembered that last night, the night that Willow, in a frenzied state, had made love to him with a wild abandon. She was not protected. They had made love, unprotected. Could she be carrying his child? Would she ever tell him?

Now, that same thought was running through Jake's mind. *Willow, how can you not know that I still love you so deeply? You must feel it. You have to hear my voice. Why are you ignoring it?*

Jake's anguished cry broke the silence in the room. "Willow, come back to me. I love you."

Four weeks after Thanksgiving, Lloyd Rivers Landscaping was sold. The last week in December, only days before the end of the year, the papers had been signed and the deal cemented. Almost immediately, Jake had the lawyers draw up the agreement taking care of Mrs. Benson and Nat's ex-wife and daughter. Jake had made only one concession before the sale became final and to which the new owners agreed. The Cove contract would not be part of the deal. Jake could not trust anyone but a Rivers, caring for the grounds. Land that had been tended by a Rivers before Jake was born. The greenhouse had been built by his father. Many of the trees and bushes had been planted by his father.

Jake had sold the contract to himself, to J. Rivers Landscape Contracts. Scott and Irene would manage the property. As instructed by Willow Vaughn before she left the Cove, maintenance would be continued by Lloyd Rivers Landscaping until further notice. Jake aimed to comply with her wishes.

It was New Year's Eve, and Jake was driving onto the snow-covered drive of Wildflowers Cove. He stopped and looked at the house before getting out of the car. The unlived-in structure was as imposing as ever. He slid from beneath the wheel and walked to the greenhouse and unlocked it. One thing he could say, all the gardeners in the employ of his father were excellent and knew their stuff. Jake needed only a glance to see that the plants and flowers were healthy and thriving. If Willow returned today, she would only have to take her pick of the beautiful blooms to paint. He locked the door and walked around the grounds as far as the woods. The snow covered the gardens and wildflower beds, but he knew that they had been prepared before the onset of winter. Of that he had no doubt. He walked to the cottage. He brushed away the snow and his fingers touched the brass key. He pushed in the door. Though the smell of oil paint was in the air, his nostrils did not sting as they used to whenever he entered the room. Gone was the smell he associated with her. No faint flowery scent hung in the air. This was a room full of ghosts. Jake smiled at his thought as he stared at the dust cloths covering the paintings. A glance at the couch evoked memories of many pleasant hours spent there.

Jake turned out the light and locked the door. When he replaced the key and walked away, he wondered whose hand would touch it next. A mover's to clean out the place for new owners? Or Willow's? Would she ever return?

For the last time, Jake looked at the house. He drove away, vowing not to let sadness overtake him again. He had promised Scott and Irene that he would drop by tonight for a few hours. They would not take no for an answer when they'd invited him to bring in the New Year with them and a few other friends. Jake had agreed only to keep them from worrying about him. He knew he was blessed to have people like them care whether he lived or died. It was more than he'd thought about himself the last few months. A heavy sigh escaped. Who knew what this New Year would bring? Another chance to grasp happiness? He laughed.

"Never," he murmured. "How many times in a life, can love like that happen? It will never happen again!"

"Hey, guy," Scott said, "you lightened Reenie's pockets by twenty bucks,"

"Oh yeah? How's that?" asked Jake.

"Me of little faith," chimed Irene. She sheepishly looked at Jake. "I bet that we'd have to go to your place and drag you over here." Her brown eyes sparkled. "I'm glad I lost that one, Jake." She kissed his cheek. "We're happy you're here."

Scott squeezed his shoulder. "That we are."

Jake looked at his two friends. "Thanks." There was nothing more to be said.

There were interesting people at the party. Some Jake had met before, others he recognized from business. Although Jake knew that it wasn't intentional because his friends knew of his feelings, a few single women were present who let him know that they were interested. At one point during the evening, Scott approached him.

"Look, Jake," Scott said, with a shrug of his shoulders. "I hope you don't think Reenie and I set you up." He indicated the guests with a nod of his head. "It just happened. Some of the ladies intended to come alone and a couple were stood up at the last minute. We know your feelings are still . . . well, you know what I mean. Just want you to know that nothing was planned."

Jake felt his friend's uneasiness. "I know, Scottie. Stop worrying about me. I'm doing just fine." His gaze covered the room. "You have some great folks here, making it a great party." He stared at a woman with whom he'd spoken to earlier in the evening. "I think we all know that tonight is just for fun."

Scott followed his friend's look to the pretty woman with smooth, dark-brown skin and naturally-styled, short black hair. He'd seen her and Jake in pleasant conversation. Later they had danced, but when the music slowed, Jake had led the woman off the dance floor. Scott knew what that was all about. Jake hadn't held another woman in his arms since Willow. He still wasn't ready to get that close. Scott sometimes wondered if he would ever be.

"Maybe," Scott answered his friend. "You're a young, good-looking, eligible bachelor, my friend. You can't blame the lady for trying."

"I don't," Jake said in a low voice. "God help me, if I ever do."

Scott clapped his friend on the shoulder. "You're going to be just fine, my friend. In time. All in time."

New Year's Day was cold and gray. Jake pulled the long wool scarf tighter around his neck as he put the snowblower away and locked the garage door. He'd already checked the Elmsford house, and now he walked cautiously on the salt he'd thrown on the cement walk. He drove carefully on the icy streets, anxious to get back home. He was chilled to the bone. And tired. He'd stayed far later at the Andersons' than he'd planned. But, he was glad that he'd gone. Bringing in the New Year with friends had meant a lot. He wasn't one to make resolutions, but he'd given a lot of thought to how he wanted to start off this year. Business, as always, was important, but so was family. There was no hope of ever reconciling with his father whenever he came out of the coma. Jake was too bitter and he was certain his father would never change. They would merely remain as polite strangers. Who knew where in the world Nat was. Jake was not interested in reconciling with his brother because, try as he did in the past, he could never like the person his brother had become. Now he hoped that it wasn't too late for the little family he had left. His former sister-in-law Annette, and her daughter, Kendra. His niece would turn thirteen this year, and Jake promised himself that he would become a better uncle.

Jake draped his damp jacket over a kitchen chair, then put the kettle on. His insides needed warming. He dropped a slice of lemon in the mug and before he could shrug out of his heavyweight sweater, the phone rang. "No business emergencies on New Year's Day, thank you very much," he said aloud. He picked up.

"Hello?"

"Mr. Rivers?" the female voice said. "This is Nurse Bartley from Mercy Hospital."

Jake clenched the phone. "Yes?"

"Your father. He's awake. He came out of the coma an hour ago. The doctor is asking for a member of the family."

"I'm on my way."

Jake was startled by the whistle from the kettle. He turned off the burner, then mechanically, shrugged into his jacket. The hospital was no more than a fifteen-minute drive, but on the treacherous ice, it would take close to an hour.

Jake drove slowly, wondering what he and his father would have to say to each other.

Twenty-four

"Mr. Rivers, I'm Dr. Pincus. Glad you could come on such short notice. Have a seat."

Jake shook hands with the doctor he'd never seen before, then took the chair across from the desk. He waited.

"As you know, your father's condition has been deteriorating these past weeks. You've been informed of that, I see," the doctor said, skimming over some pages in a folder.

"I know that, Doctor," Jake said quietly. "How is he now?"

Dr. Pincus closed the folder and looked at the serious young man. No matter what the situation or who the patient was, he would never get used to this part of his profession. "Your father is dying, Mr. Rivers."

Jake's eyelids moved slightly. "How long?" he asked.

"A week, maybe more. It's unpredictable but I wouldn't give much more than that."

Jake listened as the doctor went on in his professional voice and manner about the effects of the stroke on his father's body and the treatment and other information that Jake felt was unnecessary. Of course, everything had been done. Of course, he and his staff were sorry. What else could he say?

The doctor stood up and Jake stood with him.

"You can see him now," Dr. Pincus said. "You don't have to worry about trying to explain to him where he is, or what's happened. I've already done that. He was, of course, disoriented when he awakened. He knows what brought him here." He hesitated. "That is, everything except the seriousness of his condition."

"You mean his dying."

"Yes, his dying. I prefer to do that in consultation with the family and the patient together, if the family is agreeable."

"Must he be told?"

"That's up to you, Mr. Rivers."

"Then, can we wait on this?"

"Anything you say. This way, please. The nurse will take you to him."

He's so still, Jake thought as he stared at the thin form of his father. The once burly man with shoulders as broad as a wrestler's, now lay emaciated and shrunken. He sat in a chair by the bed.

Lloyd Rivers opened his eyes when he heard the movement by his bed. Was that his son, Jake? He looked so different. He opened his mouth to speak, but only a hoarse croak sounded. He tried again. "Jake?" His voice was a thin whisper.

"It's me, Dad," Jake answered. His eyes watered. For weeks he'd seen his father lying in that bed, unmoving. He'd become used to the quiet form. Now the movement and the speech unnerved Jake. This was the man whom he'd come to despise? Jake felt only pity now, and a sadness for their lost lives together and what they could have been to each other as father and son. His father was trying to speak.

"What is it, Dad?" he asked in a low voice.

"S-s-orry. Tell her I . . . am . . . sorry." Lloyd closed his eyes, tired from the effort. But he had to right the wrong he'd done. He was going to die and he knew it. No one had to tell him. He knew. Too late for him and his sons, but maybe, maybe they could forgive him after he was gone.

Jake was worried. What was his father trying to say? She?

Who was she? Jake frowned. Was his father trying to beg forgiveness from his dead wife?

Jake's eyes narrowed. If only Lloyd knew that he would be able to tell her himself soon. Jake was instantly contrite at his mean-spirited thought. *Forgive me Mother,* he prayed silently. *What he did to you is going down very hard with me. God rest his soul wherever it may go.*

"I . . . did it. The p-picture . . ."

"What? What are you saying? I can't hear you, Dad." Jake's heart pumped and his head began to ache. He leaned over the bed and put his ear to his father's mouth. "Tell me, Dad," he whispered.

Jake's hands had been unsteady on the steering wheel for most of the drive home. Twice, he'd skidded on the ice when he braked suddenly at stoplights. He thanked God for guiding him home safely and he immediately undressed and hit the shower. He opened up his mouth and let out the fierce yell that had been burning in his throat since he left the hospital. When his father had finally finished his story, he was exhausted. He'd closed his eyes and Nurse Bartley came and asked Jake to leave. She would call Jake if there was any change in Lloyd's condition.

Jake, in a terry-cloth robe, and nothing underneath, carried a crystal snifter and a bottle of Courvoisier to the bedroom where he set both down on the night table. He positioned himself on top of the covers, poured the fine brandy, then sipped, savoring the fruity spirit as it warmed him all over. Then he picked up the phone and dialed the number for New York City information.

"If I have to," he said aloud, "I'm going to keep this up all night until I find you." It was nearly midnight when the voice-recorded operator said, "What listing, please?"

* * *

Oscar Germany was alone in his apartment when the phone rang at nearly one o'clock in the morning. He'd just returned from taking Maria home and he was far from sleepy. He looked at the display box and frowned at the name. He'd expected this call, but at this hour? He must have just found out, Oscar thought.

"Hello, Jake," Oscar said.

"Oscar," Jake replied. Without preamble, he said, "Can we meet in your office tomorrow? I have something to tell you. It concerns Willow."

"Sure. That's not a problem. What time is good?"

"Ten? Eleven?" Jake queried. "Whatever's convenient."

"Let's make it ten-thirty," Oscar responded. "Give you time to take it slow and easy on those roads. Okay then, tomorrow. Good night, Jake."

Jake sipped the liqueur. His brow was furrowed as he thought about the strange response to his request. He never questioned me. Does he know already? Jake poured more brandy and drank deeply.

At exactly 10:25 A.M., Jake was escorted into Oscar Germany's office. Oscar met him with extended hand.

"How are you? Come in, have a seat." Oscar sat down on the couch and Jake sat across from him.

"Not bad," Jake answered. "And you?"

"Can't complain," Oscar responded. He gestured to a table. "Can I get you anything? Coffee?"

The decanter of fresh-brewed coffee was on a sideboard. The aroma was enticing.

"Yes, thanks. One sugar."

When Oscar sat down again, sipping from his own cup, he waited until Jake was ready to begin. He believed he already knew the reason for this hasty visit, but he wanted the other man to state his reasons.

Their eyes met. Jake was the first to speak.

"You know." His look was intense. The answer was in Oscar's eyes. "When?" Jake asked.

"Not for long. I was notified Christmas week. At the same time I was informed of your father's condition. I didn't know. I'm sorry." Oscar paused. "We . . . the publisher is not going to take any action."

Jake swallowed. "Thanks." He cleared his voice. "He told me most of it last night, as best he could. You can probably fill in what he wasn't able to tell me." He shook his head. "It's the damndest story, but what would he gain by lying?"

Oscar had no answer, so he remained silent.

"Remember the unorthodox way of getting mail to the post office from Wildflowers Cove?"

Oscar frowned, nodding his head as he thought of the careless trust Dorcas and Willow had put in everyone. From Willow to guests to the gardeners, someone was always "going past" the post office. There was no problem in giving mail to anyone who was leaving the Cove.

Jake continued. "That day, Dorcas gave my father the package to mail. He knew what was inside because Dorcas told him. Even showed him. Said she was so proud of her niece's latest idea. She told him not to forget to drop it off, because it was due next-day mail." Jake hesitated. "He told me that he had no intention of mailing it. The first chance he got, those pictures were going into the garbage."

Oscar raised a brow and fingered his mustache. How could the old man bear such hate for Willow? he wondered.

Jake guessed what Oscar was thinking. "My father's hatred was misplaced. Willow was an innocent victim," he said, answering the question in the man's eyes. He rubbed his forehead, wearily. "Instead of trashing the pictures, he got the idea in his head that he could do more damage by discrediting her." Jake shrugged. "He said that he'd had them in the house for a couple of days, working on them. He didn't want to mail them because of the postmark, afraid Dorcas would question him if she found out they hadn't been mailed that same day. So he delivered them himself." Jake laughed. "I didn't believe him!"

Jake was still bewildered at what his father had tried to tell him last night. The bits and pieces that he'd heard, had left him flabbergasted. The old man was on his death-bed, and what he'd told his son, angered Jake to the point of nearly getting up and walking out of there without a backward glance. Lloyd Rivers wanted forgiveness before carrying his evil deeds to the grave.

"The reason that I didn't believe him was because of his stroke. How could he possibly? Then I remembered. That whole incident took place almost two years ago."

Oscar nodded.

"My father was perfectly mobile two years ago," Jake said solemnly. He was still disbelieving at his father's crude attempt to hurt Willow in the cruelest way he could think of. He stared at Oscar, lifting a shoulder. "How did he become a suspect after all this time?"

"As you remember, when you were here last," Oscar noticed the flicker of Jake's eyes, "I told Willow that a crackerjack investigative team had been hired by the publisher. Well, as good as they are, it's taken them this long to get to the bottom of the mystery. It was a matter of painstakingly, interviewing many people in many departments, and backtracking the package from its point of entry into the building." Oscar stood up and walked to his desk and returned, handing Jake a sheet of paper. He sat back down. "There's nothing much there, just the name of the firm and a few notes I took based on what they told me. I'll just repeat everything they said, from the beginning." Oscar had poured more coffee for himself after Jake refused, with a shake of his head. After tasting the hot brew, he sat down.

When Oscar finished explaining how the trail had led to Jake's father, he watched the play of emotions on the man's face and was sympathetic. With all that Jake had experienced with the disappearance of Willow, and now this, his gut must be churning. Any words of sympathy he offered now would seem so trite, so Oscar said nothing.

Jake stood up. He didn't know why he was just sitting there, staring into space. He should be going. Go where? He had nowhere to go. No one to share this burden with him. He tried to shutter the pain in his eyes from the other man, so he walked to the window and stared outside. For a Saturday morning, the streets were not as busy as usual. He looked up. No wonder, he thought. The sky was as still as death. He shuddered against the cold wind that suddenly rattled the windows. Without turning around, Jake asked in a low voice, "Does Willow know? Have you told her, yet?" Just the sound of her name on his lips caused him pain. He hadn't allowed himself to utter it since she left. Earlier, when he'd spoken it to Oscar, it had sounded foreign to his ears.

"No, Jake," Oscar answered. "I haven't seen or spoken to Willow since Toronto."

Jake turned around, stunned. He hadn't seen her?

"Then does that mean you don't know where she is? After all these months? Suppose . . . ?" He stopped, unsure of what to say or do. Where is she?

"Jake." Oscar's voice was sharp. "Take it easy. She's okay."

"But, I thought you said . . ."

"I only said that I haven't contacted her. Not that I don't know her whereabouts."

"But . . ."

"Willow has sent me her address and number in the event I needed her on old business." He paused. "We haven't spoken."

"Then how do you know she's okay?" Jake asked brusquely, giving the man a strange look. He still cares.

"My assistant, Judy," Oscar responded. "A loyal customer wanted Willow's number to discuss a price on one of the Toronto paintings. So Judy called Willow, asking for permission to give out the number."

"Isn't that her agent's job? To haggle over prices for her? That's your job!" Jake shouted.

Oscar waited until Jake's anger subsided. "You know that's no longer true. There is no more relationship."

"No! Because it's not the one you wanted. You threw her away after all those years. She didn't have anyone else. Everyone's left her!" Jake's eyes blazed and his voice was razor-sharp. "She thought that you were her wise and good friend. Then you dropped that bomb on her. She trusted you. Why the hell didn't you just walk away in the beginning, man? Why'd you let yourself become so involved in her life?"

Oscar looked steadily at Jake. "I knew you had guessed. That day we met. You knew then."

"Hell, yes. What man wouldn't have noticed that look?" Jake said, bringing his voice under control. "Willow would have known had she seen it."

"She never knew."

"You believe that?" Jake nearly snorted. "That warm and supersensitive woman probably sensed it but chucked it off, thinking that it was only her overactive imagination at work," Jake scoffed. "She couldn't possibly think that her longtime friend was panting after her all these years."

"Stop, Jake," Oscar rapped. "I won't let you turn my feelings into something akin to a dirty old man's, which is what you're doing. Do you think I have so little respect for her? You're wrong and I'm not going to stand here and listen to you belittle what I've felt for her."

"Felt?" Jake stared, eyes like a sharp-eyed falcon's. His ears picked up the nuance of finality. A coming down of the curtain on the last act.

Oscar jammed his hands in his pants pockets and took his turn to stare out of the window and up at the dead sky.

In turn, Jake sat down hard on the couch, amazed at what he'd heard.

A slight smile played about Oscar's mouth as he listened to the awe in Jake's voice. He'd been surprised himself at the somersault his emotions took.

For weeks, since returning home from Toronto, he'd searched his soul for some answers. He'd nagged his conscience with questions. Some were answered. Some went begging. He'd been surprised at what he'd learned about himself. About the relationship between he and his wife. He knew now that he hadn't hastened to marry, to hide from his feelings for a lovely young woman. He did love Geneva, though he wished he had shown it to her sooner than he had.

"Are you okay?" The man was so still.

Oscar turned, and nodded. "Yeah, I'm fine." He made an attempt to smile, but it came off like a grimace. "Are you okay?"

Jake nodded and stood up. He walked to a chair where he'd tossed his jacket. "I've got to go. Thanks, for your help." He gestured to the air. "My father. Appreciate it." He hesitated and turned back, but before he could speak, Oscar held up his hand.

"I know." Oscar walked to his desk and opened a drawer and pulled out an index card and handed it to Jake. "Take this." he said. "Judy has a copy."

Jake looked at Willow's number and address, then back at Oscar. "Thanks," was all he could say.

"Good luck, Jake. I mean that," Oscar said, holding out his hand. When Jake took it, he added, "Too much time has been lost. You two are meant to be together. Hurry and get on with your lives. Before bitterness and cynicism become a part of you both."

Oscar sat for a long time staring at the door Jake had gone through. He fervently hoped that the two young people would find each other again before it was too late. He grimaced at that thought. It had been too late for him, to have experienced and lived passionate love. That kind of love would be lost to him forever. With Geneva, he had grown to love her in a kind, tender manner, but had always sensed that a certain fire was absent. Not only from their lovemaking but from their normal, casual, relationship. It was just not all-consuming.

Years ago, when he'd refused to run away from that first stirring of his heart, he'd watched a talented, young, delicate flower mature into a beauteous woman. He was certain that she had not suspected her womanly beauty. Then, he'd felt passion stir his soul. He'd still not run away and he had suffered.

After Geneva died, he'd never allowed himself to seek out that one passionate love. He felt incapable of ever experiencing such a love at this point in his life. Now, with his upcoming marriage to Maria Hall, he hoped that she really believed that he loved her. She was the only woman he'd met in all these years that he'd allowed inside to touch his heart. Who knows, he thought, maybe our life together will be full of surprises. And those feelings for Willow? Well, he'd buried them deep, once he saw the love in her eyes for Jake Rivers. The day that he'd watched them together in his office, he knew, that Willow had found the love of her life. The only regret he had was that he'd spoken of his feelings for her in Toronto. He'd hurt her. Since that time, he'd learned to think of her only with loving fondness. Maybe in time, she would let him be her friend once again.

He would love to be around to see the love between Willow and Jake grow deeper with time, and be shared among their children.

Jake drove straight home. There was nothing that he could think of that was pressing, especially in this weather. The Tuckahoe job site was pretty much under wraps until the cold snap broke. The same held true for other sites, in both businesses. He'd made up his mind. He would call Scott, and then Tala, immediately. He was going to Toronto.

While driving home, Jake thought deeply about how Willow would receive him. But he was determined to try one last time to revive what they'd once had. What she had once felt for him. His love for her had never died. Nor would it ever, he was convinced of that.

He shrugged out of his down jacket and walked to the phone, deciding to call Tala first, but pressed the button to clear his messages. The voice he heard made him blink with trepidation.

"Mr. Rivers. This is Nurse Bartley. Please come when you receive this message. Your father has worsened."

When Jake reached Mercy Hospital, his father was already dead. He died without waking up again since Jake had seen him the night before.

Stunned by the suddenness, Jake sat outside his father's room. He'd thought that there would be more time. A week, maybe two. Time to try and heal old wounds. But Lloyd Rivers had known last night, Jake thought, that there was no more time for him. That's why he'd stubbornly insisted on straining to tell Jake what he'd done. At the nurse's beckoning to him, he stood up and followed her to the administrative office.

"Well, old man," Jake said aloud, as he stood up. "It's between you and Him, now. I'll pray for your soul."

Twenty-five

Willow laughed so hard, the tears were coming down her cheeks. She wiped at them, trying to catch her breath and screamed again when she got suds on her face. "Mellie! I'm going to shoot you," she shouted at her friend. "Come and get him."

Mellie Pearson giggled at her friend, then went to her aid. She put her arms around the neck of the big bloodhound and started crooning to it while Willow moved away. "Now, what's wrong with you, Couscous? Your dad's going to think you're being mistreated here when he finds dried soap on your face." She spoke so softly, the black and tan dog looked at her gratefully, with his big brown eyes and licked her face.

"Face?" Willow grunted. "You can't see his face for all that wrinkled forehead." A silly thought made her laugh all over again. "When do you know when he's not worried?" Willow held her aching side and left to dry herself off. "That's the last time you sucker me into helping to bathe your critters," she said, flinging wispy curls off her cheek.

Later, she went to the front of the dog grooming shop that Mellie managed to assist the lone salesclerk. Business was slow and she soon joined her friend in the grooming room.

Couscous was dried, groomed and brushed. His coat glistened so much that it was almost a pity he wasn't doing a show. "All dressed up and no place to go," Willow said sadly. She scratched his neck and tickled his chin before sitting down on a long bench, her back against the wall. "When's his next show?" she asked, speaking of the champion dog.

"Not until the spring," Mellie answered. She dried her hands and plopped down in a chair across from Willow. She propped her feet up on another chair. "My dogs are killing me," she moaned, wiggling her toes inside her white leather sneakers.

"Literally," Willow said, then giggled.

Mellie smiled at her friend. "That's a great sound. I want to hear more of it."

Willow shrugged. "You probably will. What is it they say? Just do whatcha gotta do?" She said, "I'm just getting back to me and who I am. Guess you'd call it reverting to self?"

Mellie laughed. "Wouldn't know. They didn't teach me that in high school and I didn't stay in college long enough to learn all about the 'self.' "

"Don't give me that. You don't need higher learning to get inside yourself and know who you are."

"Oh, intuition, huh?"

"No. It's more than that, Mellie." Willow frowned. "Be serious."

"You were serious enough for both of us, my friend. Give us a break, here." Her brown eyes were accusing, then they smiled when she did. "But, you already have, and I know exactly when it happened. Thanksgiving weekend."

Willow smiled. Mellie was right. Thanksgiving Day had been blessed but also bittersweet. It was a day that Willow had thought about Dorcas. And Dolores. And Jake. They were apart on a day meant for togetherness.

But, on the sweet side, during this holiday season, was the fact that Mellie's mother had finally, after eight long years, acknowledged her granddaughter, Valerie.

"Because of you," Mellie said, as though reading her friend's thoughts. "I have my family back."

"It would have happened, Mellie."

"I don't think so, at least maybe not for many more years to come. And then it wouldn't mean very much to a grown-up young lady. I still don't know what made you go over there on Thanksgiving Day."

Willow didn't know what had made her drive from her rented house in the province of Ontario, to Mellie's old childhood home in the city either. She recalled that it was snowing that day, and the forty-five minute drive hadn't been the most pleasant.

The grand-style house was not as big as it had seemed to Willow when she was younger. She parked behind all the other cars in the driveway. All three of Mellie's brothers and their families were present, Willow assumed. All eyes were on her when she was escorted by the maid into the dining room where Dr. Pearson and his wife stared in amazement at their surprise guest.

"Hello, Doctor. Hello, Mrs. Pearson." Willow looked around the table at the surprised family. "Hello, everyone," she said, her gaze sweeping the room. She stood where she was, not attempting to remove her black, ankle-length, mink coat. She just unbuttoned it.

"Willow!" Mrs. Pearson was the first to move as she got up and went to Willow, hand outstretched. "Willow Vaughn. It's been years since you've paid us a visit. Come in."

Willow looked down at the shorter woman who Mellie was the spitting image of. She didn't smile, because she knew the woman was being pretentious for the benefit of everyone present.

"No, thank you, Mrs. Pearson. I can't stay. I'm here to tell you something and then I'll leave you to your dinner." She looked around the table, then said, "This is for all of you," her glance falling on the young men. "Andre, Corey and you, too, Roger. You all have a sister who has turned into a fine young woman."

Mrs. Pearson, sat back down, pressed her hand to her

breast and listened to the famous artist, Morgana, who'd come into her home, unannounced and uninvited. Her daughter's childhood friend.

"You have a smart and pretty granddaughter, Mr. and Mrs. Pearson. She looks like you, Doctor. And she hasn't a clue to understanding why her mother's family doesn't love her like her daddy's does." Willow walked to the table and stopped at a chair of a little girl. "Hello," she said. "My name is Willow. What's yours?"

The little girl gave Willow a smile. "Rita," she answered.

"Rita. Do you know that you have a cousin your age? Her name is Valerie." Rita shook her head solemnly.

Willow asked the same question of Valerie's other cousins. Susanna, Florence and Quentin. They all shook their head no.

Willow buttoned her coat and prepared to leave. She stopped in front of the elder Pearsons.

"Don't make the biggest, and costliest, mistake of your lifetime. You will come to regret depriving an innocent little girl of the right to know and love her family. That loss to you, and to her, will have been stupid and senseless."

Willow turned and followed the maid to the front door.

Mellie's voice brought Willow back to the present. "I'm sorry. What did you say?"

"I said, that Valerie and I can never thank you enough. My pride would never have let me go begging over there."

Willow's eyes clouded. "Sometimes pride is too heavy a price to pay, Mellie. Your mother eventually realized that." She smiled. "Now all you gotta do is see that you don't have a spoiled-rotten little princess on your hands."

"You'd better believe it," replied Mellie. "She hasn't spent one weekend with me since Thanksgiving. And forget about Christmas. She hasn't slept in her own bed but once since Christmas Day."

Willow laughed. "Let her enjoy it. She's due eight years of love and affection from a lot of people."

"Nine. Don't forget, she has a birthday this month."

"How could I forget? She's even asked me to put in a word for her on her birthday present."

"Not a chance," Mellie said, narrowing her eyes. "I can't handle a wolfhound. What makes you think that she can. And besides where would he stay in my small apartment?" Mellie was thinking of the big dog that had been put up for adoption and that Valerie had fallen in love with.

Willow's eyes twinkled. "That apartment doesn't have to remain a permanent fixture in your life. As a matter of fact, I know of an estate where he'd fit in just fine. Might even manage to accommodate his brother!"

"Oh, don't even go there, Willow. You promised me."

"Okay, okay. Calm down. I can keep my promises." She looked slyly at her friend. "But don't keep Mr. Peter St. John waiting too long. You had your hands full keeping the wolfettes at bay the other night."

Mellie laughed. "There's no such word as *wolfettes*. And besides, you had your own hands full."

"Yes," Willow sighed. "I suppose so."

"You know it was so," Mellie said softly. "You can't forget him, can you?"

Willow shook her head. "It's hard, Mellie." She stood up and walked around the room, absently picking up and putting things in their proper places.

"Willow, stop that and sit down." Mellie had moved to the couch and patted the seat cushion next to her. "Sit here." When her friend sat heavily, Mellie put her arm around her shoulders and gave her a quick hug, then sat back, giving her friend a serious look.

"You always think of everyone else more than you do yourself. What you did for Valerie and me, you can do for yourself and your sister. What's holding you back, Willow? I know that you want to."

"She probably hates me. She must think that I'm the most awful snob in the world, Mellie. How dare she call the famous artist Morgana and present herself as a long-lost relative? She probably feels like hell."

"You weren't in the state of mind to answer her calls or her letter at that time. Your own mind was in a turmoil."

"But I stood there and listened to her voice on the machine. Twice. The letter came the day before I left. I never opened it. It went in the trash the day I left that house."

"Do you want to see her?"

"Yes."

"Then what was it about pride, you said?"

"It's not pride, Mellie, it's the hurt."

"The same hurt that you rescued my Valerie from, Willow. Think about it. One relative walks into her life, only to disappear after telling her that there was another one somewhere in the world." She paused. "How many calls and letters would *you* make or send after such a long, loud silence?"

Willow tried to believe that her friend was speaking nonsense. But the truth hurt sometimes. As it did now. What she'd done for Valerie and Mellie was what she'd wanted to do for herself. But she was afraid. She couldn't shoulder another rejection. Knowing that it would be well-deserved for her own rebuffs.

"You're right, Mellie." Willow stood up. "It's time to close up, isn't it?" She looked at her watch. It was almost five o'clock.

"Are we changing the subject?" Mellie asked softly. But she also stood up, readying the shop for closing. The salesclerk was heard counting the register. "We can continue this over dinner. I'm cooking, remember?"

"I remember. Afterward, I'm driving home. I've been away for almost a week. Too much holiday can make you fat."

Mellie eyed her friend with mock disdain. "As if you had to worry about that," she sniffed.

* * *

Hours later, Willow patted her stomach. "What did you say about fat? I have a bulge."

"So? Now you know what you'll look like when you're three months pregnant. The bulge couldn't be much bigger than that," Mellie said. Instantly, she apologized. "I'm sorry, Willow."

"Don't be, Mellie." Willow's voice was soft, but sad. "It just wasn't meant to be, that's all."

"You're going to have children someday, Willow. I know it. And with Jake, the man you still love." Mellie reached across the kitchen table and held her friend's hand. "It just wasn't the right time for you to conceive. Even if you did have unprotected sex, that doesn't mean you're going to hit a bull's-eye, every time."

Willow couldn't help but smile. "What a way to put it. I'm a cow, now?"

"Oh, you know what I mean. With the emotional state you were in, your body probably didn't know which end was up." Mellie had to laugh at that one, herself. Serious, she said, "If you had become pregnant, Willow, would you really have wanted to raise his child without Jake ever being in its life? That's like history repeating itself. Think about it."

Anguished, Willow stood up. She had thought about it. Many times. When she realized on her drive to Canada, that she'd made mad love without using protection, she'd panicked at first. Suppose she'd conceived? Then, she'd remembered her vow. By the time Willow reached Toronto, she was praying that she was carrying her lover's child. She would have a part of Jake for the rest of her life.

The day she'd found out that she was not bearing his child, she'd driven, desolate, to Mellie's where she'd cried herself to sleep. Except for her childhood friend, she was all alone, again.

"No," she answered her friend. "I probably couldn't have."

"I know you wouldn't have done that to your baby. You would have been back in Irvington, lickety-split."

Before Willow left to return to her house in Kleinburg, she promised that she would not spend the rest of the weekend in a funk. She had too much planning to do. It was time she made some changes in her own life. As she drove, she hoped that she was not too late.

The phone rang as Willow was brushing her hair. She'd showered and was dressed for bed in flannel pajamas that were perfect for chasing chills.

"Okay, Mellie, what did I forget?" She was smiling as she picked up.

"Hi, Willow. It's Judy Spano. I'm sorry to call you so late."

"Judy?" Willow's heart skipped a beat. "Oscar. Is he all right?"

"Oscar's fine. He just called me. He . . . he wanted you to know, before too much more time passed. He doesn't want you to find out in a haphazard manner."

"Find out what?" Willow whispered. A million happenings ran through her mind like wildfire. What more could possibly happen to her, she thought.

"Your editor, Fran, apparently didn't share your whereabouts with anyone at the firm. She's out of the country on holiday and can't be reached. Your publisher has been trying to reach you. They finally called Oscar to try and contact you."

"Judy. Tell me!"

"They know who sabotaged your work." Judy paused. "It was Lloyd Rivers."

"What?" The phone shook in her hand as she sought to get a grip on it. She sat on the bed and closed her eyes. "You must be mistaken. How . . ." A tear squeezed through her closed lids. Did he really hate me so much? Her eyes flew open. Jake! Does he know?

"Jake," she said, her voice hushed. "Does he know?"

"Yes. Oscar told him this morning."

"Oscar? Jake, together?" Willow couldn't comprehend anything.

"Willow, listen to me. Take it easy. There's more. While Jake was with Oscar, his father died. He never recovered from another stroke he'd suffered a few months ago."

"Died?" Oh, Jake. My poor Jake.

When Judy hung up the phone, Willow cried. Not for herself, but for Jake, who must be feeling such pain. To find out that his father had done such an evil deed must have filled him with hurt and anger—but to learn of it—while Lloyd Rivers lay dying? How horrible, she thought.

Willow walked to the bathroom where she washed her tear-stained face. Jake must be feeling such hate for his father—and filled with guilt for hating. She left the room and opened her closet, dragging out her luggage. Vaguely, she remembered her same actions not so long ago. Would the pain never end? So much sadness, she thought. Too much sadness in our lives. It has to end. It has to. She walked from closet to dresser, taking only a few things. Too much time had already been wasted.

Willow was going to him. Her home was not here after all, she thought. It was with Jake, wherever he was. This time, she was really going home.

Twenty-six

Willow sat outside Jake's apartment in her rented Honda Accord. When she'd gotten to JFK Airport, she'd phoned him but had only gotten the voice mail. Leaving a message, she decided to drive straight to his home. She assumed he was still out making funeral arrangements for his father and hoped he would be at home when she arrived. Vaguely, she wondered if his brother Nat was making himself useful at this sudden, traumatic time. She couldn't help thinking that the brothers would really have to put their differences aside at this difficult time.

The nine-twenty, Sunday morning, flight from Toronto had been smooth and uneventful. The drive to Irvington had been equally quiet. Arriving at Jake's about twelve-thirty, her heart sank because she didn't see his pampered Camaro. She rang the doorbell, anyway, but received no answer. She returned to her car and waited.

It was now after one o'clock. Not knowing exactly where he was, or what he was doing, Willow wondered how long she should wait. Although the sun was bright, the temperature was a cold eighteen degrees. She didn't want to keep the Honda's motor running indefinitely, to keep herself warm. She shuddered to think about going to Wildflowers Cove to wait. She wasn't ready to face those memories alone.

Deciding to while away the time at a restaurant, Willow

drove away. As she drove, the sudden thought struck her that maybe she should check into a motel. She hadn't even considered the possibility that she wouldn't be welcome in Jake's life. She had assumed that she could walk back into his arms like nothing had happened. That he had forgiven her. What if she was wrong? What if Jake didn't want her back after the pain she'd caused him? She'd decided for them both that they couldn't have a life together. How wrong she'd been.

Instead of the restaurant, Willow drove to the nearby Holiday Inn. She had no intention of sleeping at her old home, tonight.

After checking in, and having her luggage put inside of her room, Willow left immediately to go to the dining room. The restaurant had excellent food and was a popular eatery. She and Jake had eaten at the Sarinac Room many times. Outside, she bent her head, huddling against the wind, as she hurried the few feet to the adjacent restaurant.

Jake was tired, cold and hungry. No wonder, he thought as he glanced at his watch. It was almost one-thirty. He was driving on Broadway toward home. He was passing the Sarinac Room, thinking to stop to get a bite to eat before going home. He was bone-tired and knew that he'd fall out on the bed before trying to feed himself. His cupboards were bare and he had no desire to first shop for something to eat, and then prepare it. He glanced at the parking lot, noticing the lack of spaces and kept on driving when he noticed patrons going in the door. "Forget it," he growled, giving his stomach competition. He continued home, thinking that he could have an egg fried before a waiter came to take his order.

Jake grimaced. His thoughts had been on Willow so much since yesterday that now he was dreaming her up, wondering at the woman going through the restaurant door. She had moved like Willow. He sighed. After he got some rest, he would call her.

Yesterday, when he'd learned where she was, his first thought was to go to her, to tell her that he still loved her—and hope that she still loved him.

"Hope be damned," Jake said aloud. He'd decided, that when he called her, he would tell her that he was coming to get her. She belonged here at home, with him.

Jake drove carefully on the wet road. The sun was melting the ice and slush and dirty puddles marred the once-beautiful snowscape.

Thoughtful about the arrangements he'd just made for his father, Jake being the sole decision maker since there was still no word from Nat, Jake had opted for cremation. It was scheduled for ten o'clock tomorrow morning. He'd contacted Annette and Mrs. Benson to inform them of his plans. They were both in agreement. After they'd hung up, Jake felt relieved. Both women had voiced that Lloyd would not have wanted to be stared at, nor would he have wanted the insincere attention from the few mourners that might have shown up at his funeral. Over the last twenty years, he had lost whatever friends he and his wife Olivia had made during the early years of their marriage.

At ease, Jake parked his car, and went inside. He immediately undressed and headed for the shower. He had a need to wash the feel of the funeral home from his skin.

He dressed in black sweats, and glanced at the phone. Earlier, when he'd undressed, he'd ignored the blinking message light when he entered the bedroom, and now he decided to see who'd called in his absence. Telling his stomach to wait just a little bit longer, he pressed the message button.

If Jake had not sat down on the bed, he believed he would have fallen down when he heard Willow's voice.

"Hello, Jake. It's Willow. I . . . I'm sorry about your father. Jake, I want to see you. I . . . I'm coming to you. I'm

renting a car at JFK. I should get there after twelve. I'm
so . . . sorry."

Jake nearly slapped his ears in disbelief, doubting what
he'd heard. She's here! Coming to him!

Planting his elbows on his knees, he dropped his head
in his hands An uncontrollable shiver shook his body so
hard, he thought he was convulsing. He took deep breaths,
to bring his breathing back to normal. Then he slammed
his body back onto the bed, eyes closed. The darkness
behind his lids was little bits of shadowy light that swirled
about like tiny stars. He'd just imagined he'd seen her and
now she was actually here—

Jake's eyes flew open and he sat up. That was her! That
woman had been Willow! He quickly calculated. She'd arrived here before him and then left to get something to
eat when he didn't appear. He jumped up. Willow was only
ten minutes away from him. Jake's mind raced. Should he
stay here and wait for her to return? *But, she doesn't know
where I've gone or how long I'll be. She may not return, and go
straight to the Cove, instead. But it's closed up, and cold,* he
reasoned. *She couldn't possibly think of staying there tonight.
It'd take hours to heat up that big house.*

Jake had his jacket and wool cap on and was locking the
door before he finished the conversation with himself. As
he drove, he listened to her words that bounced around
in his head. That last "I'm sorry." He believed that that
was not for his father. She was sorry for them.

Jake walked to the dining room, refusing the offer of a
table and scanned the room. After a hurried, but thorough
search, his heart sank. She wasn't there. Had he seen her?
He stood outside the restaurant door, uncertain of where
to turn. Back home? Or to Wildflowers Cove?

"Hi, Mr. Rivers."

Jake turned around to see a waiter step outside and im-

mediately light up. He was one of the young men that had
waited their table on occasion.

"Hello, Frank," replied Jake. He had to shiver, looking
at the coatless young man, puffing away on the cigarette.
"How've you been?"

"No sense complainin.' " He puffed, then grinned.
"Told Ms. Vaughn the same thing, just a while ago." He
took another drag.

"What?" Jake looked in stupefaction.

Frank looked at the excited man with a curious stare.
"Yeah, she was just in here. I asked about you and she said
she'd been away, but she'd see you soon. She took her key
card from her pocket and waved with it."

"Key card?" Jake said stupidly.

Frank crushed the cigarette out with his foot, then
stooped to pick up the butt and discard it in the trash can.
"Yeah. My break is over. See you later, Mr. Rivers." He
stepped back inside.

"She's staying here?" Jake murmured to himself. Why
would she check in here, instead of staying with me? he
asked himself. His mind a jumble of thoughts he didn't
want to contemplate, he walked the few steps to the inn
and opened the door.

As he knew, the clerk would not give out her room number, instead calling her and giving her a message.

Jake was sitting in a big lounge chair by the lobby window, lost in thought. He dreaded to entertain what her
staying here could mean. He didn't hear her approach.

"Jake?" Willow could see the dejection in his shoulders
and her eyes clouded with fear. Please let me be wrong,
she pleaded to no one in particular. Was she praying to
God, not to punish them any further?

Jake turned around. He stood up and looked into her
eyes, praying not to see what he'd feared. He held her
look for a long time. Jake was puzzled. She was afraid! Of
him? "Willow."

"Jake," Willow repeated, as she walked toward him. His

face was expressionless, and his dark eyes were unreadable as he stared at her. What was he thinking? Her knees weakened suddenly, and she sat down quietly. He sat across from her, watching. He was dressed all in black. Black sweats. Black down jacket. A black wool cap was in his hand. Black. Always associated with doom. Is this some bad omen? She took a breath before she spoke.

"I heard last night, Jake. I'm sorry about your father," Willow said softly. With a nod, he accepted her sympathy, but remained silent. "I left as soon as I could. I wanted to be with you." Her voice was but a whisper as she spoke. Her heart pounded in her chest because the veil lifted from his face. His burgundy-hued eyes were filled with sadness and hurt.

"With me?" His voice rasped as he jerked his head toward the front desk. "Then why did you check in here?"

"Because I realized that maybe your hurt ran too deep for us to . . ." His voice stopped her.

"Don't say that, Willow." Jake's voice was a soft murmur overflowing with pain, hope and love.

Willow's eyes filled with tears, when she saw his begin to water. They had both harbored the same fears. That each had lost the love of the other. How wrong they'd both been.

Neither Willow nor Jake moved as they looked at each other.

Willow remembered the last time they'd been together. Their last touch. The electricity had disappeared. She had felt nothing. What if they couldn't ever recapture the passion that they had once shared?

Jake seemed to guess her thoughts. She had her hands closed in fists on her lap. Almost as if she feared touching him. His jaw tensed. To hell with that, he thought. He loved and wanted her, electric charge or not. He was never letting her go. He stood up.

"Willow," he said in an emotion-packed voice, "Let's go home." He didn't reach out to her. He wanted her to overcome her fear of any lost feelings. He was dead certain of his.

Love and understanding for him shone in her eyes as Willow stood. She put her hands in the pockets of her slacks as she smiled. "I'll be right back," she said softly as she walked to the desk. Her eyes watered again. When she walked past Jake, the air around them had stirred. It was still there, she thought as she gave instructions to the clerk. Without a backward glance at Jake, she followed the bell-man down the long corridor to her room to retrieve her luggage. A short while later, she was following Jake out of the parking lot in her rental car. She swiped away another tear. She was really going home.

Twenty-seven

Jake put Willow's luggage in the living room, then shrugged out of his jacket. He eyed her as she shyly stood in the middle of the room, looking around as if remembering other occasions. Pleasant times, he thought, as he noticed the tiny smile on her lips. He went to her as she unbuttoned her mink coat.

"May I?" he asked softly, as he stood behind her.

Willow stood still. He was standing so close, she could smell the cold air that still clung to his face as his whisper of a breath moved a curl on her cheek. She nodded her head and waited. His hands moved over her shoulders, then slid up to the shawl collar, then down the front of the coat. The slow movement stopped at her breasts, where he pulled the coat open and slid it off her shoulders and down her arms. He never touched her. Willow felt the coat slide to the floor, where it lay in a soft pile between their ankles. She was wearing black wool slacks and a red, long-sleeve, wool sweater. When he slid his hands up her arms, Willow nearly buckled. When his hands reached her shoulders, she suddenly grasped them and held on tight, as she leaned her back against his body. She closed her eyes as he strained into her and the warmth flooded through her. With it came the familiar electric current that she'd known since the first time they'd touched. So long ago; a time that was nearly lost to her memory. He moved his arms to grasp her tightly around her waist while she hugged his arms, keeping them close. Her head rested against his broad shoulder. They cuddled and swayed, neither allowing an inch of space to separate them. Jake's whispers feathered her cheek as he tasted her salty tears. Suddenly, uncontrollable sobs racked her shoulders.

Jake turned her toward him and held her close. He picked up the coat and tossed it on a chair then led her to the sofa, where he held her in his arms. He crooned softly to her and let her cry. Just as he'd done months before. Only he knew that these were tears of happiness, because he felt like shedding some too. Finally, her chest stopped heaving and the sobs subsided. He kissed her forehead and stood up. "Be right back, sweetness."

Jake returned with a box of tissues and a warm washcloth. He handed them to her and left the room again. He put the kettle on and was about to return to the living room when his stomach growled. Jake laughed as he remembered he hadn't eaten all day. Not since he'd had one cup of coffee before his appointment this morning. He took a Chinese restaurant menu out of a drawer, dialed the number and quickly placed an order. If Willow wasn't hungry now, she certainly would be before the night was over. Guaranteed, he thought. He returned to her.

She'd kicked off her shoes but she wasn't where he'd left her. He heard the bathroom door open and her padded footsteps on the wood floor. She was wearing his burgundy, ankle-length, velour robe. She came to him and wrapped herself in his arms.

"Hello, again, my love," Willow said, looking up at him.

Jake's heart swelled. "Hello, to you, too, darlin'." Just then, the kettle whistled and Jake frowned, fearful.

Willow felt him tense up and she squeezed him tighter around the waist. "I'm fine, love. No more ghosts," she whispered.

Jake hugged her back. Willow tugged at his waist, leading him to the kitchen. There, she released him.

"You sit, I'll fix. What kind do you want?" she asked, looking in the cabinet. Before he could speak, she said, "Jake Rivers, what have you been eating?" Willow was staring at the contents of the cupboard, which was practically empty. Where before there were always several boxes of herb teas, there was a lone box. She opened it to find three individual packets of lemon tea bags. She prepared the cups and poured the water.

Jake escaped her accusing eyes when he hurried to answer the doorbell. When he returned, she was smiling the mischievous smile that he remembered. He held the bags of food out to her like a peace offering.

Willow laughed. "Okay, you're saved by the bell. This time."

Jake walked by to get the plates out of the cabinet and quickly bent and kissed her lips. "Don't listen for any bells to save you darlin'." He smiled wickedly at her and winked.

It was after five o'clock and already dark when Willow shifted her position in Jake's arms. After they'd eaten, they had returned to the sofa, where they cuddled close. In low voices, they talked of the months they'd been apart, consoling, and crooning sweet words, trying to erase the hurt.

Through the softness of the velour robe, Jake was caressing her arm, while her hand moved sensuously across his stomach and up and down his thigh. Both were content to lay and touch, basking in the feeling of peaceful serenity that had been foreign to them in the last months. There was no urgency to hasten their coming together. They were as intimate as two people can get without consummating their love.

"Jake?"

"Hmm?"

"Did you think I had gone mad?"

Jake kissed her eyelids. "No," he answered with a firm voice. "You were entitled to let your emotions run the gamut. I would have done the same, if nothing worse. So get that out of your head." He was silent for a moment.

"I wished that you would leave, go away to find some peace."

"You did?" Willow was surprised.

"Yes. But I regretted making that wish. I didn't know where you'd gone or if you were all right. I agonized over that every day. I tried hard to get on with my life, hoping that you were doing the same. Sometimes I fantasized that you'd gone back to Paris. You were happy there, once."

"I'd thought about it at times." She squeezed his thigh. "But I would have been miserable in that city without you."

After moments of silence, Willow asked in a soft voice, "Have you forgiven them?" She was referring to Lloyd and Nat. Jake had told her all that had occurred among the three men and the hatred that Jake had felt for his family. He had spoken so bitterly that she thought the anger would fester inside of him. She didn't want that kind of hurt shadowing their lives together.

Jake understood her question and thought about it before answering. Had he? There would always be some distance between him and Nat. He would never be able to forgive his brother for treating him so cruelly over the years, for no valid reason.

"I know I shouldn't harbor hate, Willow," Jake answered, "but Nat's jealousy of me all these years was unfounded and sick. I was his only sibling and he did not have enough love in his heart to care about me. He decided to deal with his own pain by taunting me. I can truthfully say that if he should come back, I will tolerate him as my flesh and blood and the uncle to my children. But that's all I can promise right now."

Willow understood and caressed his cheek. His jaw was tense and she soothed it until she felt the muscles relax. "And your father?" She wanted the air cleared of everything. He'd spoken of the heated words between he and his father that day in September. And how he'd found him unconscious when he'd returned to the house later that night.

Jake let out a sigh. "May his soul rest in peace." He fingered the curls on Willow's shoulder as he rested his chin on her head. "If the Man above can forgive, I suppose that I can. But it is something that I can never forget. Especially the way he hated you all these years. You were the innocent and he wanted to ruin you. That was harsh and evil." He grew silent, trying to blot out the anger he felt after hearing his father's whispered deathbed words.

"Jake? Would you mind if we planned a small memorial service for him?"

Jake was startled. "You would want to do that? After all that he's done to you?"

Willow nodded. "Yes. I think that it would be good. A beginning of the healing process for us and a chance for you to say a private, final good-bye. The last time you spoke would be the last thing you would always remember. Maybe, in time, you will be able to forget." She thought, and added, "It would also be good for Annette and Kendra and even Mrs. Benson. Kendra had little enough interaction with her grandfather. She needs some form of closure too. No one else need be present."

"You're probably right," Jake said thoughtfully. He bent and kissed Willow on the mouth, a deep, long, sensuous kiss that ended when he murmured against her crushed lips, "I'll love you till eternity, Willow Vaughn."

Willow sat up. Her love for him smoldered in her eyes. she said, "That's a long time, my love. But not long enough." She stood up and held out her hand and he took it, pulling himself up. "Do you think I can have a little sample of what I'll be getting for so long a time?" A smile played about her mouth and her eyes danced. "Might not be all I need to sustain me until the end of time."

Jake pulled her close, slipping his hands inside the robe to feel her lace-covered breasts. Through the black bra, he felt her quick response to his gentle touch. He smiled devilishly. "Wanna bet?" he whispered as he guided her into the bedroom.

Willow shrugged out of the robe as she walked, and at the bed, she stopped, her back to Jake. She took his hands and placed them over her breasts as she pressed into him, moving her hips in a gentle circular fashion.

Jake gasped as the warmth of her seared him even through the barriers of his clothing. He moved his own hips to match the rhythm of hers, while he molded each breast in his hands, his thumbs flicking the hardened nipples. He found the front hook and released the fabric, pushing the bra away. He kissed her skin as he slid the satin straps over her silken shoulders, letting his tongue taste her scented flesh. Her moan of pleasure hastened his exploration of her bare beasts as he cupped them in his hands. She reached behind him and held his burgeoning erection close to her and he groaned at the heightened sensation of fullness. He was filled with love. "Willow, sweetness," he whispered against the softness of her neck, "love me, now. You're killing me."

In answer to his plea, Willow turned to him and tugged at the hem of his sweatshirt and lifted it. Soon, she felt her breasts against his chest and she sighed, kissing his erect nipples. She grasped the bands of his sweatpants and his briefs. She pulled them down, and with his help he was standing naked before her. Willow sat down on the bed, gazing in fascination at him. Memories of their lovemaking came to her and she shuddered. Once again she would be fulfilled and she wondered how she could have let so much time slip by. Time was so precious and she vowed that never would there be another such stupid separation. Jake tried to sit beside her, but her hands on his thighs held him standing before her. She looked up into his eyes and smiled. "You're beautiful," she murmured, sliding her hands up and down the taut, muscular thighs, the wiry hairs, making her fingertips tingle. When she played with the tender inner flesh, she could feel the heat of him and she sighed.

Jake convulsed, and caught her fingers. "Willow," he rasped. "You're a tease." He was on the bed in a flash with her laying beside him. Her fingers were continuing in their same sensuous exploration. He gasped when she grasped his erection firmly in her soft hands, and the powerful feeling made him erupt in a shout of excruciating pleasure. He squirmed beneath her ministrations as his hand busily kneaded her breasts, bringing the berry-colored nipples to rigid peaks. Her hand was opening and closing with a strong up and down motion and Jake's body involuntarily moved with the rhythm. A second later, Jake shouted when Willow's tongue started to leave a trail of moist heat as she traced his muscled contours down to his groin. There, her tongue flicked at his inner thigh. The feathery touch on the tip of his taut manhood brought stars to his eyes and he yelped in sweet agony. He thought he could know no sweeter pain when he felt her lips close around him. Jake was lost. He gave himself up to her tender loving.

Willow loved Jake, thoroughly, and with gentle tenderness. The same way that he had always loved her. She followed her instincts on how to love this sweet man and she derived such pleasure from her giving. When she heard his soft groans, it heightened her own passion, encouraging her to bring an authority to her lovemaking of which she had been unaware. She was the sole source of his pleasure. Empowered, she touched his sensitive groin area and the sudden arch of his hips, made her moan with delight as she loved him, until finally, with one last groan, his hips sank back onto the bed. Willow felt his hands on her shoulders as he eased her up his body until her head lay cradled against his heaving chest. She rested her hand on his nipple, and he caught it, bringing it to his lips. "Don't be cruel, now," he whispered raggedly.

Willow smiled against his damp skin and her deep laugh

rumbled against him as she listened to the thumping of his heart. She snuggled close and sighed.

"Jake?"

"Yes, darlin'?"

"I do love you, more than you could know. I want you to remember that, always."

"I do know, sweetness. You've shown me, physically and mentally," Jake answered. "When you heard about my father, you never gave a second thought except to fly home to me, to help ease my distress." He kissed her mouth. "You never really left me. We were bonded through all those lonely weeks. We will always be." He propped himself up on an elbow and stared down at her, tracing a pattern of swirls across her flat stomach. "Now let me see if I have anything left. I'm supposed to be showing you how I'm going to sustain you through all eternity." He smiled broadly. "I'm not about to risk losing my bet, lady."

Willow's body answered the tune that he was playing on her stomach, so that she began to writhe to the erotic rhythm. The look he gave her and when he showed those deep dimples, the crazy things happening to her heart, made her groan in anticipation.

Jake started his exploration of her sweet, secret places, slowly, his fingers playing just outside the pulsing lips of her damp womanhood. When he touched her, slipping one finger inside, Willow sighed her contentment, tilting her hips, seeking to feel more of the pleasant invasion. Her sounds of arousal, increased the depth of his gentle probing. He could feel the mounting heat of her until his fingertips tingled. He suckled her breast, drawing each nipple deep into his mouth until she screamed his name. Her sweet woman smell mingled with her scented skin and his senses went awry. He removed his fingers and Willow cried out in anguish.

"No, Jake. Ooh, what are you doing . . . ?"

"Loving you," Jake answered huskily. He slid down her

body until he reached her mound. His tongue darted between the swollen lips, seeking, exploring until her scream told him he'd found what he'd sought. He loved her then, as he'd never before. When she arched, he increased her pleasure by probing deeper. When she rotated, he met her rhythm, until with one final arch of her hips, her hands dug into his shoulders and she screamed.

Before her scream died, Jake positioned himself on top of her and while she was still in the throes of her passion, entered her with a strong powerful thrust. The rhythm was never broken as Jake and Willow allowed themselves to love and to be loved. Their bodies moved as with rhythms of the ocean. First, gentle and lapping, then, huge white-crested waves, reaching for the sky before crashing down with a roar, only to mesh and glide peacefully out to sea.

Jake did not want to move from her but he did, falling beside her with a satisfied groan.

Willow's weakened body tingled with the ebbing flames of her desire. He'd loved her with a completion she'd never known.

Jake held her close, her head resting on his shoulder. She was so quiet. He wondered if she'd caught his thoughts. For the second time, he had not used protection before loving her. Since her return, they had not discussed the first time it had happened and the possible consequences. He'd sometimes wondered if she had become pregnant with his child. Did she abort? He hesitated to ask, unsure of how he would respond. After all, it was her body. No. His feelings ran deeper than that.

"Jake. There's something I'd like to talk about." Willow propped herself into a sitting position and Jake followed suit.

Jake took one of her hands in his and waited.

"I didn't conceive your child." Willow squeezed his hand. "I know it must have been on your mind all these months, love. I'm sorry if I caused you grief. You couldn't have known what was happening."

Surprise filled his eyes. "You know me so well," Jake said.

Her voice was sad. "All those hours on the road, I was wishing that I carried your child inside of me. When it didn't happen, I was crushed. I had lost all of you."

"Would you never have told me, Willow?" Jake's gaze was penetrating.

"I would not do that to you. Never. Too much deceit and too many lies have been a part of our families too long." Willow raised worried eyes to Jake's. "Suppose we can't have children, Jake?" Her hand dug into his.

"Shh, love. Why would you think that? We're going to have a brood." Her sudden laugh startled him.

"Why does everyone liken me to an animal where children are concerned? First a cow and now a bird or a chicken!" At Jake's bewildered look, she explained.

Jake laughed. "I think I like your friend Mellie."

"I think the feeling is going to be very mutual."

Jake's voice was serious. "Would you mind if it did happen now?"

"I'd be ecstatic," Willow answered dreamily.

Jake kissed her slowly, stirring her passions when her tongue danced around his and she moved seductively against him. "Then suppose we make certain that we get a little gleam going on in there before the night is over," he murmured against her kiss-swollen lips.

Willow's answer was to sink beneath the sheet, pulling Jake with her as she met the onslaught of his roving tongue.

One week after his death, a memorial service was held for Lloyd Rivers at a small chapel in Elmsford. As predicted, the gathering was small and reserved. Willow never spoke of it to Jake, but she could see that the healing process for him had begun. She was happy to know that he was going to be just fine. She had met Annette and Kendra and she was happy to see the rapport developing between uncle and niece. Willow intended that that relationship would be nurtured and grow even after she and Jake married.

The second week at Jake's, Willow's clothes and other personal items arrived by parcel post thanks to Mellie and her brothers. The Mercedes had arrived by private transport two days before. Most of Willow's clothes were still in her luggage. Jake's closet space was not so accommodating for both sets of clothing.

Willow was setting the table for dinner when she heard the key in the lock. It was almost seven o'clock. Her face brightened as she met Jake at the door, and kissed his cold mouth.

Jake hugged her as he kicked the door shut. "Mmm, you taste like tomatoes."

"Uh-huh, spicy, just as you like them."

Jake shrugged out of his jacket and pulled her close. "Now, how did you know that?" His fingers feathered her breasts through her lightweight sweater.

Willow slapped at his hands. "Wash up, mister. You get fed, first. Besides, I have to check the dessert."

"No dessert first?"

Willow eluded his grasp, laughing. "Not unless you want burnt tarts," she said, disappearing into the kitchen. She could hear Jake's hearty laugh as he walked into the bathroom and shut the door.

Jake and Willow were snuggled together on the sofa, watching the ten o'clock news. They'd had two kinds of dessert and they were both dreamily contented.

Jake stirred and his eye caught the luggage stacked in the corner of the living room. He decided to broach the subject Willow had not mentioned since she arrived two weeks ago. He knew that Irene had been to the Cove to check on the greenhouse. If things were not okay, Jake would have received a report.

"Willow?"

Willow had come to know Jake so well that she sensed his moods fairly accurately. Especially since they had been together constantly for a mere two weeks. She thought she was darn good with her predictions. Right now, he was serious-minded and would want a serious response to the question he was about to ask.

Willow sat up and looked at him expectantly. "Yes?" she responded.

"When are you going to visit the Cove?"

Willow was not surprised at the question. She answered truthfully. "I haven't thought about it much, Jake." Then, "I suppose I'll have to though, won't I?"

Jake nodded. "Letting a big house like that stand idle through this brutal winter, isn't the best treatment for it." He took her hand. "If you want company, I'll make myself available."

Willow was grateful. She hadn't wanted to face those memories alone. She remembered her last days there. She'd kept every light on in every room. She would welcome holding onto Jake's arm when she entered the front door. She leaned over and kissed his cheek. "I'd like that very much."

The following Saturday, nearly three weeks after Willow returned to Irvington, she visited Wildflowers Cove. It was after eleven in the morning and though the day was cold, it was not wet and gray, Willow noticed as Jake drove the big Mercedes through the iron-grill gates. Willow looked without emotion at the covered shrubs and trees. She knew whose company was responsible for the upkeep. Her management company had continued to make payments on that account. Jake had explained to her his maneuvering when he'd sold his father's company. Jake's manager was doing as excellent a job as Lloyd Rivers had done, she noted approvingly. Two days before, Willow had called the housekeeping service and advised them of her return. They'd agreed to turn up the heat to a comfortable temperature and to remove the dustcovers from the first-floor rooms. Willow also ordered a supply of staples. Who knew whether she or Jake would ever visit long enough to want a hot cup or tea or coffee, she'd thought. She got out of the car and stood looking at the house. Jake held out his hand.

How different it looked from when last she'd seen it. No lawn or porch furniture. She could almost see her aunt, sitting and rocking, sipping cool lemonade. A vision of two elderly women hurrying to their car flashed across her mind. Willow hesitated. So many memories, she thought.

Jake felt her pull back. "I'm here, sweetness," he said in a strong voice. "Come on. Let's go in."

The smell of lemon oil and floor wax hit Willow's nostrils as she stepped through the front door. She heard Jake lock it, then stand behind her quietly, watching her look around.

The room was warm from the heat in the furnace and the sun that tried to peep through the draperies. Willow opened the drapes and pale sun brightened the living room. She walked to the hallway and opened her bedroom door. She looked at the neatly made bed. The desk was left untouched with its stacks of papers. She closed her door and went to her aunt's room. As per her instructions, it remained with the dustcovers. Willow shut the door. In the kitchen, it was warm. The only thing missing was the smell of delicious food and Tommy and Dorcas' banter. The guests' dining room was sadly still and felt lonely without the chatter of the writers. Jake had followed her to every room and now stood behind her. She turned to him and took his hand and they went upstairs.

Jake walked with Willow to each room and listened to her relate her actions that last week. He heard the anguish in her voice as she told him her fears. When they returned to the living room, she took his hand and went outdoors.

Willow unlocked her greenhouse and stepped inside. She felt Jake's arms come around her shoulders and she leaned into him.

"I'm okay, love," she whispered. They left and Jake locked the door.

Willow followed the path to her studio. For the first time, Jake paid no attention to the silly place for the key. He watched Willow intently. This place was where she spent her whole life. In this little cottage she had created beautiful art for the world to enjoy. He could look back now and see her working so intently, never noticing the sly looks he'd given her while she worked. He thought he fell in love with her even before he knew it when she would smile while she painted. He stepped inside behind her.

Jake was amazed at what he saw. Willow walked around and threw more dustcovers on the floor. Then she sat down on the couch, looking around at her work.

"When did you paint these?" He was incredulous. When he'd checked the place he never touched the covers protecting her many paintings scattered around the room. At various times he'd seen the beautiful flowers she'd painted for one project or another.

"The last two weeks that I was here. All alone."

The paintings of himself, caught and held his attention as Jake looked at captured expressions on his face that even he thought he'd never had. "When did you ever see me curl my lip?" he asked.

Willow smiled. "The night you came to dinner and George Henry called you 'my man' for the umpteenth time."

Jake shook his head in amazement as he studied Dorcas with her many facial expressions; Nat at his most charming, and even Lloyd looking grumpy and hateful. One unfamiliar face caught his eye. Almost immediately he recognized it.

"You copied this from the picture?"

Willow shook her head. "From memory."

Jake looked at the exact image of her sister, Dolores Jones, and whistled in amazement.

"I'll burn most of these," she said. "I can't keep them. They were all done in that frenzied state that I was in." She waved a hand around. "They're best forgotten."

"No. Don't do that just yet, Willow," Jake said quietly. "Let them sit for awhile. Think about it. I've seen great portraits but this is not your forte and these can rank with the best portrait artist around. You can't imagine what your art will be worth when it's known that you do portraiture." His eyes pleaded with her.

"You like the curl of your lip?" She smiled at him.

"You were really studying me, weren't you, falcon eye?" Jake looked at her accusingly.

"I saw something that I liked," answered Willow. "And something that I desired."

Jake went to her and pulled her up. "Me, too," he said. "You see I wasn't trying very hard to run away."

"I'm so glad you didn't want to try, Jake," Willow murmured against his shoulder.

Jake held her. After a moment they left.

Jake locked the door and dropped the key in its place. They walked back to the house in silence.

Willow took Jake's hand and led him to her bedroom. They sat in the cozy seating area that Willow had loved.

Jake stared at her. "Okay?"

"Okay," Willow responded with a deep sigh. She looked around. "This was a happy space for me."

"You don't think it could be again?"

Answering slowly, Willow finally shook her head. "Maybe for someone, but not for me. Not permanently, ever again. I want a new place for us to laugh and make love and be sad and listen to the babies cry and coo. In a brand-new place of our own."

"Sounds okay to me." He paused. "When do you want to start looking?"

"Yesterday!"

Jake laughed. "That soon, huh?"

Willow nodded. "It's time, Jake." Willow looked at the desk. "For a lot of things," she added.

Jake followed her look. He understood. "When?" he asked.

"Yesterday," Willow answered quietly.

Jake nodded, then checked his watch. He shrugged. "It's Saturday," he said in a nonchalant voice. "Even newspaper journalists stay home to do laundry."

Twenty-eight

Dolores Jones removed her coat and hung it up in the foyer closet. She pulled off her boots and left them in the hall and padded to the kitchen where she put the kettle on. A cup of hot cocoa would go down mighty fine as soon as she shed her woolen clothing. Although the day had started out sunny, at a quarter past four, the temperature had already dropped.

She undressed and put on her robe. She stopped herself from putting on her flannel pajamas although she knew she would be in bed in a couple of hours. But she'd promised herself that she was going to try to do better. She looked at her face in the mirror and her eyes grew sad at the way she looked. She had lost weight and it was unbecoming to her. Even her coworkers mentioned that the sparkle had gone out of her eyes. They all assumed that it was due to the death of her mother and they tried coaxing her out of her funk. She had even tried going to a movie every now and then or to dinner with the other reporters. But most days, she would come straight home, eat and go to bed. Today, she had forced herself out of the house and into the mall. Bored with window-shopping because she really had nothing to purchase, she had come home empty-handed. On the short ride upstairs, she wondered who had dropped by. The doorman had said that a woman had come visiting, but left without leaving her name. She forgot about it the minute she hit the door.

Dolores went into the living room and turned on the TV. Maybe a movie would catch and hold her attention. Good, she thought, when the kettle whistled. Just in time.

She dropped a couple of mini marshmallows in the cup with the packet of cocoa and poured the hot liquid over it. Dolores carried the cup to the living room and started to channel-surf.

"Jake, there she is," Willow whispered as if Dolores could hear her. She and Jake were sitting in her car across the street from the building. Twenty minutes before, when the doorman had told them Ms. Jones had gone out, Jake and Willow had returned to the car and waited. Neither had been anxious to drive back to Irvington right away.

Willow was glad they'd waited. She turned to Jake apprehension filling her eyes.

Jake smiled and caressed her cheek. "Go on, darlin'," he said. "She's probably just as scared as you are. Go on, now. I'll be waiting right here. Stay as long as you need to."

Willow brushed his lips with hers. "I love you." She opened the door and walked across the street, praying that she could find the right words.

Dolores answered the doorman's buzz. When he announced her visitor, she froze. Finding her voice she gave permission for her sister to come up.

When Dolores opened the door to Willow Vaughn, she stared for a moment, then said, "Hello."

Willow could hardly find her voice. What's happened to her? she thought. This is not the same woman in the pictures that Dorcas took this summer!

"Hello Dolores," Willow finally said.

Dolores stepped back. "Please come in," she said. She followed Willow inside.

"I'll take your coat," Dolores said softly, watching Willow stand uncertainly in the foyer.

Willow nodded, and shrugged out of a black, knee-length wool coat and handed it to Dolores, who hung it up in the hall closet. She followed Dolores into the living room.

Both young women stood silently, each surveying the other. Willow was the first to speak.

"I'm sorry, Dolores. Please forgive me?" Her eyes begged for forgiveness and her voice shook a little. She prayed for acceptance, that finally, all the ghosts would be put to rest and they could live their lives as family.

Dolores was overwhelmed. For months she'd yearned and hoped for this moment. Now that it was here, she could not speak. Her sister was here! *I thought she didn't want me!* The thoughts whirled around in Dolores' head like a mixer. All the doubts she'd had about herself, and the kind of family that she'd been born into. She saw how nervous Willow was, and the realization brought tears to her eyes.

Dolores nodded her head. "Yes," she said in a low voice. She couldn't find more words. She took a step toward Willow and held out her hand.

The two women moved as one into each other's arms, hugging and clinging, crying and laughing.

Willow stepped back and wiped her eyes as she stood staring at Dolores. She's lost so much weight! Willow sat down and Dolores joined her on the same sofa. Dolores sniffed. She left hurriedly and soon returned with a box of tissues and handed it to Willow, who smiled.

"Good idea," Willow said softly. Dolores gave a small laugh and Willow's heart pumped wildly. She sounds so much like Dorcas!

"You look like me," Willow said shyly. "And you sound like Aunt Dee."

"I know," answered Dolores. "I wouldn't have believed it if I hadn't seen your picture and heard Dorcas' voice.

That day she visited me, I was flabbergasted, overjoyed, you name it. I had just lost my mother and her visit on top of that . . ." She sniffed again. "Well, you can only imagine what I felt." Her eyes saddened. "She visited me once more and after that, she disappeared. Then when you didn't respond to my calls or my letter, I . . . I was devastated. I think it would have been better for me if I'd never known about either of you."

"Dolores, I'm so sorry. I've been so stupid. Do you think that you could ever forgive me for being such a fool?"

"Yes," Dolores replied. "I finally realized that it must have been a shock for you too."

Willow's eyes clouded. "It was," she said. "I nearly lost the only man I'll ever love because of this whole thing." Her eyes watered again. "It took another tragedy to bring me to my senses."

Dolores had never felt so happy in her whole life as at that moment. She felt, knew, that they were going to be friends. And family.

After a moment, Dolores asked, "Have you heard from her?" They both knew who she meant.

"No," Willow shook her head. "Not a word." She looked at Dolores. "I never wanted to see her again. I never looked for her."

"Because of the letter she never gave you?"

Willow looked surprised. "She told you about that?"

Dolores nodded. "The second time she came. She told me how you were going to feel. That you would come to hate her. She didn't want to stay around to watch that happen."

Willow slumped back on the sofa. "She was right." She wearily rubbed her forehead. "I don't know what she told you, but I'll tell you everything that I've found out in the last few months."

An hour had passed when Willow stopped talking. She stood up, and paced the floor, her arms hugging her chest.

"I want her back, Dolores. We should have her back in our lives. There's only the three of us, now. We have to find her." She waved a hand in the air and grimaced. "All that's happened. That's in the past. We have to get on with our lives!"

Dolores nodded. "Do you have any idea where to start looking?"

"No," Willow answered. "I haven't a clue. Apparently, she's severed all ties here in New York." A determined look settled on her pretty features. "We'll find her. I want her at my wedding."

"Wedding?" Dolores was surprised. Dorcas had never mentioned that Willow was engaged to be married.

"Yes. It's going to be very soon, so we can't waste time in finding Dorcas." Willow gave her sister a shy smile. "Would you like to meet your future brother-in-law? He's waiting for me in the car."

Dolores could only nod in amazement.

When Jake saw Willow fairly skip to the car, he smiled and shut off the motor. He was standing to greet her when she flung herself into his arms. He held her tight, burying his head in her soft curls. It had gone well, he thought.

Willow was breathless. "She wants to meet her brother-in-law-to-be," she said. "We're going to look for Dorcas. She has to attend our wedding."

"When?" Jake asked, hugging her close as they walked into the building.

"Yesterday," Willow said, then laughed.

Jake joined her. He looked at his watch and frowned. "I think it's a little too late today," he said. "Tomorrow?"

When Dolores opened the door to Willow and Jake, both could see that she'd been crying.

Jake merely looked at the young woman to see that she was overcome with happiness. She appeared to be a shy woman and now she was feeling overwhelmed. His heart went out to her.

Once inside the apartment, and after Willow's introductions, Jake held out his arms.

"Hello, Dolores," he said quietly. "Welcome to our family."

Dolores started to cry again as she hugged Jake. Willow joined her and Jake held open his arms to hug them both.

His own emotions were stirred as he thought that the New Year was beginning with his cup very full.

Dorcas Williams was tired. She'd taken on too many private-duty cases at once, and she'd have to give some consideration to cutting back her hours. It was past six in the evening and she'd finished her eight-to-four shift at the New Haven Medical Facility.

One saving grace, she thought as she headed to the kitchen, was not traveling back and forth in ice and snow. The weather in February was a darn sight better than it had been in January, which was a killer.

She started to prepare her dinner. Lamb chops, spinach, and corn on the cob was quick enough to fix after a long day. As a single person, she knew the benefits of eating healthfully. There would be no one around to care for her if she became ill. It was bad enough that the bones were aging and a new ache was apt to appear at any time.

The corn was done and Dorcas fixed her plate and carried it into the living room. She turned on the TV for company while she ate. As usual, the feelings of loneliness enveloped her. Always at mealtime, she had to shake off the uncomfortable shroud of loneliness. In other times, she would be happily preparing meals for a crowd, pretending to scold the catering students on haphazard food preparation. She could hear her Willow's deep laugh, kidding with Tommy about who was the best dessert maker.

Dorcas banned the thoughts and tried to get interested in the old movie that was about to air.

Her meal finished, Dorcas cleaned up and took her tray to the kitchen, returning with a hot cup of tea. She glanced out the window at the darkened streets. When she'd rented this small house, she had had no idea how quiet and desolate it would be. Though she'd wanted a place out of the hubbub, she didn't think that she would feel so isolated although she was only fifteen minutes from downtown. She sighed and sat down. Although she never did it intentionally, her thoughts wandered to her life at Wildflowers Cove—and Willow. She wondered how her little girl was doing? She wondered if she and Dolores had met and were now speaking, if not friends. I guess that would be a bit too much to ask of them, she sighed.

Dorcas thought about Lloyd Rivers. "God rest your soul, old man," she said aloud. She'd read the small article about his death in the Irvington local newspaper to which she subscribed. It was a way to keep in touch with the past. In all those weeks, nothing had been mentioned of Irvington's famous artist Morgana. Only that the popular writer's retreat, Wildflowers Cove had been closed.

Dorcas felt that the book had been closed on something that had been a vital part of her past. May be just as well, she thought, and wondered exactly how she should go about planning the rest of her life. At fifty-six, it was definitely not over. Lately, she had been wondering, if she was too old to adopt. A little girl. With big black eyes that sparkled when she smiled and a mischievous grin. She closed her eyes as she began to doze off.

Willow and Jake had finally traced Dorcas' whereabouts through her professional license. They had little trouble in finding her employer and then her address. It was Willow who had been the holdup in making the trip to New

Haven, Connecticut. She'd been as nervous as when she shied away from seeing Dolores. But with her sister's and Jake's encouragement, they finally made the drive up on the second Saturday in February. As with Dolores, Willow did not want to call ahead of time, fearing the negative reception or worse, total rejection.

Jake drove the Mercedes slowly onto the deserted street as all three occupants of the car peered at the house numbers.

"There it is," Dolores said in a soft, but excited voice.

Jake pulled the car over and parked. He looked at Willow. She had been silent most of the drive. He got out of the car, walked around, then opened the doors for Willow and Dolores. They stepped out, staring at the quiet-looking house.

All were silent when Dolores put her hand on Willow's back and gave her a little push. "It's going to be fine, Willow. I can feel it."

Willow smiled at her sister and looked at Jake. He winked, and she took a deep breath and walked to her aunt's door. She rang the doorbell and waited.

Dorcas woke with a start, surprised she'd dozed off that fast. She frowned. "Now who in the world could this be?" she said, as she went to the door. Not bothering with the peephole, she opened the door and gasped as she stared at her niece. Words stuck in her throat. Willow? Her mind couldn't be playing tricks. "Willow?" she whispered.

Willow's eyes watered. "Aren't I your little buttercup?" Willow opened her arms and there were no words as the two women hugged and cried.

Jake and Dolores, arm in arm, smiled at each other as they walked toward the house.

It was after eleven o'clock at night, on the first Sunday in March. Spring was finally coming, and with it, a bright new beginning to her life. Willow was the happiest woman in the world. She lay dreamily in Jake's arms, in his big bed. In two weeks they would be moving into their new home. They'd searched, refusing to settle for anything, when they both fell in love with the same property the moment they'd lain eyes on it. Located not far away in Sleepy Hollow, the big, sprawling, rustic-style house, fit them perfectly. There was a small guest house that would become Willow's studio. Jake was adamant about where the key would be kept. Inside the house were enough rooms for Jake to have an office and there was a big room that would make a fantastic play area.

They'd also decided that they would have their wedding ceremony there in April. The huge living room would be perfect. She was filled with excitement.

"Jake?" She burrowed deeper into the hollow of his arm.

"Hmm?"

"Are you as happy as I am?"

Jake opened his eyes. He was getting sleepy, but he became alert. What kind of question was that? He stroked her arm. "You have to ask me that, sweetness?"

Willow warmed to the sound of his voice. "No," she answered, happily. "I just wanted to talk."

Jake pulled on a curl. "Then talk about the weather. Never that," he said firmly.

Willow sighed and slipped her hand inside of his pajama top. She smiled devilishly at his reaction. It wasn't too long ago that they had both fallen back onto the pillows, exhausted, but contented, from their exquisite display of love. She tugged at the hairs on his chest and he squirmed.

"Do you think that they'll be happy?" she murmured against his chest.

Jake thought before responding. Dorcas and Dolores were planning on moving into the Cove. The decision had been made without haste because of all that the house had represented to the three women. It was Dolores who had come to decide that there was a place that her roots had begun. Dorcas had been born there. And Willow. It would be foolish to let the harms of the past mar the lives of the future generations of Morgans, she'd said.

"They will be," Jake answered with conviction. "They're looking to the future. As we all are." He squirmed some more, and winced as Willow twisted her body so that he felt all of her against him. He felt himself rising.

"Jake?"

"Hmm?" he answered. He was now stroking her breasts through her satin gown. He breathed heavily.

"You really love playing godfather to Tala's and Brian's son. Right?"

"Yeah," Jake breathed. "He's a great little guy." Tala had been two weeks late, and anxious, when her son finally made his debut in mid-January. Amidst all that was happening in his own life at the time, it was all he could do to stop by and congratulate the happy parents. Maybe one day, he thought. He was thinking of his own.

Finally, through clenched teeth, he said, "Willow, I want you again. You're playing my body like guitar strings," he growled.

Willow smiled. "I want you, too, my love. But, I don't think we'll have to wonder about starting little gleams. Our little glimmer is already a reality and will be here in time for Thanksgiving."

Jake stopped moving and sat up, staring at her as if she were a dream. He cupped her chin in his hand and looked deeply into her eyes.

"No," he said in a ragged whisper. "You're not kidding."

Willow smiled and shook her head.

Jake closed his eyes. "Thank you, Jesus," he murmured. When he opened them, he kissed Willow's eyes, her nose, her cheeks, and finally captured her lips, savoring her sweet kisses. "I love you, darlin'," he said. His voice was a low tremor as he accepted his lady's love when she entwined her legs around his.

"As I, you, my love," Willow whispered.

Epilogue

The Sunday before Christmas, at three in the afternoon, in their home, Giselle and Troy Rivers were christened. Their parents and relatives and well-wishers gathered around cooing in baby talk to the two-month-old twins.

"Now, who's my little buttercup, today?" crooned Dorcas to little Zelle, as the tiny baby was already nicknamed. She rocked the baby in her arms, selfishly warding off anyone who even looked like they wanted to take her.

Dolores was sitting in an adjacent chair, her arms full with Troy, as Kendra sat at her feet playing with her baby cousin's toes.

Willow and Jake sat across the room, finally able to breathe after the hectic day was coming to a close. They both smiled at the scene before them.

Willow reached for Jake's hand. He took hers and brought it to his lips. "You're even more beautiful now, darlin'," he whispered for her ears only. "Don't know whether we can have any more like that. I'd have to beat away the competition from my front door."

Willow leaned over and kissed his lips. "Bite your tongue. The only competition you have to worry about is from yourself." She smiled wickedly. "Remember eternity?"

"Ouch," Jake said, and threw back his head and laughed.

"Now, what's she making you crack up about?" asked
Mellie. "I swear, Willow. I never saw two people crack up
at each other's jokes, like you two, do." She laughed with
them without knowing what the joke was, then drifted
across the room to the twins.

Willow looked at her friend who was a houseguest for
the holidays. The house had already been full of excitement and laughter when Mellie and Valerie had arrived
two days ago. When Peter St. John flew in today, Mellie's
love shone in her eyes. She confided that the wedding was
planned for next Christmas. Willow was happy for her
friend. She looked at her old friend and agent, now married to Maria Hall. He caught her look and raised his glass
of champagne to her and Jake. They saluted back.

"He really is happy now, isn't he?" Jake remarked.

"He is. I'm so happy for him and Maria." She thought
about the day she went into the city alone. Jake had known
where she was going without asking. He'd kissed her and
wished for the best. When Willow had walked into his office, she knew then, from the look in his eyes that her
Germany was back. That stranger she'd seen in Toronto
had disappeared. He had become her agent once again.

Willow saw the look Jake gave his niece, Kendra, and
she knew that he was thinking about his brother. "Maybe
one day, he will want to be a part of her life, Jake. But he
has to have the willpower."

Jake nodded. "Maybe. But until then, she has us." Nat
had phoned Annette from a detox center in Ohio. He
needed money to get cleaned up and pay for a room at a
Sober Station. After verifying the story, Jake had made arrangements to help, as long as his brother wanted to stay
sober. The money he was sending was part of Nat's settle-
ment from the sale of the house.

Willow walked across the room to her babies and Jake
followed her, his arm around her waist.

Dorcas and Dolores looked up, alarmed. Neither wanted to give up the bundle in her arm.

Jake grinned at them. "Don't worry," he whispered, "I'm not about to wake them up. They're all yours, for now." He took Willow's hand on their way to the kitchen. He waved to Tala and Brian and their son, and the Andersons, who were animatedly discussing an upcoming project they'd started in their new hometown in South Carolina.

Willow waved to the talkative group also and felt good inside that her husband had such loyal friends. Tala had once again taken over the reins of her company, and J. Rivers Landscape Contracts, company was in the black, thanks in large part to Scottie's and Irene's expert managing.

Walking down the hall, Jake quickly opened the door to an unoccupied room and whisked his wife inside. He caught her close and kissed her tenderly. "Just wanted some sugar, that's all. Before Zelle and Troy wake up."

Willow responded lustily. "Anytime is the right time, sweet. Our babies will never come between us," Willow said softly.

Jake hugged her. "Your mother knew that, didn't she?" he said quietly. It was only after their own children were born that his wife had finally decided to read the letter written many years ago by a distraught woman.

Jake had convinced Willow not to destroy the letter as she'd wanted to do, that maybe the words inside were not harmful or bitter. She'd listened to him and was grateful. She'd let him read it and they had said a prayer together, for a tormented wife, but a loving mother. Willow remembered the words so well.

My dearest daughter, Willow,
  I love you, my sweetcakes. Always remember that. I don't know how old you are now that you are reading this. It doesn't really matter because I only want you to

*know that you were the one true love of my life. The bright-
est ray of sunshine that I've ever known. You are Aunt
Dorcas' buttercup. I want you to forget my selfish act in
depriving you of parents in your young life. Believe me,
you would have come to hate us both had you grown up
in this house of lovelessness. I know that with Dorcas and
Thomas you will grow up to know love. You will become
a woman who will know love with a loving man who will
only love you. You will know on sight who he will be. You
will feel it. When you have your babies you will both have
more than enough love between you to go around. I've
watched you grow for four years and I know how gener-
ously you give love. Be happy, always. I love you my darling Willow.*

Love,

Mommy

Willow smiled and Jake knew what she was thinking. He
kissed her lips.

"Come, darlin'," he said. "I think the babies are calling
us."

Dear Reader,

You frequently ask which story is my favorite. I have to tell you that I can't choose. After I've told their story, some of my characters come to mind at the oddest of times.

Callie Ross and Max Ashton from NIGHT and DAY may appear whenever I spy a piece of antique silver.

Smith Richardson and Penny Norwood from NIGHT SECRETS are not far from my thoughts when I'm choosing new gemstones.

From FATHER AT HEART, I may think of Michael Kingsford when I'm riding the Q5 bus down Merrick Boulevard or Jeanne Grayson may cross my mind when I drive pass August Martin High School.

Now that you've met Jake Rivers and Willow Vaughn, I hope that you too, experienced their love and passion. I can't help feeling that Jake and Willow will be with me for a VERY long time.

Unless, of course, Adam Stone and Sydney Cox, in the July, 1999, release, HEARTS OF STONE, take center stage. An executive security manager tries to win the heart of a New York sommelier, in this sensitive, passionate tale.

Please continue to write and include a self-addressed, stamped envelope, for a reply.

Thanks for Sharing,
Doris Johnson
P.O. Box 130370
Springfield Gardens, New York 11413

About The Author

Doris Johnson lives in Queens, New York. She is a multipublished author who has written other books. She enjoys lazing on beaches, poking around in flea markets and collecting gemstones.

COMING IN NOVEMBER . . .

THE ESSENCE OF LOVE   (0-7860-0567-X, $499/$6.50)
by Candice Poarch
Once falsely accused of fraud, Cleopatra Sharp managed to flourish in her new aromatherapy shop outside of Washington, D.C. But suspicion falls on her again. Postal inspector Taylor Bradford goes undercover as a repairman at her shop, determined to keep dangerous drugs and fraudulent miracle cures out of his community. When he realizes Cleopatra is nothing but a tender, giving woman, he must choose between his head and his heart.

LOVE'S PROMISE   (0-7860-0568-8, $4.99/$6.50)
by Adrienne Ellis Reeves
Beth Jordan refused a marriage proposal from her long-time boyfriend, only to find that he was quickly engaged to another. Determined to show everyone in Jamison, South Carolina that she wasn't too flighty to accomplish anything, she took part in a community service contest. Cy Brewster, her contest partner, tested her good intentions, for now she was in it for love. And a secret from Cy's past tests whether theirs is a love that promises forever.

EDEN'S DREAM   (0-7860-0572-6, $4.99/$6.50)
by Marcia King-Gamble
Eden Sommers fled to Mercer Island, in the Pacific Northwest, after a tragic plane crash claimed her husband and left her devastated. As she searches for answers, the mysterious man who moves in next door and bears a striking resemblance to her husband, manages to distract her. Is it mere coincidence that has brought Noel Robinson to Mercer Island? Eden will discover his secrets before she submits to the love welling up between them.

ISLAND PROMISE   (0-7860-0574-2, $4.99/$6.50)
by Angela Winters
Dallas schoolteacher Morgan Breck's reckless spirit led her to make an impulsive purchase at an estate sale, that plunged her into the arms of sexy investor Jake Turner. Jake is only interested in finding his missing sister, and when Morgan stumbles onto a clue that might locate his sister, he is thrilled to be with her. But when they are on the island where his sister may be, intense passion will force Jake to surrender to love.